Ann McIntosh was born in the tropics, lived in the frozen north for a number of years, and now resides in sunny central Florida with her husband. She's a proud mama to three grown children, loves tea, crafting, animals—except reptiles!—bacon and the ocean. She believes in the power of romance to heal, inspire and provide hope in our complex world.

Kate Hardy has always loved books and could read before she went to school. She discovered Mills & Boon books when she was twelve and decided that this was what she wanted to do. When she isn't writing Kate enjoys reading, cinema, ballroom dancing and the gym. You can contact her via her website: katehardy.com.

TWIN BABIES
TO REUNITE THEM

ANN McINTOSH

AN ENGLISH VET
IN PARIS

KATE HARDY

MILLS & BOON

First published in Great Britain 2023
by Mills & Boon, an imprint of HarperCollins*Publishers* Ltd,
1 London Bridge Street, London, SE1 9GF

www.harpercollins.co.uk

HarperCollins*Publishers* Macken House, 39/40 Mayor Street Upper, Dublin 1, D01 C9W8, Ireland

ISBN: 978-0-263-30609-5

06/23

This book is produced from independently certified FSC™ paper to ensure responsible forest management.
For more information visit: www.harpercollins.co.uk/green.

Printed and Bound in the UK using 100% Renewable Electricity at CPI Group (UK) Ltd, Croydon, CR0 4YY

TWIN BABIES TO REUNITE THEM

ANN McINTOSH

MILLS & BOON

With thanks to Nicole and Heather,
whose love, marriage and devotion to each other
are an inspiration to everyone.

CHAPTER ONE

DR. SAANA AMIRI CHECKED her watch and suppressed a yawn. While the low-cost women's clinic only operated from Tuesday to Saturday, from four in the afternoon to nine at night, when coupled with her regular daytime practice, it made for long weeks. Thankfully, this would be the last patient of the night, and with the next day being Sunday, she could look forward to at least one day to recharge her batteries.

As she arrived at the examination-room door, she paused on hearing nurse Amanda Curry's voice from inside.

"Why on earth didn't you see a doctor long before this?"

It wasn't just the words, more so the hectoring tone that made Saana's hackles rise. The last thing the women coming to the clinic needed was to be berated by the very people they were depending on to help them. The hardships many of them suffered didn't need to be compounded by unsympathetic behavior on the part of the medical team.

With a quick rap on the door, she stepped into the room and took in the scene with a sweeping glance.

Nurse Curry stood with her hands on her hips, frowning at the patient, Mylie Nelson, who stared back with what could only be called a defensive glare on her pale, narrow face. Seated on the examination table, Mylie had one arm bent behind her back, hiding it from sight; nearby, in a kidney dish, was a small pile of soiled bandages. In the corner of the room lay a large, fully stuffed backpack, a small duffel bag—equally full—and a couple of shopping bags.

Before either of the other women could say anything else, Saana walked over to grab a pair of disposable gloves and interrupted the conversation.

"Hello, Ms. Nelson. I'm Dr. Amiri." Giving the nurse a cool glance, she continued, "Thank you, Nurse. I'll take over now."

Amanda Curry frowned, probably because of Saana's tone, but after a murmured agreement, she left the examination room. Apparently, though, she couldn't resist closing the door behind her with an ill-tempered snap.

Putting the nurse out of her mind, Saana turned to her patient and smiled.

"So, what can I do for you this evening?"

And there was no mistaking the reluctance with which the patient revealed the jagged wound on her arm.

As she examined the infected injury, Saana questioned how it had occurred, keeping her tone gentle and sympathetic as the story unfolded. Mylie had caught her arm on a piece of corrugated iron but, afraid to miss work, hadn't been able to have it tended to. Now, five days later, she hadn't been able to ignore it anymore.

Although she was sure there was more to the story, Saana took it at face value and was pleased when her patient relaxed.

The small mound of bags told the familiar tale of homelessness Saana had no trouble recognizing, but it was with women like Mylie in mind that she'd opened the clinic. Florida's mild winters attracted more than just snow birds, as the part-time, retired residents were called. Many transients who originally came south to avoid the northern cold ended up staying year-round.

"I'm going to need to clean the wound and tape it closed. I'll administer a tetanus shot, and you'll need to do a course of antibiotics," she told Mylie. "I can give you a voucher for the pharmacy, if you need one, and you have to take all the antibiotic tablets. Don't stop, even if your arm seems to be better. Are you allergic to penicillin or any other medications?"

By the time she'd finished with Mylie Nelson, it was almost ten o'clock, and although the clinic officially closed at nine thirty, most of the staff were still on-site. Since it was standard operating procedure for everyone to leave at the same time, under the watchful eyes of the night security guard, Saana did a quick head count.

"We're one short," she said. "Who's missing?"

"Nurse Curry left already," one of the other nurses replied.

Saana tamped down her instinctive spurt of annoyance.

"Okay, let's get out of here," she said, hitching her tote bag a little higher onto her shoulder. "Thanks, everyone. Enjoy what's left of the weekend, and I'll see you all on Tuesday afternoon."

Once in her car, Saana sighed and pushed a strand of hair off her cheek. While she was tired, her muscles aching with fatigue, her brain was still running full steam.

Amanda Curry wasn't someone she wanted to work with. Over the three weeks the nurse had been at the clinic, Saana had noticed her condescending attitude toward both patients and other staff members, as though she felt them all beneath her. Saana had given the HR team very specific instructions about hiring staff, but although Nurse Curry didn't fit the bill, it wasn't their fault. One of the nurses originally hired two months ago when the clinic opened had become ill and took a leave of absence. Nurse Curry was a traveling nurse and had been sent by an agency to fill the temporary vacancy.

As Saana headed south on US 1, she decided to contact the agency to have Nurse Curry replaced. Using the onboard electronic system linked to her phone, she set herself a reminder for Monday morning. Not that she was likely to forget, but being methodical was an ingrained part of her personality.

A vehicle swerved into her lane, making her have to hit the brakes and suppress a curse. As usual on a Saturday night, the thoroughfare, which led into the downtown Melbourne area, was busy and the driving was sometimes erratic.

As the car in front of her slowed almost to a halt although there was nothing in front of it, Saana had the urge to pull out into the oncoming lane and overtake. After all, her sports car would easily zoom past the sedan, and the speed might alleviate some of the restless energy still firing through her system.

But even as her leg muscles tensed to hit the accelerator, she forced them to relax again.

Impulsiveness wasn't something she gave in to often now, especially after the spectacular mess she'd made the last time she indulged.

Saana shook her head abruptly, annoyed, and as if to prove the wisdom of not overtaking on the double yellow lines, she spotted a police car on the verge. She would have gotten a hefty ticket, for sure.

There. *Better safe than sorry* wasn't just a maxim but words to live by, so as to not get into trouble.

Of all kinds.

It was what her father had said when she'd told him her plan to open a low-cost clinic integrated with her already thriving medical practice.

"To be frank, I think it would be a mistake," he'd said. "What you're proposing would immediately become a drain on your resources, both professionally and—knowing you— personally too."

Twirling the stem of her wineglass between her fingers, she'd tried to figure out exactly what he was saying.

"The women of Brevard County need a place to go for testing and treatment when they don't have insurance," she'd replied, keeping her voice mild but strong, so he'd have no doubt she was serious about the project. "I have the means to help provide that for at least some of them."

"I'm not saying not to do it," Dad had replied, getting up to freshen his own drink. "But be cautious and realistic about what it will cost and how you can sustain such a project without damaging what you already have."

Saana had known what he was skirting around and bit back her instinctive urge to defend herself. Yes, in the past she'd sometimes jumped into things without thinking them through, but it had been a while since she'd learned not to be so rash.

Two years, ten months and twenty-six days, to be precise. But who was counting?

Clearly, she was.

Of course, she'd taken his advice and consulted lawyers, accountants and other practitioners, especially those who specialized in low-cost care. In the end, she'd taken some of the inheritance from her grandfather and set up a trust. Then she'd hired a firm to both manage the trust and prioritize fundraising so she wouldn't need to deal with either.

All she was interested in was practicing medicine.

The first major fundraiser was scheduled in a month's time, at her parent's house, and Saana was frankly dreading it.

On being told about the fundraising party, Mom had insisted it take place at the Amiris' Merritt Island estate, where Saana had grown up. Between Mom and the party coordinator, it sounded like a magical scene had been planned, and the guest list of wealthy socialites would hopefully be moved to donate.

Saana couldn't help twisting her lips at the irony.

Thousands of dollars spent on champagne, canapés and a gourmet meal to entice people to give money to a cause that could have benefited greatly from that initial outlay. Oh, she understood it; after all, she'd grown up in this rarefied existence, where tax write-offs and social visibility trumped genuine generosity. But it still didn't sit well.

Yet she knew she had to play the game if the clinic was to be a success and outlive her, the way she hoped it would.

It was never too early to think about the legacy you'd leave behind.

She turned off US 1 and, after going over the Melbourne Causeway into Indialantic, drove slowly through the far quieter streets of her neighborhood. Smaller cottages began to give way to larger lots and houses the nearer she got to her home on the Indian River Lagoon. As soon as she was close enough, Saana hit the button to open the security gate, getting to it just as the tall wrought iron wings opened just enough for her car to go through. She was halfway down her curved driveway when she noticed a dark-colored sedan parked, facing out, at the front right-hand side of the house.

Instinctively, she eased off the gas, slowing the vehicle down as she put her finger on the panic button located on the steering wheel.

She wasn't expecting anyone, and no one had rung at the gate to be let in, because the request would have popped up on her phone.

Who was this, and how had they gained entrance to her property?

Then, before she could call for help, the driver's-side door of the other car opened, and someone stepped out.

Saana hit the brakes, and her hand dropped down into her lap, boneless.

Kenzie?

The other woman stood, unmoving, behind the car door, watching Saana's vehicle, too far away for her expression to be visible. Saana was glad for the distance.

Between one breath and the next, all the carefully constructed barriers she'd built around her heart crumbled, and she was falling apart. Battered by a rush of complex and nauseating emotions she couldn't name and didn't want Kenzie to see.

Time slowed as Saana began to shake and her brain went into hyperdrive, trying to figure out what to do.

She could hit the gate button again and reverse away through it.

Drive around to the garage and let herself into the house, ignoring and leaving Kenzie where she was.

Or I can brazen it out. Show her I don't care why she's here—only that she needs to leave again.

That thought somehow steadied her, easing the band of ice constricting her chest, allowing her to breathe as a rush of heated anger overrode everything else.

How dare she just appear like this, as though no time has passed and nothing has happened?

As if she hadn't broken Saana's heart and destroyed her faith in herself and love?

Now Saana could ascribe the trembling of her hands and wild cadence of her heart to rage, and it firmed her determination not to let Kenzie's appearance get the better of her.

After taking a couple of deep breaths, she eased off the brake and drove forward, parking her car parallel to Kenzie's. Getting out, she looked over the roof of both vehicles at her estranged wife.

"McKenzie." Saana wasn't sure how she kept her voice so cool and steady but was proud of the effect. "How did you get in here?"

Safer than asking why she was there.

Kenzie shook her head slightly, her lush lips kicking up a hint at the corners.

"If you'd changed the security code, I'd still be outside."

She'd meant to change the code. Just like she'd meant to file for divorce once she'd gotten it into her thick skull that Kenzie Bonham wasn't coming back.

Neither of those chores had been crossed off her to-do list.

Refusing to even contemplate why that was, and trying not

to let the sound of that sweet drawl insinuate itself into her psyche, she shrugged lightly. Closing her car door, she clutched her tote bag so tightly the leather straps dug into her palm.

"If I'd had even an inkling that you'd turn up like this, I would have."

Was that a flash of pain that shot across Kenzie's face at her cold pronouncement? If so, Saana felt not a shred of remorse. She hoped the barb *had* struck home since Kenzie absolutely deserved whatever discomfort she felt.

Silence fell between them for a moment, and Saana found her gaze fixed on Kenzie's face. Unable to tear it away, she took in what she could see of the other woman, the thundering of her heart giving the moment far too much weight.

Kenzie's face looked narrower, the satiny, cocoa-hued skin stretched a little tighter than usual, her cheeks not as full as Saana remembered. Her hair was longer, worn in a mass of corkscrew curls that moved gently in the breeze blowing from the ocean, held back by a simple black bandeau. Kenzie had beautiful eyes. Dark brown, gleaming with intelligence and often with ready laughter. Although she was too far away to see the expression in them, Saana's memory supplied the details—the way looking into them was like drowning in love and desire.

And those lips…

A tidal wave of arousal crashed over Saana as her gaze dropped to that full, wide mouth—unsmiling now, but no less sinfully sexy for that fact.

Against her will, her head suddenly filled with scenes, scents, sensations of being held in Kenzie's arms. There, her every sensual need had been met, ecstasy lifting her higher and higher, until it became irresistible and she was flung into the stratosphere.

Taken to the stars.

Suddenly weak-kneed once more, Saana knew it was time

to bring this surreal encounter to an end. The sustaining anger had waned, leaving her floundering and sad.

But she wouldn't allow that to show.

The one person she'd ever completely trusted had betrayed her and deserved nothing but cool dismissal.

Getting a grip on both her emotions and her traitorous body, and although her legs still felt weak, she walked around the car to the semicircular staircase leading to her front door.

"Well," she said, aware of Kenzie's gaze following her and refusing to meet it again. "This has been delightful, but I'm afraid it's time for you to leave."

She was two steps up when Kenzie replied.

"Saana, I need your help."

Pausing, Saana felt the words echo, shockingly, between them. In fact, it was almost impossible to believe she'd heard them correctly.

Unable to resist, she looked over her shoulder, saying, "As surprising as it is to hear you, Miss Independence, say that, I'm sorry. I'm not interested in offering assistance."

Then, as she turned to climb to the next step—wanting to hurry now, to get away—she heard Kenzie say, "I'm pregnant with twins. And I really need your help."

She froze where she stood, trying to process the words, her first impulse to spin around and look at Kenzie to judge whether she was telling the truth or not. To let loose all the questions firing around her brain.

Pregnant? By whom? Had she started a new relationship without telling Saana? Decided she wanted a family with someone other than the wife she'd promised to love and cherish always but had then left behind?

The hand she'd laid on the banister tightened until even the bones hurt. Behind her, a car door slammed, and her already racing heart sped up even more. If she spun around now, Kenzie would be completely visible, and perhaps Saana could figure out how far along she was.

But hadn't she learned her lesson? Impulsive behavior—which she knew herself to be prone to on occasion—not only often got her in trouble but had, more specifically, gotten her into the present situation.

They were standing, watching the water show outside the Bellagio, Kenzie's arm around Saana's shoulders, their heads close together. It came to Saana that she'd never been happier. Never felt more secure, comfortable—loved. She'd only known Kenzie for five days, and these were the last few hours they'd spend together before the other woman went back to Texas.

"Marry me," she said, unable to stop the words from emerging, though she knew it was crazy to even suggest it. "I can't imagine my life without you now."

Those dark, gleaming eyes, wide with surprise, turned to search her gaze, and Saana's heart beat so hard she felt sick.

Then, shockingly, she said, "Yes..."

But it had all turned out to be a mistake. A mirage.

One she didn't dare allow herself to be pulled back into, lest she find it impossible to extricate herself.

"No..."

But it came out like a sigh, too quiet to be heard by the woman standing behind her, and even as she said it, Saana knew she'd have to force herself to mean it.

That the emotion Kenzie had awoken in her had never faded but now would have to be ruthlessly suppressed.

CHAPTER TWO

KENZIE LEANED AGAINST the side of her car, needing the support to stay on her feet.

You'd think she'd be steadier. After all, she'd had lots of time to prepare for these moments, from the first stomach-churning instant she realized the trouble she was in to the two-day journey from San Antonio to Indialantic. It was a desperate plan to begin with, and she knew it may not work, but she'd been determined to at least try.

And she'd reminded herself, over and over, that her feelings for Saana didn't matter. Not anymore. Not when she was responsible for the lives growing in her belly.

The babies had to come first. Always.

Yet thinking she was ready to face whatever she found here in Florida had been a lie.

Just the approach of Saana's vehicle created a wave of such mingled love, desire and sadness that it had taken all her strength to get out of the car. Then, on seeing her wife again, it had taken every ounce of control to keep her voice even, when all she wanted to do was round the vehicles and pull Saana into her arms.

Kiss her, never wanting to stop.

Find home again in her embrace.

Now, looking up at Saana where she stood on the staircase,

Kenzie was once more reminded of all the reasons why their marriage didn't—couldn't—work.

Saana was so elegant, so incredibly beautiful that Kenzie could hardly believe she'd ever been lucky enough to touch her, much less be married to her.

Even casually dressed in a slim-fitting pair of tailored trousers and a long-sleeve cotton shirt, simple gold hoops in her ears, she was all graceful sophistication. Saana had cut her hair since the last time Kenzie saw her, and thick, dark strands feathered around her face, emphasizing the gorgeous bone structure and wide-set hazel eyes. The honey-toned skin, as smooth as velvet, just begged to be touched.

In contrast, Kenzie's low-slung jeans, sleeveless and shapeless plaid shirt and dusty cowboy boots proclaimed, loud and clear, her country-girl heritage.

And it wasn't hard to feel, once again, that she didn't belong here in this hoity-toity neighborhood, where people weren't just rich but insanely wealthy.

That was a concept Kenzie had never considered until moving to Florida to be with Saana over two and a half years ago. Up until then, in her mind, people were either rich, middle-class or poor. Sure, she knew there were gazillionaires, but to her they were sort of like unicorns—mythical and never to be experienced in real life.

Once she'd gotten a taste of what wealth truly meant, she knew she didn't understand it. Nor would she ever truly fit in, and there was no way to explain that to Saana fully without hurting her. Kenzie had been careful not to tell her wife about the rudeness and snubs she'd experienced from Saana's friends.

It had taken her months after leaving to realize just how beaten down she'd been by those interactions; how low her self-esteem had fallen. Not to mention how Kenzie being with her would be detrimental to Saana's image.

If she couldn't be an asset to her wife, then it was better she stay out of Saana's life.

No. If there was any other way to protect the babies, she wouldn't be here.

No matter how much she loved Saana—wanted, *needed* her—it would never be enough. She couldn't live her life constantly feeling inferior to her surroundings. A fish out of water. A source of embarrassment to the woman she loved.

A woman who hadn't moved in over a minute.

"Saana—"

Saana's hand chopped downwards, obviously to cut off whatever Kenzie was going to say, and when she turned around, Kenzie felt a trickle, like melting snow, down her spine.

Her face was calm, untroubled, but her eyes—flashing with anger—belied that unconcerned facade.

"Your condition has nothing to do with me," she said, her voice as cold as the sensation growing in Kenzie's chest. "I think you should leave."

The curt dismissal fired through the air like bullets but was nothing less than Kenzie knew she deserved. Although she wanted to walk—no, *run*—away, that wasn't an option.

"Please, Saana. Will you at least let me explain what's going on?" God, why was it so hard to ask for help, especially from the regal woman in front of her? Didn't Saana know how difficult this was? How behind the eight ball Kenzie had to be to even ask? "You know I wouldn't be here if I had any alternative."

Saana's eyes narrowed, and her lips tightened, and for an instant Kenzie thought she might, for once, lose control. Maybe even shout or curse. Show some outward evidence of strong emotion rather than keep it all inside.

Then her expression smoothed out, and she gave one of her

characteristic shrugs, shoulders moving forward, then back, her chin tilting to one side.

"I'll hear you out, but your problems aren't my concern, so don't expect my help."

Then she turned and walked slowly up the stairs, like a queen having dismissed her subject, and Kenzie trailed behind, scared but determined.

Only the babies mattered, she reminded herself, even as her heart ached with sadness and with love for the woman walking in front of her.

The house loomed before her, as unwelcoming as she remembered. It was a mansion, with so many rooms some of them were closed up because they were unused. Filled with things that were beautiful and obviously expensive, it had felt like a showpiece rather than a home to Kenzie. She'd been afraid to touch anything, hadn't wanted to put up her feet anywhere.

The only place that held any meaning to her here was upstairs, in the bedroom. There, Saana and she had explored each other with the type of abandon Kenzie hadn't expected but had relished.

She shivered, trying to push thoughts of their lovemaking aside, and now the interior of the house seemed to scowl at her as she stepped inside and closed the door. Her stomach clenched, and her hands started trembling. Stuffing her fingers into her pockets, she called out to Saana, who had continued on into the sitting room.

"I just have to run to the john."

"You know where it is," came the cool reply.

Yeah, she did. She'd lived in the house for ten months, and nothing seemed to have changed in the two years since she'd left.

With her overwrought nerves, the clack of her boots across the marble foyer sounded extraordinarily loud, each echoing pop seeming to emphasize her unsuitability to be in the house. It was a momentary relief to step onto the thick runner that covered the floor of the hall, and then Kenzie couldn't help glancing back to see if she was leaving dirty footprints on the cream fabric.

"Get over yourself," she muttered under her breath as she opened the door into the powder room and flicked on the light, illuminating a space larger than most people's bedrooms. If she was to have any hope of convincing Saana to help her, she'd need to move past her little ego trip and be logical.

Now wasn't the time to allow the nagging sense of unworthiness that had dogged her life here to take over.

Saana had closed herself away, all emotion locked tight, and it would take everything Kenzie had to break through that barrier to gain her sympathy. And without doing that, there was no way Saana would agree to help.

The unreality of the situation suddenly struck her anew as she tugged down her jeans and sat on the john, then leaned forward to put her hands on either side of her head.

Who could have known a random encounter in Las Vegas would have led to this moment?

Their relationship had, at the beginning, seemed like an extension of the fantastical aura surrounding her all-expenses-paid seven-night trip. Kenzie had never won anything in her life and had entered the radio-station contest on a whim. Flying into Vegas, seeing the lights beneath the wing, had made her not even care that she'd been guilted into taking Ashley with her instead of the friend she'd originally wanted to. Nor had her cousin's words, as they stood outside the hotel, felt like more than a pinprick.

"Stop gaping, Kenz. You look like even more of a hick than you are right now. Take my bag up to the room, will you? I'm heading to the casino."

She was used to Ashley's nonsense and hadn't wanted the

hassle of an argument, so she'd done as commanded and spent most of that evening walking the strip, just taking in the sights.

Then, the next morning, she'd met Saana.

It had seemed totally right.

Despite the obvious differences between them—Kenzie had known right away that Saana was way too good for her—they'd also had a lot in common. They were both in medicine and loved romantic comedies, real Mexican food, strawberry everything and watching ice-skating. Even their differences had seemed more amusing than barriers to their holiday romance. They'd argued over the best types of music and books, which led to them sharing headphones, faces close together so they breathed each other in.

Everyone else on the tour bus could have disappeared right then and there, and neither of them would have noticed. Or cared.

Back then, Saana had seemed so open and free. The only hint of reticence had arisen when Kenzie—who, by then, wanted the other woman more than her next breath—had initiated their first kiss. For a brief instant, Saana had stiffened, her lips unmoving against Kenzie's. Thinking she wasn't into it, Kenzie had started to pull away—but just then Saana had pulled her closer, and that delicious mouth opened, accepting the entrance of Kenzie's tongue.

Later on, she realized what she'd seen as shyness about sex was really just Saana expressing a preference for submission. While to the outside world she presented a confident, no-nonsense facade, in bed she preferred to surrender and be told what to do. It had been so in-line with Kenzie's own more dominant style that she'd seen it as a perfect match.

Lying in bed, limbs twisted around each other, Kenzie had initiated a conversation on the topic, wanting to know everything she could about the fascinating woman she was falling for.

"I was a bit of a late bloomer," Saana had admitted. "I spent all my time trying to be the perfect daughter and granddaughter, the very best student, and sometimes I think it was because I was confused about my sexuality. I knew the guys I was dating weren't really fulfilling me, but because I'd spent so much time with my grandparents, I had a very conventional attitude toward sex."

Stroking her hair, Kenzie had asked, "When did you figure it all out?"

"In my mid-twenties, after being away from home for a while. I thought maybe I was bi, because I don't dislike being with men, but then I had an affair with a female classmate, and that was it."

Kenzie had tamped down the little rush of jealousy that twisted in her belly and the thought that she wished she'd been Saana's first. "Was it hard, coming out to your family?"

Saana had shifted, rolling over and propping herself up on her elbow so she was looking into Kenzie's eyes. "Not really. They're good people, with open minds and hearts. The hardest part for me was figuring the rest of it out. Especially when I got told that I was boring in bed."

Kenzie had been unable to prevent the little bark of laughter breaking from her throat at the thought.

"You know better now, don't you?" Kenzie had said, sliding down in the bed so she was flat on her back and cupping a hand around the back of Saana's neck. "Or will I have to prove to you that you're anything but boring?"

Saana's eyelids had drooped, veiling her gaze, but she couldn't hide the flush staining her cheeks when Kenzie licked her lips…

"Stop, stop, stop," Kenzie told herself, getting up and straightening her clothes with hands that had once more grown shaky at the memory of how that night had gone. "This isn't helping."

Maybe it would be better to remember arriving at this unwelcoming mausoleum and finding out that Saana was even more above her pay grade than Kenzie could ever have imagined.

It was as if she could hear Aunt Lena's voice in her head again, as she had back then.

"Honey, I don't know what kind of hoodoo this woman cast over you, but getting married and leaving everyone you know behind after only knowing someone for six days is madness. Are you sure it's not some kinda scam?"

Kenzie hadn't known whether to laugh or get angry. "I looked her up on the internet, Auntie. She's legit a doctor in Florida, just about to open up her own clinic. I can't see why *she'd* want to scam *me*."

Aunt Lena had shaken her head, the sadness on her face heartbreaking. "Well, I hope I'm wrong, but I think you're makin' a big mistake. Just remember that if things don't work out, you can always come back here."

In hindsight, she should have taken those prophetic words to heart and kept her big butt in Texas. Not that doing so would have changed anything, really.

She would still be heartbroken by the loss of Saana and probably still pregnant.

The babies. You gotta forget everything else and concentrate on them.

Staring at her reflection in the mirror, she repeated the words one more time in her head and then added softly, out loud, "Remember, you're not plannin' to be here forever. Just long enough to straighten everything out. I love her, but we don't belong here. Remember that, okay?"

And she'd have to remind herself continuously just how impossible it had been to fit into Saana's life back then and how depressed and dispirited she'd been when she finally left. For the sake of her unborn children, she couldn't allow herself to get back to that state.

This time, if she ended up staying, it would be different.

It *had* to be.

CHAPTER THREE

I SHOULDN'T HAVE let her come in.

Saana stood by one of the living room windows, looking past her own reflection to the gardens, lit for the night by low spotlights, mentally kicking herself for agreeing to hear Kenzie out.

It was outrageous for her to show back up like this, asking for some type of favor, ripping the dressing off the wounds she'd inflicted.

Making Saana remember all the things she'd tried so hard to forget.

How it felt to be happy. In love. Content in a way she'd never been before.

All I need to remember is the pain.

That would bolster her against whatever pleas Kenzie might make.

There was the sound of the powder room door opening down the hallway, the tap of Kenzie's boots on the hardwood floor as she came into the formal living room, but Saana didn't turn around.

"I needed that, badly," Kenzie said, and the sound of her voice made goose bumps fire out over Saana's back, chest and down her arms. A heated rush of arousal tightened her nipples and had tingling desire flooding her belly.

Get a hold of yourself.

Putting a bored expression on her face, she finally looked over at the younger woman, raising her eyebrows.

"Did you drive straight through?"

"I didn't think it would be wise." Kenzie hadn't sat down. In fact, she was hovering just inside the doorway, poised as though unsure whether to come in or not. "I stopped overnight in Pensacola."

Such banal conversation, ignoring the fact the air between them was thick with tension. Muffling a sigh, Saana walked over to an armchair. As she sat, she gestured to the nearby couch.

"Sit down, and let's get this over with."

She'd been trying not to look too closely at Kenzie but couldn't seem to stop her gaze from roaming over the curves and valleys of the other woman's body. Looking for the differences, she told herself. Trying to gauge how far along she was in her pregnancy.

But that really wasn't what registered.

Instead, she noted the sweet swing of Kenzie's hips as she strode across the room, the innate grace of her movements and the way she ran her hands down the outer seams of her jeans. She always complained about how sweaty her palms could get, making it a sure sign of nerves.

And the renewed burst of heat in Saana's belly had nothing to do with anger. Instead, it stemmed from the intimate memories she'd refused to let herself dwell on but now battered at her control.

The ones that arose in her dreams and left her twisting with unslaked desire.

Pushing them aside, she frowned across at Kenzie.

"Well?"

Kenzie rubbed a hand across her mouth, and Saana could see weariness in the movement. In the past, Kenzie had always been easy to read, her thoughts writ plain on her face and in her eyes. She'd been easygoing by nature, slow to anger, hard to rile, so there was seldom any reason for her to hide her emotions. Now Saana realized there was a barrier between them, making her strain to parse out what, exactly, the other woman was feeling.

"A year ago, my cousin Ashley asked me to be her surrogate."

Saana held up her hand, stopping the recitation. "This is the cousin who had cancer as a young woman?"

Kenzie nodded. "Yeah, that cousin. The treatment made her infertile, and she wanted me to donate eggs as well."

Saana didn't comment, but she remembered Kenzie saying Ashley was spoiled rotten and always wanted her own way over everything.

"I initially told her I wasn't interested, but then…" Kenzie looked down for a moment, her fingers curling into her palms on her lap. "Well, let's just say I finally agreed to do it."

"Why?"

Kenzie looked up, her brows pinched in, wrinkling the skin above her nose.

"Does it matter?"

Saana smoothed one hand down the opposite sleeve thoughtfully. Kenzie's resistance to being questioned made Saana want to push at the other woman in a way she knew she'd hate.

Shrugging, she replied, "If you don't want to tell me, then I guess the conversation is over."

Kenzie's lips tightened in annoyance, but then she inhaled deeply, clearing trying to take control of her temper. That in itself showed how emotional she was, since anger was usually her last defense. When she'd exhaled, she met and held Saana's gaze.

"Aunt Lena was dying, and she asked me to do it. She said Ashley's husband, Darryl, was a good man and would take care of his family." She blinked rapidly, clearing the moisture that had gathered in her eyes. "I knew that was true, so even though I also knew Ashley probably wouldn't be a very good mother, I agreed to the IVF, using Darryl's sperm."

There was no need to question that decision. Kenzie's aunt had raised her from when she was very young, and it had been obvious how much Kenzie loved her. If Lena had asked it, and it was at all possible, Kenzie would do it.

A situation her cousin Ashley probably hadn't hesitated to exploit. From what Kenzie had said in the past, Lena had done everything she could to make Ashley's life comfortable, probably out of a misplaced sense of guilt over her daughter's illness. And Ashley had taken every advantage of the situation.

In fact, when Kenzie and Saana had met in Las Vegas, Ashley had been there, too, because Lena had asked Kenzie to take her cousin on the trip. If she hadn't, she and Kenzie probably would never have gotten together, since Ashley spent all her time in the casino, leaving Kenzie to her own devices.

If Kenzie had been with the friend she'd initially wanted to take, she wouldn't have been alone on the bus tour. Would most likely have been unavailable to Saana.

Memories of that week tried to impose themselves on her, but Saana shook them off fiercely.

This was no time to contemplate the joys of the past, and even though the sound of Lena's name sent a jagged pain through Saana's chest, she found herself saying, "I'm sorry for your loss." Then, not wanting sentimentality to come too strongly into the conversation, she asked, "So what happened?"

"I got pregnant during the first cycle of IVF, with the twins. But when I was twenty weeks along, Darryl, whose family owns a technical-supply company for the oil industry, was killed in a freak accident on the oil platform he was visiting."

She paused, rubbing her hand over her mouth again, and Saana felt a pang of sympathy.

"That must have been a shock."

Kenzie nodded and closed her eyes for a moment, as though reliving the moment.

"It was, but there was worse to come. Right after the funeral, Ashley told me she didn't want the babies. She'd never really wanted to be a mother; had only agreed to the arrangement to make Darryl happy."

Kenzie bit her lower lip, her gaze affixed to Saana's, probably waiting for a reaction or question, but although there were many things Saana wanted to ask, she kept silent.

It wasn't her job to make any of this easier.

After a moment, Kenzie continued. "Of course, I decided to keep them, and Ashley signed away her rights."

Then she looked down at her lap, and Saana knew they were getting to the crux of the discussion. Yet there was a part of her that didn't want to hear the rest—that was whispering warnings about the pain she was opening herself up to just by engaging.

Rising abruptly, she walked over to the sideboard to pick up the decanter of brandy. As she poured a splash into a snifter, she was about to offer Kenzie some when she remembered her condition, and the reality of it slammed home.

They'd never gotten around to discussing children during their brief, impetuous marriage, but in the back of her mind, Saana had imagined them going through the process. Deciding which of them would carry the baby, picking a donor, helping each other through the IVF, lovingly growing their family.

Together.

Another dream shattered.

Her hand was trembling when she set down the decanter and, without turning around, she asked, "Can I offer you some water or juice?"

Waiting for Kenzie's reply was a good way to give herself a moment or two more to get her emotions under control.

"No." The reply was abrupt, and Kenzie's voice sounded

high and strained, as though she, too, had had enough of the stressful encounter. "Saana, listen—Darryl's parents have filed suit to gain custody of my babies when they're born."

She considered that for a moment, trying to work out the ramifications, to figure out just where she, of all people, came into it.

"So what do you want from me?" There could really only be one answer. "Money?"

The sound Kenzie made was impossible to interpret, especially with Saana's back still turned, but sounded like an outraged bark of laughter. Almost manic in nature.

"Hell no. Darryl gave me a lump sum of money when I agreed to the IVF, and even if he hadn't, I make—well, up until two weeks ago *made*—enough to support myself and my children."

She should have known better. The one thing Kenzie had never seemed interested in was Saana's considerable fortune. In fact, it seemed to have been something of an unpleasant surprise when Kenzie had found out exactly how wealthy her new wife was.

Taking a sip of her brandy, hoping the liquor's burn would steady her nerves, Saana finally turned to face Kenzie again. Leaning back against the sideboard, she braced herself, while the thunder of her heart in her ears made her voice sound far away.

"So what *do* you want?"

Kenzie stood up, seemingly no longer able to stay still, but instead of coming nearer to Saana, she walked away, toward the door.

Was she leaving?

It should have been a relief, but Saana had to stop herself from calling her back.

Then Kenzie turned on her heel to face Saana again and ran both hands down the outer seams of her jeans. Even from across the room, Saana could see the deep inhalation the other woman took, and then, in the midst of a long, rushing exhalation, she said, "I need you to pretend for the court that our marriage is solid and we'll be providing a good home environment for the babies."

And for the second time that evening, Saana's heart stuttered, a cold void opening in her belly as she stared in disbelief at the love of her life and her greatest heartbreak.

It took everything she had to hold on to her cool and not rage at Kenzie for even thinking up such a crazy, dangerous plan. Not to mention the sheer gall it took, after walking out on their marriage, to waltz back in and suggest they could pretend all was well between them. Just the thought of having Kenzie back in the house—back in her life—sent Saana's brain into a spin and her body into hyperdrive.

Yet, somehow, she stayed impassive and simply said, "No."

Kenzie had seen this side of Saana before. The coldly ruthless side she usually employed only when politeness, reason and all other lesser forms of discussion had failed.

Yet she'd never been the target of it, and that one icy word stung more than anything else she'd experienced that night.

But she couldn't allow Saana's attitude to deter her, even if the entire venture seemed like a lost cause. This was too important to take her refusal without a fight.

"Saana…"

The other woman turned away, putting the glass to her lips and tipping the entire finger of booze into her mouth. That uncharacteristic move gave Kenzie a tiny glimmer of hope.

Saana hardly drank anything more than a glass or two of wine.

"Darryl's parents are rich and well-connected in San Antonio. They've already laid out their argument, and my lawyer says it might very well work." The words tripped over each other as Kenzie tried to make her own case. "They said I was only ever meant to be a surrogate and had agreed to hand over the babies to Darryl and Ashley, so I shouldn't try to argue that now I want these children for myself."

Saana didn't seem to even be listening. Instead, she'd picked back up the decanter and was pouring herself another finger of whatever it was she was drinking.

"I'm just a poor nurse," Kenzie continued, making no effort to disguise her fear. Her desperation. "I don't own a house or have a lot of resources. Mr. and Mrs. Beauchamp know that."

"You should ask your cousin for her help." Saana could have been discussing the weather, her tone flat and disinterested. "I'm assuming she inherited her husband's estate and isn't hurting for resources. Since she was the one who put you in this position, the least she could do is help to get you out of it."

The familiar anger she felt whenever she thought about Ashley's complete lack of interest colored her voice when Kenzie replied.

"She doesn't give a damn. As far as she's concerned, she doesn't see the problem. Her advice was simply to hand the babies over after they're born and walk away."

Swirling the alcohol in her glass around and around, Saana shrugged lightly.

"Maybe that's the best thing for you to do. After all, from what you've said, the Beauchamps raised their son well, and they can give the children whatever they need to thrive."

Balling her hands into fists until her short nails dug into her palms, Kenzie fought for control.

"That's not an option," she said, hearing her voice waver and despising herself for it. "Once Darryl died, I knew I had to take responsibility for the twins. After all, they're mine too."

Something flashed behind Saana's eyes, and her lips tightened, but all she did was shrug again.

"Then there's the argument you need to make when you

go to court. It will probably be cut-and-dried. You donated the eggs, ergo the children are as much yours as Darryl's. If he's not here to take care of them, the responsibility is yours, and you're willing to take it on. I doubt the court would deny you that right."

Unable to stand still, Kenzie paced across the room, her heart hammering, fear stalking right along beside her. When she got to the French doors leading out onto the terrace, she paused, staring out into the darkness. In the distance, the lagoon gleamed as moonlight touched the waves, while the lights from buildings on the landward side sent slivers of silver onto the water.

All this she noticed vaguely while she scrambled for a stronger argument to convince Saana.

What more could she say—what could she do—to get the help she knew, in her heart and soul, was necessary?

The Beauchamps were determined to get their grandchildren and, in a way, she couldn't blame them. They'd lost their son, and the twins were the last connection they had to him. If she were in their position, Kenzie wondered if she wouldn't do the same thing too. Fight for the right to take and raise the babies since Darryl had lost the chance to do it himself.

And they had the resources and the connections to sway the court to their side, while Kenzie...

Well, all she had was the bone-deep knowledge that these children were hers and she'd move heaven and hell to keep them and raise them.

She already loved them.

From the first flutters of life, which, coincidentally, came just a few days after Darryl's death, something warm and sweet had bloomed in her chest, and she'd known. It had made her cry, that precious moment. She—who never cried, who'd trained herself to be strong in every circumstance—had sobbed like a child, and she'd made a promise to herself, the twins and to Darryl that she'd be there for them.

That she'd be a good mother and give them the maternal love she'd never had.

Bolstered by that thought, she turned just in time to see Saana down the last of her drink and put the glass down on the sideboard with a little snap.

"McKenzie, I meant what I said: I cannot help you."

"Can't? Or won't?" she fired back, her stomach twisting with disappointment and that never-ending fear.

Again, that dismissive shrug, which made Kenzie want to scream.

"Is there a distinction I'm missing?" Before Kenzie could reply, Saana chopped her hand through the air. "It doesn't really matter. You got yourself into this position, and you'll have to work it out yourself."

She headed for the door, then paused momentarily to add, "If you need a place to stay tonight—by all means, use the pool house, but I expect you to leave in the morning."

Then she strode out of the room, and Kenzie stayed where she was. It was only until she heard Saana's bedroom door close on the floor above that she moved, sinking down onto the floor and resting her cheek against the glass door.

Shaking.

Once more fighting tears.

What do I do now?

CHAPTER FOUR

HAD A NIGHT ever seemed so long? Saana couldn't think of another that had stretched on—pain-filled and debilitating—as though never to end, except for the night after Kenzie had walked away from their marriage.

Yet this one had been different, Saana realized as she sat on the edge of her bed and contemplated the hours just passed. Two years ago, she'd curled into a ball, arms wrapped around her belly, trying to hold herself in one piece. Although part of her had held on to the hope Kenzie would come back, she'd cried until, devoid of even one more tear, exhaustion had dragged her into sleep. In comparison, last night she'd been too wired and angry to doze for more than a few minutes at a time, her brain spinning like a top with what she should do.

Go downstairs and tell Kenzie to leave immediately.

Follow her to the pool house and demand to know the real reason she'd decided to end the marriage. It wasn't the first time Saana had been cruelly rejected by a lover, but she'd been so head over heels for Kenzie that her leaving had shattered whatever confidence Saana had. Didn't she deserve to know what it was about her that made her unlovable?

And then there was the venal part of her brain, which didn't seem concerned with *why*s and *wherefore*s but kept sending erotic messages to the rest of her body. All it was interested in was the potential ecstasy Kenzie could so effortlessly provide if Saana were willing to demand it... Maybe in exchange for the help the other woman had asked for?

That idea was so ridiculous Saana had scoffed at herself.

From the moment Kenzie's lips had touched hers in Vegas, Saana had been lost. And when she'd realized Kenzie instinctively understood exactly how to take Saana past pleasure to the heights of ecstasy, there had been no looking back. No other lover had ever figured out the perfect mix of control and complicity that rendered Saana compliant and undone by need.

Wrestling with the combination of anger and desire had made the night seem to stretch to eternity, and she'd paced back and forth, emotions like a tornado tearing through her mind and body.

Now, as she made her way into the bathroom to clean her teeth, she was no closer to any kind of reconciliation with her feelings, which seemed volatile enough to cause an explosion.

She'd never considered herself an emotional person. To her, life was something to enjoy, work hard at, think seriously about, but she'd never felt *immersed* in it the way she'd observed others to be. Yes, there were highs and lows, but she'd never wailed over a lost relationship, gotten hysterical with joy or fallen so in love that she'd lost her head.

Until she'd met Kenzie.

Pausing with her toothbrush buzzing away in place in her mouth, she let herself remember their first meeting, on a bus tour to Lake Mead and Hoover Dam. As she'd stepped onto the bus, she'd immediately spotted Kenzie, sitting by herself and staring out the window. Something about her profile had made Saana's heart stutter, and she'd slowed, her gaze affixed to the beautiful, dark-skinned woman, willing her to look up. As she got closer, she'd noticed the plaid shirt, worn like a loose jacket over a black tee but unable to fully disguise the lush figure beneath. Short, curly hair stuck out from beneath a ballcap, and as Saana paused beside the seat, she could see the smooth skin of one thigh between the rips in Kenzie's jeans.

Even her well-worn cowboy boots caused Saana's instant fascination to increase.

Then those gorgeous, umber eyes had turned her way, and Saana's knees weakened.

Hanging on to her cool by a thread, she'd smiled and asked, "Anyone sitting here?"

Kenzie had blinked up at her for what seemed like forever and then smiled back, sending Saana's heart rate through the roof.

"I guess you are."

Saana had thought of that moment often, classifying it as love at first sight. *Un coup de foudre*, as her French teacher called it. Something Saana had never believed in.

Until that first glimpse of Kenzie.

All she'd wanted when she went to Vegas was a simple holiday. One that wasn't on the Riviera or anywhere that would necessitate evening gowns and meetups with old school friends or relatives. The stress she'd been under in getting her practice ready to open had been enormous, and she'd known once she opened the doors, she would only get busier.

Having a quickie romance hadn't even been on her radar. Falling in love? If someone had mentioned that, she'd have laughed herself silly.

But didn't love last forever instead of dying, leaving only anger behind?

And, if she were being honest, lust.

Kenzie had been the best lover she'd ever had, and even now, angrier than before, remembering the things they'd done together drove shards of arousal deep into Saana's body.

Finished in the bathroom, she went to her closet to pull out a sundress. After she tugged it on, she crossed the room to the windows and, once there, opened the curtains facing the pool house. It was attached to the main house by an enclosed walkway and was sometimes used to house guests, as well as all the paraphernalia needed for days on or by the water.

The blinds were drawn, and there was no sign of life.

Had Kenzie left already?

Saana was about check the security feed to see if her car was still parked out front when the door to the pool house opened, and Kenzie stepped out into the early-morning light.

A shiver climbed Saana's spine as she watched her estranged wife walk down the path, through the flower garden and to the dock. Kenzie was wearing her usual casual attire, which consisted of colorful board shorts with a plain white T-shirt that hung down to her hips and rubber flip-flops on her feet. She hadn't taken off the satin sleep bonnet she wore to stop her hair from getting tangled, which brought back another rush of memories and made Saana smile despite herself. For a moment, rage slipped away, leaving her to savor Kenzie's confident stride, the roll of her hips, the straight-backed posture that silently proclaimed that she was a force to be reckoned with.

And she was that—an immovable force. Independent to a fault, despite her easygoing nature. Determined. Self-reliant.

All this, Saana had learned quickly during their first few days together as spouses, which made Kenzie's plea for help that much more powerful.

Yet it was impossible to disregard the past, especially in light of not being able to understand it. There had been no closure—no proper explanation. Saana had tried to give Kenzie whatever—everything—she could possibly want or need, and yet it hadn't been enough. Instead, she'd been left feeling as though she'd failed—a sensation Saana wasn't used to and hated with every cell in her body.

It was impossible to put the pain aside, but something deep inside whispered that she was being hypocritical. She, who constantly talked about helping others, was turning her back on someone desperate enough to put her considerable pride and independence aside to ask for her assistance.

The person Saana had loved with every fiber of her being.

Already, despite her bone-deep resistance to the ramifications, a plan was forming in her head, and for the first time in her life, she cursed her habitually methodical nature. It laid itself out before her, presenting itself as the most natural thing in the world. She would help Kenzie the way she'd asked and perhaps, in so doing, might at least be able to put a period on this painful, distressing part of her life.

Yet there were numerous stumbling blocks, she thought, watching her wife sit on one of the benches overlooking the water and rub the small of her back as if it ached. The one thing Kenzie valued above all else was her autonomy, and if she accepted Saana's conditions, she'd have to surrender it— lock, stock and barrel.

And Saana herself would have to keep the tightest control ever on her own emotions. There could be no sliding back into a real relationship. The reminder that once Kenzie got what she wanted she'd leave again had to be kept at the forefront constantly.

Saana knew herself well enough to admit that, given the slightest chance, she'd fall for her enigmatic, frustrating, absolutely wonderful wife all over again.

Turning away from the window, she went to finish getting ready, already regretting the impulse to help. Caught somewhere between hoping Kenzie refused that help and longing for another chance to spend time with the woman who'd captured her heart.

Kenzie sat on one of the benches near the dock, looking out over the water, still trying unsuccessfully to figure out what to do next.

Return to San Antonio?

Stay in Florida?

Take off and start over somewhere else, hoping the Beauchamps wouldn't find her? Maybe head south to Mexico since she was fluent in Spanish? Her savings would definitely go further there.

She had no idea what would be best, but she did know coming here had been a terrible mistake.

Returning to the house in Indialantic had brought back all those feelings of inadequacy she'd run from before, and she despised herself for it. No matter how out of place she'd always felt here, this was no time to be dwelling on it.

Everything she did from now on had to be in the twins' best interests, and if Saana had agreed to her crazy plan, Kenzie would have had to just suck it up.

But Saana had turned her down flat, so she could go on hating the house as much as she wanted.

Not that it was ugly or a monstrosity, despite Kenzie's habit of thinking of it as a mausoleum. In fact, the rambling two-story structure, built in a vaguely Spanish style, with its elaborate gardens and massive pool in the back, was probably someone's dream home. Especially being set on a two-acre riverside lot—almost unheard of in this small enclave—and having a private dock and boathouse.

But she'd felt lost and insignificant in the house, particularly when Saana was out and Kenzie was there alone, which happened often in those early days. The great room was twice as big as the entire downstairs of the house Kenzie had grown up in, and it was just one of three sitting rooms on the ground floor. And there was also a formal dining room, a breakfast room, a large library and office, and a room Saana referred to as *the parlor*.

Kenzie could agree that, viewed from the angle of a disinterested outsider, it was palatial, if old-fashioned and far too big. One weekend afternoon, while they were swimming, she'd asked Saana why she lived here, and her reply had been enlightening.

"My grandfather left it to me," she'd said with unmistakable fondness in her voice. "Under his will, Gran had a life interest in the house, but she moved to Palm Beach right after he died, so I moved in."

"Don't you find it too big?" Kenzie had asked, really meaning that she thought it too huge for just the two of them, but Saana had shaken her head, obviously not hearing the subtext.

"It's my family home," she'd replied, moving closer to Kenzie in the water until her hands brushed against Kenzie's thighs. "My mother was raised here, and I spent a lot of time with my grandparents when I was growing up, so it holds wonderful memories for me."

Then she'd grinned. "Besides, it's a historic house, built in the 1940s by a Hollywood producer as a place to entertain movie stars. Can you imagine what they got up to down here? All the crazy parties they must have had, far from the prying eyes of the press?"

"All the orgies, you mean?" Kenzie had asked, completely distracted by the sight of Saana's lovely breasts bobbing just below the waterline, barely covered by her skimpy bikini top. "All the skinny-dipping and naughtiness... Like this?"

She'd been untying Saana's top as she spoke, and her wife's shuddering sigh of agreement had been more than enough for her to let the conversation fade away.

Okay, those memories weren't helpful right now. They made her want to squirm with the ever-present desire for Saana—that inescapable current of arousal that flowed in Kenzie's blood for her, no matter how far apart they were.

They were perfectly matched between the sheets. Unfortunately, that harmony hadn't existed outside the bedroom.

Besides, that was all in the past. Right now, what she needed to do was concentrate on the present and, most importantly, the future.

The sound of a door closing had her looking over her shoulder, and her heart gave a shudder at the sight of Saana walking down the path toward her. Dressed in a vividly patterned dress that hugged her breasts and flowed like water around her lithe figure, she made Kenzie's mouth water and a burning lump form in her stomach.

No matter how hard she'd tried, she hadn't been able to forget.

Not just the way it felt to make love with Saana but what it felt like to love and be loved.

The tenderness.

The sensation of having someone to care for and knowing Saana had cared about her too.

She knew she'd never experience anything like it again because she'd given her entire being over into Saana's hands, and there was no getting it back.

But she couldn't let the other woman know the effect she still had, so from somewhere deep inside, she found the ability to appear calm and unconcerned as Saana got closer. She even tore her gaze away and turned back toward the water.

"You always loved it down here," Saana said as she took a seat on the other bench. "I figured this is where you'd be. We need to talk."

There was something different about the way she spoke. Her tone was still cool, but also, beneath the control, there was a hint of something else. Not hesitancy but maybe close to it.

"I plan to leave soon," Kenzie said, unwilling to explain that she didn't have the first clue about where to go. "So don't worry that I'll be hanging around too much longer."

"Actually, I came to tell you that I'm reconsidering your request."

Kenzie's head whipped around, seemingly of its own free

will, so she could see Saana's expressionless face. Her heart stopped for an instant before galloping back into action, and her breath hung suspended in her chest long enough to make her light-headed.

Finally forcing her lungs to work again, she stammered, "Wh…what?"

Saana shrugged, coolly dismissive.

"I've decided to help you after all. But there is a number of important conditions you have to agree to."

The surge of excitement that had roared through Kenzie waned slightly at Saana's words, replaced by suspicion laced with an undercurrent of fear, although she wasn't sure what she was afraid of.

Swallowing that dread, reminding herself this was the best outcome she could hope for, she licked her bottom lip and asked, "Like what?"

"The first is that no one, and I mean no one, can know what we're doing. Our subterfuge must be completely and utterly believable to any onlookers."

Kenzie ran her tongue over her suddenly dry lips, trying to think through the consequences of Saana's words.

"Did you have anyone in particular in mind?" she asked.

Saana's nostrils flared slightly as she drew in a sharp breath. "My family. Delores."

"But shouldn't they know the truth?"

How on earth could they keep the true nature of their relationship from people so close to Saana? Delores, her housekeeper, was at the house every weekday. Keeping up the facade of a happy marriage in front of her would be almost impossible.

"They are the *last* people who should," Saana said, the steel in her voice unmistakable. "Think about it. If the case against you goes to court and they are called to testify, are you expecting them to perjure themselves for you?"

If she were being honest, Kenzie knew she would ask just

that, in a heartbeat, but she could see Saana's point. So, reluctantly, she agreed. "You're right."

It struck her, then, that she would be giving up her autonomy to Saana again, and it wasn't in her nature to give over control of her life so easily.

"I'll need to work," she said quickly, wanting Saana to know she didn't intend to sponge off her just because she was in a bind. "I have to think about the future, and that means not sitting around for however long it takes to get the legalities cleared up."

There was a long pause as Saana's gaze searched hers until Kenzie was fighting the urge to look away. Then another of those careless shrugs.

"I know of a clinic that needs a nurse right away. I can put you in touch with the HR lady on Monday, if you want."

"Yes." She knew it was petty to add neither *please* nor *thank you* to the acceptance, but although she'd been the one to request the assistance, having to accept it made her hackles rise. "That would be great."

After another long look, the corners of Saana's lips twisted, and she got up.

"I'll take care of it, but now I have somewhere to be. While I'm gone, there's plenty of food in the kitchen, so make yourself at home."

Her mouth twisted again, and Kenzie bit her lip as the unintentional barb hit her straight in the solar plexus.

Or *was* it unintentional? From Saana's expression, it seemed that way, but Kenzie was having a hard time reading her.

Before she could answer, Saana continued. "We'll discuss the situation further when I get home this afternoon. You should take your bags up to the bedroom and start getting settled in."

Again, Kenzie found her breath caught in her throat, trapping whatever she was going to say next, as the full truth of what she'd agreed to exploded in her brain.

"The bedroom," she parroted like an idiot, waves of heat and cold running uncontrollably over her skin.

That gained her a haughty, eyebrows-raised glance from Saana.

"How else will we convince everyone that we're back together if we're not sharing my bed?" Saana asked before turning and walking away.

CHAPTER FIVE

HOW LIKE SAANA to simply carry on with her life as if nothing unusual had happened, making an earth-shattering pronouncement, then leaving Kenzie reeling in her wake.

What could be more important than sticking around and hashing out the situation now that she'd decided to help?

However, it didn't surprise Kenzie that her wife had dropped a bombshell and left, sticking to her schedule no matter what. Saana lived an almost regimented life. Nothing could be allowed to interfere with her plans. Oh, she could be spontaneous on occasion, but once she'd come up with an agenda, it was written in stone.

Which always made Kenzie want to mess those plans up.

But as she watched Saana go back into the house, Kenzie faced the agonizing fact that her wife was right. While Saana was close to her parents and brother, back in the day there hadn't been a lot of family get-togethers. Unless that had changed, the Ameris weren't Kenzie's biggest problem. Delores would be the hardest to fool since the housekeeper came Monday to Friday, arriving about ten in the morning and leaving at four in the afternoon.

She'd not only potentially see Saana and Kenzie interacting, but she'd also see all the little signs of how they lived. Whether one bed had been slept in or two. Where Kenzie had her clothes hanging or if one of the myriad guest bathrooms had been used.

There was no way to get around Delores.

A familiar oily sensation suddenly arose in the back of her throat, bringing Kenzie out of her unhappy thoughts. Looking down at her stomach, rubbing it with both hands, she dredged up a smile from somewhere.

"You guys are hungry, huh? Yeah, Momma's been neglectin' you, but we'll go rustle up some grub now, just to keep you happy."

After getting up, she made her way toward the mansion slowly, wondering if Saana was still there or had already left.

And she couldn't help the feeling of mingled annoyance and relief when she heard Saana's car start up and then drive away.

As she ate, Kenzie tried to figure out some way to keep up the pretense of the marriage being back on the right track without sharing a bed.

The last thing she needed was to be that close to Saana.

The need to touch, to arouse, to feel that lithe, sexy body coming apart beneath her hands and lips might well pound all her good sense to dust.

There must be some way to make their lies believable without getting all tangled up together that way again.

From the beginning, they'd been unable to keep their hands off each other. They'd actually slept together the day after they met, and if Kenzie had had her way, it would have happened the first day instead. But she'd realized right off the bat that Saana wouldn't want to be rushed. She'd thought Saana wasn't as comfortable with physical intimacy as Kenzie was, but that reserve, near hesitancy, had made her even more attractive.

And when they'd finally gotten into bed together...

The deep shudder that fired through her body had Kenzie shutting those memories down and pushing her plate away.

She had to forget the past and concentrate on the present

ANN McINTOSH 49

and future. Her babies were depending on her, and right now, she needed to figure out the best way to make the situation with Saana work without making everything worse.

Maybe they could negotiate once Saana decided to get her behind back to the mansion and discuss it, but in the meantime, Kenzie accepted what she had to do.

After bringing her car around to the garage, she pulled out her bags. For the first time, she was glad there was an elevator in the house, which she'd silently scoffed at before.

"Did your grandparents have mobility issues?" she'd asked Saana when she first saw it.

"No," she'd replied with a chuckle. "It was put in when the house was built, back in the forties. Apparently, no one wanted to climb stairs if they could ride up instead."

And it was so elaborate, with gold paint all over everything, including the carved woodwork and the folding grill at the front.

Ridiculous but useful now, when she had a couple of hefty suitcases and a pair of babies in her belly that caused her to think—and overthink—everything she did. While the doctor had told her she was healthy and shouldn't change her lifestyle, it was impossible not to worry.

These babies were precious and, in her mind, a miracle. Kenzie would do everything in her power to keep them safe and bring them into the world as strong as possible.

At the door to Saana's room, Kenzie's breath hitched, and she found herself rooted in place, battered by memories— both good and bad.

The room looked the same. Large and bright, it was decorated with sleek furniture and soothing colors. But Kenzie felt anything but relaxed as her gaze tracked from the bed to the chaise longue, then the dressing table, each bringing to mind a moment of past tenderness or passion. There, in front of the fireplace, they'd lain with entangled legs and caressing hands, whispers of love barely audible above the crackle of the flames.

Wandering in, Kenzie blinked against the tears filling her eyes. She'd stood behind Saana at the vanity, brushing her hair, which then had fallen halfway down her back. Watched with sweet delight the way her wife's eyes had drifted closed in pleasure.

There was even a lingering scent that was fundamentally Saana, and each time Kenzie inhaled it was like taking a little of their past back into herself.

It was heartbreaking and enticing all at once, and Kenzie knew she shouldn't indulge in this soppy emotionality.

Giving herself a mental shake, she quickly unpacked, placing her clothes in the ample walk-in closet, and then high-tailed it out of the room and back downstairs. Once there, though, the weight of the house seemed to press down on her, and the anger she'd felt toward Saana earlier returned.

Why should she stick around, cooling her jets while Saana was off doing whatever?

And wouldn't it serve Saana right to come home and not find Kenzie waiting like she expected?

With a toss of her head, Kenzie went back upstairs to change. Then, without any real idea of where she was going, she locked up the house and took off.

Driving south, she ended up at the Sebastian Inlet State Park and, after stopping at the commissary to buy a couple bottles of water, went for a long walk on the beach, followed by lunch at the beachside restaurant.

Determined not to be at the mansion when Saana got home, she took her time meandering north on Highway A1A later that afternoon, stopping here and there, reorienting herself. In the past, she'd been so wrapped up with Saana and her studies she hadn't really explored as much as she could have.

Yet she knew she was really just dragging her feet in the

hopes that Saana would get home and, finding her gone, realize Kenzie wasn't sitting around waiting for her.

The joke was on her, though, when she returned to Indialantic after having dinner and Saana wasn't there. Eventually, when the exhaustion brought on by her travels and day out was overwhelming, she admitted defeat and went to bed, fuming.

The next morning, when she realized Saana hadn't come home at all, she was forced to face a thought that hadn't even occurred to her before.

Was there someone else in Saana's life? Someone she'd run to, so as to get away from Kenzie?

And the rush of jealousy was both unwanted and far too strong to be ignored.

Saana woke up, disoriented, to find her cheek on something hard, her arms above her head on the same flat surface. It was only when she straightened, groaning at the pain in her neck and back, that she realized she'd fallen asleep at her desk. For a long moment, she couldn't understand why she was in her Suntree clinic office; then it all came rushing back.

Kenzie was in Florida, at the house.

Pregnant and wanting help.

Saana shook her head, rubbing her sore cheek, as she acknowledged that she'd run away yesterday, scared by what she was agreeing to, what it would do to her emotional equilibrium.

But she'd spent the whole day before trying to figure out another way to help Kenzie without her staying in Florida—at the Indialantic house—and had come up empty.

And she was honest enough to recognize that she didn't really want to find an alternative. That there was a huge part of her that reveled in the thought of being around Kenzie again. Having her back in her life.

She must be a secret masochist. Hadn't the past pain taught her anything?

When Kenzie had said she was going back to Texas for an undetermined period of time to take care of her sick aunt, Saana tried to find some other way to solve the problem.

"I can hire a nurse to take care of her," she'd told Kenzie. "Or we can find a really nice long-term care facility."

"Aunt Lena doesn't need either of those things yet." Kenzie had hardly seemed to be listening, intent on her packing. "What she needs is someone to be there with her. Someone she knows and trusts."

"What about her children?" Saana had heard the desperation in her own voice and despised herself for it. "Why aren't they taking care of her? They live in San Antonio, don't they?"

Kenzie had just shaken her head, rejecting every suggestion, refusing to say how long she'd be gone.

"Listen, with the pandemic, both Raul and Justin have formed a bubble with their families, and Ashley's as useful to her mom as teats on a bull. I *have* to go."

And she'd refused to say she'd come back at some point.

Saana had seen it as another example of her wife's stubbornness and overreaching independence. Her aunt was her responsibility, and she wouldn't consider any ideas other than what she'd come up with, even if it meant abandoning her marriage.

Abandoning Saana, who loved her beyond reason.

And there was no getting around the fact that this was, once again, a temporary situation. Once Kenzie got custody of her babies, she'd take off.

That was what Saana had to keep front of mind, no matter how her silly heart was already trying to get involved.

A quick glance at the clock showed it was just after six, giving her ample time to get home and back to the office in time for her first appointment at nine.

There was a lot she had to do today, along with her usual clinic appointments, and the first would be talking to Kenzie.

Had she wondered where Saana had spent the night? Had she slept in their bed, the way Saana had told her she needed to?

Saana forced herself to shrug at the idea and ignore the wash of heat climbing her spine.

Just because they'd be sharing a bed didn't mean this bone-deep longing would—or should—be assuaged. In fact, making love with Kenzie would be the very worst thing she could do.

Things were complicated enough, she thought as she headed out into the already bright morning light, without throwing any more knots into the puzzle.

Hopefully, the HR manager at the Eau Gallie clinic would get her message first thing this morning and contact Kenzie regarding the job there.

Saana stopped as she was driving out of the parking lot.

Did Kenzie still have the same number? She hadn't thought to ask. Hitting the button on the steering wheel, she recorded a text message.

Is this still your phone number, McKenzie?

Then, without waiting for a reply, she headed for home, running through everything she wanted to get done over the next couple of days.

If she could keep thinking about the practicalities, she would be okay.

Hopefully.

It took twenty minutes to get home, during which Saana sent a slew of text messages, trying to get life into some semblance of order. There was nothing worse than feeling as though things were topsy-turvy, and with Kenzie's sudden return, she needed everything else to be under control.

Just as she was approaching the gates, her phone pinged with a one-word reply from Kenzie:

Yes.

Kenzie at her laconic best, and it put Saana on alert. You knew there was trouble on the horizon when Kenzie became quiet instead of her usual easy, slightly chatty self.

It caused Saana to be ready for some type of battle when she entered the house through the garage and followed the sound of the kitchen radio playing.

Although her back was turned and she was chopping something on the counter in front of her, as soon as Saana stepped into the kitchen, Kenzie said, "Mornin'. Want some breakfast?"

Not quite what she was expecting, so it took Saana a moment to catch up and reply. "Yes, please. I have to get ready for work, though."

"No problem. I haven't started cooking yet. How long will you be?"

"About twenty minutes?"

She made it a question and got a wave of Kenzie's knife hand in reply. "That'll work."

Feeling dismissed, Saana headed upstairs to shower. By the time she came back, breakfast was on the table, and they both started eating.

"Mmm..." Saana closed her eyes for a moment in pleasure as the flavor of the egg white, spinach and cheese omelet burst on her tongue. "This is so good. Thank you."

Kenzie gave a nod, acknowledging the compliment, but Saana saw a flash of amusement cross her face.

Suddenly, it was easy to read Kenzie again, and Saana remembered a conversation they'd had before, when Kenzie had realized Saana didn't know how to cook.

"How do you get to thirty-two without being able to cook?" she'd asked, laughing but with raised eyebrows that hinted at her horror. "I was in charge of making dinner at Aunt Lena's since I was eight or nine."

It had been one more reminder of just how different their upbringings had been and the responsibility Kenzie had shouldered at a young age. Not wanting to show how touched and saddened she felt at this glimpse of her wife's previous life, she'd given a dismissive shrug.

"I never had to learn and wasn't very interested anyway."

It had made her want to do everything for Kenzie. Wrap her in cotton wool and give her any and everything she'd had to do without.

Well, that wasn't in the cards anymore, and she wasn't planning to even pretend she still wanted to cosset Kenzie.

Clearing her throat, she banished those thoughts and got back to practicalities. "You'll need an ob-gyn here. I can give you a list of the best ones, and you can see if any of them will take you as a patient."

Kenzie hesitated and then lifted her chin a notch. "I was going to ask you if you could get me in with whichever one you thought would be best for me, in my situation. If I just call and ask if he or she is taking new patients, I might get turned down."

It was hard to keep her instinctive reaction of shock off her face, but Saana thought she did a good job of it.

"I can do that, if that's what you want."

"It is," Kenzie replied, her chin still at a combative angle. "I want the best for the babies."

Apparently, there was nothing Kenzie wouldn't do for those babies—even ask for more help.

"I'll reach out to Dr. Ramcharam," she replied. "She's the

best in my book, and a maternal-fetal medicine specialist too." She glanced at her phone, then pushed back from the table. "I have to go. My first patient is at nine."

"So I guess you don't have time to talk now?" The question was mild enough, but Saana wasn't fooled. The crease that appeared in Kenzie's forehead told the true story.

"No, I have to get to work."

"What do I say to Delores? Do I just brazen it out?" No mistaking the hint of temper in her voice. "We haven't even decided what we're going to tell everyone."

Battling a rush of unaccountable anger, Saana shrugged.

"You figure it out," she replied, hearing the frost in her own voice but unable to suppress it. "All I told everyone was that you had gone to nurse your aunt, who had terminal pancreatic cancer. Just let me know what you decide our story is going to be."

She'd been hopeful at first that Kenzie would come back. Then hope had turned to sorrow, which had to be hidden so no one would feel sorry for her. Afterward, she'd simply felt embarrassed at having made a fool of herself over a woman who clearly didn't love her the way she'd claimed.

Angry as she thought about all she'd been put through by the beautiful woman across the table from her, she walked away before she could say something she might regret. But she was brought to a halt at the door by Kenzie's voice.

"One last thing. Are you seeing anyone? Because, if you are, I'll find some other way to deal with the situation."

How tempting it was to lie and say she was. It would be the perfect out, wouldn't it?

"No. I'm not seeing anyone right now."

And she didn't wait for Kenzie to reply.

CHAPTER SIX

KENZIE TURNED IN to the parking lot at the Eau Gallie clinic twenty minutes early and looked around. Just a block away from US 1, the area was mixed residential and commercial, although the majority of the businesses seemed to have failed, since the buildings she could see were mostly abandoned. The few remaining houses looked sad and unloved, some with boarded-up windows and overgrown yards.

The clinic itself was housed in what looked like an old strip mall, and that, at least, looked clean and well maintained. The sign above the door was fairly small and simply said *Preston Medical*, and inside she could see a figure standing by the door. It looked like a guard.

Tilting the rearview mirror, she checked her face and hair and then sat back in her seat and took a deep breath.

She hadn't felt this frazzled in a long time. And while she'd be the first to admit life had been throwing a lot of stuff at her over the past ten months, she placed the blame squarely at Saana's feet.

Once faced with the situation they were now in, the Saana of old would've put together a plan and presented it as being written in stone. Her way or the highway. Now it seemed she was leaving it all up to Kenzie to sort out. Not that Kenzie was quarreling about that. After all, it was what she was used to from everyone else in her life.

Just not Saana, who was hardwired to take control of any situation involving someone she cared about. Methodically plan everything within her ability and do whatever it took to make that plan work. Abdicating the responsibility of figuring out what they should say demonstrated just how little she cared—Saana was no longer in love. It explained everything.

Which should be a good thing, right? They both knew their impulsive marriage had been a mistake and that it wouldn't have lasted, even if Kenzie hadn't gone back to Texas to take care of Aunt Lena.

It was better this way, especially for Saana, but it still hurt like hell.

Not that she was looking to revive their marriage, Kenzie reminded herself sternly. All that was important was to put on a good performance for the courts and have them decide in her favor.

That was what had galvanized her earlier to get their story straight since Saana hadn't.

The best thing, she decided, was to keep it simple and just add a few details so it all made sense. She'd texted Saana the concocted story, asking if she had anything to add, and gotten one word in response.

No.

Thankfully, the call from Marion Nunez, the HR lady at Preston Medical, had come at nine. Setting the appointment for ten thirty gave Kenzie an opportunity to get out of the house before Delores got to work.

She hadn't felt competent to deal with the housekeeper just then.

Now, with another glance at the time, she decided to go in.

The man inside opened the door as soon as she got to it, asking her name and checking the clipboard before stepping back so she could fully enter the waiting area. Then he called Ms. Nunez to let her know Kenzie was there, and within a couple of minutes, a short, older woman with bright pink hair came bustling into the reception area.

"Ah, McKenzie," she said with a broad smile. "It's so nice to meet you. Thank you for coming on such short notice."

"My pleasure," she replied, shaking the outstretched hand.

"Come on, then. Follow me, and we'll have a chat."

The HR office was to the left, down a corridor, past some examination rooms and a couple of doors with brackets on them, clearly to hold signs of some type. Once they were seated on either side of Ms. Nunez's desk, Kenzie found herself the focus of the other woman's sharp blue gaze.

"I was looking over your CV before you came and was interested by the fact that you've only been qualified for two years. Can you tell me about your path to nursing?"

Ouch. She was going straight to the weak spot in the CV, and Kenzie felt her heart sink even as she kept the smile on her face.

"Well, ma'am, I always knew I wanted to be a nurse but also knew I'd have to keep workin' while I studied so as not to be in debt when I left college. So it took me longer than most to get my degree. As you can see, I did work as a nurses' assistant at the hospital before I qualified, and that experience has been invaluable."

Ms. Nunez nodded seemingly happy with the explanation. "I do see that, and it's telling that the same hospital you worked at before immediately hired you on after you graduated." She steepled her fingers under her chin. "You were told that, if hired, this would be a temporary position?"

"That's all I'm looking for at this time." Kenzie knew it was against labor laws for the other woman to ask if she was pregnant, but she didn't offer that information either. She really wanted something to do, to make money, until the babies arrived. There was no way she'd give them a reason not to hire her.

"Good." Seemingly satisfied, Ms. Nunez leaned back in her chair. "Let me tell you a little about the clinic and the work we do here."

Kenzie had looked it up online while she was getting dressed to come to the interview, and she knew about the Preston Trust and the fact that it was a low-cost facility, but Ms. Nunez was able to tell her a great deal more.

"We treat women who've been referred to us by shelters, other clinics, emergency rooms, etcetera, but our goal is not just to treat immediate wounds or issues but develop a care plan for the patients. To this end, we partner with labs, specialists and pharmacies to ensure a holistic approach."

She paused, making sure Kenzie was following, and after receiving a nod, continued.

"We have a radiologist, endocrinologist and ob-gyn on-site once a month, offering mammograms, diabetes clinics and pelvic exams. But the mainstay of our clinic is the nurses, who are charged not only with assisting the doctors, but are also our eyes and ears when it comes to patient needs. The directors believe that the only way to truly serve the community is to allow the women coming here to express their needs. To become, in effect, stakeholders in the clinic."

"I understand," Kenzie said slowly. "I grew up in a poor neighborhood when I was a child, and people there often used the emergency room as their primary care facility. A place like this would allow more women to have their medical needs met without clogging up emerge."

"Exactly." Ms. Nunez smiled and then, totally unexpectedly, added, "Can you start tomorrow afternoon?"

Caught off guard, Kenzie could only stare like a deer caught in the headlights and grin like a fool.

"Yes. Yes, I can," she finally said, causing Ms. Nunez to lightly slap her hands on her desk and push to her feet.

"Perfect. Let me show you around."

An hour later, Kenzie left, feeling as if she were walking on air. She'd been hopeful about the job but hadn't dreamed she'd be hired on immediately. And this was exactly the type of facility she'd have picked to work at. Not only was it set up to do good for women in need, but also it operated during the afternoon and evening. Saana worked during the day, while Kenzie would be working at night, thereby limiting the amount of time they spent together.

A win all round.

Just as she settled into the driver's seat, still grinning, her phone rang.

Speak of the devil.

"Hi, Saana. What's up?"

"Just checking to see if you heard from the people at the clinic yet."

Kenzie couldn't hold back the little bubble of laughter that rose in her throat. "I just finished the interview. I start tomorrow."

"Congratulations. You can tell me all about it later, before we go to my parents for dinner."

"What?"

"No need to shriek in my ear." Having just about caused Kenzie's heart to stop, Saana had the audacity to sound amused. "We're going to have to face them sooner rather than later. I called Mom and told her you were back, and she invited us over. They're expecting us at six-thirty."

"I was hoping for later rather than sooner," Kenzie muttered. "But will you be back from work in time to get there?" In the past, Saana had often worked until eight or nine at night.

"Yes, but tonight's the only night I can, so we have to go. See you at the house at about five. Bye."

Kenzie cursed under her breath and stared at the phone for a moment more before tossing it on the passenger seat.

It was too much for one day. Clearly in agreement, one of

the babies rolled over, making Kenzie gasp and rub the spot where a little elbow—or was that a foot?—poked out from her side.

"Yes," she crooned, kneading the little bump. "You agree, right? Getting all dressed up to go see the Ameris isn't high on our list of fun things to do."

Although she had to admit Saana's parents had never been mean to her or made her feel unwelcome. What they *had* made her feel was like a country bumpkin. Not by anything they said but simply by being their habitual, elegant selves.

Speaking of which…

"What the heck am I supposed to wear?"

Nothing she had from when she lived here before would fit, and just the thought of driving to one of the elegant boutiques in Viera to look for something was exhausting. Looking back at the early days of their marriage, she recognized her own desperation to fit in, to not embarrass Saana, and she kissed her teeth in annoyance.

Reality now was, they were playing at being together for the babies' sakes, and Kenzie no longer felt the need to bend over backward to pretend she belonged. She never would, and that, in its own way, was freeing.

They could take her as she was.

But that didn't mean she could turn up at Saana's parents' home in a T-shirt and board shorts or the scrubs she'd worn to the interview.

"We're goin' shopping, babies. But don't worry," she added, starting the car, "it won't take too long. I promise."

Of course the one day she absolutely needed to leave work on time, Saana found herself running late with a patient, not getting home until almost five forty-five.

"I won't be long," she called to Kenzie, who was in the small TV room off the great room.

The only answer she got sounded suspiciously like a snort, but she didn't have time to investigate.

After a quick shower and having gotten dressed, she hurried back downstairs, calling, "I'm ready."

The TV went off, and Saana heard the distinctive clack of cowboy boots approaching.

"You're gonna be late for your own funeral," Kenzie drawled as she came down the hallway, her tone light but her chin tilted up at a pugnacious angle.

She was dressed in jeans and cowboy boots but had on a soft cotton short-sleeved tunic in swirls of greens, blues and copper that clung to her breasts. Then it furled softly down over her belly to her hips. Her hair was a riot of twisted curls around her head, framing her face, and she'd added a simple pair of copper-toned earrings and a chunky bead necklace that nettled right in her cleavage.

Saana's breath caught in her throat, and for a moment, she couldn't speak. Couldn't move. And her heart was racing so hard her entire body flashed hot.

Molten.

Like wax dripping from an upended candle.

Kenzie came to a halt in front of her, eyes flashing, chin still at that combative angle, but Saana didn't have the presence of mind to understand what the problem possibly could be.

Instead, instinctively, she blurted, "You look amazing."

Kenzie's lips parted as though she were about to speak, hung open for a second and then snapped shut again.

Shaking her head, she brushed past Saana and muttered, "Thanks. You look nice, too, as usual. Now, let's go. We're gonna be late."

Why was it so hard to get her legs to move? She all but stumbled after Kenzie to the car, trying—and failing—to keep her gaze off the swing of the other woman's hips.

By the time they got going, Saana's mouth was as dry as sawdust and her brain was a whirligig.

"What did you tell your parents?"

Kenzie's question forced Saana to pull herself together, but she had to moisten her lips before she could speak.

"What you suggested: That before your aunt passed away, you'd been asked to be surrogate for your cousin. We talked about it and I didn't have a problem, and you planned to come home as soon after giving birth as possible. Then, when your cousin didn't want the babies, we decided to keep them ourselves."

Kenzie didn't answer immediately, and when Saana glanced over at her, she had her chin on her hand and was looking out the side mirror.

Then she sighed.

"I want you to know I'm really grateful for your help. I know I'm causing you all kinds of trouble—"

Unable to bear it, Saana cut her off.

"It's fine. Really." A lie, but told in her own best interests. No way she'd let Kenzie know just how much having her around again was playing havoc with her senses. "I can understand your need to protect your babies, and I said I'd help, and I will."

"Yes." Kenzie sighed again, but quietly, probably hoping Saana wouldn't hear it. "I do know how committed you are once you make a decision."

Saana waited to hear what else she'd say, but Kenzie fell silent and stayed that way all the way to the Merritt Island estate.

As they walked toward the entrance to the house, Kenzie stuck her hands under her tunic and swiped them down the sides of her jeans. Saana tried to ignore the tender sensation the gesture caused to bloom in her chest but couldn't.

Reaching out, she snagged Kenzie's hand and laced their

fingers together. When the other woman stiffened, Saana squeezed gently.

"We're supposed to present a united front," she murmured. "Remember?"

And Kenzie shook her shoulders, as if to loosen up tight muscles.

"Sure," she replied just as the front door opened, revealing Mom and Dad waiting for them.

Saana really hadn't been sure what reception to expect from her parents, but immediately, when they stepped into the foyer, she knew it was going to be all right.

"McKenzie," Mom said, her welcome obvious as she pulled Kenzie in for a hug. "It's so good to have you back. I'm so sorry to hear about your aunt."

"Thank you, Mrs. A."

"But now we have so much to look forward to! Twins on the way? Do you know what you're having?"

The shock of hearing her mother say *we* made Saana freeze, and then she was horrified to realize she hadn't even thought to ask the sex of the babies.

"Oh," Kenzie said, smiling, although Saana could see signs of strain around her eyes. "At least one boy—but each time they do an ultrasound, the other baby is hidin' the naughty parts, so I'm not sure what the final outcome will be."

"Surprises are always good," Mom replied with a laugh. Her hands were hovering on either side of Kenzie's belly, not touching, but clearly longing to make contact.

Kenzie stiffened, her back arching just a little, and she gave a sharp inhale.

"Someone is turnin' somersaults in here," she said. Then, without hesitation, she reached out and took one of Mom's hands, placing it just to the left of her navel.

And Saana had to blink against tears at the sight of the two women joined together in that tender moment and the look of wonder and delight on her mother's face.

And later, when she finally went to bed, having given Kenzie a chance to fall asleep before she went upstairs, that was the image that followed her into sleep.

No wonder she awoke just as the sun was coming up and found herself spooning Kenzie from behind, her hand cupped around the sweet swell of the little lives within her womb.

Drowsy, good sense still lulled by sleep, she allowed herself to savor the scent and feel of the woman she'd always loved and the miracles she carried within.

Then Kenzie stirred, and reality intruded, causing Saana to roll away to her own side of the bed.

Into the emptiness.

CHAPTER SEVEN

THE FIRST DAY at a new job always brought butterflies to Kenzie's stomach, but when she got to the Preston Clinic for her first shift, she felt no nervousness at all. She was just glad to have something to do to take her out of the Indialantic mansion and help her not think about the muddle she'd created by coming back to Florida.

The guilt gnawing at her as she remembered Mrs. Ameri's excitement over the babies.

And she'd forgotten—or tried to forget—just how demonstrative Saana was in public. Touching Kenzie's hair, arm or leg as she talked. Even kissing her cheek as they sat on her parents' enclosed patio, watching the last rays of the sun disappear into night.

Not to mention the suppressed longing she'd felt when she'd woken up in Saana's arms this morning. Although Kenzie was the more demanding one in bed, Saana had always been the big spoon when they snuggled, and the sensation of being held that way once more had immediately ignited her desires.

Not just for sex but for love too. Lying there, Kenzie had found herself pretending everything was the way it used to be, and the urge to roll over and hold her wife tightly was almost impossible to resist.

It was too big, too much of a tangled mess, for her to contemplate right now, so it felt good to sign in for work and introduce herself to the head nurse, Minerva Hartley.

"Nice to meet you," Minerva said, giving Kenzie a firm handshake. "I know you got shown around before, but I'll show you where we keep the important stuff."

This was, of course, a more comprehensive and useful tour of the store cupboards, examination rooms and reporting system.

"We use an old-fashioned filing system," Minerva explained. "But everything gets entered into the computer by an outside firm." They were coming to the end of the tour, by the nurses' desk, and the clinic was about to open—patients were already filling the waiting room beyond the plexiglass barrier. "Each afternoon, you'll find your personal clipboard in your slot, and the front sheet will tell you which doctor you're assigned to for the shift."

As she spoke, Minerva pulled out a board and glanced at it.

"You're working with Dr. Ameri today."

"Ameri?"

It was impossible not to screech the name like a pup whose tail had been stepped on, and Minerva gave her a startled look.

"Yes. Dr. Saana Ameri. Do you know her?"

"Yes, we know each other."

The cool, controlled voice coming from behind her had Kenzie spinning around so quickly she stumbled, and an electric strike fired into her arm from where Saana steadied her.

Pulling away, she glared at her wife, who lifted an eyebrow in return.

"Is everything okay, Dr. Ameri?" Minerva asked, caught somewhere between caution and curiosity.

"Perfectly fine. I'll show McKenzie which rooms are ours, and then she can bring in our first patient."

With that, she turned on her heel and, after swiping her

card, walked through the security door without checking to see if Kenzie was following.

"We'll be using exam rooms three and four," she said, once Kenzie had gotten herself under enough control to take off after her.

"What are you doing here?" Managing to keep her voice low enough not to be overheard was a struggle.

"I work here in the evenings," came the bland reply, as if it should have been self-evident. Opening the door to the exam room, she waved Kenzie through. "Actually, since you'll probably eventually hear anyway, I was the one who set up this clinic."

Shocked, Kenzie found herself gaping at Saana and snapped her mouth shut. "You own it?"

Saana closed the door behind them and leaned against it.

"The Preston Trust owns and operates the practice, but I set up the trust." Kenzie tried to speak, but was cut off when Saana continued. "We don't have time to hash this out right now. There are patients waiting. You've been told what to do?"

That tone clearly said Saana was done talking, so, still steaming, Kenzie replied coolly, "Yes, Doctor."

But it took a moment for Saana to move from in front of the door, during which time they stared each other down. Even through her annoyance, Kenzie felt the pull of those gorgeous eyes and had to fight the urge to pull her wife close and kiss her senseless. Then Saana opened the door and stepped out, holding it for Kenzie to come through behind her and go call on the first patient.

Tearing her thoughts away from Saana and the bombshell she'd just dropped, Kenzie firmly put her mind on the upcoming shift. In comparison to working in a busy hospital urgent care clinic, the Preston Clinic was going to be a breeze as far as Kenzie was concerned, even if it meant being in constant contact with Saana. And the ability to interact more with the patients rather than rushing them in and out was a definite plus.

During the tour earlier, Minerva had explained, "We're expected to ask questions and advise the patients about the various services offered. Have they had a mammogram recently? Pelvic exam? Very often, at a doctor's office, patients are expected to only talk about the one issue they came in for, unless it's a yearly checkup. But many of these women don't have primary care, much less yearly exams, so it's up to us to mention these things. It allows them to think about it for a little while and not be taken by surprise when the doctor brings it up."

With all that in mind, Kenzie went to the waiting room and called her first patient, Miriam Durham. She was sixty-two, was complaining of extreme pain in her knees and had been referred to them by a community group specializing in assisting indigent members.

The lady, who came forward at a slow shuffle, had on what looked like several long-sleeved shirts, topped off with a knitted hoodie. Unusual in the Florida heat but not unheard of. Kenzie made a mental note to try to find out why Miriam was dressed that way. The answer could, to Saana, be important.

"Hi, Ms. Durham," she said as the patient finally got to her. "My name is Kenzie. If you'll come with me, I'll get your information, and then the doctor will be with you."

"Thanks, darlin'," the other woman said, shuffling alongside Kenzie into the back corridor.

At the general staging area, Kenzie said, "Let's just get your weight."

"Ugh." Miriam leaned heavily on Kenzie so as to step up onto the scale. "I don't even wanna know what I weigh now. It's just crept on over the last ten years and won't stop comin'. Guess I'm just at that time of life, huh?"

"Could be," Kenzie replied, noting the numbers on her chart

and then helping Ms. Durham back down. "But it's something you should mention to the doctor when you see her."

"I planned to since I'm here about my poor knees. They hurt like the blazes, and I figured it might have something to do with my weight."

"When did you last have a full checkup?"

Miriam gave a rueful smile. "Chile, not since I left North Carolina about five years ago. With one thing and another, I just never had the chance. By the way, where're you from?"

"Texas." Kenzie opened the door to the examination room and steered Ms. Durham in.

"I thought I recognized that drawl," the older lady said with a chuckle. "I followed a boy to Fort Hood when I was young. Married him too. First of my three marriages and probably the best, although it didn't last."

Kenzie laughed with her and then, after carefully helping her up onto the exam table, set about taking her blood pressure, oxygen-saturation level and pulse rate. The entire time, Miriam chatted about her three ex-husbands and her son, whom she said she'd come to Florida to be closer to.

"It's been hard, though," she said, no longer smiling. "His wife don't like having me around, and I hardly get to see my grandbabies. I lived with them for a little while when I first came here but eventually moved on because I was causin' trouble in the marriage, ya know? Like my momma used to say: two hens can't rule the same kitchen."

"I'm sorry to hear that." Kenzie patted Miriam's shoulder and then made a couple more notes on her chart. "Do you get to see him sometimes?"

"Yeah," Miriam said, but it was impossible not to hear the sadness in her voice or miss the gleam of tears in her eyes. "He brings Tia and Mikah to see me at a park near where I live, but only every now and then. It's hard to plan anything since I work shifts and he's busy all the time." She gave a little sniff. "I wish I could see them more—even look after them sometimes—but that can't work."

The door behind her opened just as Miriam added, "It's hard, being away from my grandbabies like that. They and my son are all I have left in the world."

"Hello, Ms. Durham. I'm Dr. Ameri."

The sound of Saana's voice, the brush of her shoulder as she stepped past, made a hard shiver fire along Kenzie's spine. Instinctively, she stepped back and held out the clipboard for Saana to take.

"Thank you, McKenzie."

There was no mistaking the dismissal in her tone, so Kenzie took the hint and left.

Saana shook Miriam Durham's hand and then, hooking the wheeled stool with her foot, pulled it close and sat on it.

"So, what can I do for you today?"

"Oh, it's my knees, Doctor. They're acting up something terrible. After my shifts at work, I can hardly walk, and the pain keeps me up at night too."

"Is it just your knees?" she asked as she scanned Kenzie's notes quickly.

"Oh, no, honey. It's everything—my back, too, and shooting pains down my legs—but the knees are the worst."

"Okay," she said, putting down the clipboard and meeting Miriam's gaze. "If you have the time, I'd like to do a full examination and send you down to our lab to have some blood drawn for testing. I see here that you haven't had a full physical in five years?"

As Saana spoke to Miriam Durham, she was drawn back to the tail-end of the conversation she'd overheard between Kenzie and her patient. For some reason, hearing Miriam speak so sadly about her grandchildren lingered in her mind.

After getting some more details and the older lady's consent for the full physical, Saana got up and said, "If you'll undress down to your underwear, put on this gown and get up on the table, I'll be back in a little while."

Miriam blinked at her with an expression of rueful concern. "I'll try, but it'll take me a while. I'm not moving as fast as I used to."

Pausing on her way out the door, Saana asked, "Do you need some help? I can send the nurse back in."

"Yes, darlin'," came the reply. "Or we'll be here all night."

Smiling to herself over the patient's spicy wit, Saana exited the room in time to see Kenzie coming out of exam room four.

"Finished with Ms. Durham already?" she asked, the words carefully casual.

"No. I want to do a full examination while she's here, so I left her to put on a gown. She was asking if you could assist her in getting undressed and back up onto the table."

"Sure." Kenzie held out the chart in her hand, continuing, "Your next patient should be ready for you in a moment."

"Thanks." Taking the chart, she scanned it, again noticing the scope of Kenzie's notes. She wasn't content to just jot down the patient's blood pressure, oxygen saturation and pulse rate, but, in this case, also had *habitual smoker, diagnosed COPD three years ago*, and *not on medication initially prescribed*. All this, despite the fact the woman had come in with a stomach complaint.

Before she could say anything complimentary about the extra notations, Kenzie had already slipped past, and she heard the door shut behind her.

Suppressing a sigh at the thought of the fight they'd probably have later now that her involvement in the clinic had been revealed, Saana made her way to room four and her next patient.

It was going to be a longer night than usual, but she had only herself to blame.

She'd known how Kenzie would react but, at the time, hadn't cared. In fact, she'd been glad, thinking of it as another way to tweak at her wife's independent spirit. Now? Well, the joke was on Saana since it was coming home to her in a most unsettling way what it would mean for them to work alongside each other.

But she actually found Kenzie to be an almost ideal assistant during the shift. Of course, there were a few times her wife didn't know where to find something or a correct procedure, but the main thing in Saana's view was the way she communicated with the patients.

They all seemed perfectly at ease with her, and there were no complaints from either them or the other staff members.

Saana took a break at about seven o'clock, sitting down to finish writing up some notes and resting her feet in her office. When a knock came on her door, she sighed before calling, "Come in."

Somehow, she wasn't surprised it was Kenzie who marched in, shutting the door behind herself with a snap.

"Saana, I'm handin' in my resignation to HR tomorrow."

Leaning back in her chair, Saana gave a shrug that belied the way her heart rate kicked up, then replied, "That's up to you, but may I ask why?"

"When I said I wanted a job, I didn't mean for you to manufacture one for me. It's nepotism."

Battling annoyance, Saana kept her expression neutral, her voice cool. "What makes you think I manufactured this job for you? You wanted a job. The clinic needed a temporary nurse. I recommended they interview you, and you were hired without, may I add, any coercion from me. I put off telling HR that you're my wife for just that reason. I'll tell them tomorrow, but you got this position all on your own."

"It doesn't feel right." Kenzie's eyes were narrowed, and her lips firmed into a line.

"What about any of this feels right, Kenzie?" Suddenly exhausted, Saana rubbed a hand over her eyes, closing the lids tight for a second before meeting her wife's gaze again. "You wanted a job, and I found one for you. If you're unhappy about having to work with me, that's just too bad. Get over it."

When Kenzie looked set to start fussing again, Saana held up a hand.

"Listen, while I remember, Dr. Ramcharam has agreed to take you on as a patient. She's asking that you have your file transferred to her by your previous obstetrician, and her office called to make an appointment for this Friday morning at eleven."

"Oh." Kenzie looked startled by the change of subject and pulled out her phone. "Will you send me the address? And I'll need the information—an email, I guess—for where to send the file."

"I'll send you the phone number and email address. As for where her office is, I'll take you to the appointment myself."

"You don't have—"

Saana shook her head.

"You want us to pretend to be a couple? That means I go to all your prenatal appointments and classes. Otherwise, what's the use of this charade?"

Even she heard the bitterness in her own voice, and so wasn't surprised when Kenzie shook her head and turned away, toward the door.

And left without another word.

CHAPTER EIGHT

SOMEHOW, THAT FIRST night of working with Saana became a turning point for Kenzie, bringing to light long-hidden truths she knew she'd have to face.

She'd harbored some misconceptions about her wife once she found out about her wealth.

In the beginning of their marriage, Kenzie had felt the relationship would work out, without doubt, once they were living in the same place. Everything had seemed wonderful, the future stretching shiny and new before them, while she was wrapping up her life in Texas in preparation for the move. Their daily telephone and video conversations had been sweet—loving. Learning about each other, sharing secrets and hopes. Looking back, she realized hints of their ultimate incompatibility had been blatant, but she'd refused to see them.

She'd already been a little intimidated by the fact Saana was a doctor who was on the verge of opening her own practice, while Kenzie had still been working on her nursing degree.

"You're only four years older than me," she'd pointed out.

Saana had shrugged it off.

"I was lucky enough to have parents who helped me get through med school," she'd replied. "It doesn't matter. At least while you're here, you can just concentrate on finishing your degree rather than working as well."

Saana had sounded so sure, so determined, that Kenzie

hadn't disagreed. After all, at that time she'd had enough money saved up for the final two semesters of college and didn't have to depend on Saana to provide that for her. But all her adult life, since she'd gotten her first part-time job at fourteen, Kenzie had been used to providing for herself. Even at that young age, she'd given Aunt Lena money toward the household expenses and bought her own clothes and necessities.

She wasn't used to depending on anyone else to do for her, and she had been uneasy about the thought she might have to ask Saana for anything.

Yet she'd put that worry aside, reassuring herself it would all work out.

That had been her mantra during those weeks of wrapping up her life in San Antonio.

It will all work out.

But she hadn't known—couldn't have imagined—what she so eagerly drove toward back then.

That Saana was rich and lived a life Kenzie couldn't have even visualized. So foreign it would seem like science fiction in her wildest dreams.

And for the first time in her life, she'd severely doubted her ability to do what she'd put her mind to.

Building a life with Saana.

Making her happy.

Looking back, Kenzie knew everything she'd done, and everything Saana had done, had been seen through the framework of Saana being rich. With that much money, how could she not be out of touch with reality? And how could Kenzie ever hope to find a space for herself in that fantasy?

Seeing Saana at work—especially finding out she'd set up the clinic and trust that ran it—gave Kenzie new appreciation for her character.

The way the clinic had been set up showed a firm grasp

on what the women it served really needed. So often with endeavors like this, the actual end users weren't really taken into consideration, but at the Preston Clinic it was obvious the patients were really listened to and catered to also.

And that was because Saana had the foresight to find out their needs and make sure they would be met.

It wasn't an urgent care clinic but a place where disadvantaged women could receive the full spectrum of medical intervention—from preventative to diagnostic and specialized care, if necessary.

She was calm and listened to each patient so as to make sure they received the best treatment possible. It was truly an extension of Saana's logical and yet compassionate nature—the very nature Kenzie had been depending on when she made her desperate flight from Texas to Florida.

Deep inside, she'd known Saana wouldn't let her down. That she could depend on her wife to agree to help, even if it was to come up with another plan. One that had a better chance of working.

Everything she'd asked of her, Saana had done.

And how had Kenzie reacted in return?

Like a bit of a brat, really.

So busy thinking of herself and the babies—even though she'd been the instigator of the entire situation—that she'd spared little thought for the upheaval in Saana's life.

Yes, it was the most stressful situation Kenzie had ever been in, but the fact was that she'd caused it herself.

It was time to stop acting the fool and start being grateful for the help she was getting.

Besides, now that she knew Saana was working over twelve hours, four days a week, she was also worried. She'd always pushed herself hard, but working at both clinics was, in Kenzie's opinion, too much.

Not that she had any right to say anything about it. After all, nothing had changed from the past she'd run away from, and this situation was still temporary. Kenzie wasn't enough of an idiot to think otherwise, no matter what personal revelations she might have or her continued love for Saana. But what she could do was stop making things more difficult and even try to make Saana's life easier in whatever small ways she could.

It was hard sometimes to figure out what that might be since the distance between them lay cool and wide…

Except at night…

They'd gotten into a routine of sorts. Kenzie would say she wanted to watch the news and that Saana should have her shower first. Then Saana would come down in her robe to tell Kenzie she was finished and stay downstairs until she thought Kenzie was already in bed before going back up.

But even with that careful maneuvering, and although they started out on opposite sides of the bed, somehow Kenzie always awoke with Saana snuggled against her back—snuggled in so tight she imagined she could feel every delicious curve—and they breathed together as though they were one.

It was sweet torment to have one long arm and one leg thrown over her body, cocooning her in fragrant warmth. Reminding her of the nights when they'd made love until they were satiated, then lain that way, talking until they'd both fallen asleep.

Each night, she lay as still as possible, not wanting to move in case Saana woke up and rolled away. Torturing herself until her heart seemed fit to beat its way out of her chest and her body began to shiver with suppressed need. Only then did she move, knowing that if they stayed that way any longer, she'd roll over into Saana's arms, either courting rejection or the type of explosive encounter that could only lead to more chaos.

Now, as she put together breakfast, just thinking about those nightly encounters made a hard tremor fire down her spine.

The sound of footsteps alerted her to Saana's approach, and Kenzie took a long, deep breath in preparation.

"Hungry?" she asked when she knew her wife was within earshot. "I'm cookin' oatmeal."

"You don't have to cook breakfast for me every morning," Saana replied as she went for the coffeepot. "I usually grab something on my way to work."

Kenzie snorted. "I have to eat soon after getting up, or the babies make me feel miserable. It's no big deal to cook something for you too."

"Well, then, thank you." Pouring herself a cup, she asked, "What are your symptoms?"

"Huh?"

"When you don't eat on time. What happens?"

"Oh, a bit of nausea," she replied. "At the beginning, I was worried I'd develop hyperemesis gravidarum, the morning sickness was so bad, but it got better over time. Although, if I don't pay attention, it'll nudge me. Or the babies will."

"You're probably soon going to have to limit how much food you eat at any one time," Saana said as she moved to sit at the table. "We can come up with a diet plan to make sure you get all the nutrition you need without getting indigestion. You could mention the continued nausea to the doctor when you see her later."

"I will, although my previous obstetrician said not to worry unless it becomes unmanageable, and when I eat on time, it's fine."

After dishing out two bowls of oatmeal, Kenzie carried them to the table, where she'd already put out honey, almond milk and some mixed berries she'd found in the fridge. Sliding Saana's bowl over to her, she sat down on the opposite side of the table.

Neither of them spoke for a while as they ate, but Saana seemed to be taking her time over breakfast, and Kenzie found herself checking the clock repeatedly. Finally, unable to stop herself, she said, "Hey, if you don't get a move on, you'll be late for work."

Saana didn't look up from where she was adding a few more berries to her bowl.

"I'm not going in this morning. I got reception to reschedule my patients since I'm taking you to your appointment."

"Oh." Kenzie turned that over in her mind and then added, "Okay."

Saana's lips tightened for an instant. "I told you I was going with you. Didn't you believe me?"

"Sure did. But I just thought you'd go to work as usual and we'd meet there. This is good, though. Better."

"Why better?" Saana asked, tone still cool but seemingly unable to resist her curiosity.

"Well, you work twelve-hour days for most of the week. A little time to yourself probably isn't a bad thing."

Saana's gaze lifted then, and Kenzie found herself suddenly breathless. Then Saana glanced down again.

"It is tiring," she admitted, her voice low, making it seem like saying the words out loud was somehow taboo. "But the clinic is still so new. I have to be on top of things."

Kenzie snorted before she could stop herself. How like Saana to have to be in control all the time, even when it might not be completely necessary.

"It's true," Saana interjected before Kenzie could reply. "Right now, there aren't enough doctors on staff for me not to be there."

"Can't the trust hire some more staff?"

Saana pushed her bowl away and leaned back, crossing her arms.

"Hopefully, they will be able to soon, but for the time being, we have the make do with the doctors we have."

It brought to mind a question Kenzie had been pondering

since learning about the clinic, and she didn't see the harm in asking.

"How did the whole clinic idea come about, anyway?"

Saana relaxed, her arms falling away from their defensive posture.

"I worked in a free clinic when I was in med school, initially just for the experience, but then I saw just how necessary places like those can be. Yet the entire time I was there, I kept thinking how I would improve on the services, widen the scope, if it were mine. I shelved the idea for a while so I could build up my practice, but it was always in the back of my mind."

It wasn't hard to see Saana having an idea and just going for it. Focus was another of her character traits. "Okay, but that doesn't explain the name. How did you come up with that?"

There was a part of her—the part that had jealously come up with the idea that Saana had found someone else—that expected not to get a reply. Somewhere, deep inside, Kenzie thought she knew the answer: that the clinic and trust had been named for whoever it was her wife was now in love with, even though Saana had claimed there wasn't anyone else.

"That was easy." A ghost of a smile tipped the corners of Saana's lips. "It's Mom's maiden name, and I got the money I used to set up the trust from my grandfather George. His will stipulated that I couldn't touch the principle until I turned thirty-five, so I had to wait."

She'd turned thirty-five the year before, and a sudden rush of sadness for not having been there to celebrate the milestone pushed aside Kenzie's elation at knowing the origins of the Preston name.

Obviously, being around this woman was turning her into a mess, emotionally.

As usual.

Needing to lighten her own mood, she forced a grin and

joked, "Grandpa didn't trust you not to spend all that cash on wine, women and song, huh?"

For the first time since Kenzie had been back in Florida, she saw Saana throw back her head and laugh. Not a chuckle or a restrained smile but a full-on riot of laughter. Seeing it brought a rush of love and want so strong it took everything Kenzie had not to round the table and absorb that humor through her kisses.

Saana was still chuckling as she replied, "Could be. Truthfully, though, I think it was just one of those things they usually do when there's that much money involved, to avoid taxes or something. He set it up the same way for Robbie, too, so at least I know it wasn't because I'm female. And I was allowed to withdraw some of the interest each year if I wanted or needed it. That helped with the maintenance of the house, but I really wanted as much as I could for the clinic, so I didn't dip into it very often."

She didn't want to talk about the house, so Kenzie kept the conversation on the clinic.

"So, you set up the trust, but it isn't enough to hire more doctors?"

Saana leaned forward, her face alight with enthusiasm.

"It cost a bomb to buy all the equipment I wanted for the clinic, and the financial advisors were honest about how long the clinic would be able to operate if the trust wasn't increased. I don't want the clinic to only last for twenty or thirty years. I want it to exist for as long as it's needed. Which reminds me: we're having a fundraising gala at Mom and Dad's house next month, and I'd like you to go with me."

Startled, Kenzie asked, "Me? Why?"

Saana raised her eyebrows. "I thought it would be obvious. You're my wife. Being there will show your support, both for me and for the clinic itself—especially since you're now working there."

"I don't think my bein' there will be a benefit to either you or the clinic," Kenzie said slowly, while her heart went a million miles an hour, and an anxious flush overwhelmed her body. "I'm sure it'll be real fancy, and we both know I'm anything but. I wouldn't even know what to wear, or…or…" She wracked her brain for the worst thing she could think of. "Or what fork to use at dinner."

Saana just shook her head, and the look on her face made Kenzie's heart rate go up a notch but not out of fear.

"I've never asked you to be anything but yourself," she said quietly while Kenzie drowned a little in those gleaming eyes. Then Saana's expression smoothed out, becoming cool again, and she gave one of those *I don't really care* shrugs. "And I know a place in Orlando where we can get you something appropriate to wear. It would look strange if you, as my wife, aren't in attendance, and it's that type of situation we need to avoid, isn't it?"

Recognizing the trap but unable to avoid it, Kenzie swallowed and then nodded.

"Yeah, I guess it is," she acknowledged since her brain couldn't come up with a good reason to get out of going. "Nobody else would care, I don't think—but your parents would think it weird, anyway."

"Exactly."

Pushing back her chair, Saana got up and stretched, making Kenzie's mouth water at the sight. There was something about that long, sleek body, those firm breasts rising on a deep inhalation that created inescapable hunger deep in Kenzie's heart and soul.

And especially in her body.

Then one of the babies kicked, as if to remind her of its presence, and, ridiculously flustered, Kenzie got up too.

"What time do we have to leave to get to Dr. Ramcharam's office?" she asked as she gathered up the dishes.

"Ten fifteen at the latest. I'm sure although they got your records, there'll be forms to fill out before your appointment."

"Yeah. Okay." She was at the sink now, her back to Saana, so she was able to draw in a deep, slightly tremulous breath without it being obvious. "I'll be ready by then."

"Why don't you leave the dishes for Delores?" Saana asked. "Come join me by the pool for a little while. I'm going to enjoy being outside for a change."

For a minute, Kenzie hesitated, tempted beyond all reason.

For the first time since she'd come back, they were talking the way they used to—openly, without the barriers that had built up while they'd been apart. Kenzie had been determined to keep her feelings in check, and if you didn't count during those embraces at night, she'd succeeded pretty well.

But just now, she was raw, each nerve a receptor, not of physical sensation but of emotion, and she knew if she wasn't careful, she'd lose her head.

Again.

As she reached for the sponge, she found her voice and replied, "You go ahead. Maybe I'll come out when I'm finished."

That was a lie, though.

She needed time to pull herself together and rebuild those defenses against the love and need washing through her system.

She held her breath until she heard Saana's footsteps retreat into the distance, and then she let it out with a whoosh.

She'd be spending most of the rest of the day with her wife. Best take some time to regroup and get herself under control.

As if agreeing, one of the babies—or was it both?—did something that felt like a karate kick.

"Yes," she muttered. "Just think of the babies, and you'll be okay."

Only the babies.

Nothing else.

CHAPTER NINE

Kenzie seemed particularly quiet on the drive over to the obstetrician's office, and Saana made no effort to fill the silence. Although they'd always been able to sit together without talking, to her the air in the car felt heavy, heralding that some undefinable change had taken place between them.

Finally, unable to resist breaking the tension, Saana asked, "Nervous about your appointment?"

A glance caught Kenzie giving an ironic little smile.

"Nah. I feel good, and I know the babies are growin' like crazy. My belly's gotten so big I'm guessing I'll have to start using a rideshare service to get to work soon. The steering wheel's getting closer and closer."

"Well, you do have a workmate who can drive you in each afternoon."

She said it lightly, trying to get back that easy camaraderie they'd seemed to achieve this morning over breakfast but had lost again somehow.

"That doesn't make sense, considerin' where your other office is in comparison to the house and the clinic. It shouldn't cost too much, so don't worry about it."

Classic Kenzie, unwilling—almost unable—to accept even the slightest bit of help.

Except when it came to the lives in her uterus.

So, although she wanted to argue, Saana let it drop.

At Dr. Ramcharam's office, Kenzie filled out the requisite forms, and thankfully it wasn't long before they were called back to the exam room. When Saana got up with her, Kenzie seemed to hesitate for an instant before following the nurse, and although Saana felt a spurt of annoyance, she again kept quiet.

After the weigh-in and the other usual tests and questions, the nurse handed Kenzie a gown and said, "Strip down—although you can keep your bra on, if you want—and put this on, please. Dr. Ramcharam will be with you in a few minutes."

It was then Saana recognized the position she'd put herself in and frantically wondered how to get out of it.

"Do you want me to…"

Already having pulled her blouse off over her head, Kenzie glanced over and cocked an eyebrow.

"What?"

"Um… I was wondering if you wanted me to leave while you got undressed?"

By then, the baggy shorts Kenzie had been wearing were already in a puddle around her ankles, in preparation of her stepping out of them.

"Nah. There's nothing you haven't seen already," she said, but Saana thought her voice sounded strange. A little deeper than usual. "Besides, you know I ain't shy."

Her drawl was more pronounced, but Saana hardly noticed, her gaze intent on Kenzie's body, so enthrallingly changed and yet so gloriously familiar.

Pregnancy suited Kenzie, in every way. Saana had always loved her wife's bountiful curves, but somehow now she looked even more enticing. It wasn't something Saana had ever considered before, but who knew pregnant women could be so terribly arousing?

In what seemed like slow motion, Kenzie pushed down her

tiny tap pants and, once they were off, stooped to pick them and her shorts up.

It was like watching a gorgeous statue come to life. Strong thigh muscles, round bottom, full breasts and the prominent bulge of her belly were emphasized in the movement. It was a moment she had no doubt she'd remember for the rest of the life. Kenzie arose, her body once more showcased in profile, and heat flashed from Saana's chest into her face, her mouth going dry as her heart thumped like a mad thing in her chest.

Standing with hands on hips, Kenzie met Saana's gaze.

"Why're you lookin' at me like that?"

No mistaking the gravel in those drawled words, but it took a moment to actually comprehend what Kenzie had asked.

"You're so damn beautiful…"

Kenzie's eyelids drooped, but then she shook her head and turned away to grab the smock.

As she thrust her arms into the sleeves, she said, "Thanks, but wrong time and definitely wrong place."

Will there ever be a right time and place again?

But even as she opened her mouth to ask the silly, hopeful question, there was a knock on the door, and Maria Ramcharam came in.

"McKenzie? I'm Dr. Ramcharam," she said, coming in with her hand outstretched. Then she noticed Saana, and her dark gaze tracked from one woman to the other as she shook Kenzie's hand. "Nice to see you, Saana."

It came out more like a question than a statement, and Saana couldn't help smiling slightly.

"Kenzie is my wife, Maria."

The slightly curious expression on the doctor's face was wiped away, leaving it expressionless. "Oh. Lovely. Hop up here, McKenzie, and let's take a look at you."

Kenzie chuckled. "No hoppin' goin' on here right now. Not with this belly in front of me."

As Kenzie went to step up on the footstep, Saana held out her hand to offer support and was pleased when Kenzie immediately took it.

"I had a look at your records," Maria said, glancing at the laptop where her nurse had entered Kenzie's results for weight, blood pressure, glucose levels and O-sat. "And I'm quite happy with your progress. Of course, I'm sure you know that going forward, your twins will be gaining weight rapidly."

As she asked questions and listened intently to Kenzie's responses, Maria measured Kenzie's belly and then palpated it.

"One head here," she said before running her hand along Kenzie's left side. "Bottom here. And… Here we go. There's the other head. I'm going to do an ultrasound, just to see how things are shaping up inside. It's important, with twins especially, to keep a check on the amniotic fluid."

"It'll be nice if the second baby decides to let me know their sex," Kenzie said with another chuckle.

"I noticed one was hiding the information in the last ultrasound," Maria said, smiling as she prepared the machine. "Let's see if we can encourage him or her to solve the mystery."

Kenzie hissed as the gel was applied, drawing Saana's gaze from the monitor to her face. She was obviously eager, and her delight—apparent in the sweet curve of lips and twinkling eyes—made Saana's heart melt.

"Here's your little man," Maria said. "And…"

She paused, and Saana saw Kenzie's eyes widen.

"A girl!" It was Kenzie who said it, and sudden radiance made her expression joyous. "It is a girl, isn't it?"

"Yes."

And Saana was unbearably moved when Kenzie, still looking at the monitor, reached blindly for her hand and said, "Oh, Saana. One of each. Isn't that awesome?"

"Beautiful," Saana replied, although all she could see was Kenzie's smile. "Absolutely beautiful."

The clinic was busy that Friday evening, but Kenzie was still buzzing with happiness and didn't mind being kept hopping.

One of each!

When she'd first been told that two of the four implanted eggs had taken, she'd immediately hoped for a girl and a boy. Back then, she was glad for Darryl and Ashley's sake. Now, she was ecstatic for her own.

It just felt *right*.

All of it.

None of her fears and apprehension could touch the happiness rushing through her blood. Not about how quiet Saana had been on the drive back from Dr. Ramcharam's office, nor what was going to happen with the custody. Not even what leaving Saana again would do to her heart.

None of it could touch her tonight.

As she walked swiftly down the corridor to call the next patient in, Kenzie was humming a country song under her breath.

"You're in a chipper mood tonight," Minerva said as they met up at the main desk.

"Feelin' like a million bucks," Kenzie replied with a grin. "Babies doin' well, and the little girl finally decided to let us in on the secret of her sex. It's a good day."

Minerva grinned back and nodded once. "Sounds like it."

That was all the time they had to chat, though. The waiting room was full, but thankfully, there were four doctors in the clinic that night, so they should be able to get to everyone.

Most of the patients were referrals and had appointments, but there were also a few walk-ins—women who'd heard about the clinic and came there in hopes of being seen. While they could always go to the emergency room of any of the local hospitals, word had gotten around that the clinic was an easier alternative if you were in that area. What Kenzie realized was that the women were coming in with their complaints earlier than they might have gone to the hospital. Coming in while their ills were still fairly easily treated rather than trying to stick it out until they were too sick to go on.

If that was the only reason the clinic existed, it would be a really good one, in Kenzie's opinion. Some of the patients she'd seen in the ER back in San Antonio, who knew they couldn't afford a doctor or medicine, had waited until it was too late.

As she went to the door separating the waiting room from the nurses' station, she heard someone shout, "Can we get some help here?"

Pushing the handle to open the door, Kenzie rushed to the aid of an older woman, who was supporting a younger, taller and heavier one around the waist, obviously straining under the weight.

"What happened?" she asked, putting her arm around the sagging woman from the other side, bracing to help hold her up.

"I don't know," the woman on the other side replied. "She just came through the door, stopped, then looked like she was going to fall over."

Minerva, seeing what was happening, came running with a wheelchair, and between herself and Kenzie, they were able to ease the young woman into it. When they settled her in the chair, her head lolled back so Kenzie was looking into unfocused eyes.

"Get the door," Minerva said, and Kenzie ran ahead to do just that. Then, as the chair rolled through, she hurried to catch up and reached for the woman's wrist, feeling the rapid pulse.

"Get one of the doctors," Minerva snapped to the receptionist as they rushed past the front desk. "And you better call an ambulance too."

Kenzie pushed open the door to exam room one, which

she knew was empty, and Minerva maneuvered the wheel-chair through. Between them, they were able to get the patient onto the examination table, and both nurses started preliminary tests, calling out to each other so as not to double up and waste time.

By the time they'd taken BP, O-sat and pulse rate, the door burst open, and Saana came barreling in.

"What do we have?" she asked before she even got to the table.

"She collapsed just as she came in through the door," Minerva replied before reading out the levels they'd already collected.

"BP is high. Glucose?" Saana asked as she lifted first one, then the other of the patient's eyelids to check her pupils.

"Normal," Kenzie said, having just got the reading.

"Minerva, please check to see if anyone came in with her, and call an ambulance."

"Ambulance should be on the way," Minerva said as she headed for the door. "I'll see if anyone knows her."

"Hey," Saana said, tapping the patient's cheek gently. "Hey, can you hear me?"

The patient muttered; then one eye opened.

"Hi, there." Saana leaned closer, making sure she was in the other woman's line of sight. "Can you tell me your name?"

Her mouth opened, but what came out was a garbled mishmash of sound, and her fear was unmistakable. Her right hand came up, grasping at Saana, who took it in her own hand.

"You're okay." She made her voice soothing. "I'm Dr. Ameri, and we're looking after you."

The patient, instead of calming down, grew more frantic, babbling and moving restlessly on the table. Kenzie moved up close to Saana.

"I'll keep trying to calm her down so you can go on with the examination."

They switched places, and as Saana turned toward the cupboard where the instruments were, Kenzie saw the patient's hand lower so that it rested on her belly. The familiarity of the gesture—fingers cupped below the navel, thumb above—made her heart jolt.

"Saana," she said quietly, forgetting professionalism in the urgency of the moment. "I think she might be pregnant. That's what she's been trying to tell us."

As the wail of the approaching ambulance ratcheted Kenzie's tension higher, Saana turned to meet her gaze, and for an instant the same fear she felt was reflected back at her. Then her wife spun away to reach into the cupboard and grab a fetal Doppler.

Minerva came back in just then.

"Someone in the waiting room thinks they know where this woman lives. She's run to the house, to see if anyone's there."

Minerva paused, seeing Saana with the fetal heart monitor, and her lips tightened for a swift second. Kenzie could see the flashes of red lights coming around the edges of the blinds and tried to pull herself together. She felt disembodied. Mentally and emotionally adrift, as recognition of what was happening to the young patient forced itself onto her consciousness.

Saana didn't have to say anything. Neither did Minerva. Kenzie saw all the signs of some type of cerebrovascular incident—whether it was a stroke or aneurysm wouldn't be known until she got to the hospital—but a pregnancy would make the emergency all the more urgent.

Then came the *whoosh-whoosh-whoosh* of a tiny heartbeat, and Kenzie's stomach clenched.

"McKenzie." Minerva's voice startled her back to the moment. "Go and lead the paramedics in. Make sure they hurry."

She didn't reply. Her throat had closed with the type of emotion she normally didn't allow herself at work. Rushing out of the exam room, she hoped to collect herself before anyone noticed how shaken she was. Cutting through a short passageway leading to the nearest emergency exit, she used her cloth-covered shoulder to wipe her eyes before pushing the door open.

The paramedics were pulling the gurney out of the back of the vehicle when she called, "This way."

But when they got to the exam room, she didn't go in with them but instead slipped away to the bathroom, where she stripped off her gloves, then washed her hands and face. The face that looked back at her from the mirror looked older than the one she'd seen in the morning—but she shrugged the thought away.

"Pregnancy hormones," she said to herself as she dried her hands. "That's all."

With one last deep breath, she tossed the paper towels into the bin and went back to work, determined to regain, and maintain, her workday persona.

She thought she'd done okay until later that night, when her restless sleep was interrupted once more by the sensation of Saana snuggled against her back. Where before it had been arousing, tonight she felt tears threaten once more because it felt like home.

Like safety.

As if no matter what, the woman whose arm was wrapped around her wouldn't allow anything bad to happen.

It was frightening. She'd always known she could take care of herself. At least, that's what she'd told herself and anyone else who would listen.

But tonight, she didn't have the strength. So, when Saana finally stirred, seemingly about to roll away, Kenzie gripped her wrist and held on.

Saana didn't hesitate, but placed her hand back over Kenzie's belly and went back to sleep. And Kenzie, feeling the stress leech away, followed suit.

CHAPTER TEN

SATURDAY MORNING DAWNED overcast and gray, strangely echoing Saana's mood. The emotion she'd felt the night before, even before Kenzie's fingers closed on her wrist, had kept her awake for hours and even now lingered.

Her mind, usually so ordered and meticulous, couldn't seem to stop spinning—swinging wildly from one thought to the next.

It had been easy to see the effect their emergency patient had on Kenzie. Just the expression on her face, the fear in her eyes, had sent a shock of apprehension through Saana's body too. For the rest of the evening, although Kenzie had been her usual capable self, there'd been an atmosphere of disconnect between what she was doing or saying and the flatness of her affect. Her words didn't match her expression. Smiles didn't seem natural or reach her eyes. The empathy she usually displayed had still been there but from a distance.

That anxiety was as contagious as the flu and had awakened all Saana's protective instincts. But just because Kenzie had been obviously shaken by their patient's situation didn't mean anything had changed. Kenzie wouldn't be grateful if Saana started coddling her, the way she wanted to. In fact, it would probably cause more tension, increasing the problem.

It would be so much easier if she just didn't give a damn. If she could maintain some kind of detachment from Kenzie.

Yet she was forced to acknowledge that each and every day they were together made Kenzie even more fascinating than she'd been before.

Made Saana fall even further in love.

Sighing, she swung her feet off the bed, wondering how best to handle the increasingly complex mess they'd created together. None of her experience in life had prepared her for this conundrum.

In the past, she would have simply taken control. Or tried to. She'd have marched downstairs and told Kenzie to stop working, for the sake of her emotional well-being and the well-being of the babies.

She couldn't stop the little snort of unamused laughter that broke from her throat at that thought. It would never have worked. Kenzie valued her independence far too much to give in to such a suggestion. In fact, she'd have fought it tooth and nail in her quiet, implacable way.

And who could blame her, really?

Kenzie had been working since she was a teenager. Longer, if you count being her aunt Lena's right hand since she was even younger. Unless the doctor put her on bed rest, she'd keep working until the twins were born. She'd be climbing the walls with boredom and fretting about her future finances if she stayed home with nothing to do.

But…

It didn't mean Saana was totally without resources when it came to protecting Kenzie. She just had to be strategic about it and keep her own emotions out of the equation.

In reality, that would be the hardest part.

Determined but still apprehensive, she went downstairs, expecting to find Kenzie in the kitchen or the small den she favored when at home, but she wasn't in either place. Moving into the great room at the back of the house, Saana looked out toward the river and saw Kenzie sitting by the dock.

Funny to think it had been only a week since the last time she'd walked down the garden path to speak to her wife about her request for help. It felt as though those intervening years when they'd been apart had faded way. Become insignificant.

Dangerous territory, in line with the Santayana quote about those who forget the past...

Not something she could afford. So she forced her emotions down deep, pulling her cloak of cool control around herself. Hiding beneath it.

Kenzie looked over her shoulder at Saana's approach, and the dark shadows beneath her eyes were obvious.

"Mornin'," she said with a small smile.

"Good morning." Saana sank onto the bench next to her, making no attempt to hide the way she was scrutinizing her wife. "You didn't sleep well last night, did you?"

Kenzie looked away, over the water.

"Got some sleep. I'm okay."

"Really?" Letting her skepticism show, she shook her head. "Could have fooled me."

The sound Kenzie made was neither amused nor annoyed but seemed to fall somewhere in between.

"Why not just say I look like hell on wheels and be done?"

A shrug seemed the appropriate response, and it was easy to keep her tone cool when those dark eyes weren't focused on her. "Because you never look like hell on wheels, but you do look tired. I have to run out to get something. Why don't you come with me, and we can go to Ernest's Tavern, where they have those delicious egg Bennies, for breakfast?"

"I can make breakfast here."

"I know you can."

No use pushing. Better to let Kenzie make the decision herself.

"I wonder if they ever found out that young girl's name."

She didn't have to specify. Saana had suspected it might be

weighing on her mind, which was why she'd called the hospital before heading down to the dock.

"Yes, they did. They were able to treat her quickly enough and think she'll make a full recovery. She was able to tell them her name and where to contact her boyfriend."

"And the baby?"

"Doing well." It had been on the tip of her tongue to add *so far*, but she bit the words back. Not so much because she thought she'd be shielding Kenzie, who would no doubt know the continued risk, but so as to keep the news upbeat. Hopefully, that would lift Kenzie's spirits.

Kenzie let out a breath as if she'd been holding the air in her lungs while waiting for the reply. Then, with a little shake of her shoulders, she rose.

"Yeah. Let's go get some breakfast. Then maybe I'll take a nap before work this afternoon."

Relieved, Saana got up too.

"It'll just take me a minute to get ready," Kenzie said as they headed back to the house.

"Take your time. There's no rush. I'm going to grab a coffee."

As Saana went into the kitchen, she was genuinely surprised both by Kenzie's actions and the relief she felt at them. She'd been wondering how to get Kenzie to relax, maybe even sleep a little before work, but hadn't had to do much except invite her to breakfast.

Apparently, cool and controlled was the way to go when trying to manage her wife. It went against everything Saana wanted to do, but if that was what it took, she'd have to keep it up.

As glad as she was that the young woman patient had been successfully treated and that her baby was fine, Kenzie couldn't shake the sense of gloom that had been dogging her since the night before.

As she started getting the examination rooms prepared for the evening clinic, her brain kept cycling back to the fear in the other woman's eyes.

The desperation.

And, like the refrain of a song when the record kept skipping back, she heard Aunt Lena's voice in her head: *"You never know the luck of a mangy mutt."*

Most people used it in a positive way, meaning that just because you were down and out didn't mean something good couldn't happen. But Aunt Lena used it both as an expression of hope and of warning.

Just because you were down and out didn't mean something worse might not happen.

Luck was capricious.

Life was capricious.

Not that Kenzie didn't already know that. She'd been through enough in her lifetime to realize how little control she had over the really important issues. But it wasn't something that had affected her emotionally. Not the way the thought of something happening to her and the babies was scrambling her brain.

To the point of being so scared she felt completely and utterly powerless.

The early part of the day had passed in a blur. At breakfast, Saana had kept the conversation going, chatting about inconsequential things while Kenzie picked at her meal and tried to respond appropriately. She'd like to think it was tiredness from a disturbed night of sleep making her feel like she was underwater, but it was much more than that.

Not even a nap before work had made it go away.

The door to the examination room swung open, and Minerva came in.

"Everything okay in here?"

"Sure," Kenzie replied, trying to sound like she meant it. "I've restocked both rooms, and we're ready to rock and roll."

"Good." The head nurse took a quick look around, as she did each evening before the clinic opened. "Hopefully, tonight won't be as eventful as last night was."

Kenzie was glad to have her back to the other woman so she wouldn't see her wince.

"Yeah," she finally said, when she was sure her voice would be normal.

As Kenzie turned to head out the door, Minerva hitched her hip on the wall and said, "By the way, I realized you and Dr. Saana knew each other from before but didn't realize you were such good friends."

"What do you mean?"

Taken by surprise, that was all she could think of to ask.

"Well, I saw you getting out of her car this afternoon."

It hadn't even occurred to her that their traveling to the clinic together would cause any kind of stir, and now she was left floundering to think of what to say.

How much easier it would be to simply admit they were married, but they hadn't discussed the matter, and Kenzie was reluctant to be the one to out them.

So instead, she pulled herself together to say, "She was nice enough to offer me a drive since we were coming from the same direction."

Minerva's eyebrows went up.

"You live in the same neighborhood as Dr. Ameri?" Her skepticism was clear. Then her hand flew to her mouth, and her eyes widened. "Oh my God, McKenzie. I'm so sorry. That sounded horrible. I didn't mean—"

After a snort of laughter, Kenzie replied, "No worries. I'm not surprised. I'm definitely not in the same league as Saana."

"Stop that," Minerva said, sounding caught somewhere between horror and amusement. "You're a lovely person. It's just that I know the doctor's family is loaded…" She stopped and shook her head, her hands flapping as if she was trying to shut herself up. "I'm making it worse, aren't I?"

Kenzie just laughed and opened the door.

"Don't worry about it. You haven't hurt my feelings."

Saana was right outside the door, and both Kenzie and Minerva paused when they saw her standing there, her head slightly tilted, as though in question.

"'Scuse me," Kenzie muttered, sidestepping her wife while trying to avoid that interrogative look. "Time for the first patient."

Walking away, she could swear she felt Saana's gaze boring into her, but even as the skin at the back of her neck heated, she kept going without looking back.

At least the conversation with Minerva had given her something else to think about other than her fears and allowed her to better concentrate on her patients' needs as the evening wore on.

Finally, the final patient had been seen, and they cleaned up the examination rooms, doing a quick restock as needed. Saana was sitting in the cubicle off the nurses' station, writing up the last of her notes, when Minerva stopped Kenzie as she was walking toward the lockers.

"Hey, do you need a ride home?"

From the corner of her eye, Kenzie saw Saana's head come up and knew she was listening.

"No thanks, Minerva. I'm good."

"You sure? It's not a problem."

Saana stood up, and Kenzie said quickly, "I have a ride already, so thanks but no thanks."

"Okay—but you know, if you need a ride, you can always call me rather than bothering Dr. Ameri."

"Sure. Thanks," she said quickly, starting to walk away, not wanting to get any deeper into the conversation.

But a quick look back showed Saana striding in the opposite direction, and something about that prowling gait rang all kinds of alarms in Kenzie's head.

There was nothing said on the ride home, but the air between them hummed with a kind of electricity that had Kenzie wondering which one of them was giving it off. Her previous gloomy mood was submerged beneath this new jumpiness, and she would be hard-pressed to say which of those feelings was worse.

Getting to the house, Saana parked her car in the garage, and they went inside, still silent. Tired to the bone, Kenzie made a beeline for the stairs, but Saana called her name, halting her flight.

"I could see you were upset by the situation last night, so I bought a blood pressure monitor for you," she said, as cool as ever. "I'll be monitoring your BP morning and night, just to be on the safe side."

"Thanks," she mumbled, turning away so Saana couldn't see the tears welling in her eyes. Somehow the thoughtfulness coupled with that emotionless delivery was more painful than she'd expected.

"No problem." Kenzie's foot was on the first step when Saana's voice once more made her stop. "Why didn't you tell Minerva that you lived here with me?"

Surprise had Kenzie turning to face her wife.

"What?"

"When Minerva was offering you a ride home, why didn't you just tell her we were married?"

"It's none of her business, for one," she replied, strangely glad for the change of subject, which took her mind completely off Saana's consideration. "And second, I didn't want to stir up any trouble at work. I'm only going to be there until your original nurse comes back, so why make it difficult?"

"Difficult?" Saana pronounced the word as if she wasn't sure what it meant. "For whom?"

Kenzie rolled her eyes. "For either of us. You want folks chatting behind our backs, sayin' whatever they feel like about our relationship?"

"I don't really care what anyone says about our relationship." Her voice had gone from cool to icy. "Why should I?"

"Wow." The spark of anger heating her stomach at Saana's arrogance was welcome. "Easy for you to say. Let's be honest here... No one's gonna give you sideways looks and whisper about *your* motives for being in the marriage. I'd be the one taking the heat, right? Bein' called a gold digger or worse."

Saana's eyes narrowed, and her lips tightened.

"Do you really think it's wise to try to pretend we aren't married?"

"I'm not pretending we're not married," Kenzie replied, her voice rising to match the racing of her heart. "I'm just not tellin' every Tom, Dick and Harry we are. What's wrong with that, especially when I'm gonna be gone again in a while? Wouldn't *you* prefer they didn't know, under those circumstances? When we both know this isn't a long-term situation?"

"What I would prefer isn't of any importance. And the long term doesn't concern me. It's the short term I'm thinking about." Saana moved closer so they were within touching distance, and Kenzie could have sworn she felt the heat coming in waves off her wife's body. "You want to make it seem our marriage is solid for the sake of your children. That means being open about it, not hiding because you're worried what people will say. It also means publicly being my wife."

Then she gave one of those dismissive shrugs that said oh so clearly how little she cared about any of it. "Besides, in three weeks, when we have our first fundraiser, I expect you to be there. Not as an employee of the clinic but as my supportive, loving wife. So no matter how difficult it might be, I suggest you start acting that way."

The jolt Kenzie felt when Saana brushed past her to head up the stairs stole her breath.

Saana raised her hand to grasp the banister, her back as straight as a board, defiance and dismissiveness blatant in every line of that slim, sexy body.

A rush of emotion—love, anger, want—made Kenzie's blood boil, but a little voice in the back of her head whispered a memory and kept her rooted in place...

She was walking alongside Saana down the strip in Las Vegas, wondering why the woman who'd been so warm and enticing earlier in the day had turned cool and somehow distant. A gust of wind rustled past, causing Saana to raise her hand to brush a wisp of hair off her face, allowing Kenzie to see how her fingers trembled.

And it was then Kenzie recognized the attraction between them had grown past just liking but that Saana wasn't sure what to do about it. How to express her needs. Instead, it was bottled up inside, vibrating through her, just like it fired in waves through Kenzie too.

There was a little recess beside where they were walking, and Kenzie impulsively reached for Saana's wrist, tugging her into the niche so they stood face-to-face, bodies brushing with each inhale.

"I want you."

Kenzie made it a statement and a question all in one, sensing Saana needed her to take the lead but wanting her to feel comfortable enough to refuse.

"Come back to my room."

"Yes."

It was barely a whisper, and Saana leaned closer so the word brushed like a feather against Kenzie's lips.

"Yes."

How had she forgotten that moment until now? Let the knowledge slip away of how her wife dealt with desire when she wasn't sure it would be reciprocated?

Until seeing the unmistakable trembling of Saana's fingers as she reached for the banister.

Kenzie wondered how to handle the situation even as her heart galloped and arousal became a flame threatening to incinerate her from the inside out. She wanted Saana, desperately, but hadn't she decided complicating the situation by making love to her would be stupid? Did she really want to compound her heartbreak by getting that close?

But hadn't they already stepped past the rules they'd imposed on the situation? And mightn't it actually be better to deal with this overwhelming desire rather than let frustrations create arguments and discord?

Even as she thought it, Kenzie knew she was just finding excuses to do what she wanted.

Make love to Saana, no matter where doing so might lead.

So determination and erotic intent overcame common sense, and she set off after her wife.

CHAPTER ELEVEN

SAANA STRIPPED DOWN and stepped into the shower, shivering as the water hit her over-sensitized skin.

It was very probable, she thought, that she was losing her mind in increments each day Kenzie remained in the house. Lying beside her, night after night, was torture, especially since her slumbering self couldn't seem to stay on her own side of the bed, instead giving in and seeking the closeness it craved.

Saana moaned under her breath, remembering the sensations of Kenzie's body against hers, the firm satin skin under her hands. No one had ever demanded her surrender until Kenzie, and no one else had ever given her the type of ecstasy she'd experienced under her wife's concentrated, passion-inducing attention.

No one else had been able to make her lose all control. Get her so aroused she wanted to beg for orgasm and yet knew if she waited, gave in to the desire, she would experience all the release she could ever need.

Often multiple times.

And no one but Kenzie had made her inhibitions fall away until there was nothing Saana wouldn't do to give her wife the same pleasure she'd meted out.

Kenzie had introduced her to a side of herself—a wanton, rapacious side—that Saana would have hitherto absolutely denied.

The side that had died when Kenzie left but now was rampaging behind the calm facade Saana presented to the world.

With another muffled groan, she lifted her face to the water streaming from above and reached for the tap to decrease the hot water flowing through. But before she could make the change to the cold shower she so desperately needed, the bathroom door opened, freezing her in place.

Beyond the glass enclosure, crossing the bathroom, came Kenzie, gloriously naked.

The effect on Saana was immediate. Goose bumps arose all over her body, her breath got trapped in her lungs and her muscles tightened, affected by the wild spurt of adrenaline into her bloodstream induced by the fight-or-flight instinct.

Yet, as Kenzie pulled open the door and stepped into the shower, Saana neither fought nor fled.

"Wh…? Wha…?"

Kenzie reached for the body wash and scrubby, her lips tilted into a smile.

"You said I was to act like your wife, so I decided to come and wash your back. It was one of the things I always used to do, so I figured it would be a good way to get back into the role." Then she lifted one eyebrow. "Do you want me to do it or not?"

Unable to find her voice, Saana turned her back to Kenzie and stood shivering under the water.

"I thought this might help," Kenzie said as she squirted soap onto the scrubby. "We both know where our relationship is goin'—or in our case, not goin'—but it doesn't mean we're not still attracted to each other. All this sexual tension makes it hard to act naturally when we're together, don't ya think?"

Think? Kenzie wanted her to think while they were naked

in the shower together, and Saana knew those hands—so skilled in the art of love—would soon be on her body?

She tried to laugh, but it came out a weird, strangled wheeze. Then Kenzie stroked the scrubby down the length of her spine, and Saana braced against the wall to hold herself up.

"Now, I can wash your back and leave," Kenzie said, her drawl getting slower. Sexier. "Or I can stay, and we can relieve a bunch of the stress that's been building up the last few days. It's completely up to you."

Saana cursed silently. How much easier it would be if Kenzie just took over without giving her a choice. But although Saana knew her wife was definitely more dominant in their sexual relationship, Kenzie had never pushed or forced.

She'd always asked for consent.

For the type of complete complicity that turned Saana on more easily than anything else.

After clearing her throat, Saana whispered, "It might make it worse, though. I'm struggling, trying not to get pulled in any deeper with you, Kenzie, but you're making it so difficult."

Kenzie froze for a moment, then gave a wry chuckle. "I know what you mean. It all went so bad the last time, but I doubt our situation could get much more complicated, no matter what we do."

"Why did it go wrong? I've never really understood."

Even raising that minefield of a question couldn't douse the heat under her skin as Kenzie shifted, her breast gliding across Saana's back.

"I'm not really sure." Kenzie's voice was low and rough, as though the admission hurt to make. "But what I do know is that I'm goin' crazy, sleeping beside you every night, trying to stop myself from touchin' you. If you're havin' the same problem, then let's do somethin' about it. We can sort the rest of it out another time, when my head is clear. Right now, all

I can think about is touching you. Tasting you. Making you come so hard you can't help crying out."

If she refused, she thought she'd just go up in flames and burn away to ash with frustration; yet still, Saana hesitated, trying to find the willpower to walk away. But with each stroke of the scrubby—now working sideways, going lower to her waist, almost to her bottom—Saana fell deeper under Kenzie's spell.

She'd always been under her spell, she thought almost despairingly. No one had ever gotten under her skin, into her head and heart like Kenzie. Wishing she could explain that while for Kenzie, it might be just sex, for her it was so much more. It had been clear from the moment they met. Sexual attraction was a big part of it, for sure, but what Saana felt in her heart for her wife far surpassed that.

It was love, pure and simple, with all the care and concern, the longing and fear and desperation and anxiety that came with it. But right now, with her heart pounding and need clawing at her, she had to accept the truth.

There was no use in lying when she knew Kenzie was right. If they went on like this for much longer—aroused and unfulfilled—they'd be at each other's throats soon.

So she took a deep breath, turned to face her wife and said, "Stay."

The first time they'd kissed, Kenzie had felt like the world had stopped and it was just the two of them left in motion. Every thought, every movement, every breath had been about Saana. And every time after, there'd been the lingering sensation of that moment in their kisses, making each touch of lips on lips a special occasion.

This time, though…

Oh, this time was like being thrown back to the very first kiss but with the sensations magnified by each instant they'd been apart.

They clung together, bodies still fitting perfectly despite her belly, and she hugged Saana as tightly as possible without hurting her, physical desire subsumed by emotional need.

It was ridiculous to pretend that when she'd made that head-long, fear-filled flight from Texas, it was simply to go to someone she trusted. No. She'd known, in her heart, that what she'd needed was Saana to hold her, to be with her through the crazy and leech the fear away.

When she was holding Saana, she felt unstoppable, able to face anything.

But this was her submissive girl, who needed to be coaxed and aroused until she forgot her need for control, so Kenzie broke the kiss and picked up the scrubby again. Then she slowly bathed Saana, using the otherwise mundane task as foreplay.

"Turn around, babe."

She made her voice strong, even while inside she was melting with desire.

Exhaling a shuddering breath, Saana did as bid, facing Kenzie but leaning on the wall like her legs didn't want to hold her up.

Slowly, Kenzie worked the suds over Saana's arms, then shoulders. Paying special attention to those firm, high breasts, circling until the already tight nipples contracted to dark points and Saana's breath rasped in her throat. Down to her belly, teasing now, skimming over flesh glowing rosy from her attention.

Then she started to stoop to wash her legs, and Saana held her shoulder, stopping her.

"My turn," she said, her voice gone husky and her eyes gleaming.

Kenzie made no argument. After all, she'd been longing to have her wife's hands all over her. And there was something absolutely soul-shaking to see the care with which Saana rubbed the soap across the bulge of Kenzie's belly, as if fascinated by it.

Then she looked up and said, "I never knew how beautiful a pregnant body could be until I saw yours."

Kenzie tried to chuckle, but her throat felt too tight to let the laughter through. Instead, she finally replied, "I'm glad you feel that way."

"I do." Saana's soapy hands were on either side of Kenzie's belly, moving in slow, tender circles. "I just about fell down in Maria's office when you took off your shirt and I saw the changes in your body. So sexy."

Her wife's words were melting away her restraint, and Kenzie gently took the sponge away from Saana and backed the other woman under the water to rinse off. Once she was sure Saana's back was soap free, Kenzie turned her to rinse her front. Lightly biting the nearest shoulder, Kenzie reached around to put her hand between Saana's thighs, and her wife's moan of pleasure made her arousal kick up a notch.

Wet heat enfolded her fingers, and the inner muscles contracted. Avoiding Saana's clitoris as best she could, Kenzie slowly pushed deeper inside, then pulled back out.

"I remember all the things you like, babe," she said against the damp nape. "And if you're a good girl, I'll do as many as you want."

"God, Kenzie." Saana had her hands flat against the wall, her entire body trembling, seemingly already on the brink of coming.

"Do you still have the toys I bought you?"

"Yes…"

It was a whispered groan, and Saana shuddered again as Kenzie pinched her nipple.

"I'm not using them tonight," Kenzie said. Saana had said no one had ever talked dirty to her until Kenzie and admitted it made her hot. "Tonight, I'm using my hands, and mouth, and tongue, and I'm gonna make you come until you tell me to stop."

Without waiting for a reply, she reached out and turned off the water, then tugged her wife out of the shower. Grabbing towels, they dried off hurriedly, and then they were kissing again, and Kenzie, unable to resist, pushed Saana up against the wall and gave her the first orgasm of the night.

"We didn't even make it to the bed," she said with a laugh as Saana sagged in her arms, trying to catch her breath. "Are you ready to go again?"

"You're so bad." Saana straightened, pushing her hair out of her blushing face.

"That doesn't answer my question."

Shaking her head, her face getting even rosier, Saana said, "Honestly? Yes. I'm always ready with you."

Giving her a hard kiss and taking her hand, Kenzie replied, "Good girl. Let's go and set that bed on fire."

And she was rewarded by her wife's huff of laughter as she led her into the bedroom.

She didn't want to think about the question Saana had asked earlier—about what had gone wrong between them. Just thinking about it made the dark thoughts about her own unworthiness to be here with Saana rise up to strangle her self-respect.

So, instead of dwelling on them, Kenzie concentrated on her wife's pleasure.

Pulling Saana down onto the bed, Kenzie took her hands and guided them to the headboard.

"Hang on to that," she said, making it a demand. "When you want me to stop, let go and I'll stop."

It was a game they'd played before. One that had left them both aroused, then wild with lust.

"Kenzie…" It was just a sigh, but Kenzie's body tightened in anticipation.

She played Saana's body like a well-remembered instrument, finding and loving on all the places she knew would ratchet her wife's need higher and then higher still.

Then, as she kept her hovering just on the brink of release, Kenzie had a moment of déjà vu so strong she forgot to breathe.

Here, at this point, with Saana's shudders firing into her own flesh, making Kenzie almost come in sympathy, would be when she used to say, *"Tell me you love me..."*

The words hovering on her lips, she froze, the need to say them almost as strong as her desire. Saana's eyes were closed, her body bowed off the bed, trembling and jerking, obviously yearning for the final touch that would push her over into orgasm.

Tears flooded Kenzie's eyes, but she refused to let them fall. Instead, she eased Saana back and then, before her wife could respond, buried her head between Saana's thighs and sent her crying out over the edge.

And she kept her head there, wringing out another orgasm from Saana, until she was sure no evidence of her tears remained on her face.

CHAPTER TWELVE

SAANA WOKE UP on Sunday with the sun blazing in through a chink in her curtains and the unmistakable sensation of her world having been severely rocked.

They'd made love late into the night. Each time Saana thought she couldn't carry on a moment more, Kenzie would touch her or make some erotic demand that set her afire all over again.

Although she didn't agree that nothing had changed after their passionate night, she couldn't bring herself to regret it. Maybe Kenzie had been right about everything being easier if they got the physical out of their system.

Saana sat up and stretched, laughing ruefully at herself.

She'd never get Kenzie out of her system.

Kenzie had apparently woken up way ahead of her and already gone downstairs since her side of the bed was cold except for where Saana herself had been lying. After rushing to wash and dress, Saana made her way downstairs.

Not surprisingly, Kenzie was in the kitchen, which smelled deliciously of bacon and pancakes.

"Mornin'." Kenzie smiled over her shoulder, lush lips a sly, conspiratorial curve. "Sleep okay?"

"Like a log, when someone finally allowed me to go to sleep," she quipped in response, feeling her cheeks heat.

Kenzie chuckled and turned back to the stove, leaving Saana

wondering if it would be appropriate to kiss her good morning. Then she mentally shrugged. She was as invested in the situation, in her own way. If she wanted to kiss her wife good morning, why shouldn't she?

And Kenzie didn't seem to object, since she curved her free hand around the nape of Saana's neck and held her in place for a kiss that made Saana's toes curl.

"Mmm…yeah. Really good mornin'," Kenzie murmured with another sly smile as Saana backed away. "By the way, your phone's been ringin' and pingin' for a while. Hopefully, it wasn't anythin' too important."

"Probably Mom," she said, looking around, wondering where she'd left the damn thing. "Do you have anything planned for today?"

"Not really. Although I thought I'd just lounge around. Maybe take a swim."

Heat trickled along Saana's spine as a memory of the two of them swimming together in the past surfaced.

"Is there something you need me to do?" Kenzie continued when Saana didn't reply.

"Oh, no. I just thought we could drive over to Orlando and find you an outfit for the gala. It's coming up fast, and I heard you at the clinic telling Shelley none of your clothes fit properly anymore."

Kenzie snorted. "Even if they did, I'm pretty sure I don't have anything appropriate for a gala." She turned off the stove before bringing the patter of pancakes and crispy bacon to the table. "So, yeah, if you want me to be there and not embarrass you, I guess we better look for somethin'."

Saana's mouth watered at the sight and scent of blueberry pancakes and bacon—two things she didn't often eat—and as she reached for her fork, she replied, "You wouldn't embarrass me, no matter what you wore."

Kenzie didn't answer, but when Saana looked up, she saw the skepticism on her face clearly.

"I mean it," she said. It felt a little like stepping into a mine-field, but she couldn't help adding, "Do you think I care how you dress?"

Kenzie shrugged, but her gaze was searching as she admitted, "The clothes were just a part of it. I always thought I had to fit in with your friends and family and knew I never did."

"I didn't realize you thought I was so shallow," she said slowly, in part hurt but, more importantly, feeling the conversation held an important clue to what had gone wrong before. "So whenever I offered to buy you anything, you were thinking I was trying to make you somehow more acceptable to the other people in my life?"

Kenzie still held her gaze, but her chin tilted up. "It's in the past, Saana. I'm not worried about all that now, so it doesn't really matter."

Saana nodded, wanting time to think it over before continuing the conversation, and she didn't object when Kenzie changed the subject.

Just as they finished breakfast, Saana's phone rang again, and she got up to grab it.

"Hey, Mom. How are you?"

"Fine, darling. Just fine. I was wondering if you and Mc-Kenzie would like to come for lunch. I have something I want to talk to you both about."

She knew if she told her mother they had just eaten breakfast, she'd want to know what they were doing getting up so late, and just the thought made Saana blush.

"Sorry, Mom. We're just about to head over to Orlando to do some shopping."

"Oh." The disappointment in her mother's voice was marked. "That's fine. I just wanted to talk to you about the nursery. Have you done anything about it yet?"

The question gave Saana an emotional jolt, and she couldn't help her gaze flying to Kenzie's face. In response, her wife raised questioning eyebrows, and Saana shook her head reflexively.

"No, Mom. We really haven't made any firm decisions about it. What with work, you know, there hasn't been a lot of time."

"That's why I'm offering to help. I thought you could get the door into your grandfather's old dressing room—you know the one you had sealed off—reopened, and that would be perfect for the nursery. Right next door, for when they wake up in the night."

Kenzie was still looking askance, but Saana was strangely reluctant to clue her into what Mom was saying. Although, it was inevitable it would be brought up at a not-too-much later date.

"That sounds like a good idea. Let me talk to Kenzie and get back to you."

"That's fine, darling, but don't wait too long. With first babies, and twins too, you might not have as much time as you think."

When Saana hung up, Kenzie asked, "What's your mom have up her sleeve?"

It was said with a certain tone of fondness, but Saana still felt a little defensive as she replied, "She was asking about our plans for the nursery."

Kenzie's eyes widened. "Damn," she muttered, getting up abruptly and picking up the plates off the table.

Surprised, Saana followed her over to the sink.

"What's the matter?"

Kenzie ran the hot water over the plates to wash off the maple syrup and didn't respond until after she'd turned the tap off. Then she turned, placing her back against the counter and crossing her arms.

"Honestly, I'm startin' to feel pretty guilty about your mom." She frowned and shook her head. "I never expected her to be so into this whole baby thing. I hate to think how she'll feel when I leave again."

Determined not to make a big deal out of it, Saana shrugged. "She'll get over it. She's been dropping hints about grandchildren for a while, so I should have known she'd be excited. I suppose I should have warned you."

Kenzie's brows knit for a moment and then she straightened and turned back to the sink.

"Well, nothin' to be done about it now. Any way we can hold her off on the nursery? Seems a shame to waste the money."

Saana's heart clenched, but she made her voice cool as she replied, "Money isn't an issue. And when you're ready to move on, you can take the furniture and everything with you so you don't have to worry about starting over from scratch."

"Kind of ya." Saana couldn't decide whether her tone was disgruntled or sarcastic. "But that's a bit more than I could accept."

"Well, then, how about you think of it as the best thing for your babies instead of immediately letting your pride lead the way?"

There was no mistaking the way Kenzie stiffened, but then she exhaled and her shoulders slumped.

"You're right. I'm being a brat and not thinking straight. But I need you to know…" Grabbing a towel, she faced Saana, drying her hands as she continued. "When I came here, I wasn't expecting to gain anything other than the custody of my babies. That was the only thing I was thinking about."

There was something so poignant about the way she said it that Saana couldn't help squeezing her shoulder and saying, "I know. If there's only one thing I know about you, I know you're not avaricious."

That seemed to strike Kenzie as funny, and she grinned. "I'd say you know a lot more about me than that…"

Saana found herself blushing again under that teasing gaze, and she quickly said, "Let's get ready and go to Orlando before it gets any later. If we get back early enough, we can still spend part of the afternoon in the pool."

Kenzie's laugh was frankly sensuous, and Saana thought if her cheeks got any redder, they'd burn right off as her wife said, "I'm lookin' forward to that…"

They headed off to Orlando as soon as they'd gotten dressed, and Kenzie found herself more relaxed than she'd been in ages. The idea of Mrs. Ameri being excited about setting up a nursery for the babies still niggled at the back of her mind but couldn't dim the glow she'd gotten from the night before.

Adjusting her dark glasses, she leaned back in her seat and stretched her legs out as far as she could. Funny how, although she generally disliked shopping, she was looking forward to the trip with Saana. She'd only ever passed through Orlando, and Saana had suggested they go to the outdoor shopping-and-dining mall outside one of the theme parks for lunch. It would be more fun if they were going to the park to enjoy the rides, but there was no way Kenzie would do that with the babies on board.

Maybe one day, when they were older, she'd be able to take them for a vacation.

Somehow thoughts like that, which usually made her a little anxious about the future, today made her smile and feel hopeful.

"After our conversation this morning," Saana said suddenly as they were getting onto I-95 and she was merging with the traffic. "I was thinking you might want to consider staying in Florida once you get custody of the babies."

Kenzie sent Saana a sharp look, wondering why she'd suddenly come out with that.

"What're you suggestin'?"

"Just that you don't have any family back in Texas to be interested in your children when they're born. At least, that's what I've gathered from what you've said."

"With Aunt Lena gone, yeah, that's true." She wasn't close with any of her cousins, and in fact she had wondered whether it would be safe to move back into close proximity to Darryl's parents.

She shivered at the thought of them potentially kidnapping the babies and then berated herself for being silly.

"Well, then, it would make sense to stay fairly close by—not necessarily in Melbourne or on the East Coast—so that my parents can fulfil the grandparent role."

"Would they even want that?" she asked, really wondering *why* they might want to.

"I should think so." Saana sounded completely sure. "Besides, they already consider the babies mine as well as yours. Even though our relationship was rekindled only because of the legal problems, they don't know that."

Kenzie blew out a breath, not even ready to think about those particular complications coming about because of her need to protect her children.

"It isn't something you need to decide right now, but keep it in mind when it comes time to make any decisions."

"Sure."

But she knew staying close to Saana, having her in her life, wasn't something she wanted to have to deal with.

And she was glad when Saana dropped the subject.

When they got to the outdoor mall, Saana drew up to the curb, and a couple of valets came running up to open their doors. Kenzie swung her legs out and gratefully took the young man's hand so he could help her get out and to her feet.

Kenzie couldn't help laughing at herself. Any day now, she would get stuck in Saana's little sports car if she wasn't careful. Even her own larger, slightly higher sedan was becoming a chore to navigate. Besides, she really couldn't ask Saana to drive her old beater, with its finicky starter and questionable brakes, just because Kenzie had gotten so unwieldy.

Just imagining her elegant wife, who was casually used to the best of everything, even as a passenger in that decrepit old car made her grin again.

As they strolled into the first avenue between the stores, Kenzie sniffed at the fragrant air. It even smelled expensive.

Best to get the situation straight from the get-go.

"Saana," she said quietly, not wanting to embarrass herself or her wife by being overheard. "I can't afford anything in here. You know that, don't you?"

That earned her a sideways glance, and her wife didn't even miss a step.

"I didn't expect you to buy anything," she replied. "I'm asking you to go with me to the gala, so I'm buying your outfit."

She didn't like it, but Kenzie knew that was for the best. It would be bad enough having to mingle with Saana's friends, without sticking out like a sore thumb because of what she was wearing.

"There's a shop along here that has maternity wear for all occasions, if I remember correctly." Saana turned down another wide avenue that ran at right angles to the first. "Ah, yes. Here it is."

The store was bright and light, with racks and racks of clothes, and Kenzie balked, stopping just inside the door.

"Go on," said Saana, resting a hand on the small of Kenzie's back and giving a little push. "Look around and see if there's anything you like. If not, there are other places we can try."

So Kenzie prowled around the store, trying to figure out which of the garments might suit her and not make her feel like a faker. After all, her usual dress code was either casual with a hint of cowboy, casual with a lot of hip-hop—like the shorts and tee she had on—or scrubs, none of which was represented in this chichi store.

Then, hanging on a wall, she saw a shimmery shirt with swirls of bronze and gold, and she paused to look closer at it.

Now that might work, if she could find some drapey pants to go with it. The only problem was that as she lifted one side of the front, she realized it was split from just below the bust. She'd seen pictures of expectant women wearing shirts like that, with their bellies on display, and wasn't sure she had that type of confidence, even if Saana declared it suitable.

"Is there something I can help you with?"

At the sound of the haughty voice behind her, Kenzie turned and met a pair of obviously scornful eyes.

"Yes," she said, emboldened and annoyed enough to try on the blouse she had just decided wouldn't work. "I'd like to try on this top."

The woman tilted her head, eyes artificially wide with fake innocence.

"That won't fit you. In fact, I'm quite sure nothing we have here will be in your size."

Funny how a few words combined with a certain attitude could take you right back and make you feel six years old again.

Six and small—not in physical size, but inside, where it really matters—making the comment hurt more than you had even imagined anything could.

Too small to do anything but walk away, knowing you were nothing but dirt—and cheap dirt, at that.

Then Kenzie looked across and saw Saana standing near the door, waiting for her, and everything inside rebelled against letting this sneering woman get the better of her.

Drawing herself up to her full height—only then realizing she'd unconsciously slumped—she stared down the woman.

"That's a shame," she said, letting her drawl deepen so the words dragged mockingly. "Do you work on commission?"

The woman hesitated, as if she didn't want to answer. Then she admitted, "I do."

Kenzie shook her head with pretend sorrow. "You've lost out today, then, girlie, since I guess my wife and I'll have to go somewhere else. We've got a fundraisin' gala to host and a mess of cash to spend, but definitely not in here."

"Did you see anything you like?" Saana had come up behind the saleswoman, and the woman turned quickly to see who was speaking.

"Afraid not, darlin'." Kenzie sent her wife a smile and then took her arm. "This ain't the place for us."

And she was so happy she could have cried when Saana didn't ask any questions but simply walked out beside her, their arms linked.

CHAPTER THIRTEEN

LIFE SETTLED INTO a routine after that first full week of Kenzie being back in Florida, with work, doctor's appointments, and visits to and from Saana's parents. Not terribly exciting on the surface, except for the nights spent together, making love whenever they could.

For the first time in memory, Saana found herself resenting how busy she was with work. It would have been nice to have more time with Kenzie, especially when she considered how short their time together probably would be. But because of their routine and new-found closeness, Saana found herself sinking into a lovely fantasy that this was how things would continue to be in the future.

Willful amnesia, she thought, if she thought about the situation at all.

However, it was easier to simply *not* think about it and just continue to drift through the days, enjoying Kenzie's company and the feeling that having her there made her house a home.

Mom had completely taken over the decoration of the nursery after intensive consultation with Kenzie.

"Darling," she said in that conspiratorial way she had, "it makes absolutely no sense to ask Saana what she'd like. Whenever I do that, she gives me the blankest look, as though she doesn't even know what paint *is*."

"She is rather more scientific than artistic," Kenzie had replied, sending Saana a teasing glance. "I do think, of the two of us, I'm the more imaginative."

Saana had immediately been transported back to their bed, images of some of their more adventurous sex-capades flashing into her brain. And she'd had to turn away so her mother wouldn't see her reddened cheeks.

"Any ideas on theme?" Thankfully, her mother had continued on, unaware of her daughter's randy thoughts. "We could do a jungle theme—I think that would be so pretty, and gender neutral too—or a fairy tale, although that's a little more difficult for a boy, I think. Or am I just being old-fashioned?"

"I think you're kinda right," Kenzie agreed. "When I think fairy tale, I imagine princesses and castles, although there are knights and dragons and stuff, too, huh?"

"Is there anything you're thinking of?" Mom asked, almost absentmindedly stroking the side of Kenzie's belly. It never failed to amaze Saana how enthralled her mom was with Kenzie's growing middle and how Kenzie put up with her ignoring the concept of personal space.

"Actually... I kinda do, but you might think it's dumb." Kenzie's gaze flicked back and forth between Saana and Mom.

"Tell me," Mom insisted. "I'm sure I can work with it."

"Well, I don't know if you knew this, but my great-grandmother was Native American, and I've always loved the Old West and native patterns and themes."

"Oh, yes." Mom had actually clapped her hands in excitement, making both Saana and Kenzie chuckle. "Leave it to me."

But, of course, she'd run every decision past Kenzie, and Saana again wondered about her wife's patience.

It would have driven Saana crazy.

By then she'd shown Kenzie the room, now used as a catch-all for luggage and whatnot, and the door to their bedroom next door.

"Back in the day, both husband and wife had separate dressing rooms," she explained. "But when I got the house, I converted what had been my grandmother's into the walk-in closet and closed off the door to my grandfather's since I didn't need the space. All I need to do is have a carpenter come and remove the drywall, and we'll have easy access to the babies once they move to the nursery."

"It's definitely big enough," Kenzie said, walking over to the curtains and opening them up. "And nice and bright too. But are you sure you want to go to all that trouble? It's not like it's on the other side of the house. I can walk out into the corridor and down the hall just fine."

Saana shrugged but smiled too.

"Hey, it won't take a lot to open the door up again, and it wouldn't take much to close it back off. I'm sure it would make it much easier for you after the babies are born and they're old enough to have their own space."

One Sunday, on a whim, they drove down to Vero Beach and walked around, had lunch, and then stopped at an outlet mall and bought two bassinets, along with a bunch of baby clothes. Kenzie kept saying they had enough things, but Saana, who'd never considered herself even remotely broody, couldn't help picking out one cute outfit or toy after another.

"You're a menace," Kenzie said as they left the store almost staggering under the weight of the bags. "Between your mom and you, y'all gonna spoil these babies."

"And what's wrong with that?" she couldn't help asking. "If I'm not mistaken, you're going to be a complete disciplinarian. These kids are going to need somebody to be on their side when you get going."

Kenzie had given her a sideways glance, as though trying to decide how to respond. Then she'd laughed and shaken her head, choosing to argue about which of them would be stricter rather than point out that Saana probably wouldn't be around to intercede on their behalf.

They'd been on a conference call with the lawyer in San Antonio, who'd advised them Darryl's parents seemed to be waiting for the babies to actually be born before they filed suit.

"It makes sense," she'd explained. "They'll want to have the names on the legal papers, rather than just 'infant child.' Besides, if anything were to happen to either McKenzie or the babies, their plans would certainly change."

"Are you sure they're even still planning to sue for custody? They might have changed their minds."

Hearing Kenzie ask that had been one of the few times over the last weeks that Saana had been forced to acknowledge that although she was enjoying their time together, Kenzie may not be. Not as much, at any rate.

"Unfortunately, I don't think there's much hope of that. And although I've offered mediation, they won't hear of it."

"I don't blame them," Kenzie had said fiercely. "I'm not willin' to negotiate with them over my children, so I'm not surprised they don't want to either!"

"Well, if I hear anything more, I'll contact you. And do let me know when the babies are born."

They'd hung up, and Kenzie huffed.

"I can't believe they're still pursuing this," she'd said. "I was hoping once they knew they'd have a fight on their hands, they'd give up."

Saana hadn't known what to say. They both knew Mr. and Mrs. Beauchamp wouldn't give up on the chance to raise their son's children now that they'd lost him. But each time Saana tried to work her way around to urging Kenzie to compromise, she'd been shot down.

Kenzie still wasn't in the mood to even contemplate it.

The day before the fundraising gala, while they were at

work, Saana noticed Kenzie was moving a bit slower, and her smile was strained.

In between patients, she cornered her in the exam room.

"Are you okay?"

"Yeah," Kenzie said. "Just achy. I think I'm having Braxton-Hicks contractions."

Saana's heart leapt and then started to gallop.

"We should call Maria, see if she can take a look."

That made Kenzie chuckle.

"Saana, it's seven o'clock at night, and I'm quite sure it's nothing. If it gets worse, I'll ask Dr. Preston to take a look to make sure, but I'm pretty certain it's false labor."

She hadn't been happy about it, but Saana had backed off, having to be content with keeping a sharp eye on Kenzie for the rest of the night.

Later, when they got home, they showered together, after which Saana rubbed Kenzie's belly with cocoa butter lotion, as she'd started doing each evening. It often turned into foreplay, but that evening, when Kenzie made it known she wanted to make love, Saana refused.

"You didn't sleep well last night," she said. "And the Braxton Hicks must be exhausting. Get some sleep, okay? We have some running up and down to do tomorrow before our hair and nail appointments and then a late night at the gala, and I know you never sleep past seven in the morning."

Kenzie lay back with a disappointed groan. "What does any of that have to do with us gettin' it on tonight? Our appointments aren't until midday. What else do you have going on?"

Saana made sure to turn her back so Kenzie couldn't see her expression because she knew it would give away at least a hint of her secret.

"I just need to pick up something I ordered," she said, making her voice unconcerned.

"Are you sure it's more important than giving your wife orgasms?" Kenzie asked in a teasing, enticing tone. "And getting a few yourself?"

But Saana wouldn't budge, even though her skin tingled and heat gathered in her belly at the thought.

Next morning, Saana had to exert all the control she could muster not to act like a giddy fool and alert Kenzie to the fact there was something other than the normal going on. Getting her wife into the car at ten was a chore since Kenzie was, by then, grousing about how early they were leaving home.

When they drove to Cocoa Beach and Saana turned into the car dealership, Kenzie didn't even look interested; she was probably thinking Saana was just having something on the car checked.

"You better come in with me," she told Kenzie as she turned off the ignition. "It's too hot for you to stay out here, and I don't want to leave the car running."

"Sure." Kenzie opened her door and swung her feet around, but by the time she was trying to lever herself out, Saana was there to give her a hand. "Damn, I'm like a beached whale. I might need to get a jack of some kind to hoist me in and out of vehicles soon."

Saana laughed and said, "I'll take the video so in the future, you can show the kids just what they reduced you to."

"Ha ha." But she was smiling as they walked through the door and into the lobby. "Yeah. I'm thinking I'll have enough ammunition to guilt trip them for the rest of their lives."

"Sit here and wait, if you want," Saana told her, still chuckling. "I won't be long."

Then she hurried over to the desk, too excited to wait even a moment more.

Kenzie watch Saana stride over the reception desk and wondered what was going on. She's been acting a little strange the last couple of days, and Kenzie couldn't put her finger on the source.

She wasn't sure whether to be worried or not.

Sometimes Saana was incredibly difficult to read. Kenzie didn't think she'd ever met someone so able to conceal their thoughts as effectively.

Sighing, rubbing at her back, she tried to find a comfortable position in the chair. Over the last few days, she'd become aware of a change in her body and, actually, her mental state too. The Braxton Hicks had surprised and scared her at first, but that was probably normal. The babies weren't due for another five weeks but—as everyone kept reminding her—with first babies and especially multiples, anything was possible.

In reality, she was mentally holding her breath until she passed her thirty-seventh week. Not that the babies wouldn't probably be healthy if they were born now at thirty-five, but the longer they stayed in her uterus, the better. All she'd ever wanted was for them to be healthy, and going to term was obviously the best outcome. However, she was quickly getting to the stage where she felt like she was floundering around, constantly overheated, either thirsty or needing to pee—sometimes both at the same time.

Now she completely understood women who said they were ready to give birth two or three months before their due date!

She looked up as Saana and one of the dealership employees walked toward her, but she didn't bother to get up, expecting them to go past her and out to Saana's car. Instead, they came straight over to her and stood, looking at her.

"Come on," Saana said.

"Oh, you're all finished?"

"Not quite, but you need to come with me."

"Ugh," she replied, sliding her butt to the edge of the seat, then using the armrests to get herself onto her feet. "Couldn't I just sit here until you're done?"

Saana just shook her head, her deadpan expression some-how annoying. "No."

Back out into the heat they went, Kenzie trailing behind the other two, not really paying attention, so that when Saana stopped abruptly, Kenzie almost ran into her.

"What do you think?" Saana waved her hand toward a sport utility vehicle parked in front of the building. "Do you like that color?"

Kenzie frowned at the high-end vehicle, wondering why she was even being asked about someone else's car. Then, know-ing she was being a total grump but unable to help it, she said, "Nah. It's too bright a red. Looks trashy."

Saana shot her a strange look while the man with them made a sort of gurgling noise, as if he'd been throat punched.

"Really?" Saana asked, her eyes suddenly twinkling and her lips twitching, like she were trying not to laugh. "I thought that was your favorite color."

"It is," she said, wrinkling her nose. "But not on a car."

"Okay." Saana turned to the man beside her to ask, "That'll teach me to try to surprise my wife. What other colors do you have? But I want the same features we discussed last week."

"Um, I'll have to check, but it's a custom paint job. I don't know…"

Then, and only then, as Saana told the man in no uncertain terms that none of that mattered, did it come home to Kenzie what was going on, and she felt her knees get weak.

"Saana, wha…?"

"I bought this car for you." She said it casually, glancing over then quickly coming to put her arm around Kenzie's waist. "Are you all right?"

"You… You bought this? For me?"

Kenzie suspected her wife would have shrugged if her shoulder wasn't being used to prop her up.

"You can hardly get in and out of either of the cars, and

when the babies are born, you're going to need a vehicle that can accommodate two car seats with ease, so yes. I bought this for you. But if you hate it, we can get something else—"

"Are you kiddin'?" Kenzie knew she was shouting but didn't care. "I love it! Don't you dare change a damn thing!"

And it was only later she realized she hadn't even balked for a second at the expense of the gift or thought about being beholden to Saana even more than she already was.

Instead, what came to mind was how considerate and wonderful the woman she married really was and how much she loved her for it.

But while in the past she'd have thought those emotions injurious to her own peace of mind, just then she couldn't work up the strength to care.

CHAPTER FOURTEEN

THE EVENING OF the gala was warm and muggy, making Kenzie glad her top was sleeveless and had a deep V-neck, and her pants were almost gossamer-fine silk. She was even more pleased to find out that instead of being held outside in the Ameris' extensive and beautiful gardens, they'd set everything up indoors.

"I wanted to wait until later in the year," Saana's mom had said to Kenzie a couple of weeks earlier. "Then it would be cooler, and all our friends from up north would be here for the winter. But getting the trust and the work Saana's doing in front of people's eyes as soon as possible was so important we decided to do this now."

Taking out the necklace that was the only thing she'd inherited from Aunt Lena, Kenzie slipped her wedding ring onto it and then put it on, adjusting the band and heart pendant so they lay nicely in her cleavage. She'd tried to put the ring on, but it no longer fit.

Looking at herself in the mirror, Kenzie frowned.

She didn't look very much like herself, and it wasn't just because of her pregnancy. Her hair had been cut and styled in an expensive salon, and the mani-pedi she'd gotten had almost put her into a coma of pleasure. The clothes and shoes she was wearing cost more than a months' pay and made her feel guilty, even as she ran an appreciative hand over the sleek gold fabric of her blouse.

When she'd asked Saana if she'd be expected to wear makeup, her wife shrugged.

"That's totally up to you," she'd replied. "If you don't want to, then don't. You don't need it."

A comment that made her tingle with pleasure, even as it annoyed her as well.

She'd met a few of Saana's friends when she first came to live at the mansion, and they'd all looked at Kenzie like she'd crawled out of the bottom of a pond. Mind you, they'd made sure Saana wasn't aware of that, the hypocrites. Obviously, staying on Saana's good side had been first and foremost on their agenda. But a few times, as if realizing Kenzie wouldn't rat them out, they'd made their snide remarks when Saana was out of earshot.

"Where on earth did Saana dig you up? Vegas? Somehow, I'm not surprised."

"You're from Texas? Are you legal?"

"Do you have indoor plumbing where you're from?"

Just rude, stupid comments that made Kenzie feel like poop on the bottom of someone's shoe, even as she held her chin up and gave them the stink eye.

The image looking back at her from the mirror was nothing like the usual board shorts–wearing, flip-flop-loving woman she knew herself to be. In fact, she almost felt she was inside someone else's skin. A skin she needed to be able to get through the night without embarrassing Saana and her parents, or damaging the Preston Trust.

"Hey, are you ready?" Saana called from the walk-in closet. "Can you zip me up, please?"

Somehow the sound of Saana's slightly harried voice eased the band of anxiety around Kenzie's chest, and she said, as she walked over to the door, "You're gonna make us late, as usual."

Then, as she stepped into the closet, she halted, her heart turning over and desire flashing out to flood her veins.

Saana's dress was a simple column of coral silk that draped her body like a second skin, except where it flowed in soft pleats from one shoulder, across her bare back to the opposite hip. It hugged every curve and dip, bringing to Kenzie's suddenly feverish brain images of the sinuous, sexy way Saana moved as her arousal climbed, threatening to peak.

"Dear lord," she murmured, moving closer so as to run her palm across that bare, warm skin, tracing the line of her wife's vertebrae, feeling goose bumps fire up beneath her fingers. "How am I gonna keep my hands off you all evening? This is the sexiest dress in the world, and all I wanna do is take it off you."

Saana's blush made Kenzie lick her bottom lip, and her wife's cheeks turned even pinker.

"Stop that," she muttered, trying and failing to wrestle with the zipper at the side of her dress. "Now you're the one who's going to make us late, and don't think I won't blame you for it. Mom likes you better than me, anyway, so I'll happily throw you under the bus to avoid her fussing at me."

"Mm-hmm," Kenzie replied sarcastically, still wondering if they had time for one quick sexual encounter before the party. Nah. Unfortunately. She batted at Saana's hand. "Lift your arm. Let me do you up."

When Saana obeyed, Kenzie bent quickly to place a kiss right on the exposed edge of her wife's breast, eliciting a soft gasp. Then, before she changed her mind, she pulled up the zipper, tucking the tiny tab into the bodice so it became invisible.

"There," she said, unable to resist giving that truly wonderful ass a quick squeeze too. "Are you all ready to go? Your mom gave us strict instructions to be there by six thirty, and it's almost six now."

"Yes." God, that husky note in Saana's voice got her every time. "I'm ready."

"Me too," she replied, knowing Saana understood the double meaning when another wave of pink flooded her face. "But we have to go."

"Wait." Saana's voice, with its sharp edge, stopped Kenzie in her tracks. "Is that your wedding ring?"

Reaching up, Kenzie lifted it and nodded. "Yeah. I wanted to wear it tonight but couldn't get it on my sausage finger."

And although Saana didn't say anything more, her smile was all Kenzie needed.

"Oh, earrings!" Saana exclaimed, turning back into the closet abruptly. "Mom says no outfit is finished without some."

In two twos, she was back, fastening gleaming diamond drops to her earlobes as she quick-stepped into the hallway.

Kenzie suppressed a grin. When they'd first met, she'd thought Saana was just one of those people who always walked fast—in a rush to get to where they were going. It was only later on she realized that her wife's speed had more to do with her constant lateness than anything else.

Climbing into the SUV, Kenzie said, "Have I adequately thanked you for buying this? It's so much easier to get into and out of than the cars. That automatic drop-down step is the bomb."

"It was this or a crane," Saana teased. "And I thought this would be more useful in the long run."

Laughing, Kenzie had to agree.

When they got to her parents' house, Saana drove around to the back entrance, where a guard let them in so they could park near the stand-alone garage. Inside the house, it was a hive of activity, with Mrs. Ameri and the party planner like army generals in the middle. When Mrs. Ameri saw them, she bustled over.

"There you are!" They both were hugged and received air-kisses, so as to avoid the spread of unwanted lipstick, Kenzie suspected. "Just in time to start greeting guests. Saana, that color looks lovely on you, and McKenzie, you're absolutely glowing. Gold suits you. You look like a Renaissance portrait."

She rushed off again, leaving Kenzie to ask, "Was that a compliment?"

Saana laughed, threading her arm through Kenzie's and leading her toward the great room at the back of the house, where a band was already playing.

"Yes, it was. You look fabulous. I've told you, pregnancy suits you."

Then there was an influx of guests needing attention. Saana kept her arm through Kenzie's for a while as she greeted them—mostly by name—and introduced everyone to Kenzie. They'd been there for about forty-five minutes when Saana let go to hug someone she called Uncle George, and Kenzie eased away. When she realized Saana hadn't noticed, she took another step back, then another, until she could unobtrusively set off to find a quiet place away from the limelight surrounding her wife.

"Is everything all right, McKenzie?"

At the sound of Mr. Ameri's voice, Kenzie started guiltily.

"Yes. Sure. I just wanted to sit down for a moment. My back's been sore the last couple of days." His look of concern had her quickly reassuring him that it wasn't anything serious.

"Ah, good." He looked around and then guided her toward a table near the front of the room. "Let me get you seated and get you something to drink. Knowing Mariella, the cocktail hour will be brought to a close exactly at eight, and dinner will be announced." He sent his wife a fond glance, before continuing, "She's a martinet when it comes to hosting these affairs. Positively frightening."

With a wink, he left her as Kenzie laughed quietly. Even though she had no idea what a martinet was, she could make a pretty good guess, having seen Mrs. Ameri keep everyone around her on their toes.

And, just as he'd predicted, in fifteen minutes—at eight exactly—Mrs. Ameri announced that dinner would be served and asked everyone to take their seats.

"There you are," Saana said as she slid into one of the remaining seats at the table. "I wondered where you'd run off to."

She was glowing, and Kenzie felt her heart turn over as she was the recipient of that beautiful smile.

"Sorry. Had to get off my feet for a while. I know I should have been mingling, but—"

"No worries," was all she had time to say before her parents and two other couples interrupted by coming to take their seats.

Dinner was sumptuous, but Kenzie merely picked at her food, more worried about her table manners not being up to par than about eating. The conversation swirled around her, but it wasn't about anything she could comment on or contribute to, and the old self-conscious feelings started creeping up on her again.

"Have you been to Paris, McKenzie?" Mrs. Guilder suddenly asked, surprising her so much Kenzie almost choked on her food.

It seemed there was a general lull in the conversation because it felt as if everyone at the table was suddenly looking at her, and heat gathered at the back of Kenzie's neck.

She didn't dare look at Saana or her parents, and for a long moment, she had no idea what to say. This was just the sort of thing she'd tried to avoid—to warn Saana about—but here she was anyway, on the spot and in the fire.

Well, then, to hell with it.

"No, ma'am," she said, rolling the drawl out like a rug. "Haven't been anywhere much and never outside of the States."

There was a choking sound from somewhere in Mr. Ameri's

direction, but Kenzie kept her gaze fixed on Mrs. Guilder, who looked almost comically startled.

In for a penny, in for a pound.

"My parents both had substance abuse problems, so I was pretty much homeless until I was six. Then my mother was incarcerated, my father disappeared. My aunt took me in, although she already had three kids of her own. I was an orphan by the time I was ten, but I think I was damned lucky because I still had Aunt Lena givin' me a roof over my head and makin' sure I had food to eat."

Everyone at the table was listening now, and Kenzie had never felt more inferior in her life—surround by the wealthy, with their total lack of understanding of reality. But it was no use stopping now. Better to at least make her sad, sordid tale relevant to why they were supposedly all here and regain some semblance of pride.

Firming her lips, which felt like they may be about to tremble, she lifted her chin and looked around the table at everyone except Saana.

She didn't want to see her wife's reaction to her words.

Her bad behavior.

"Which is why I'm so proud to be a part of the Preston Medical Clinic staff. I know what it's like to be without a home, insurance and medical care. My aunt told me that when my father dropped me off at her home after my mom went to jail, just before he disappeared, I was so sick she wasn't sure I'd make it."

Once more, she let her gaze wander around the table, and this time she forced herself to look at Saana. Her face was still, unmoving, but the expression in her eyes—a burning, angry look—made Kenzie's stomach fall.

But she'd started something Kenzie knew she had to finish, so she took a deep breath and continued.

"Turned out I had viral meningitis, and if Aunt Lena hadn't

taken me to the emergency room, I'd have probably died. But the cost of the treatment and the hospitalization was something she couldn't afford and had to pay back over a very long time. That's not right, ya know? To have her kindness be so costly that when her own daughter got cancer, it almost bankrupted her. That's why we need places like Preston Medical."

Her hands were trembling by the time she'd finished, so she kept them under the table, where they couldn't be seen, trying to keep her defiance at the forefront. Hoping all any of them would see was her dignity, not her fear.

"Well said, McKenzie." Surprisingly, it was Mrs. Guilder who spoke, and when Kenzie looked at her, she was nodding. "And please forgive me for putting you on the spot with my question. Of everyone here, I should have known better. We do like to pretend we've all grown up wealthy, and of course, some have, but I come from a hardscrabble town in Oklahoma, and if I hadn't met and married Myron, I'd probably still be a waitress, hardly able to make ends meet."

"Someone would have snatched you up," her husband said, taking her hand and kissing the back. "I'm just glad I saw you first."

And the conversation turned to the clinic and what else Saana wanted to achieve through the trust, but although Kenzie was brought into the conversation, she again avoided looking at Saana.

It was hard not to think her revelation, in front of all these people, hadn't caused a shift—perhaps even a break—in their relationship.

Kenzie had always avoided talking about her parents; there didn't seem to be anything to gain from bringing them up. To her, her life had started and been saved the night Aunt Lena took her in.

No one would have blamed her if she'd turned her sister's no-good husband away and told him to take his child with him. Lena had been widowed just two or so years before, and although her husband had a small life insurance policy when he died, it had only been enough to bury him and pay off a portion of the mortgage.

One more mouth to feed had been the last thing she'd needed.

Thank goodness she hadn't thought that way.

Without her, Kenzie didn't know where she'd be.

What—who—she would have ended up as.

The rest of the evening passed in a bit of a blur. Feeling emotional wasn't one of Kenzie's favorite moods. It was exhausting. But although she longed to go home, she knew Saana had to stay to the end.

Thank goodness for Mrs. Ameri, who ushered the last of the crowd out the door at half-past eleven on the dot.

"I think that was a resounding success," she said happily as they sat together in the den, while the catering staff finished cleaning up. "I'm looking forward to hearing the total donations tomorrow, but according to Jean, everyone was very generous."

"Thank you, Mom." Saana got up and crossed the room to kiss her mother on both cheeks. "We couldn't have done it without you."

The fondness in Mariella Ameri's smile as she looked at her daughter made Kenzie have to blink back tears.

"You're very welcome, darling. I'm so very proud of you and all you're doing. But I think you should take poor Kenzie home. She looks exhausted."

Saana gave Kenzie what she could only interpret as a brooding look and nodded. "Yes, we should go."

And so, after saying goodnight to the Ameris, they went.

CHAPTER FIFTEEN

SAANA WASN'T SURE how to approach the subject of Kenzie's revelations during dinner.

At first, as she'd spoken, Saana had felt hurt that she was hearing this story for the first time, along with people who were little better than strangers to her wife.

Why hadn't Kenzie told Saana about her early life? Was it a matter of trust—or, more precisely, lack thereof?

In all the time Saana had known Kenzie, the only person who'd she'd ever spoken about in a parental role was her aunt Lena. Although she'd been very young when her aunt had taken her in, did she remember being with her parents? What had she seen? Experienced?

Had that time in her life left scars that maybe even Kenzie wasn't aware of but that had contributed to her extreme independence?

What else had it caused?

All those questions were flying through her mind, but Kenzie looked so exhausted that Saana hesitated to bring it up.

"I'm sorry I embarrassed you earlier."

Kenzie's voice surprised Saana out of her reverie, but she didn't sound terribly sorry, rather more defensive. Saana shot her wife a quick glance, and seeing her chin at that combative angle for some reason made her heart ache.

"You didn't," she said softly, trying to gauge how best to proceed.

"Then why were you so angry?"

"I wasn't angry."

Yet even as she said it, she knew it wasn't true.

Clearly, Kenzie did, too, because she snorted rudely.

"What does that sound mean?" Saana asked, unable to rein in her own annoyance.

"I'm trying to figure out whether you're lying to me or yourself. I know you well enough to know when you're angry."

"I was shocked to hear your story, McKenzie, and—"

Kenzie snorted again, interrupting her. "You weren't shocked. You were definitely angry. You're still angry. You only call me McKenzie when you are."

That was, in Saana's mind, a step too far.

"Don't you dare tell me what I felt or thought." She couldn't help the coolness of her tone, and from the corner of her eye, she saw Kenzie turn to look at her. "I was angry because of what you went through and, if you want the entire truth, because you seemed willing to tell the story to strangers but had never told *me*."

"Maybe because I didn't want to." The words were like a dart through Saana's heart. "Because I don't want your sympathy or to be looked at as a victim of my parents' bad choices. That has *nothing* to do with who I am."

"I know that." Saana said it although she didn't really mean it. The weight of love sitting directly on her heart made her want to cry. "But it's a part of you—your history—and I'd have liked to hear it from you, in private, rather than in front of everyone else."

"Sorry." It was grudgingly said, but Saana's anger faded.

"It's okay. I understand why you'd feel that way."

"Thanks. I appreciate you sayin' so."

Kenzie yawned, turning her head to the side, looking out

the window, and after a few moments of silence, Saana realized her wife had fallen asleep.

Sighing, Saana turned the conversation over in her head.

Now that she knew what Kenzie had gone through, she was forced to look at her own reactions to her wife's behavior.

If she were honest, early in their marriage, she'd been unable to understand why Kenzie, at her age, was still studying to become a nurse. There were grants, and scholarships, and loans she could have taken out, allowing her to go to college and finish quickly rather than have it take forever and a day. As much as she'd loved her, Saana acknowledged now that she'd also judged her without having the first idea of why she was the way she was.

Saana had even found herself getting annoyed at the way Kenzie wouldn't accept the help, particularly the financial assistance, she offered. After all, Saana was rich and a doctor. Any normal woman would be pleased to be with someone who not only had the means to give them whatever they wanted but also was generously willing to do so.

Wow. Thinking about it now, in light of her new understanding, Saana actually felt ashamed. And incredibly proud of all Kenzie had been able to achieve.

Having pulled into the garage, Saana turned off the ignition and gently shook Kenzie awake. When her eyes opened, she looked around, seemingly disoriented.

"We're home." Saana's kept her voice as soft as the hand that skimmed Kenzie's cheek. "You're going to have to awake up. Unfortunately, I can't carry you inside."

Kenzie chuckled, seemingly having put their argument behind her. Rubbing her eyes, she straightened from her sideways slump.

"You'd definitely hurt yourself if you tried," she replied, taking off the seat belt after Saana unlatched it. "Let's keep it that only one of us has a backache, okay?"

As they meandered slowly into the house, Saana was left wondering if Kenzie would accept or resent the new, tender feelings growing ever stronger in her wife's heart. Things had been so good between them Saana was truly reluctant to even try to find out.

She already knew that Kenzie wouldn't hesitate to take off if she didn't like the way things were heading, although Saana didn't know, really, why she'd run in the first place. That, too, would take some thinking about, in light of these new revelations—Kenzie's childhood, what she'd said earlier about trying to fit in, in particular.

Kenzie undressed and fell into bed while Saana was still taking off her makeup, and although Saana was tired, too, she found herself lying in the dark, still thinking about the evening. Kenzie had spoken her truth with more than a hint of defiance, daring those listening to judge her life or look down on her experience.

Instead, it had filled Saana with helpless rage as she listened to Kenzie talk about her parents, and also pride at the resilience of the woman she loved so dearly.

And it was the sense of pride that had her rolling over to spoon around Kenzie's back and finally fall asleep.

She was dreaming. One of those dreams you know is a dream and yet seems incredibly real.

They were standing on the Eiffel Tower, Kenzie and she. Not on the observation deck but literally on the Eiffel Tower. Outside, being buffeted by the wind, hanging on to a pole or antenna.

"We need to get down," she shouted to Kenzie. "It's too dangerous. You might fall."

Kenzie tilted her head, as though unable to hear what Saana had said, and shouted something back.

Saana couldn't hear her either.

Looking around, she tried to find the way down, but there

were no steps or lifts, nothing to indicate how they'd gotten up there in the first place. Desperate now, her heart pounding, she tried to stoop down, hanging on to the pole for balance, thinking that if she did, the change in perspective might show her where to go.

From the corner of her eye, she saw Kenzie move. When she looked around, she instinctively screamed, seeing her wife had let go of the antenna, the only thing keeping her tethered. She was being pushed backward by the wind, about to go over the edge—

Jolting awake, Saana lay panting, trying to determine if she was still dreaming or actually awake.

"Saana." Kenzie's voice came to her out of the dark. "Saana, it's all right."

Was it? Would it ever be again?

"I…I'm okay."

"You were dreamin', babe. Sounded like a bad one." A hand, soft and soothing, stroked her shoulder, then her hair. "You shouted."

Swallowing her fear, she composed her voice to calmness.

"I'm sorry I woke you."

Kenzie made a rude noise that made Saana smile, even though her heart was still hammering.

"Don't worry about it."

"Go back to sleep, Kenzie. I'm okay."

But Kenzie's hand drifted to her throat, lingered there, fingers finding and measuring her pulse.

"Your heart's racing and not in a good way." Her lips replaced her fingers, and the wet heat of her tongue fired goose bumps over what felt like every inch of Saana's skin. "I won't promise to calm you down, but you'll be excited in a far better way."

Saana wanted to object, to say Kenzie needed her sleep,

but they were kissing, and every other thought, every other concern, fled her mind.

All she felt were those full, sensual lips on hers, the wet, slick slide of their tongues against each other.

With Kenzie, Saana's need didn't build slowly. Instead, it flamed instantly, ignited by her wife's touch, her kisses, the sound of her voice demanding complicity. And in its path was all Saana's fears and inhibitions, incinerated.

Some nights, Kenzie demanded Saana give her pleasure, with the promise of ecstasy returned two-, three-, fourfold. On others, like this night, Kenzie caressed and kissed and aroused Saana into a sensual stupor, holding her there.

"Open wider."

Her legs fell to the sides as if the words were strings and she were a marionette. Those fingers, long and strong and oh so knowledgeable, slid home, stroking through the wetness of arousal, finding a spot deep inside that, until her, had been secret. Kenzie had found it, as sure as a musician finding the right note, and had learned how to play it until Saana arched, and strained, and craved orgasm more than air.

"Relax." Kenzie's voice was passion-rough, her fingers equally so, both combining to push Saana incrementally closer to the edge. "You're almost there, baby. Relax. Let me get you there."

She stroked faster, a little harder.

Just right.

Perfect.

Perfect.

Ahh...

As her body convulsed, she bit her lip to stay silent. To stop the words of love filling her heart from coming out.

Coming down off the high, she suddenly realized something was wrong. Instead of cuddling up close to her still,

Kenzie was sitting on the side of the bed, barely visible in the darkness.

"Kenz?"

There was no immediate answer. Saana rolled onto her knees so as to put her hand on Kenzie's back. The muscles were rigid, shivering slightly. Then Saana felt her take a deep breath.

"I think I'm in labor."

They'd been warned about it, but Saana wondered if, like her, Kenzie had put the thought of premature labor out of her mind.

"African American women, women who've had IVF and women carrying multiples are all at risk of premature births," Maria Ramcharam had reminded them. "And of course, McKenzie is in all of those high-risk groups. As soon as you have any thoughts that you might be in labor, I need you to contact me and head to the hospital."

So that's what they did.

It was three in the morning when Saana helped Kenzie out of the SUV outside emerge, where they were met by an orderly with a wheelchair. Only years of practice keeping a cool head during emergencies carried Saana through with any kind of dignity. What she really wanted to do was abandon the vehicle right where it was and rush into the hospital with Kenzie.

As though knowing that, her wife looked back over her shoulder and blew Saana a saucy kiss.

Driving way too fast for a parking lot, she parked the car and dashed into the hospital.

And the waiting—and the extreme stress—began.

A nurse practitioner examined Kenzie and declared she was five centimeters. As Saana was helping her get comfortable, adjusting her pillows, promising to find the fluffy socks to warm up her feet, Kenzie grabbed her wrist and let out a curse.

"Water just broke," she said when the contraction had passed.

At five o'clock, Saana called her parents to let them know what was happening. By then Kenzie had only progressed to seven centimeters, and both she and Saana were watching the babies' heartbeats anxiously.

"It's too early. Too soon for them to come now," Kenzie kept saying.

"You're almost thirty-six weeks." Saana was trying to reassure her, even in the face of her own fear. "They'll be fine."

But there was no denying the fact they were both scared stiff.

At seven, Maria Ramcharam arrived, having been kept apprised of Kenzie's condition and wanting to check on it herself.

At that point, with each contraction, one baby's heart rate slowed dramatically, and although it picked back up when the contractions passed, Maria suggested they err on the side of caution.

"I'm recommending you have a Caesarean section, but because you opted not to have an epidural or spinal block, we're going to have to do it under general anesthesia."

Kenzie immediately agreed, and Maria left the room to arrange for the operating room.

One of the nurses bustled around for a while and then left the room. As soon as they were alone, Kenzie grabbed Saana's wrist.

"I need to ask you a favor. A huge favor."

"Another one?" she asked, trying to keep it light, not liking how serious Kenzie looked.

"I'm serious."

"I think by now you know I'd do pretty much anything for you."

"If anythin' happens to me, I want you to keep the babies."

"Kenzie—"

"I mean it. I don't care if you let the Beauchamps see them or not, but I want you to raise them. If you do that, you can tell them about me, and they'll know I loved them and fought for them and *wanted* them so very much. If you give them to their grandparents, no matter what happens, they'll always feel deserted. Abandoned by the people who gave them life."

Saana swallowed, unable to stop the tears filling her eyes, and nodded.

"I'll do it, but nothing's going to happen to you, Kenzie. You'll be okay, and then you're going to feel silly even asking me."

"Doesn't matter," she said, shaking her head. "I don't care if I look like a fool right now. It's a parent's responsibility to try and cover the bases so as to protect their children. That's what I'm tryin' to do."

The nurse came back in just then.

"We going to move you now to prep you for surgery. You're going to have to wait in the surgical waiting area, Dr. Ameri."

Then another nurse came in with forms to be signed, and Saana knew she couldn't take the chance of losing Kenzie without telling her how she felt one last time.

But another contraction hit just then, and the chance to say she loved her passed before the words could be uttered.

"Dr. Amari…"

"Yes. I'm going."

Then, with one last look at first her wife and then the monitor, she swiftly left the room.

In the corridor, just standing there, unnerved and more frightened than she'd ever been before, she waited, wanting to see Kenzie go by before making her way to the surgical area of the hospital.

"Saana."

Her mother's voice jolted her out of her funk, and she turned to see her parents coming toward her, almost identical expressions of concern on their faces.

Then the door opened, and Kenzie was wheeled out.

"McKenzie."

Mom and Dad reached out, touching her hand and arm as the nurses wheeled her by, and Kenzie smiled a slightly lop-sided smile and called out, "Thanks for being here. Take care of your daughter. She looks a little pale."

As the love of her life disappeared down the hallway, all of a sudden, a thought crossed Saana's mind, and she pushed past her parents to go after the gurney.

"Kenzie. The names."

But it was too late. They'd already turned into the eleva-tor, and the doors had closed, leaving Saana a trembling, ter-rified mess.

CHAPTER SIXTEEN

SHE NAMED THEM Leanna and Darren.

"Leanna was Aunt Lena's given name," she told Saana late on the evening she'd given birth, after she'd come out of the anesthetic. "And Darren because I prefer it to Darryl."

"Makes perfect sense," Saana replied, her gaze stuck like glue to Leanna and Darren, who were both asleep on Kenzie's chest.

They'd been born without complications—Leanne at six pounds, four ounces and Darren at seven pounds flat—but Maria Ramcharam had said she'd be keeping Kenzie in the hospital for four days, worried about the chance of an embolism. Leanne had a touch of jaundice and had spent part of the first day in the NICU.

In Kenzie's mind, they were the most beautiful babies in the world, although she suspected every mother thought the same thing. Her only regret was having been out of it when they were born.

"I can't believe you got to hold them before I did," she groused, looking up in time to see Saana smile.

"I didn't, really," Saana replied. "You held them for almost nine months."

Darren wriggled, his eyes opening a crack, but then went back to sleep.

Kenzie wished they would wake up, although she knew

she'd probably look back on that thought and laugh at its craziness sometime in the future.

"Mom and Dad were asking if they could come by during visiting hours to see you all."

The way Saana stroked a gentle finger down each baby's cheek in turn threatened to completely melt Kenzie's heart.

"Your parents are welcome anytime. You know that."

Glancing up, Saana grinned suddenly, replying, "You might not want to tell them that. We might go home tomorrow and find them living in our house."

Kenzie chuckled with her, then shifted slightly, trying to ease a sudden muscle cramp in her arm.

"Can I take one of them for you?"

"Sure," Kenzie said on a yawn.

Perching on the edge of the bed, Saana expertly lifted Darren and cradled him in one arm, looking down to coo at him, "Who's the sweetest little man who ever was, hmm?"

Then she glanced up, meeting Kenzie's gaze, and there was no mistaking the way the shutters came down over her face, making Kenzie's heart give a little jolt.

"I think we should hyphenate the babies' last names. If Darryl's parents are waiting to get word of their birth, it would probably be wise to give them a firm indication that you're not fighting them alone. If they're the kind of people who like to know what they're up against, they'll investigate, hopefully finding out the Ameris aren't going to just roll over to their demands."

There was that cool tone, which told Kenzie there was something being hidden. With Saana, it usually meant some unwanted or secret emotion, but that couldn't be the case here. Perhaps she just wanted to sound businesslike—in fact, removing the emotion from the discussion altogether?

"I'll think about it," she said with another yawn. "But I can't wrap my brain about what else that would mean right now."

"What else it would mean?"

"Yeah. The consequences for all of us, you know?"

Just then, Leanna let out a wail that seemed so completely out of proportion to her size that it startled her mama into laughter.

"Maybe she's ready to eat? Leanna, please don't wake up your brother. I haven't got this whole breastfeeding thing down yet, and I don't think I can handle both of you at the same time."

"Relax, babe. It'll be fine. And if it doesn't work, that's why we have bottles."

The words, so warm and understanding, made her tear up a little. During her obstetrics rotation, she'd seen so many new mothers driven to anxiety attacks because they couldn't get their babies to nurse, and no one offered the right support.

"One of the nurses said to call her when it was time. Can you ring the bell for me?"

Saana did as she was asked and then, apparently thinking Kenzie might not like her hovering, moved over to the visitor's chair on the other side of the room.

Intellectually, Kenzie had known she may have issues breastfeeding, but by the time she finally got Leanna latched on and had gotten over the rush of painful pins and needles, she was frazzled.

And as soon as the nurse left the room, Darren started fussing.

"You could probably tandem feed." Saana was bouncing Darren, trying to keep him calm. "Should I call the nurse back?"

Close to tears, Kenzie shook her head. How she hated seeming—feeling—so weak.

"No. Maybe you should go and get him a bottle." There was no way she could handle any more right then, with her inci-

sion making it impossible to shift positions and Leanna, just then, losing her grip on the nipple.

Kenzie cursed and started to cry, adding her sobs to both babies' wails.

"Aw, babe." Saana came over, and although her words were tender, her tone brooked no argument. "I'm going to tell the nurse to bring two bottles, okay—but in the meantime…"

Kenzie didn't even realize what Saana was doing until she found herself with Leanna back on the breast but now lying on a pillow, her body curled back, almost under Kenzie's arm. And she made no objection when Saana positioned Darren the same way on the other side, tickling his tiny mouth with her nipple and guiding his head until, miraculously, he, too, latched on.

"Will you be okay while I go and get the bottles?"

Kenzie snorted, unable to laugh because her nose was stuffy, and she was afraid to cough because of the pain. She'd need someone to press the pillow into her middle, and all pillows were otherwise in use just then.

"I think it's clear I don't need them anymore. Why did I bother with the nurse when you've proven to be just as efficient?"

Saana shrugged. "I just hate to see you upset and not do anything about it." She glanced toward the door and asked, "Will you be okay for a little? I want to go and head Mom and Dad off at the pass until you've finished breastfeeding."

"Sure. I'm all right just now." A jolt of anxiety made her add, "But don't be long, okay?"

And when Saana replied, "I won't be. I promise," Kenzie felt herself relax.

Saana called her parents and asked them to wait at least half an hour before leaving to come to the hospital. Then, when the babies finished feeding, Saana offered to take one of them for the recommended fifteen minutes of skin-to-skin bonding and was thrilled when Kenzie agreed.

"I was wonderin' how I was goin' to manage both of them," she said. "The nurse just made it sound so easy. 'Remember to spend time cuddling your babies after feeding.' I want to, but right now I'm a little overwhelmed."

"Understandable. I'm feeling a bit that way myself, and I didn't have a C-section this morning."

Laying Leanna down in the cot for a moment, Saana undressed to the waist, subduing her natural shyness about public nudity. This was, after all, a special and important circumstance. Rolling the cot over to the comfortable chair beside the door, glad that she'd insisted on a private room, she sat down to unswaddle the baby.

The sensation of that soft, fragile life against her chest made all the air leave her lungs in a rush, and the wave of tenderness that crashed through her made tears fill her eyes. When she tucked the blanket around them both and Leanna relaxed into a sweet, boneless little heap, Saana knew she was in all kinds of trouble.

It wasn't that the babies hadn't seemed real to her. They most definitely had—but in a completely intellectual and rather distant sense.

In her head, they had been Kenzie's babies. Nameless, faceless, future problems. They'd only become human—precious—in those fraught moments when Maria lifted them from the unconscious Kenzie's womb, and Saana had taken hold of them. Heard their first cries. Looked into their wrinkled, vernix-coated faces and seen not "the babies" but new and glorious lives filled with personality and potential.

Falling in love with them hadn't been high on Saana's list of priorities, but in those moments, she'd realized she hadn't been given a choice.

And she doubted she could love them any more than she already did.

After the nurses had chased her out of the room and were wheeling Kenzie to recovery, Saana had gone into the bathroom, locked the stall door, and cried from sheer and overwhelming emotion.

What had started as an act of altruism seemed set to be both the best and the worst thing she had ever done, but she was powerless to change any part of what had already gone.

And if she were honest, she didn't think she would, even if she could.

Mom cracked open the door cautiously, poking her head through just after Saana had put the babies back in their cot and, thankfully, redressed. Saana put her finger to her lips, pointing to where Kenzie lay asleep.

After a quick tiptoe closer to get a glimpse of Leanna and Darren, Mom gestured for Saana to come out into the corridor so they could talk.

"Have you decided on their names yet? When can I hold them? Are they letting McKenzie go home tomorrow or keeping her in longer?"

When Mom got this excited, it was sometimes hard to get a word in edgewise, so Saana held up both hands in surrender.

"Mom, slow down! Kenzie decided on Leanna and Darren, but there are no middle names yet. We discussed it and would like you to wait until at least tomorrow before you can cuddle them. And Dr. Ramcharam wants to keep Kenzie here at least three days to make sure there are no complications after the C-section."

"I'm so glad you got the bassinets when you did. I was telling your father that I have to get the nursery finished. It's mostly done. Just a few finishing touches. Things that hadn't been delivered yet but will be tomorrow. Oh, I can't wait to snuggle those babies."

Mom ran on for a while more, so enthusiastic neither of them had the heart to interrupt. Dad stood there, smiling the smile he reserved just for his live-wire wife, and Saana made all the appropriate noises while also keeping an eye on Kenzie through the glass at the top of the door.

"I'm not sure how long Kenzie will sleep," she said when Mom finally stopped to draw breath. "She's pretty exhausted."

"You look like you are too." Dad patted her shoulder. "When did you last eat?"

Saana shrugged, glancing back in at her sleeping wife. "Um, maybe around lunchtime?" She actually couldn't remember whether she had or not.

"If your mother promises not to actually touch the babies, why don't you let her sit with McKenzie for a while and you come with me to the cafeteria? You look like you need sustenance."

"I'm fine," she insisted. The memory of Kenzie's meltdown while trying to breastfeed was foremost in her mind. "But maybe I'll go get a cup of coffee. I'm planning to stay as long as they'll let me this evening."

"Go with your father." When Mom spoke in that tone of voice, it was a rare person who refused, no matter their age. "I'll just sit by the bed in case she wakes up, and I promise not to touch the babies. I'll just look."

Unable to find any good excuse not to do as ordered, Saana found herself walking down to the elevators with her father. Glancing across at his profile, Saana felt another jolt of tenderness, this time directed at the quiet, thoughtful man who had always been there for her, through thick or thin.

As her mother had often pointed out over the years, they were actually very much alike. Neither of them wore their heart on their sleeves but used logic to try to make sense of whatever life threw at them. Even when Saana didn't want to talk about things, she'd often found herself seeking out her father just to be around him. They'd play a game of golf or take the boat out and just spend the day hanging out.

And when she'd needed advice, he'd always been the one she turned to.

Riding down in the elevator, Saana leaned against the wall, fighting the feeling of being overwhelmed and scared by everything happening in her life. Trying, as she always did, to hide her fear. To be strong and reliable.

Kenzie and the babies needed her now more than they had before, and she knew she couldn't let them down.

"Parenthood is a scary job," Dad said after they'd sat at a table and Saana was nibbling on a rather unappetizing sandwich. "But just think of all the people who've done it, with varying levels of success, over the centuries, and it won't seem as frightening."

She tried to laugh, but it was a harsh, truncated sound that came from her throat, and her father's gaze sharpened.

"I know there's something going on you're not telling us about, Saana." He held up his hand when she opened her lips to speak, effectively stopping her. "You do know that whatever you need, your mother and I are there for you, don't you? And no matter how old you are, if there's anything you can't handle, we're here to lend a hand. The same goes for McKenzie."

Shaking her head, concentrating on the paper plate in front of her, she replied, "It's fine, Dad. Really. We just have a lot going on right now. Things we need to work out."

He tapped his fingers on his coffee cup and then took a sip before speaking.

"Both your mother and I have noticed how things have changed—how you have changed—since McKenzie came back. Not in a bad way—not at all—but in a good way. You're more relaxed, more well-balanced, less inclined to work yourself into the ground. But there's been a change in the…" He hesitated, as if looking for the right word. "A change in the dynamic between you two, and that is something I can't make up my mind about. It would be a good thing if it heralds maturity in both of you, but I can't be sure."

She forced a little laugh.

"We were in our thirties when we met, Dad. I'm a pretty well-respected doctor, and you heard what Kenzie has been through in her life. I don't think a lack of maturity is one of our problems."

He grimaced, leaving her to wonder if it was because of what she'd said or the taste of the coffee.

"You were sheltered, and somewhere along the line, you lost confidence in yourself as a person outside of your profession." He shrugged, and suddenly it was like looking into a mirror and seeing herself but in masculine form. "When you first introduced us to McKenzie, told us you were married, both your mother and I were understandably worried. You were obviously in love, and she was in love with you, but what the songwriters and poets don't tell you is that it's never enough. There has to be substance, understanding, the willingness to sacrifice and learn who the other person is, to back up the emotion.

"What we didn't see, back then, was a coming together— a meshing of lives, which always involves honesty and compromise. You were still working flat-out, as though nothing in your life had changed—"

"I was building my practice, Dad. Do you think I should have neglected it?"

"Neglected it? No. But there was no need to throw yourself into it so completely it was to the detriment of everything else in your life, including your marriage. Especially when you married a woman who must have needed your help to fit into a very different life than she was used to. She looked so uncomfortable all the time, Saana, and you didn't even seem to notice. When you told us she was going back to Texas to look after her aunt, I wondered if, in reality, she was running not so much away but back to a place that made sense to her."

Having lost her appetite, Saana pushed her plate away.

"You might be right, Dad, but things have changed. We have the babies now…"

Just saying it brought a rush of mingled love and fear and sorrow. She couldn't force anymore words past the burning lump in her throat.

"What's really going on?" Dad's voice had lost its softness and taken on a steel-sharp edge.

"I can't tell you." Now it was her time to don the cool, remote mask she used to shut out intrusion. "To do so would be to betray a trust and put us all—you included—in a bad spot. Don't ask me again, Dad."

For a long moment, their gazes clashed, battled, and then her father dipped his chin, apparently acknowledging her right to her secrets.

"All right, Saana. I won't push, but I will give you one piece of advice: decide what it is you want out of this relationship and then fight for it." Glancing at his watch, he tipped the last of his coffee into his mouth, then stood up. "We better get back up there before your mother can't help herself and starts petting those babies. I haven't seen her this excited since I don't know when. McKenzie's going to have to take a hard line with her, or she'll be moving in with you!"

From somewhere, Saana dredged up a smile and followed him back to the elevator, his words ringing in her head.

CHAPTER SEVENTEEN

HOME.

When on earth had she started thinking of the monstrous mansion in Indialantic that way, Kenzie wondered as the SUV drove through the gates, and she found herself sighing with relief.

Sore, still apprehensive about her new responsibilities, frankly overwhelmed, the last thing she expected was to view the house as a sanctuary, but that was exactly how she felt.

After driving around to the side of the house, Saana opened the garage door and drove inside.

"Just stay there a minute," she said as she turned off the engine. "And I'll come around to help you out before we liberate the babies."

Kenzie couldn't help chuckling at her turn of phrase.

"You make it sound like they're in jail rather than in their car seats."

Saana paused halfway out of the vehicle and said, "With what it took to get them into those seats, I think they are rather like prisons."

And Kenzie felt her heart lighten a little more.

Saana carried both the babies, still strapped into the detached seats, into the house, while Kenzie shuffled slowly along after her, feeling as if a truck had driven through her belly. By the time she got into the house, Saana had the elevator waiting so that Kenzie could step right into it.

"The first time I saw this thing, I thought it was ridiculous," she admitted. "Who on earth actually has an elevator in their house when there are only two floors? Now I've never been more grateful to the guy who put it in."

Saana snorted. "I have to agree with you. I don't think I've used it more than three or four times since I moved in, although when I was a child and visited my grandparents, Grandad used to lock it to stop me riding up and down in it all day."

She could almost picture it, and the mental image made Kenzie smile.

Everything seemed perfect at the moment. The babies being born healthy. Saana being attentive and helpful, far beyond what Kenzie would have expected. Not because she wasn't generous—nobody knew Saana's generous and giving nature better than she did—but she'd had the feeling during her pregnancy that Saana was keeping a mental distance. It was even in the way she'd always referred to them as "your babies," or "your children." Now, watching as she unstrapped and lifted Leanna out and placed the sleeping baby in the bassinet, there was no mistaking the tenderness in her every touch.

"Lie down," she said, nodding toward the bed. "Take a nap while these little ones sleep. You need your rest."

There it was again—that wonderful sense of being taken care of and treasured. A sensation she wasn't sure was real but was too incredibly tired to figure out.

And as the next few weeks passed, Kenzie found herself increasingly reluctant to do anything about either the Beauchamps or the situation between her and Saana. Instead, she took care of her children and basked in her in-laws' and, especially, Saana's gentle care. For the first time in her life, she felt part of a family complete rather than a lone wolf, circling the outskirts, hoping for scraps of connection.

Then she felt guilty for feeling that way. Hadn't Aunt Lena done the very best she could for her? Even when she had her own problems and issues and little time to cosset Kenzie in any way, she'd at least always been there.

She'd taken Saana's advice and hyphenated the surnames so the babies were registered as Bonham-Ameri, which actually sounded pretty good. If she and Saana were a real couple instead of in the midst of a crazy farce, Kenzie thought she'd change hers to that too.

But that wasn't in the cards. Not even to give her children a sense of belonging, knowing their mother shared the same name as them.

When Saana had brought it up again before the babies' names were registered, Kenzie had hesitated.

"What happens when we're no longer together? How do I explain it to them when they get older?"

That had gained her a shrug and a laconic reply.

"Kenzie, anything we do legally can be undone." After getting up, she'd walked across to look out the window and continued. "When the time comes, we can change the names back, if you want. Remember, right now we need to make it clear we're family."

It was then that the pleasant bubble of domesticity started to thin.

The lawyer had advised that rather than wait to be compelled to produce the birth certificates, they be proactive and send copies to the Beauchamps' attorney, which they did. Kenzie knew things would soon be coming to a head but refused to think about it too much. Enjoying this time with Saana, Leanna and Darren seemed far more important.

Saana was the one who consistently followed up with the

lawyer, asking why they hadn't heard anything from their opponents.

"I thought we would have heard from them by now," she said. She had the lawyer on speaker, and was joggling Leanna on her shoulder while talking. "Either through their lawyer, or the courts. Do you have any idea what they might be doing?"

"None," the lawyer admitted. There was a bit of a hesitation, and then she added, "Perhaps they're trying to gather more information before they move."

Both Saana and Kenzie froze, exchanging a worried glance.

"Information? Like what?" Kenzie asked.

"I don't know for sure, but I don't think hiring a private investigator would be out of the question."

After that, Kenzie found herself scrutinizing every vehicle or person she noticed near the house.

"Do you think they might try to kidnap the children?" Saana asked Kenzie after they'd hung up, in that clear, cold way she had of speaking when she was really angry.

"I…I don't think so."

But her heart was pounding just from hearing the words.

"Don't worry," Saana said, putting her arm around Kenzie's shoulders and pulling her in for a hug. "This is a secure neighborhood and house. Don't let it stress you out."

But after Saana went back to work, it was hard not to dwell on it, although Delores was there during the day to keep her company in between her chores.

"These babies are the sweetest," the housekeeper said almost daily, even though they were beginning to realize Miss Leanna already had a temper, which she wasn't afraid to unleash. If she was hungry or needed a diaper change, she didn't leave them in any doubt.

Darren was quieter, more easygoing.

"Takes after you," Saana said one night while they were

lying on the bed together, both babies between them. "A laid-back guy who doesn't want to cause any trouble."

Kenzie shook her head.

"You might want to rethink that statement," she said, only half joking. "You have to admit I've caused you—and keep on causing you—all kinds of trouble."

Saana only smiled, her brown eyes soft with an emotion Kenzie didn't know how to interpret. "Right now, lying here like this, I can honestly say I really don't mind."

Making Kenzie remember exactly why she'd fallen so hard for Saana and how much it was going to hurt to give her up again.

Impatient didn't begin to describe the way Saana felt as she hung up the phone after talking with the lawyer yet again.

She'd set herself a weekly reminder to call the woman in San Antonio, and never failed to make contact for a status update.

No doubt the recipient of her Friday-morning calls was probably getting fed up, but if they didn't get the question of Leanna and Darren's custody settled soon, she thought she might lose it.

There'd been time during her leave to think long and hard about what her father had said the night the babies were born. To look back at those early days and—with the new insight she'd gained into Kenzie's character and her own—figure out some of where things went wrong.

He'd been right to say she hadn't done much to help Kenzie assimilate into her new life. If she were honest, with uncon-cern and arrogance, it hadn't even occurred to her that either her wealth or her ambition would be a problem. While she'd been ecstatic to realize Kenzie had no interest in her money, deep inside, there'd been part of her that secretly thought her wife was actually happy to have married into wealth.

After all, wasn't that pretty much standard? And every-one knew having too much money was far better than hav-ing too little.

But that wasn't Kenzie. What Saana had put down as an almost ridiculous level of independence was actually a self-defense mechanism. One that had allowed her to somehow survive and thrive in a situation that would break most other children.

Kenzie may have loved and been grateful to her aunt, but in Saana's book, the older woman had done the minimum while expecting the maximum in return. Not that she'd ever say that to Kenzie. No. Now that Lena was gone, it was best to let it all lie.

Instead, it was time to look to the future. And that wouldn't be possible the way Saana wanted until the custody battle was over. To her way of thinking, that needed to be settled before she could ask Kenzie to stay and keep this beautiful family they'd somehow ended up creating intact.

In the meantime, she was doing her best to show Kenzie how much she cared about her and their children. Because she really did think of them as hers as well as Kenzie's. Every day, each time she looked at them, cuddled or played with them, she fell in love a little more. When she looked back at the night they were born, when she arrogantly assumed her feelings for them were already at their peak, she had to laugh at herself.

She honestly couldn't imagine her life without them. With-out Kenzie. She'd do any and everything in her power to pro-tect them all.

Why, why, why hadn't the Beauchamps already made their move?

Until they did, they were all stuck in limbo instead of being able to move forward.

Even though she was back at work, she'd rearranged her schedule to avoid the twelve-hour days she'd been working and found, to her relief and chagrin, that both clinics continued to function perfectly well.

Apparently, she wasn't as completely irreplaceable as she'd so conceitedly thought. Tonight she was working at the Eau Galle clinic, and one of her patients was Miriam Durham, who'd been Kenzie's first patient at the clinic. They'd been able to diagnose her with hypothyroidism and had put her on a course of treatment that seemed to be working well.

By now, not only did everyone working at the clinic know Kenzie was Saana's wife but somehow, through the grapevine, many of the patients did too. Including Miriam.

So it was no surprise when the first thing she asked when Saana entered the examination room was, "How's your wife? Got any pictures?"

Laughing, Saana pulled out her phone, asking, "Do seagulls steal your lunch? Here're the latest. I took them last night."

And Miriam *ooh*ed and *ahh*ed over them until Saana insisted they talk about her disease and treatment schedule rather than the babies.

"I got your latest blood-test results back, and I think the dosage of the medicine is working well," she said after she'd taken a look at her vitals. "Are you seeing any improvement in the joint pain and fatigue?"

"Oh, yes." Miriam beamed. "I feel so much better already. Hard to recognize myself after only two months on the meds. I'm even able to work a full shift and then go to the park or visit with friends. Before, all I could do was go home and collapse on the couch."

Saana took another look at Kenzie's notes from the first visit Miriam had made to the clinic, seeing *Depression over alienation from son/grandchildren.*

"And how're things with your son? Are you seeing him and his children more often?"

Miriam's smile wavered slightly, but Saana, although watching carefully, didn't see any signs of sadness.

"Still on and off, but things are gettin' a bit better, I think. It's hard on us all because it would be easier on Marlon and his wife if I could take care of the kids regularly, but I can't just yet. I told him about what you said and how much I've improved so far, and I think he'll talk to his wife about me seein' my babies when I'm not working."

Talking to Miriam once more brought home to Saana just what the Beauchamps must be feeling, but she had to put that aside so as not to get distracted.

"I hope it works out for you and your grandbabies," she said, gaining herself another broad smile.

The clinic ran late, so it was almost ten o'clock before Saana headed home. She yawned, glad she wasn't working the next day. She'd made the decision to keep the weekends free as much as possible, although loosening the reins of her businesses had created some anxiety. However, she told herself hopefully, it was just as well she start doing that now so that when the kids got older and had weekend activities, she could be involved.

She was almost home when her phone rang, and her heart leapt when she saw her father's number. Pressing the button on the steering wheel to answer, she slowed down, pulling close to the curb.

"Dad? Is everything okay? Is Mom okay?"

"We're both fine," he said, but there was more than a hint of steel in his voice. "But I need to speak to you—and Mc-Kenzie."

"Now? I'm pretty sure Kenzie is sleeping already. Leanna and Darren wake up at all hours, so she'd taken to turning in early."

She was babbling, worried by that tone in his voice and the fact he wanted to speak to them both rather than just her.

"It can wait until tomorrow morning, but I wanted to make sure you'll be at home when I get there. It's important."

"Why not just tell me what it's about instead of all this cloak-and-dagger business?"

He was silent for a long minute, and then Saana thought she heard him exhale.

"I just got off the phone with a man named Andrew Beauchamp. He told me a story about his son and McKenzie, and seems completely convinced that your marriage is a sham."

Saana stopped the car, too intent on the conversation to pay attention to where she was going.

"Really." Her brain was whirling, and cold rage made her fingers tighten in a vise grip on the steering wheel. "Did he say where he got that erroneous information?"

"He didn't say, and I didn't press him. That part of it seemed irrelevant to me."

"So what did he say he wanted?"

"He asked me to help him get custody of his grandchildren. I refused, of course, but what I need to know is why the *hell* you didn't tell me what was going on from before?"

CHAPTER EIGHTEEN

KENZIE WOKE UP at the first mewling coming from the bassinet and rubbed her eyes before sitting up. The room was still dark, with just a hint of dawn at the edge of the curtain and the glow of the nightlight.

"I'm coming, Mr. D.," she whispered, glad to be woken up by his soft sounds rather than her daughter's lusty howls.

Glancing over, she realized Saana's side of the bed was empty and wondered where she was. Usually, on the mornings she didn't have to work, she would lie in bed with them while Kenzie nursed the babies, either singly or in tandem.

Because Darren woke up first and wasn't fussy, Kenzie was able to change his diaper before his sister set to howling. After a quick diaper change for Leanna, too, Kenzie made herself comfortable and fed them both.

There was still no sign of Saana, so when the babies fell back to sleep, Kenzie put on a robe and went downstairs to look for her.

She eventually looked out toward the river and saw her sitting on one of the benches, bent forward with her elbows on her knees. Something about her posture made Kenzie's stomach drop, and for a moment, she considered going back upstairs.

Pretending she hadn't noticed her out there.

Then, telling herself she was being silly, she let herself out of the house and walked down the path, her flip-flops almost silent on the gravel.

It felt like a full-circle moment but in reverse. Rather than her sitting on the bench, wondering what to do next, it was Saana.

But there wasn't anything for Saana to decide, was there?

As she got closer, her wife straightened and glanced back for an instant.

"Hey. You're up early."

"Yes. I couldn't sleep and didn't want to disturb you, so I went downstairs." Ordinary words, but her tone was off. Cool, but in a newer, icier form. Kenzie shivered. "The babies woke you up?"

"Yes." Strangely weak-kneed, she sat on the other bench. "I fed them, and they've gone back to sleep. What's wrong?"

Saana rubbed her knuckles under her nose, a gesture so unlike her usual poise that fingers of cold ran down Kenzie's spine.

"I've finally found out what the Beauchamps' next move will be. Actually, *has* been."

Kenzie's mouth went dry, and she felt light-headed but forced herself to inhale deeply—once, twice, three times. When she knew she wouldn't pass out, she licked her lips and asked, "What happened?"

"Mr. Beauchamp called Dad last night. Told him that our marriage wasn't real and asked for his help 'convincing' you to give up the babies."

Maybe she should be panicking, she wasn't sure. But instead, a deep, numbing calm came over her.

"Oh."

Saana looked over at her, and when their gazes clashed, Kenzie couldn't read her wife's expression. It reminded her of the night of the gala, when Saana had listened to the story of Kenzie's young life and said nothing, hiding her reaction.

"Dad wants to talk to us, so he's coming over this morning." Her lips tightened, and her nostrils flared on a breath. "What do you want to tell him? We need to get our stories straight."

This was it, then. The moment she'd known instinctively would one day come, no matter how she'd dreamed it wouldn't or pretended to herself that it would never come about.

"We tell him the truth. Your father—your parents—deserve that."

No matter how much they might hate her for it.

Saana nodded, turning to look back over the water again, as yet untouched by the weak dawn light, so dark and gloomy looking, fitting the mood of their conversation perfectly.

She wanted to ask if she should pack and leave; if Saana would expect that of her, but the words stuck in her throat. Funny how initially she'd been completely prepared to raise the babies by herself, but now the prospect filled her with pain.

No one needed to tell her how much Saana loved Leanna and Darren. It was obvious in every interaction, in the gentleness that went beyond just an adult being careful with a child. The tender way she looked at them, spoke to them, held them.

Losing them would devastate her, but what was the alternative? Because they were a package deal—the babies and her—and Saana couldn't have one without the other.

No matter how much she loved her wife, Kenzie wasn't willing to give her children up to her just to make her happy, and Saana had given no indication she wanted Kenzie to stay. Not to stay for the sake of the babies, but because Saana wanted her for herself.

A while ago, she'd suggested Kenzie consider staying in Florida, letting the Ameris stay in contact and continue to act as grandparents. But that seemed even less viable than it had in the past.

Back then, they'd viewed Kenzie as their daughter-in-law.

A part of the family. Now that they knew it had all been a lie, why would they want anything to do with her or her kids?

Suddenly, Kenzie realized she was shivering, almost hard enough to make her teeth chatter, and she got up, pulling the neck of her robe closer to her throat.

"I'm goin' inside. What time is your father comin' over?"

Saana shrugged. "He didn't say, but I suspect it'll be quite early. I know he wants to sort this out ASAP."

"Okay."

That was the best she could manage. The adult part of her was saying she should stay. That they needed to talk this out. But the little girl wanted to run and hide, the way she had in the past when things got too hard to handle.

She needed time to think, is what she told herself. But even as she walked back to the house, she knew the truth.

This was nothing more or less than the ultimate coward's escape.

Saana couldn't remember a time when she'd been quite so angry. Enraged, really.

It wasn't just a matter of her and Kenzie having their hand forced, but even more so the violation implicit in Mr. Beauchamp's actions. He'd clearly had them watched. Investigated. How else would he have known to contact her parents?

Was that even legal, since both sides had lawyers involved? Even if it was, it was underhanded in the extreme. The type of maneuver men of wealth and power probably wouldn't hesitate to use when up against women, in the hopes of intimidating them into compliance.

But while Saana's brain was going too fast just then for the kind of cool planning needed, there was one thing she knew for sure.

The Beauchamps had bitten off more than they could chew.

Where previously she'd had some sympathy for them, now she was ready to plot their downfall.

Family was everything, and by messing with hers—spying, and scaring, and overstepping the bounds of decency—they'd set themselves up for a bitter disappointment.

Family.

In the past, that had been her parents, grandparents and brother. Now... Now her whole heart and soul was up there in the house, and she wasn't going to give any of it up without a fight.

She loved Kenzie. Always had. But now she had a deeper understanding of what made her tick, what her fears might be, what they needed to make a go of their life together. It meant not only stepping outside of her sexual inhibitions, the way Kenzie had taught her, but also outside of her emotional ones too.

Opening up, expressing her feelings, no matter how raw or ugly, wasn't something Saana was good at. She'd rather hide behind cool logic, even when she was a screaming mass of emotion inside.

But she couldn't help remembering what her father had said the night the babies were born. The things he said every relationship needed to survive and thrive.

Honesty.

Communication.

Compromise.

Willingness to sacrifice.

He'd intimated that for all she'd achieved, she'd never fully grown up. But now she knew that if there was ever a time to do so, with her marriage and her family—her children—on the line, this was it.

And she'd have to start with Kenzie.

Enigmatic Kenzie, who also had the uncanny knack of keeping her own council, leaving Saana guessing as to how she really felt when things got serious. How arrogant Saana had been when she so blithely assumed that Kenzie's easygoing ways made her simple to read. She was anything but simple or easy. In fact, she was one of the most complex women Saana had ever met.

Sitting up suddenly, she wondered what that complicated mind was thinking and planning right now. Was Kenzie's mind spinning the way Saana's was, trying to come up with an answer to the problems they'd created?

Did that answer include keeping their family together or tearing it apart?

That thought had her on her feet in an instant and almost running toward the house.

She took the stairs two at a time, tearing into the bedroom, coming to a halt when she found it empty except for the babies, still asleep in their cots. And checking the walkin closet proved unfruitful, so she went across to open the door to the nursery.

Kenzie was standing just inside the room, her arms crossed tightly over her waist, looking at the mural Mom had commissioned. It depicted a southwestern landscape, made dreamy by the light colors used, with a variety of animals scattered throughout. While it certainly wasn't a traditional baby's room look because of the palette and subject matter, it really worked.

"I love it," Kenzie said, and Saana couldn't miss the sadness in her voice. "Your mom really outdid herself, didn't she?"

"Yes." Saana edged closer until she was directly behind Kenzie. "I'm glad you love it. And it'll be good for word illustration too. Leanna and Darren's first words will probably be *horse* instead of *mama*."

The shuddering breath Kenzie took was audible. "I'm not leaving them here with you. I'll keep fighting for them, and when I go, they'll be coming with me."

Shocked, Saana said, "What are you talking about?"

Kenzie spun around to face her, and the sorrow on her face was unmistakable.

"I know you love the babies, and your parents do too. And I also know y'all probably despise me for all the chaos I've caused and want me to leave. I'll go, Saana, but I can't leave my babies behind, even though I know you can give them a far better life than I could."

Shaking her head, Saana said, "Nobody is going to tell you to give up your babies, Kenzie, me least of all. I'm ready to fight with everything I have to make sure Leanna and Darren grow up with their mama—with you."

Kenzie's lips parted, but before she could speak, Saana put a finger against her lips, halting the words.

"I need to tell you something else. I love you. I've always loved you. And I know I haven't always been what you've needed, but if you love me and decide to stay with me, I'll do whatever I can to make it up to you. You don't have to say anything now, just bear all that in mind when you're deciding what you want to do."

Kenzie shook her head, not saying anything, just as the doorbell rang.

"That must be Dad. I'll go let him in. Will you come down?"

Kenzie's chin lifted even though her eyes were damp, and her voice was shaky when she replied, "Of course. I just need to change. But, Saana…"

Her voice faded, and Saana held up her hand as she went through the door, saying, "Later. We'll talk later."

There was no way she'd be able to hold it together if Kenzie rejected her right now, and she wanted to present a strong front for her father.

To her surprise, when she got downstairs, she found both her parents on the doorstep. Dad looked furious, while Mom looked like she'd been crying.

"Come in," she said, and then, when they were both inside, she kissed them each on the cheek. "Let's go into the kitchen. Kenzie's just changing, and the babies are sleeping. Do you want some coffee?" she asked as they walked down the hallway.

With habitual politeness, both her parents refused, and Mom started a rambling dialogue of small talk as they each took a seat around the kitchen table.

Surreal, to be acting as if there was nothing wrong, when nothing felt right and wouldn't feel right until she knew what Kenzie wanted to do.

They'd just sat down, Mom still rambling on, when Kenzie came down the back staircase, pausing just at the bottom for an instant. Mom spluttered to silence as Kenzie walked over to sit.

Holding up her hand, she said, "I have somethin' I want to say, before we get into the nitty-gritty of this crazy situation." Suddenly, Saana found herself the focus of her wife's gaze, and her heart began to race. "I love you, Saana. I loved you from the first moment I looked up and saw you standin' in front of me on the bus to Hoover Dam, and I'm pretty damn sure I'll love you forever.

"I didn't realize it, when I lit out from Texas, comin' back here to you, but I was runnin' towards the one person who made me feel safe. The one person I knew I could trust and depend on. I didn't know whether you'd want me back or not, but I knew you'd help me if you could."

Suddenly, Saana didn't even care that her parents were sitting there, watching. She needed to kiss her wife, so buoyed by relief she felt her happiness would cause her to float off into heaven.

When she leaned forward, Kenzie met her halfway, and they exchanged a long kiss, redolent of love, spiced with their passion and sweetened by newly renewed commitment.

As their lips parted, Dad cleared his throat and said, "Well, I'm glad that's all dealt with. Now, what are we going to do about the Beauchamps?"

CHAPTER NINETEEN

KENZIE KNEW MR. AMERI was a businessman, but it had never really sunk in just how serious he could be. Each time they'd met before, he'd been in gracious host or laidback-father mode. Now, suddenly, with what he seemed to perceive as a threat to his family, his nice-guy persona fell away to be replaced by a pit bull.

She couldn't believe she'd ever hear herself defend the Beauchamps in any way, but when Mr. Ameri started talking about suing them for slander, she felt she had to intervene.

"It's not that I don't understand how they feel," she explained. "Darryl was their only son, and I know losing him was a horrible blow, but they just assumed I'd hand the babies over without any conversation. As if they were entitled to them."

"Bullies is what they are. I can't stand a bully. They should have given some thought to what they would do if someone started messing around and threatening *their* family before they decided to mess with ours. Don't worry, McKenzie, I'll take care of it."

Hearing him say it that way had made her quite emotional. The Ameri family was claiming her as one of their own, circling the wagons around her and the babies, and the feeling was wonderful.

"Don't worry," Saana murmured so her parents couldn't

hear. "Mom will be the voice of reason. Once Dad calms down, she'll work on him and make sure he doesn't go off the rails."

"Go off the rails?"

Saana chuckled. "When he fixates on something, especially if he believes he's righting a wrong, he sometimes doesn't know when to stop. Mom will redirect him to the appropriate solution."

Somehow, knowing the Ameris were behind her somewhat lessened the fear she'd harbored that the Beauchamps would find a way to take her children. It was becoming obvious neither Saana nor her father would ever allow that to happen, and so she felt she could consider a compromise.

"I don't mind letting them see the babies—have some kind of relationship—but the visits would have to be supervised when they're little."

"Definitely not." Mr. Ameri's voice was cool and controlled even though Kenzie knew he was anything but inside.

Now she knew where Saana got that particular characteristic.

Mrs. Ameri just shook her head and said nothing until Leanna let out a lusty yowl from upstairs, and she asked if she could go up with Kenzie.

"I was hoping they would wake up before we had to go," she said when Kenzie happily agreed. "I do love them so."

"I'm glad you do," Kenzie admitted. "Everyone needs family."

Mrs. Ameri picked Leanna up and checked her diaper.

"Oh, darling. You're absolutely soaked. Let's get you cleaned up. Is it feeding time yet?"

"I shouldn't think so," Kenzie replied, following Mrs. Ameri over to the changing table. "We'll know once she's dry. If she stops crying, then you know she isn't hungry."

Sure enough, once she was changed, she lay quietly in Grandma's arms, kicking her legs for a few minutes before nodding off. Mrs. Ameri settled in the upholstered chair and happily rocked the sleeping baby.

It felt like the right time to speak to her while they were alone, in case she wanted to say anything she didn't wish Saana to hear.

"Mrs. Ameri, I want to thank you for accepting me into the family the way you have. I know I'm not in the same league as Saana—"

The older lady clicked her tongue. "We love you, Kenzie, and think you're good for Saana. If you make her happy, that's all I'm interested in."

And one more small corner of her battered heart was healed.

Later that evening, after Saana's parents had gone home and the babies had been bathed and fed, they lay side by side on the bed, Kenzie holding Darren, and Saana, Leanna. The atmosphere in the room radiated peace, and the love both of them had tried to deny and now finally acknowledged and reveled in.

"What a day," she said. "Stressful and amazing, all at the same time."

Saana gave her a long look.

"I want to say something, and I want you to believe me."

Kenzie's heart did a little flip, but she held Saana's gaze as she nodded.

"Mom had a word with me before she left, telling me that I'd obviously omitted to explain exactly how I feel about you, since you're still worried about what she delicately termed our 'difference in backgrounds.'"

"Oh, Lawdie. I love your mom, but I wish she hadn't said anything."

Saana shook her head, and she didn't smile. Instead, her gaze was intense and serious.

"I've never cared about where you came from, how you dress or any of that. The first time I saw you, all I noticed was how beautiful you were. When we started speaking, I felt I'd found something I hadn't even known I needed—a friend, love, a home for my soul. It never even occurred to me that our backgrounds would have any bearing at all on our relationship. If I had, I'd have told you about the money and all of it. But just like you never thought it was important to tell me about your parents and what you'd experienced as a child, I didn't think my wealth would make a difference."

Then she took a deep breath and straightened slightly before she continued.

"Actually, if I'm honest, I arrogantly thought if my wealth was going to make a difference, it would be in a good way rather than a bad. I apologize for that, and also for not giving you the attention and help you needed to actually settle in when you moved here."

Kenzie exhaled, her heart steadying from the rolling gallop it had taken up when Saana started to speak. It took a moment to work through all Saana had said and figure out what she, in turn, needed to say. All the time, Saana was watching her, and Kenzie felt her gaze like the warmth of the sun.

"I think, looking back, that it was a good thing you didn't tell me how rich you were when we met," she admitted. "If you had, I probably wouldn't have gotten involved with you. Everything about this house, the way you lived, made me feel small and worthless, but I know that was my lack of confidence rather than anything you did."

It was a hard thing to admit, but she felt strong enough—safe enough—to unburden all the emotions she'd been hiding.

"When I left to go take care of Aunt Lena, I really meant to come back. But when I got to Texas, I fell back into my old way of life, and the longer I stayed, the harder it became to imagine ever belongin' here. Every conversation with you felt like it was happening over a wider distance every time. Eventually, I just couldn't do it anymore. It just hurt too bad.

"I know I hurt you by staying away and not taking your calls or staying in contact, but I honestly believed you were better off without me."

"Oh, babe." The pain in Saana's voice was evident, and when she brushed the back of her hand across Kenzie's cheek, it felt like a benediction. "I'll do whatever it takes to make you comfortable. We can sell the house, if you want. Move into somewhere more to your taste."

Now, without a doubt, Kenzie knew Saana truly loved her if she was willing to give up her beloved family home. But it didn't seem important anymore.

"No." She gave her wife a soft smile, so filled with love her throat was tight. "I'm happy here, with you, now. And I know how much you love it."

Saana shook her head slowly, her lips twitching, as though she wasn't sure whether to laugh or do something else.

"You never did say whether you'd stay with me or not." Now the movement of her lips was clearly caused by suppressed laughter. "If you don't want to live with me, you could always move in with my parents. I think they love you more than me."

"Nah. Love 'em, but they don't make my heart pound or make me think naughty thoughts."

Saana laughed lightly then. "Glad to hear it. That's my job."

"I'm sorry, babe, but you're truly stuck with me." Leaning close, she gave Saana a lingering kiss, and when it ended, she whispered, "I'm here to stay."

EPILOGUE

KENZIE LOOKED AROUND the room, trying to find her boots.

"Don't tell me I left them at home," she muttered to herself as she rummaged through the cupboard where her clothes had been stowed. Then, with an exclamation of satisfaction, she found them. "Thank goodness!"

Outside the window, there was a steady stream of chatter from the Ameris' garden, and from down the hall came a sudden shriek she recognized as what they called *Leanna denied*. Quickly pulling on the white cowboy boots, she went out into the hall.

There, she saw Delores trying to wrangle a squirming Leanna, who was firmly embedded in the terrible twos. When combined with that temper she'd been exhibiting since birth, it had become a particularly trying time.

"Leanna Mariella," she called. "Please behave yourself."

"Mama!" Darren was the one who came running toward her, arms outstretched, to be picked up. "Ms. Delores said there was cake, but Lee-Lee and me haven't got any."

"Ahh." Now she understood the problem. "Nobody's had cake yet, and nobody will until after dinner."

Coming toward her, Leanna in tow, Delores gave Kenzie a grin.

"I shouldn't have mentioned it, but it seemed like a good idea at the time."

Kenzie shook her head, returning the older woman's smile as she placed Darren back onto his feet. "You shoulda known better."

"I should," came the reply as Delores took Darren's hand. "Come on, let's go downstairs you two. Your moms will be coming down soon." She raised an eyebrow in Kenzie's direction. "Right?"

Kenzie chuckled. "I'll go and hurry Saana along, or who knows how long the guests will have to wait."

True to form, when Kenzie entered Saana's room, it was to find her wife almost dressed but struggling with her zipper.

"Babe, everyone is waiting for us to come down. Why aren't you ready?"

"I'm almost ready," Saana said, smiling and looking totally unrepentant. "Oh, you look delicious."

Kenzie smoothed her hand down the silk of her cream jacket, enjoying the slip of the fabric against her palm. The lovely sensation reminded her of Saana's skin.

"You look real tasty yourself."

They'd decided to wear outfits made from the same cream fabric, but although Kenzie had opted for a pantsuit, Saana looked elegant in a sheath dress. Both were trimmed with a hint of gold thread, adding to the festive nature of the outfits.

Perfect for a blessing ceremony and renewal of their vows.

"Lift your arm, and let me zip you in," Kenzie said, stepping close to fit deed to words. "Did you remember your earrings?"

"Yes. I just have to find them."

As she hunted for them, Kenzie went to the window and looked out at where their guests were waiting.

Mrs. Ameri was shooing everyone toward the chairs, which were set out in a semicircular pattern. Even from this distance, Kenzie could pick out most of the people there. They'd opted for a small ceremony rather than a large bash. After all, this was their fifth anniversary, and neither of them wanted any-one there who wasn't terribly important to them personally.

"You better hurry. Your mom is getting everyone settled, and you know how punctual she is."

"Are the Beauchamps here?"

"Yeah. I see them down there."

It had taken some time, but they'd come to terms with the Beauchamps, and the older couple had agreed to come to Florida to see their grandchildren periodically. Maybe, when Leanna and Darren were older, they'd be allowed to go visit in Texas, but it wouldn't be for a while. While everything seemed on the up-and-up, both Kenzie and Saana had trust issues about them.

It was hard to forget what they'd been willing to do to take the children.

"Happy, love?"

Saana came up behind her, fitting her body against Kenzie's back, her arms around her waist.

"Ecstatic," Kenzie admitted, smiling with the realization it was true. "I'm about to marry the woman I love all over again. I can't think of anything better."

Saana's arms tightened fractionally.

"Neither can I. Shall we go?"

"Yes. Let's. I can't wait to kiss the bride."

She turned and faced Saana's sweet, seductive smile.

"You don't have to wait, you know."

And Saana had to reapply her lipstick before they could go down to join their family and friends and once more pledge their love to each other.

* * * * *

AN ENGLISH VET
IN PARIS

KATE HARDY

MILLS & BOON

For Gerard—
one day we will get to the top of the Eiffel Tower!

CHAPTER ONE

'ANT, I NEED your help.'

Why would the Zoo de Belvédère's head of human resources need his help? Antoine Bouvier was more used to one of the zookeepers coming in to ask him to check on an animal. Unless Marie was worrying about the health of one of her own pets, perhaps, and wanted his professional advice; but he couldn't remember her ever mentioning a cat, a dog or even a goldfish. 'What's wrong?' he asked, saving the file of the notes he was writing up.

'I brought you coffee just the way you like it.' She set the mug on his desk.

Uh-oh. This was phase one of Marie getting what she wanted: softening him up with a kindness. Ant had seen her do this with other people. Next, she'd use his name a lot: too much, in fact. Then she'd get to the subject of what she wanted and spin it to sound as if it was his idea. Finally, she'd close the deal before he could object, thank him, and swan off again before he had a chance to say a word. 'Thank you,' he said, polite yet wary. 'What did you want?'

'It's the English vet.'

The one who was starting on Monday for six months' job enrichment; their zoo in Paris was twinned with a zoo in Cambridge, and Geraldine Milligan, one of the junior vets from the English zoo, was joining his team. 'She's changed her mind and she's not coming?'

'No.' Marie looked awkward. 'The problem's with her accommodation, Ant. The windows in her apartment were meant to be replaced this week, but the builder found asbestos. The surveyor says it needs to be removed safely before anyone can live there. We're talking weeks. And finding her suitable accommodation at this late notice...' She shook her head and grimaced. 'I was wondering, Ant, could she possibly stay with you?'

'With *me*?' Ant stared at Marie, surprised.

'You have a spare room, Ant,' she pointed out.

In the townhouse in Montmartre that he'd inherited from his grandmother, two years ago; he'd been hugely grateful at the time, because it had cushioned him from some of the fallout from the wedding-that-didn't-happen. At least he'd had somewhere to go. Somewhere to lick his wounds. A space to call his own that didn't have any memories of Céline.

'And it would be a kind gesture, Ant, as well as helping the team to bond,' she added.

All of that was true but, apart from the annoying overuse of his name, Ant had a major reservation. 'Surely it'd be awkward for her to stay with a man she's never met or had any real contact with?' The zoo's veterinary director, whose job involved negotiation and admin rather than working with animals nowadays, had arranged the secondment; Ant was simply going along with it as part of his job.

'You're both professionals, Ant,' Marie said crisply. 'I can't see why it would be a problem for her to stay with a colleague.'

'Wouldn't it be better if she stayed with one of the

female members of staff?' He thought of their younger veterinary nurse. 'What about Valerie?'

Marie narrowed her eyes at him. 'Valerie lives with her parents. I can hardly impose on them, Ant.'

But she could impose on him?

As if she'd guessed what he was thinking, she said, 'It's only for a few weeks, Ant. I'm sure Dr Milligan won't be any trouble.'

Yeah, right. A woman he knew little about, other than that she was a qualified vet, had a Masters in Exotic Veterinary Medicine, and his counterpart in Cambridge was impressed enough with her skills to suggest to their director that she'd be a good addition to the team. Plus Ant had grown used to having his own space. Sharing with someone else would be strange.

'And, at this time of year, Ant, finding a hotel wouldn't be easy,' Marie continued.

Spring in Paris. The time the tourists loved most. She had a valid point.

'A few weeks,' he said. Which meant what exactly?

Before he could ask for clarification, Marie beamed at him. 'Excellent. I knew we could rely on you, Ant. Thank you very much.'

Wait, what? He hadn't agreed to anything—had he?

But he also knew that Marie was a bulldozer. It was great when you needed something done and she was working on your team; the flip side was that it was rather less great when you were on the receiving end of her pushiness.

'I wouldn't have asked you if I had another solution, Ant,' Marie said.

He didn't think that was strictly true, but he wasn't

going to waste time with an argument he knew he'd never win.

'Her train gets in to the Gare du Nord at three on Sunday afternoon.' Marie gave him the sweetest of smiles.

'I'll meet her at the station.' He didn't really have much choice. If Dr Milligan was staying with him, she'd need a key to his apartment. He could hardly tell her to wait on the doorstep or in a nearby café; besides, it wouldn't be fair to expect her to take the Métro across Paris and then find her way from the station at Montmartre to his place, particularly with a pile of luggage. 'Perhaps you could let her know the situation. And ask her for permission to give me her phone number so I can contact her to make arrangements. Give her my number, too, in case she needs to contact me about anything urgently.'

'Thank you, Ant. You're one of the good guys,' Marie said. She patted his shoulder and breezed—*hurricaned*, he thought ruefully—out of the office, her mission accomplished and leaving Ant's thoughts in complete disarray.

Sharing his space for a few weeks.

Even if Dr Geraldine Milligan turned out to be the easiest houseguest in the universe, it still meant a huge change to his life. Something that brought back memories. Something that filled him with trepidation.

The notes could wait a while. He needed to get his head round this. And the best way he knew of dealing with things that made him antsy was to go and see the tigers. Specifically Bianca, the white Bengal tiger who'd joined the Zoo de Belvédère on the same day that he had, eight years ago. As the zoo vet, Ant wasn't supposed to have favourites, but he loved the big cats, and he'd seen Bianca through three litters of cubs now; he'd been keeping a closer eye on her for the last few months, since she'd developed a liver condition. Maybe the walk over to the tigers' enclosure would help him clear his head enough to work out how he was going to deal with the situation.

The Betjeman statue at St Pancras Station was the perfect place to say goodbye to her family, Geri thought: public enough to stop her bawling her eyes out. And she really appreciated the fact that her parents and her little sister were here to wave her off.

'Geri, are you *sure* you're doing the right thing?' her father, Ben Milligan, asked. 'It's OK to change your mind if you need to. We can sort everything out.'

It reminded Geri of the speech her dad had made on her wedding day, about marrying Mark and she could change her mind. She'd said she was sure, back then. And here she was, five years later: divorced, and heartbroken…

She shook herself. Enough of the pity party. You couldn't change the past, but you could make the future better. And of course she'd made the right decision. She'd had a bit of a wobble on Friday, when the head of HR in the Zoo de Belvédère had called her to say that there was a problem with her flat and she'd be staying with Antoine Bouvier, the senior vet, instead; but then again maybe it would be good to stay in a family home rather than feeling completely alone and a bit homesick in a strange city.

Focus on the positive, she reminded herself. And the positives were always there. You only had to look for them.

'It's Paris in the spring, full of blossom and good coffee,' she said brightly. 'And it's only for six months, Dad. A secondment. A fresh start—' she forced her smile not to wobble '—and, hey, with any luck I'll be looking after a pregnant panda. Being a zoo vet doesn't get any better than knowing you're going to be one of the first to see a tiny panda cub.'

Alex, Geri's younger sister, raised her eyebrow. 'You're only taking one suitcase. Paris fashionistas will never let you get away with that.'

Geri laughed. 'I don't need to be a fashionista. Trust me, a sharp suit and Louboutins have no place when you're anaesthetising a tiger. Anyway, if I need something posh, I can always go shopping.'

Sally, Geri's mum, looked worried. 'I know we've been through this—but Paris feels so far away, love.'

'It's only a couple of hours on the train. Our girl will be fine,' Ben reassured her. He smiled at Geri. 'If you need us, just ring—any time, day or night. We'll be straight over.'

'I will,' Geri promised, mentally crossing her fingers because she knew she needed to stand on her own two feet again. Living with her parents last year while she'd done her Masters in Exotic Veterinary Medicine had meant that she'd relied way too much on them. Even this past year, after she'd moved to Cambridge, they'd fussed over her. 'Love you, Dad. Mum. Alex.' She hugged each of them in turn. 'Stop worrying. Dr Bouvier is meeting me at the station. It's all going to be fine.' Though she was aware that she was trying to convince herself as much as her family.

'Love you, Geri.' Sally held her tightly.

'Enjoy every second of Paris,' Alex said. 'Remember, your mission is to find the best crème brûlée in Paris, and then invite me over for lunch. In between the tigers, the pandas and the penguins, that is.'

'Got it.' Geri gave her parents and her sister a last hug. 'I need to go, or they'll close the gate. I'll let you know when I arrive in Paris.' Though she was pretty sure her mum would be frantically checking the location sharing app on her phone and would know the precise moment that Geri arrived at the Gare du Nord. She smiled, hoping it masked her apprehension. 'Speak to you soon.'

Had she made a huge mistake, agreeing to a six-month secondment at the zoo in Paris? Or was this the thing that would finally help her move on from the past? The way she saw it, if she was brave enough to live in a country where she hadn't spoken the language since her schooldays, then she could also be brave enough to be honest with her emotions. And that meant, the next time round, she'd pick someone who really did want the same things that she did. Someone who'd grow and change with her, rather than growing apart from her.

Besides, Paris in the spring would be beautiful. Plus Geri had been fascinated by giant black and white pandas since she was a tiny child, and now she had the chance to work with a panda in the zoo's breeding programme— that was definitely a dream come true. Putting herself back out there, looking for the good things in life, would be a Very Good Thing. This year, on the anniversary of the day her life had fallen apart, she'd be somewhere with no sad memories; and maybe this year she'd cope better and finally start to put it behind her.

She didn't look back at her family, knowing that it would test her resolve a little too much; she scanned her ticket and her passport at the barrier, then headed for the departure lounge.

Once she was settled in her seat and the train had departed, she texted Antoine Bouvier to let him know her estimated arrival time at the Gare du Nord. Then she opened the historical thriller she'd bought for the journey, but she couldn't concentrate. Had she brought the right kind of gifts to thank her hosts? She hadn't bought flowers, not wanting them to wilt on the journey; and bringing wine to a French family would be woefully easy to get wrong. In the end, she'd settled for some really good chocolates and a tin of biscuits from Fortnum & Mason, and maybe she could take them all out for dinner one night this week.

She silently practised the phrases she'd learned that week while brushing up her language skills: *Bonjour, monsieur et madame. Merci beaucoup pour me recevoir chez vous.*

Oh, for pity's sake. She needed to ignore the apprehension causing a mass butterfly stampede in her stomach and enjoy the anticipation. This was a chance to do something she'd wanted to do for years. She was perfectly capable of negotiating life in a new city, even if her language skills were a bit rusty since her schooldays, and she'd got on well with her colleagues in Cambridge. Why would it be any different in Paris?

Stop whining and think of the positive stuff, she told herself sternly. *You're perfectly capable of doing this.*

The train journey passed swiftly, and when they came out of the other side of the Channel Tunnel there was a message on her phone from Antoine Bouvier.

Turn right when you get off the train. I'll wait for you on the west side of the station concourse.

He'd been thoughtful enough to send her a photograph of himself on Friday to help her recognise him at the station, along with a message.

Looking out for me might be a little easier than looking out for a placard with your name on it.

Geri had been surprised to see how young Dr Bouvier was. He was good-looking, in a brooding way; his dark hair had a sprinkling of grey and was cut short, his eyes were dark, and his olive skin was shadowed by a faint stubble. With a mouth that beautiful, he could've been a model for a perfume ad.

Not that she should be thinking of him in those terms. He was her new colleague—senior enough to be her boss, really—and he'd been kind enough to offer her a place to stay with his family.

She'd shaken off the stirrings of attraction and sent him a photograph in return, so he could look out for her on Sunday, too; and that had been the limit of their conversation until today.

At last, the train pulled into the Gare du Nord.

This was it.

Paris.

Her new start.

Adrenalin made her fingers tingle and she nearly dropped her suitcase. Cross with herself for the wobble— she wasn't going to let the past get in the way of her new adventure in Paris—she hauled her case off the train and turned right, scanning the crowd for a glimpse of her new colleague.

Ant surveyed the people coming from the train. He recognised Geraldine Milligan from her photograph straight away, though she was a little taller and slighter than he'd expected. Her fair hair was pulled back from her face in a scrunchie; her eyes were wide and almost navy-blue, and her mouth was a perfect Cupid's bow. She was dressed casually, in jeans, a long-sleeved T-shirt, canvas shoes and a light fleece jacket, and she looked very English.

The fact that she only had one suitcase with her surprised him. It wasn't much for a six-month stay. Or maybe she was hedging her bets and seeing how the first few weeks went; moving to another country for six months was quite a life change.

He took a deep breath and walked towards her, holding up a hand in greeting.

She smiled when she saw him. *'Bonjour, monsieur et...'* She tailed off, before rallying with, *'Merci beaucoup pour me recevoir chez vous.'*

He hadn't expected Dr Milligan to speak in French, and he appreciated that she'd made the effort. *'De rien—'* And then he had to stop. Was she *mademoiselle* or *madame*? A quick glance told him she wasn't wearing a ring, but that didn't necessarily mean she was single. Not wanting to get it wrong, he switched to English. 'You're very welcome, Dr Milligan.'

'Call me Geri, please.' She held out her hand.

'Antoine.' He took her hand to shake it, and it felt as if he'd been galvanised. He'd never reacted to anyone like that before, even Céline, and it threw him for a moment.

'I wasn't sure how much luggage you'd have,' he said, dropping her hand and hoping that she couldn't tell how much she'd momentarily flustered him. 'Parking isn't great around here; I thought it'd be easiest to get a taxi back to my apartment,' he added. 'The queue moves fairly quickly. Shall we?' He gestured towards the taxi rank, then went to pick up her suitcase.

'Thanks, but I can manage my case myself,' she said,

with the kind of smile that made it clear she wasn't being difficult.

Independent, rather, he decided. He liked that, as long as that independence was tempered with knowing to ask for help when you needed it. The welfare of the animals came before anything else, in his view. 'Of course,' he said.

In real life, Antoine Bouvier was even more attractive than his photograph, Geri thought. When he'd shaken her hand, it had sent a shiver of awareness down her spine, making her feel off balance; she really shouldn't react like that towards her new colleague, particularly if he was married. The unexpected whirl of her feelings had made her a little bit snippy about her suitcase, but hopefully he wouldn't hold the slight rudeness against her.

She followed him to the taxi rank; as he'd said, the queue moved fast, and soon he was opening the door for her to get in the back of the taxi while the driver put her case in the boot. He gave the address in rapid French, then sat next to her. Geri followed his example and looked out of the window, enjoying the views: the tall buildings with their shuttered windows and ironwork balconies, the wide cobbled streets, and the trees dappling the streets with shade. It was a far cry from the ancient narrow streets in Cambridge, dominated by the colleges and the ubiquitous cyclists.

The taxi pulled over to the kerb, and Antoine had dealt with the fare before Geri even had the chance to offer to pay. And then she was standing on the pavement, her suitcase beside her, looking up at the row of five-storey townhouses. They were built from pale stone, with wrought-iron balconies at the bottom of tall windows; there were trees along the cobbled street, and streetlights which looked like old-fashioned lanterns.

Before she could stop herself, she blurted out, 'What a beautiful building. It's so Parisian.'

Oh, way to go, Geri. How to make your new colleague think you're a babbling idiot.

'Thank you.' He shrugged. 'I guess it's easy to take it for granted. My apartment's on the top two floors. *Bienvenue à Montmartre.*'

'*Merci,*' she said with a smile.

He unlocked the door and led her through to the lobby. The lift was tiny, and the two of them only just managed to fit inside, together with her case. Geri was very, very aware of his closeness; and even more aware that the frisson down her spine was completely inappropriate. There was a huge difference between noticing the gorgeousness of a random stranger and being attracted to a new colleague who was being kind enough to let her stay with his family.

She made herself concentrate on the lift instead. It felt very French, with the glass doors looking through an ironwork grille as they rose very slowly towards the top of the building. The creaks and grinding noises sounded ominous to Geri; Antoine looked completely unbothered by them, so she decided to take her lead from him.

Not wanting to risk blurting out something inane again, she waited for him to start the conversation. Except he didn't. By the time the lift pinged to say they'd reached their floor, she was starting to feel really awkward. Maybe Antoine was the kind of dedicated vet who was brilliant with animals but not with people; hopefully his partner would put her more at ease.

He unlocked the front door, and she followed him into a hallway.

'We'll leave your case here while I give you the guided tour,' he said. 'I guess my apartment's a little upside down—the bedrooms, bathrooms and my study are on this floor, and the living quarters are on the floor above.' He gestured to the first door. 'That's my room, but feel free to choose whichever you like of the guest rooms.'

'Thank you,' she said.

'I'll show you upstairs first,' he said.

Wide stairs led up to the top floor. The walls were painted a pale biscuity colour, toning with the light wooden parquet flooring. All the ceilings had moulded cornices—the kind Geri associated with ancient European palaces—and old-fashioned wrought-iron and glass chandeliers; the tall windows meant that the rooms were full of light. The dining room was at the front of the apartment, overlooking the street, with a narrow wrought-iron balcony that ran the length of the building and held terracotta planters stuffed with red geraniums. There was a table and six chairs in the centre of the room, a traditional French sideboard that she guessed was antique and a grandfather clock that ticked loudly.

The dining room led into the living room, which was furnished with a couple of sofas, a thick Persian rug and an armoire; there were framed botanical prints on the walls, and an ornate mirror above the mantelpiece. Geri couldn't see any personal touches: no bookshelves, no photographs, or anything to suggest that this was a family home. This was strange. She was sure Marie had said Antoine Bouvier was married...or had she assumed it, because he was the senior vet at the zoo and her own boss in Cambridge was married with grown-up children?

'The fireplace is gorgeous,' she said. The old-fashioned black-leaded fireplace had a stone hearth with two wrought-iron sphinx firedogs flanking it. 'Do you have an open fire in winter?'

Antoine shook his head. 'My grandparents did, when I was small, but central heating's much less messy. Though I couldn't quite part with the fireplace during the renovations. Come and see the terrace.' He led her through to an enormous kitchen with a red-tiled floor, old-fashioned shelving and cupboards and a butler's sink but what looked like very high-tech white goods. He unlocked the back door, and she was thrilled to see a comfortable roof garden shaded with huge plants in equally huge pots, and a wrought-iron bistro table and a couple of chairs.

'It looks like the perfect place to sit and read on a summer evening.'

'With a glass of wine,' he agreed. 'Yes, it's pretty much perfect.'

'I'm really grateful to you and your partner for letting me stay,' she said. 'Finding another flat at such short notice would've been a bit daunting.'

'Yes,' he said. 'Though I should perhaps advise you now that I don't have a partner.'

She winced. 'I apologise. I thought...' Wrongly. Hideous embarrassment at her gaffe flooded through her, and she could feel the colour bursting into her cheeks. 'I'm terribly sorry.'

'Not a problem,' Ant said. 'I should've mentioned it earlier.' Though, if his fiancée hadn't fallen in love with his brother, then he would still have had a partner. Maybe they would've had a baby, by now. A little girl who'd sit on his shoulders and beam in delight when he took her to see the tigers…

But things were as they were. And he needed to put his houseguest at her ease.

He took a deep breath. 'I did suggest to Marie that you might be more comfortable sharing with someone who wasn't a single male you'd never met before, but she seemed to think we could both be professional about the situation.'

'Of course,' Geri said swiftly.

'If you prefer, I can call in a favour and stay with friends until you've found somewhere.'

'No, no—it's fine.'

Though it clearly wasn't, because she looked flustered.

'You're perfectly safe with me,' he said, wanting to reassure her that he wasn't going to make unwanted advances.

A tide of deep red swept through her face for the third time since he'd met her. She definitely wasn't the type who could hide her feelings easily, then.

Unlike Céline, who'd hidden a huge, *huge* secret until their wedding day—and then it had all come out in the most hurtful way.

Not that he was going to think about his ex. Or his brother. It was over and finished with.

'Of course I know I'm safe with you. I wouldn't have thought anything else,' Geri said. 'I'm very grateful that you're letting me stay here, even though it's all been last-minute and it must be putting you out. And it was really kind of you to meet me, though I still owe you for the taxi.'

'De rien,' he said, realising that he hadn't managed to stop her feeling awkward. His sister was right: he needed

to brush up his social skills. 'It's fine. Really. The taxi was the least I could do. May I offer you some coffee? Wine?'

'Coffee would be lovely,' she said, looking grateful.

'I'll make it while you choose your room,' he said. Hopefully that would give them both some breathing space.

She followed him into the kitchen, where he took beans from the fridge.

'You don't need to go to that much trouble for me,' she said. 'Instant coffee's fine.'

'Instant?' He rolled his eyes. 'This is Paris.'

'There's nothing wrong with instant coffee.'

Oh, but there was. He had experience of English instant coffee, and it wasn't something he wanted to repeat. 'Let's agree to disagree,' he said. 'I'll make coffee. Go and have a look downstairs. Oh—and you need a key to the apartment.' He took the spare one from the kitchen drawer and handed it to her.

'Thank you,' she said.

He'd ground the beans and the coffee was brewed to perfection when she came back into the kitchen. 'I chose the smaller guest room,' she said. 'I hope that's all right.'

The room furthest from his. Which was a good thing—and a bad one, at the same time. He'd wanted her to choose the room because she liked it, not for any other reason. 'That's fine.'

'And I brought these from London as a small gesture of appreciation for having me.' She handed him a tin of biscuits and a box of chocolates; both bore the logo and signature colour of a very upmarket London department store. 'I thought I could take you out to dinner, to say thank you.'

'That's kind of you, but there was really no need to bring me anything. I'm sure you would've done the same for me if I'd come to Cambridge on secondment and stayed with you. Do you take milk, sugar?' He gestured to the coffee pot.

'Neither, thanks.' She accepted a cup of coffee and let him usher her onto the terrace.

'You have a beautiful apartment,' she said. 'I love the mix of ancient and modern. You said you renovated it?'

'Not all with my own hands. I hired builders to do the structural stuff,' he said.

'They did a good job. It's beautifully decorated—I loved those voile drapes at the window in my room. And the bathroom—the shape of the tiles on the floor reminds me of a honeycomb.'

'I was very nearly forced to include tiles with bees.' He rolled his eyes. 'They were my sister Amélie's choice. It's her room.'

Geri's eyes widened with obvious anxiety. 'Oh! Sorry. If you need me to move into a different room…'

'Not at all,' he said. 'She doesn't come to Paris that often, and only at certain times of the year. Fortunately for me, most of the time she's too busy making wine to come here and boss me about.' Or nag him about the family rift. He was trying to put it behind him, but he still wasn't in a place where he could forgive.

His houseguest seemed to relax again. 'I can relate to that, though actually I'm the bossy sister.'

Ant couldn't imagine Geri Milligan being bossy. If anything, she'd seemed a little lost as she'd walked through the train station. Or maybe that was because she was making such a big life change, moving to a different country for six months. He wondered what had driven her to do that. What made her tick.

'What kind of wine does your sister make?' Geri asked.

'Sancerre.' He lifted a shoulder in a half-shrug. 'It's the family business. My grandparents were winemakers, and my dad took over when they retired. When we were small, Amélie was the one who was interested in the soil and the plants; and then, as a teen, in the way the chemistry of the wine changed. I was more interested in the vineyard's dogs and cats—and our neighbour's rescued Poitou donkey, Bertrand,' he added wryly.

'It sounds as if you were always going to be a vet.'

'Yes.' And, when he was younger, he'd thought about going into partnership with Jean-Luc: the Bouvier brothers, veterinary surgeons. Just as well he'd been drawn to zoo medicine as a student, or his career would've gone the same way as his personal life.

'I used to bandage our poor Labrador on a regular basis when I was tiny,' Geri said, 'but he always put up with it because I'd give him a biscuit as "medicine".'

Ant could imagine that. And, for a moment, he could see a small child in his mind's eye, copying her father in being a vet and 'looking after' the family pets... Except he wouldn't be the child's father. He pushed the thought away. 'Are either of your parents vets?'

'No. Dad's an accountant, Mum works in admin, and my little sister's a fitness instructor.'

'And you're really the bossy one?' He still didn't quite believe her.

She laughed. 'Alex is bossy in her classes. I couldn't move, the day after I did one of her aerobics sessions.

But outside that she's a bit scatty.' She smiled. 'I'm under instructions, though, to find the best crème brûlée in Paris for when she comes to visit.' Her smile broadened. 'Which is going to be fun—both the search and her visit.'

Her laugh was lovely. Bright and sparkly. Geri was clearly close to her family, and telling him about them had taken away that lost look. Ant felt a flicker of something in his veins, something he couldn't quite pin down. A feeling so old and neglected that he barely recognised it.

He shook himself. They were talking about crème brûlée and her sister's visit—by which time Geri would be settled in her own apartment.

'Indeed.' He lifted his coffee cup in a toast. 'Welcome to Paris.'

'Thank you. I've been looking forward to this hugely.'

'It's a big change,' he said. 'What made you decide to come to Paris?'

Her face shuttered slightly. It was clearly something she wasn't comfortable talking about. He could appreciate that; he didn't like talking about bits of his life, either.

'I've always been fascinated by pandas,' she said. 'When I had the chance to work with the international breeding programme, I jumped at it.'

That was fair enough. He was thrilled to be part of it, too. And work was a safe subject. He could handle that. 'I'll introduce you to the pandas and their keeper tomorrow. I thought you could shadow me for the day, to get a feel for our routine and a chance to meet the rest of the team—and I include the keepers in our team, because they're the ones who notice when something isn't quite right with one of the animals and tell us, meaning we can treat a problem at the earliest stages.'

'That's how we work in Cambridge, too.' She looked pleased. 'I'm really glad of the chance to broaden my knowledge. And I hope I'm bringing experience with me that will be useful to others.'

'I'm sure you will,' he said. 'I'm cooking dinner for us tonight.'

'Thank you.' She paused. 'While I'm staying with you, perhaps we can take it in turns to cook—it'd be a bit of a waste of time and energy for us to cook separately, wouldn't it? And I'm very happy to do my share of the chores.'

'I have a cleaner,' Ant said. 'There's no need for a chore rota. But, yes, if you like, we can take turns in cooking.' She didn't need to know that he usually grabbed something from the staff canteen at lunchtime to eat at his desk and made himself a sandwich in the evening. His family had always been excellent hosts, and he intended to keep that tradition going. 'Are there any dietary requirements I need to know about?'

'No. I eat most things,' she said.

He suppressed the unexpected urge to tease her by suggesting frogs' legs. And that in itself was unsettling, because it was a long while since he'd been tempted to tease someone. 'I was thinking something simple. Chicken Provençal, followed by cheese and fruit?'

'That sounds lovely,' she said. 'Can I do anything to help?'

'No. Take your time to unpack and settle in,' he said. 'Dinner will be ready at seven. Would you prefer red, white or rosé wine?'

'I like all three. Whatever you feel goes best with dinner,' she said.

'*D'accord*. See you later.'

CHAPTER TWO

HER NEW COLLEAGUE was an enigma, Geri thought as she unpacked and put her things away. Antoine Bouvier had been perfectly polite to her, but she was aware that he was keeping his distance. Marie had intimated that he'd offered to let her stay with him, but his comment earlier about thinking she'd feel more comfortable staying with someone who wasn't a single male made Geri wonder whether it was more like he'd been pushed into making the offer.

She'd have to make the best of the situation. And there was a lot to be grateful for. The room was gorgeous, with voile curtains and teal drapes at the windows; the bed had a white-painted wooden frame and a duck-egg-blue patterned duvet cover. There was a white-painted wardrobe, dressing table and bedside cabinet, and a pretty blue rug was spread across the pale parquet flooring. Best of all, Geri could actually see a bit of the Sacré Coeur from the window.

Of all the places to stay in Paris, Montmartre must be one of the prettiest, she thought, and took a snap of the view to send to her family.

She glanced at her watch. There was still another hour before dinner. Antoine had made it very clear he didn't want any help in the kitchen, and she didn't want to make him feel as if he needed to entertain her. The last thing she wanted was to be an intrusive, demanding guest, even though right at that moment she felt lonely and a bit homesick and could really do with a hug. Instead, she sent cheerful messages to her family and friends along with a picture of her view, determined not to give in to the melancholy that threatened to drain her energy, then worked on her list of places she wanted to visit in Paris. If the conversation stalled over dinner, maybe her list would be something to talk about.

When she walked upstairs, the dining room table was meticulously laid with silver and crystal. She headed for the kitchen to find her host, and paused in the doorway. 'Dinner smells lovely.'

'Perfect timing,' Antoine said, not acknowledging her compliment.

'Can I take anything through?'

'The wine,' he said, taking a bottle from the fridge and uncorking it.

He brought in the food, then gestured to her to serve herself.

'This is wonderful,' she said after her first taste.

'I'm glad you like it.'

She took a sip of the wine. 'This is lovely, too. Is it one your sister made?'

'Yes.'

He didn't take the conversation further. The silence felt too awkward to bring up the topic of her Paris list, but she didn't want to eat in complete silence, either. She fell back on what she hoped would be a safe subject: work. 'You said earlier that I'd be shadowing you tomorrow. May I ask what's on the agenda?'

'I'm usually at the zoo by eight,' he said.

Just as well she was a lark rather than an owl, Geri thought.

'I'll introduce you to the team. First thing, we look at the daybook and discuss the active cases, and from there we decide what the plan is for the day. I have some things scheduled in already—we have an elephant who was stung on the eyelid yesterday, and I want to check him for swelling, plus we have an okapi with a swollen jaw who needs an X-ray.'

'Are we looking at sedation?'

'No. We've been working with conditioned behaviour,' he said. 'Okapis are quite unpredictable when they're under anaesthetic. We're doing the X-ray while she's still conscious.'

'How?'

He smiled, then, and it took Geri's breath away. When he wasn't being polite and anonymous, or silent and brooding, Antoine Bouvier was utterly gorgeous.

'She's been trained to stand still for a treat,' he said.

'That's brilliant—it reduces the stress on the okapi and takes out the risk of anaesthetic,' Geri said.

'Plus it gives the okapi some stimulation, because the keeper will do some target training first and then the okapi will stand still for the treat. Do you not do that in Cambridge?'

'We don't have okapis,' she said.

'It doesn't have to be okapis,' he pointed out. 'Any animal responds to conditioning.'

'Like Pavlov's dogs,' she said.

He smiled in acknowledgement, and her heart skipped a beat. Talking about animals was clearly a subject he liked. Wanting to keep him talking, she asked, 'Which animals are your favourites?'

'As a vet, I'm not supposed to have favourites.'

She ignored the rebuke; every vet she knew had favourites. She gave him a pointed look.

He sighed. 'All right. The tigers. We have a white Bengal tiger, Bianca. She joined the zoo the same day that I did. I'm very fond of her.'

'I look forward to meeting her,' Geri said. 'And the pandas.'

'The pandas are your favourite, I assume?'

'Absolutely. My earliest memory is seeing the pandas at London Zoo. My parents bought me a panda cuddly toy, and a book that I made them read to me every night until it fell apart.' She smiled. 'Obviously there are still pandas at Edinburgh Zoo, but not at London; since that first visit I've had to travel to get my panda fix. I got to see the babies at Berlin, the other year, and that was amazing.' She smiled at the memory. 'I'm still blown away by the fact that a cub might only weigh ninety grams at birth—around a thousand times smaller than their mum.'

'Hopefully we'll have a cub here,' he said. 'Zhen's exhibiting behaviour that means she's coming up to her fertile phase.'

The incredibly short window of two to three days in a year was one of the reasons why panda numbers were in decline. 'Perfect timing for me to join the team, then,' she said. 'Are we looking at mating her naturally with the male?'

'No. We've tried for the last two years. The year before last, Bohai—our male—was a bit clueless and didn't seem to know what to do, even when we built him a special ramp to help him. Last year, he seemed to get the idea, but Zhen wouldn't have anything to do with him,' he explained. 'This year we're going to try artificial insemination. We don't know the best timing to collect eggs from a female panda or when to transfer an embryo; AI is the only technique we can use right now.'

'I've done that with cows,' she said.

'Then you'll know about frozen sperm and thawing. Good.' He paused. 'Though it's a little different from cows, because we need to anaesthetise the bears for the procedure, and we use a catheter rather than an AI gun for insemination.'

'But it's still done slowly, I assume.'

He nodded.

'You said you anaesthetise both bears?'

'Yes. We'll take fresh sperm from Bohai under anaesthetic, mix it with thawed frozen sperm from the international cryopreservation bank, and then inseminate Zhen under anaesthetic. Four students are coming in from the university to observe, though I think it'll be useful for them to have a bit of hands-on practice.' He raised an eyebrow. 'I assume you're experienced with anaesthetics?'

'I worked with large animals at my practice, before I did my Masters and switched to zoo medicine,' she said. 'Although obviously I haven't worked with a panda before, a lot of the principles are the same.'

'Very true,' he acknowledged. 'What made you switch to zoo medicine?'

Because working with farm animals had led to an event that had changed her life utterly—and broken her heart. Not that she was going to dump that on a stranger. 'I'd always been interested in exotics,' she said. 'After my divorce, I took a long look at my life and what needed to change.'

And making a big career change had helped to distract her from the misery of the miscarriage, the shock of realising that she and Mark wanted very different things, and the hard to face knowledge that having the family of her dreams might be a lot more difficult now. Not that Antoine Bouvier needed to know that; she didn't want his pity. She wanted him to see her for the competent professional she was. 'Can I ask why you're using a mix of fresh and frozen sperm?' she asked.

'Bohai might not produce enough fresh sperm; the frozen acts as a safety net. The mixture helps with genetic diversity and increases the chance of pregnancy, because the sperm cells in the frozen semen are already activated,' he explained.

'And then we wait,' she said. 'If it works, Zhen will have the cub somewhere in the next fifty to one hundred and sixty days, depending on when the egg implants. It still amazes me that pandas have embryonic diapause.' The fertilised egg started to divide, and then the process stopped; the embryo might not attach to the panda's uterine wall until weeks later, and only then would the embryo's development continue.

'Not only pandas,' he reminded her. 'Kangaroos, mustelids and other species of bears do the same thing.'

'Which is very likely to do with waiting until it's the optimum time for the embryo's survival,' she said. 'Though it makes it hard for us to know what's happening.'

'Especially because pandas often have pseudopregnancies, where they exhibit the same behaviour and similar hormonal changes as if they're actually pregnant,' he said. 'This is going to be an interesting project for you.'

'And I'm a sucker for babies,' she said. 'There's nothing like a cuddle from a kitten or a puppy.'

'Do you have pets back in England?' he asked.

'No,' she said. 'With the hours I worked—' not to mention that Mark had liked their home to be absolutely pristine, which in hindsight should've been a warning sign '—I didn't have the time a pet deserved.' She'd made a fuss of her patients instead: from the cattle to the farm dogs and cats, and the pigs to the sheep.

The sheep that unwittingly had been her downfall.

'As I can't see any evidence of a dog, do I assume you have a sleek Parisian cat who's prowling the rooftops somewhere?' she asked, trying to push the memories away.

'No. Like you, I work long hours; I don't think it's fair to have a dog or cat.' He shrugged. 'But I enjoy my job—and my patients.'

But even work turned out to be a subject that died out by the time they got to the cheese and fruit course, and when she asked him about his tastes in music, cinema and books she felt as if she were prying rather than trying to get to know a new colleague and housemate.

'What time do we need to leave tomorrow?' she asked.

'It's a ten-minute walk to Pigalle station, then about twenty minutes on the Métro to the zoo. We don't have to change lines,' he said. 'I'm sorry, I should've bought bacon and eggs for your breakfast.'

'Actually, I usually have cereal—though toast is fine by me,' she said. 'Or whatever you usually have for breakfast.' She didn't want to be a difficult guest.

'Coffee and a baguette with conserves,' he said.

'That sounds lovely,' she said. 'As you cooked dinner, I'll wash up.' Before he could voice the protest she could see in his expression, she reminded him, 'We agreed to share the chores.'

'I don't leave the dishes for my cleaner,' he said, 'but I do have a dishwasher.'

And she'd bet he was fussy about how it was stacked.

As if her thoughts had shown on her face, he said, 'It will take me two minutes to stack it.'

Though he did at least let her help bring the crockery through. 'If you'll excuse me, I have some paperwork to catch up on,' he said. 'Feel free to use the television, though I'm afraid I don't watch it much and I'm not sure what kind of English programmes you can access.'

'I think I can access my streaming account abroad, but that's probably easiest on my laptop,' she said.

'*D'accord.* Sorry, I should have given you the Wi-Fi password earlier,' he said. 'Let me get that for you.' He grabbed his phone, and a couple of seconds later her phone pinged with a message that was clearly his Wi-Fi code.

'Is it all right to make myself a cup of tea?' she asked. 'I assumed you drink coffee rather than tea in France. I brought some Earl Grey teabags with me.'

'Please, make yourself at home,' he said. 'I do have some tisanes—chamomile and peppermint—but I'm afraid I didn't think to buy English tea.'

'I don't expect you to buy things especially for me,' she said. 'And I'd prefer to go halves on the shopping while I'm staying with you. I'm cooking tomorrow night, though I could do with some pointers about where to shop.'

He dipped his head in acknowledgement. 'There's a

row of shops in the next street—the baker, the butcher, the greengrocer and the *fromagerie*—and the supermarket's ten minutes away. I'll send you the addresses. Then you can find them on your phone's map.'

'Thank you. Is there anything you don't eat?' she asked.

He shrugged. 'I'm not fussy.'

'All right. I'll see you tomorrow at breakfast then, I guess,' she said.

Unsettling. That was what Geraldine Milligan was.

Ant wasn't sure what it was about her that disconcerted him. The keenness of her blue eyes—especially as he had a nasty feeling that she could see right through him. The brightness of her smile. The way she hadn't let him retreat into silence but had persuaded him to chat to her; he was more used to being left alone to brood under his dark cloud.

And all that meant she had the ability to turn his quiet, ordered life upside down. He'd need to be very, very careful. He couldn't face that kind of disorder and unhappiness again.

The next morning, Antoine had already made a pot of coffee before Geri came upstairs. She joined him in a breakfast of toasted baguette and a sharp yet incredibly fruity orange marmalade; then they took the Métro to the Zoo de Belvédère. The train was too noisy and crowded for them to talk on the journey; he seemed to switch into tour guide mode when they reached the park, and he pointed out various bits of interest for her.

At the zoo, he introduced her to the rest of the veterinary team and senior keepers; then they checked the daybook, and the jobs were shared out.

'We'll start with the okapi,' Antoine said, and took her over to the enclosure along with the portable X-ray machine. 'Geri, this is Sylvie, who looks after the okapi. Sylvie, this is Geri from the Cambridge zoo, who's working with us for the next six months. We'd like to X-ray Nia.'

'Then we can get to the bottom of that sore jaw. Excellent.' Sylvie smiled warmly. 'We'll do a little bit of target training with her, first, and then she'll stay still for the X-ray.'

'She's beautiful,' Geri said as they went over to the training enclosure. 'With those stripes, you'd think okapis were related to zebras rather than giraffes.'

Sylvie nodded. 'Especially as only the males have the ossicones. It still amazes me that we've only known about their existence for a little over a century.'

'Are you OK to operate the X-ray?' Antoine asked Geri.

'Of course,' Geri said.

She was fascinated by the way Sylvie used a piece of wood as a target; Nia touched it with her nose and got a treat of acacia leaves as a reward. Sylvie repeated it a couple of times.

'Is acacia their favourite food?' Geri asked.

'And some fruits.' Sylvie grinned. 'Hey, you know what a giraffe's favourite fruit is? A neck-tarine.'

Geri laughed. 'Love it. I'll remember that one.'

But Antoine, she noticed, barely cracked a smile at Sylvie's joke.

Did he hate bad puns? Or was he simply reserved with everyone at work? Geri couldn't quite work out what made him tick.

Finally, Sylvie finished the training and Nia stayed still while Geri sorted out the X-ray, and then Sylvie gave the okapi more treats.

'We have a dentist in the next *arrondissement* who specialises in animal teeth,' Antoine told Geri. 'We'll send the X-rays over to her for assessment, and then we'll know what's happening with Nia's jaw and what we need to do next to make her comfortable again.' He gave Sylvie a brief nod. 'I'll come and see you as soon as we hear something. Thanks for your help.'

They paid a couple more visits to animals who needed checking—the elephant who'd been stung on his eyelid, where Antoine was happy that the swelling was going down and no extra treatment was needed, and a tortoise with a broken toenail, where thankfully it wasn't infected and she'd be fine.

'And now for the bit you've been looking forward to,' he said, taking her to the panda enclosure. 'This is Pierre, who looks after our pandas.'

'Zhen's our female,' Pierre said. 'Her name means "precious". And Bohai's the male; his name means "sea".'

'Good names,' Geri said. She got as close to the glass as she could. 'And oh, they're *gorgeous*.'

'How are they doing?' Antoine asked.

'Zhen's a bit restless,' Pierre said. 'She's wandering in the enclosure, walking backwards with her tail up and playing in the water.'

These were all signs that the panda was heading towards ovulation, Geri knew.

'She's vocalising more,' Pierre said, and as if on cue Zhen started to bleat and chirp.

'Bohai's vocalising, too, and keeping her in his sight,' Pierre added. 'I'm waiting to grab today's urine samp—'

He broke off as Zhen started to urinate. 'I'll be back in a minute,' he said.

'She's definitely getting closer,' Antoine said. 'Hopefully Pierre can manage to get that urine sample before it all soaks into the earth, and we'll check the lab results against yesterday's sample.'

'I'm really excited about this,' she said. 'Getting to know the pandas and being involved in the breeding programme.'

'It's a privilege,' Antoine agreed.

Pierre managed to get the sample. 'For the last week, I've kept a sealed bag with a sterile syringe in my pocket,' he said wryly.

'Just as well,' Antoine said, and put the labelled phial into his bag before taking Geri around a couple more enclosures.

At lunchtime, Antoine grabbed a sandwich along with the others in the staff canteen, but left early, saying that he needed to catch up with paperwork. 'Stay and take your full break,' he directed Geri.

'Don't take it personally,' Valerie, the junior veterinary nurse, said. 'It's amazing that he stayed with us for as long as he did. He normally eats at his desk.'

'He's a bit remote with everyone, then, not only m—?' Geri stopped and grimaced. 'I'm sorry. I didn't mean to be rude and judgemental.'

'Of course you didn't. Antoine's fabulous with the animals, patient and kind,' Valerie said. 'But it's fair to say he's not really a people person.'

'He used to be,' Émilie, the senior veterinary nurse, said. 'Before—' She wrinkled her nose. 'No, it's not fair to gossip.'

'I won't say anything,' Geri promised. 'But if there's

something I ought to know so I don't...' She stopped, her vocabulary deserting her, and circled her hand to show she was searching for the right phrase.

'*Faire une gaffe?*' Valerie supplied.

Émilie nodded. 'Let's say his ex broke his heart, a couple of years ago, and he doesn't let anyone close now. Except maybe his parents and his sister, and they live in the Loire.' She gave a very Gallic shrug.

Geri knew how that felt. Been there, done that— but her family and friends hadn't let her withdraw, and she'd tried hard to find the sunshine ever since. 'That's a shame,' she said quietly. 'I'll be tactful. Thank you for warning me.'

The conversation turned to Paris and advice from everyone about the best times to visit the more popular tourist spots, as well as suggestions for places she might enjoy exploring. At the end of her lunch break, she headed back to Antoine's office.

'What's the agenda for this afternoon?' she asked.

'More rounds,' he said. 'Though I need to make a couple of phone calls, first. The urine sample's exactly what I hoped it would be—her oestrogen levels have peaked. It looks as if she's ovulating. Tomorrow morning, we're doing the AI.'

'That's fantastic news,' she said.

'I'll do the initial sedation,' he said, 'and then we'll have the usual team of three on anaesthesia—one on airway management, one monitoring the anaesthetic drugs, and one doing the record-keeping—while I do the insemination procedure. That means you, Jacques and Émilie.'

'Which do you want me to do?' she asked.

'Your choice,' he said.

'Airway management,' she decided.

'That's fine.'

In between the rounds, Geri met Marie, the head of HR, who seemed warm and effusive.

At the end of the day, the veterinary nurses left—as did Jacques, the other vet.

'What time do you normally leave the zoo?' she asked Antoine.

He spread his hands and shrugged. 'It depends on the paperwork. Unfortunately, today is a big paperwork day. Will you be all right getting back to the apartment on your own?'

Geri wondered if he was using the paperwork as an excuse to avoid her company, but smiled sweetly. 'Of course. What time would you like dinner?'

His eyes widened slightly. 'I, uh…'

'Seven?' she suggested.

'You really don't have to cook for me.'

'I can take you out to dinner, if you'd prefer,' she said.

That was definite panic in his eyes, then, and she remembered what Émilie had said. This wasn't about her; Antoine was clearly still hurting from whatever had happened with his ex. She knew how that felt. Mark had moved on, and she was glad he was happy; at the same time, she wished things could've been different. That they'd wanted the same things. That her fertility wasn't in question, post-Q fever. 'I'll make something flexible,' she said. 'Text me when you're twenty minutes away, and it'll be ready five minutes after you get in.'

'*D'accord,*' he said.

Geri navigated the Métro and, with the help of her phone and the maps, found the shops Antoine had recommended. He was probably expecting her to cook something stodgy and English; she planned to surprise him.

* * *

Ant found it hard to concentrate on his paperwork; he knew it was because of Geri. She just *unsettled* him.

Eventually he closed down his computer, headed for the Métro, and texted Geri to let her know when he was twenty minutes away.

He could smell something delicious as soon as he walked into the apartment. For an odd moment, he felt as if he should've brought flowers. But this was his apartment and Geri was his houseguest; bringing flowers for her would've been inappropriate and made them both feel embarrassed.

When he walked upstairs, she appeared in the kitchen doorway and smiled. His heartbeat went up a couple of notches, and he had to breathe deeply to bring it down again. This was ridiculous. A smile shouldn't make him feel like this. He'd been perfectly fine on his own, these last couple of years. He wasn't looking to change his situation. At all. And definitely not with someone who was only here temporarily.

'Hi. Is your paperwork all wrestled into submission?' she asked.

'Something like that,' he said. 'Dinner smells good.'

She went pink and looked pleased. 'I hope you like it. You did say you ate anything.' She gave him a wicked smile. 'Though I did think about cooking roast beef and Yorkshire pudding.'

'Les rosbifs.' The phrase slipped out before he could stop it.

She laughed. 'Yeah. That's how I thought you'd react. One of my best friends at uni taught me her mum's recipe for Keralan chicken curry. I made flatbreads to go with it, but I'm also cooking rice and dhal. And I thought we could eat on the terrace, as it's a nice evening.'

'Can I do anything to help?'

'Sit down. It'll be ready in five minutes. Oh, you could take the jug of lassi out of the fridge, if you like.'

She'd even made a traditional Indian drink? 'That's impressive.'

She smiled. 'It's really not that difficult.'

Geri's smile definitely had the power to scramble his brain. Ant knew he'd need to be careful. Especially because, when he went out into the roof garden, it felt incredibly intimate. She'd laid the bistro table with simple bowls and his everyday cutlery rather than the family silver, and it felt like the perfect cosy evening for two. It was something he hadn't done since Céline, and it made him feel awkward.

But then he stopped having time to feel strange about it, because she brought out the dishes of food and loaded the table.

The curry was excellent; the spices were beautifully balanced. 'I don't often eat Indian food,' he said. 'This is really good.'

'You're welcome. I know I made way too much, except for the rice, but it's freezable—or maybe we can have leftovers tomorrow night.'

'Leftovers sounds good to me,' he said. 'Did you enjoy your first day at the zoo?'

She nodded. 'And I'm really looking forward to tomorrow.'

'We'll be doing the annual health check for the pandas as well as the AI procedure,' he said. 'Weight, height, teeth and bloods, for starters.'

'That makes sense,' she said.

They chatted about the pandas—a welcome safe subject—until they'd finished eating and cleared away. Ant made a pot of coffee, and they returned to the roof garden.

'I was checking the roster today,' she said, 'and it says I have Wednesday off.'

'Do you have any plans?' he asked.

'I'd like to start ticking things off my Paris list,' she said. 'The roster said you're off on Wednesday, too. I was wondering…' She looked at him shyly. 'Would you like to come with me?'

He really hadn't expected that, and it knocked him off balance.

Part of him wanted to go with her; but part of him didn't want to let her get any closer. He had a feeling that Geri Milligan could be seriously dangerous to his peace of mind. 'It's kind of you to ask,' he said, 'but, actually, I was planning to go in to work on Wednesday— I want to check on the pandas myself, as it'll be the day after the AI.'

She smiled brightly at him. 'No problem. Just a thought.'

But he'd seen the momentary sag of disappointment in her shoulders, and he knew he'd caused it. Guilt flickered through him. Would it be that difficult to show her round the city? He could even dress it up as work: helping his new colleague settle in and make her feel part of the team. It would be the kind thing to do.

Though it would also mean letting her past his barriers, and he wasn't ready to let anyone in. And he could do with a tiny bit of distance between them right now, too. Before he let her tempt him. 'You cooked,' he said. 'I'll clear up.'

Her expression showed that she knew it was an excuse to avoid her, and guilt washed through him again. It wasn't her fault. But explaining to her was too complicated. 'I'll see you later,' he muttered, and headed for the kitchen.

CHAPTER THREE

TUESDAY MORNING WAS full on. Antoine had started an hour and a half earlier than usual to give himself time to check on any animals that needed urgent help, and then checked the operating theatre so everything his team needed was in place. Just before the operation was due to start, he made sure everyone knew what their role was: Geri on airway management, Jacques on anaesthesia and Émilie on record-keeping.

'I'm trying to keep the number of people around minimal while the pandas are awake; then they won't feel crowded and it's less stressful for them. The zoo directors and the visiting lecturer can observe the actual operations while the pandas are under anaesthetic, and the four students can help with the procedures under our direction. Does that work for everyone?' he asked.

The team all murmured their assent.

He was efficient, without being abrupt, Geri thought, and it was clear that the animals were his top priority. She liked the fact that he put them before any office politics—and she really appreciated that he noticed the moments where she was struggling to keep up and quietly translated from French to English for her, without making a big deal of it.

'Good. Any questions or issues?' He paused for a moment. 'OK. I'll bring the students in now.' He disappeared and returned with four final-year veterinary students, then introduced them to his team.

'Pierre, I know we've had the keeper team monitoring the pandas overnight, but can you confirm that Zhen and Bohai haven't eaten or drunk anything for the last twelve hours?' Antoine asked.

'They haven't eaten or drunk anything,' the keeper said, 'and they're both a bit grumpy about missing their breakfast. We'll supplement the bamboo this afternoon, once they're round from the anaesthetic.'

'Good.' Antoine looked at the students. 'I'm sure you all know this, but why am I asking about food and drink?'

'To avoid any risk of regurgitation or pulmonary aspiration of the stomach contents during anaesthesia,' one of the students said.

'Exactly.' Antoine gave one of his rare smiles, and Geri was unsettled by the sudden flash of heat down her spine. This was *work*, she reminded herself. She needed to focus on her job.

'Some of the team are giving the enclosure a thorough clean while the procedures are being done,' Pierre said. 'We'll be draining the pools, disinfecting the floors and the rock features, then refilling the pools and the feeders.'

Antoine nodded. 'Let's get going. I prefer to use a hand syringe for the anaesthesia, where I can, rather than a dart. We'll start with getting Bohai—our male,' he explained to the students, 'in the restraint cage.'

Ant glanced at Geri, hoping she'd pick up the cue to ask a question. 'Why do we use the restraint cage?' she asked.

'It keeps them safe—so they won't fall or hurt themselves during a procedure,' one of the students said.

She smiled. 'That's one reason. And another?' When none of them answered, she said, 'I have a very soft spot for pandas, but are they as cute and cuddly as most people think?'

Good question, Ant thought. She was making them consider the reasons behind the clinical decisions. And he liked the fact that she was practical, even though the pandas were her favourite.

'No. They're bears,' a student said. 'They're dangerous.'

'Just like a black bear or a polar bear, though pandas aren't quite as heavy,' Geri agreed. 'Using the cage means we're out of reach of their claws and their teeth.'

'Absolutely,' Ant said. 'We need to be safe, too, or we can't treat our patients properly.'

They left the examination room for the panda enclosure, with the four students in tow. Pierre encouraged Bohai into the cage; then Ant knelt by the cage with the bear's back towards him and gently scratched the panda's back. Bohai grunted with pleasure, and Ant kept talking to him calmly while he administered the injection. He continued soothing the bear and giving a running commentary to the students while they waited for the sedative drug to take effect; a couple of minutes later, Bohai's head started drooping, and within a quarter of an hour it was safe for them to open the cage. Ant checked the panda's level of consciousness and vital signs, took a phial of blood, then covered the bear's eyes with a blindfold. 'I know he's under anaesthetic, but this helps to minimise external stimuli,' he explained to the students.

Geri put a face mask on the bear. 'Why do we need this?' she asked. When none of the students answered, she said, 'We need to keep his oxygen saturation levels up during transport. Where's the best place to put the pulse clip?'

'His tongue or his cheek,' one of the students said.

'Why not an ear?' she asked.

Again, Ant liked the way she challenged the students. He rather thought that she could challenge *him*, if he gave her the chance. She'd push him out of his comfort zone and make him engage with the world again; and he wasn't sure if the idea intrigued or terrified him more.

'Because the reading won't be good enough, and it's also too easy for the clip to slip off,' one of the others said.

'Perfect.' She smiled at the first student who'd answered. 'Put the clip on his tongue, and then I'll check it.'

Once the clip was in place, between them they gently put Bohai onto a tarpaulin, checked his weight and height, then transported him to the main examination room.

'I'm putting a cuff round his forelimb to track his blood pressure,' Geri said.

As they expected, Bohai's blood pressure had risen initially, but finally Geri was happy that the bear was relaxed and ready for intubation. With the help of two of the students, she prepared his jaw to check his upper airway. 'Dental check, first,' she said, and let the students all check the bear's teeth.

'It all looks fine to me,' the last one said.

Geri checked, too. 'No problems—no chips or cracks, or anything that makes me think we need to X-ray him,' she said. 'Now, we'll spray lidocaine on his vocal cords, to reduce the risk of his larynx going into spasm as we intubate him,' she explained. She inserted the tube, inflated the cuff and used a stethoscope to check his breath sounds, before getting the students to listen and check it too.

'Bilateral breath sounds OK,' the last one confirmed to Antoine.

Antoine gave Geri a nod of approval that made her feel warm all over. They might be a bit awkward with each other outside work, but they were definitely on the same page when they were at the zoo.

Once the airway was secured and IV access was ready, Jacques gave the bear a balanced electrolyte solution to help keep his fluids up. Finally, Antoine did the electroejaculation procedure to collect the sperm from Bohai, explaining to his audience what he was doing and why, and then Jacques administered an antiemetic.

'Are we ready to wake him?' Antoine asked.

'Ready,' Jacques and Geri confirmed.

Between them, they moved Bohai to the recovery cage; as soon as his swallowing reflex returned, Geri deflated the endotracheal tube and withdrew it carefully. They monitored him until he lifted his head, and finally got to his feet again. Once Antoine was satisfied that the bear was safe to be back in his enclosure, they took him back; one of Pierre's team stayed to feed Bohai his usual breakfast of bamboo.

They went through the same process to anaesthetise Zhen, ready for the insemination, and do her health checks.

'We're using a mix of fresh semen from Bohai and thawed frozen sperm from the international cryopreservation bank,' Antoine told the students. 'A panda has a small uterus; we need to empty Zhen's bladder first with a catheter, then insert the semen via an inseminating catheter.'

Once the procedure was done, they reversed the anaesthesia, kept a check on Zhen as she recovered, then finally took her back into her enclosure.

During the debrief, Antoine patiently answered every question from the students, and made sure that Geri, Jacques, Émilie and Pierre also had the chance to answer questions. This was a different side of Antoine, Geri thought; given that he'd seemed a bit distant with his colleagues yesterday, she'd expected him to have little patience with the students. Today he appeared more relatable—and much more likeable. She noticed that the female student kept giving him covert glances; in her shoes, Geri rather thought she would've been doing the same. Not only because Antoine was good-looking, but because he was clearly passionate about his work, and that passion was captivating.

What would it be like if Antoine showed that same passion outside his work? She couldn't help wondering, and again it sent a wave of heat through her.

Once their visitors had left, they carried on with the rest of their normal day's routine, though she noticed that Antoine skipped lunch and the afternoon break to check on the pandas.

He was reluctant to leave, only agreeing when Pierre promised to call him at home if his team was in the slightest bit worried about the pandas.

It was too noisy on the Métro to talk, but once they were back at Antoine's flat Geri looked at him. 'Sit down. I'll make some fresh flatbread and rice, and heat up yesterday's leftovers. We were in early, and you didn't even stop for lunch.'

'I wanted to keep an eye on the pandas,' he said. 'Anaesthesia's always a worry.'

'Is this the first time we've performed panda AI at our zoo?'

He nodded. 'The pandas have been at the zoo for four years now. The first year, we missed Zhen's fertile window; the next two years, as I told you earlier, mating naturally didn't work. This year, we wanted to give her the best chance of having a cub.'

'Let's hope we're lucky this time,' she said. 'I guess we'll know at some point in the next six months.'

'If the embryo implants, and provided Zhen doesn't have a pseudopregnancy,' he said. 'We'll have to persuade her into having an ultrasound in three months' time. According to Pierre, she'll do a lot for honey water or sweet potato.'

'More Pavlov stuff,' she said lightly.

'And enrichment,' he said. 'The panda team put the bears' favourite fruit and veg in puzzle cubes and hide them around the enclosure. As well as having to hunt for the cubes, the pandas have to figure out the right angles to hold them to get the treats.'

'It's a million miles from how zoos were when I was a child,' Geri said.

'And me,' he said. 'I always thought I'd work with farm animals—after Bertrand the Poitou—but I had the chance to do a final-year project here when I was a student, and that was it for me.'

It was similar to her own career progression, but Geri didn't want to talk about the farm animals she'd loved working with and the way her life had subsequently imploded. She changed the subject. 'You were good with the students.'

'I enjoy teaching. Especially when the students' questions challenge me to further my own knowledge.' He shrugged. 'But I prefer practice. You were good with the students, too. Very clear in your explanations.'

'I like working with people as well as animals,' she said. 'But I'm enjoying the challenge of zoo medicine—using what I know and applying it to different animals.'

'Indeed.'

She could tell he'd gone remote on her again, but she wasn't going to take it personally. 'I'll go and sort dinner,' she said.

The next morning, Ant left early. He felt a bit guilty about abandoning Geri on her first day off, but reminded himself that she wasn't his responsibility; she was an adult, and she was perfectly capable of sightseeing in Paris on her own. But all the same he nipped over to the boulangerie in the neighbouring street before he went to the zoo, to buy her a couple of croissants, and left her a little note next to the bag in the kitchen.

Thought you might like these for breakfast. Enjoy sightseeing. I'll sort dinner tonight. A

By the time he arrived at the zoo, she'd texted him.

Merci beaucoup pour les croissants. À bientôt.

He liked the fact she was trying to do as much as she could in French rather than relying on her own language all the time. And the unexpected friendship growing between them made him feel warm inside.

To his relief, Zhen and Bohai had no after-effects from the anaesthetic, and he spent a busy day doing rounds and checking on a penguin with a possible case of bumblefoot. He was scanning recipes and deciding what to cook for dinner when his phone buzzed.

He glanced at the screen and frowned. His sister didn't normally call him at this time of day. 'Is everything all right, Mélie?'

'Yes, fine,' she said. 'Well, mostly.'

'What's wrong?'

'I, um… I know one of us should've told you earlier.'

Dread knifed through him. 'What's happened? Is Maman or Papa ill?'

'No, nothing like that.' She dragged in a breath. 'It's not bad news. But it's going to hurt you, and… I'm sorry for that. You know I wouldn't hurt you for the world. You're my brother and I love you.'

'I know,' he said. 'Mélie, just tell me.'

'Jean-Luc. He and Céline…um…had a little girl this morning.'

The little girl that should've been his.

And nobody in his family had breathed a word to him throughout the whole of Céline's pregnancy. They'd shut him out. For a second, Ant couldn't breathe. It felt as if he was in some kind of vacuum; the only thing that existed was stinging hurt.

But he didn't want his sister or his parents worrying about him. He pulled himself together. 'I see,' he said.

'Ant, I know one of us should've told you before.'

Yes, they should've done. But he knew why they hadn't. 'You all still tread on eggshells around me,' he said. 'I take it you were the one who drew the short straw.'

'Ant, you know we all love you. And we miss you.' She sighed. 'I *knew* I should've come to see you about this instead of phoning you.'

'We're both busy at work. Why waste a day travelling? You were right to phone me instead.'

'I'm still sorry. I know how much you loved Céline. And I wish things were different.'

'Things are as they are,' Ant said. 'You can't help who you fall in love with.'

'Just why did she have to fall in love with our brother?'

Yeah. He'd asked himself that, so many times. The whole thing was a mess. The gap they'd left in his life was still there, and he still didn't know how to deal with that.

'Are you OK?' Amélie asked.

'Yes.' Because he was going to stuff all the feelings down in a little box in a corner of his heart, and lock them up tightly before they could do any more damage. 'Mélie, I love you, but I need to cook dinner. Geri will be back soon.'

'Geri?'

'The English vet. I told you about her last week,' Ant reminded her. 'She's staying with me—in your room, actually—because the builders found asbestos in her flat, and I have room here. Marie thought it would be a good idea if she stayed with me until the zoo can find her another place.'

'Is she nice?'

'She's good with the animals. I think the secondment will go well.'

Amelie sighed. 'That isn't what I asked.'

He knew that, but it was all she was going to get. 'I'll speak to you soon,' he said. 'Give Maman and Papa my love.'

'Why don't you come and tell them yourself?'

'Because I'm really busy at the zoo.' And because his parents would naturally want to see lots of their firstborn grandchild, and Ant didn't want to risk bumping into his brother or his ex. Not until he'd had a chance to process this news and work out how he felt.

But, despite telling his sister that he was absolutely fine, he was very much out of sorts. To the point where he burned dinner. Twice. Deciding to give up and order a pizza or something when Geri came back from her sightseeing, Ant scrubbed the kitchen. Which didn't help, because cleaning didn't occupy his head anywhere near enough. He had no paperwork from the zoo to do—at least, nothing he could access from home—and he'd never really been one for watching the television.

Nothing would push the pictures out of his head.

Céline, holding a baby, her face glowing with love...

By the time he heard the front door close behind Geri, he was in a thoroughly foul mood. One which got even worse because she was bubbling over about her day as a tourist in Paris.

'The Louvre is amazing!' she said. 'I admit the *Mona Lisa* was a little bit disappointing, because I didn't expect it to be that small. But I saw tons of beautiful paintings. And the Tuileries were full of blossom—like pink fluffy clouds, and the scent was incredible. It didn't matter that it poured with rain while I was in the queue because then there was an enormous rainbow, and more rainbows inside by the upside-down pyramid, and—'

'You really are *un petit rayon du soleil*, aren't you?' he cut in.

As soon as the words came out of his mouth, he knew how horrible he was being. How unfair. None of this was her fault and she didn't deserve him venting his spleen on her. But he couldn't stop himself.

Her eyes narrowed as she translated it mentally. 'Says

the man who's determined to be the rain—and spill the gloom over everyone else's parade.'

He knew he probably deserved that, but it still rankled.

'What's your problem, Antoine?' she asked.

'Nothing.' He turned away.

'Oh, no. You're not getting away with that,' she said. 'Snapping at me and then pretending there's nothing wrong—when you've been scrupulously polite and kind with me. A bit distant at times, yes, but always polite. And you were sweet enough to buy me croissants for breakfast this morning. Has something happened with the pandas?'

'No. Everything's fine at the zoo.'

'I'm glad to hear it—but everything's clearly not fine with you,' she said. She sniffed, then frowned. 'Bleach and burned toast.'

It was obvious. He might as well admit it. 'Burned chicken, actually.'

She raised an eyebrow. 'I can't believe that someone as meticulous as you would forget that you were cooking something.'

She was too perceptive for his own good. 'I just had some news that...' He waved a hand in a circle, hoping it would be enough to explain.

'Upset you enough to burn dinner and snap at me?'

He winced. 'I apologise. I shouldn't have taken out my temper on you.'

'No, you shouldn't—but, even though I don't know you very well, this feels out of character.' She looked concerned. 'Can I do anything to help?'

'No.'

'No, because it's not something fixable, or no, because you're out of sorts and want to brood about it on your own?'

Razor-sharp perceptive, he amended mentally. 'Both, I guess.'

'Don't move,' she said. 'I'll be back in a couple of minutes.'

He heard the kettle boiling and some banging around; he could definitely smell vanilla—or was it chocolate?—and then the microwave pinged.

What was his houseguest up to?

A few moments later, she came back into the living room with a tray.

'The English answer to everything,' she said. 'Tea and cake.'

'That's *tea*?' He looked at the cup with its extremely pale beige contents. It looked like no tea he'd ever been served before. And what exactly was in the mug with a teaspoon balanced on top?

'It's Earl Grey, and probably not how a fastidious Frenchman would drink it,' she said. 'Actually, I'd get flayed in England for making tea like this, too, but I like mine weak and milky. And the cake's a chocolate mug cake. Best thing ever when you need a quick carb fix.'

It looked appalling, and it really wasn't the sort of thing he'd eat; but it was an incredibly kind gesture, and right at that moment Ant didn't know whether to laugh or cry. 'Thank you,' he said. 'I don't deserve this.'

'You're a bit of a panda,' she said. 'Not very sociable. But you've clearly had a rubbish day, and I wouldn't be a very good houseguest if I left you to stew.'

She thought he was like a panda? A solitary beast who didn't socialise?

Then again, she had a point. Since the day of the-wedding-that-wasn't, he'd kept everyone at a distance. Including his family. He hadn't been able to bear seeing the pity in their eyes, even when they tried to hide it—and he hated that his family was split. Yes, his brother was technically in the wrong; but, as he'd told his sister, you couldn't help who you fell in love with. Jean-Luc had tried to resist his feelings. So had Céline. But it had been too much for them.

Ant didn't even know where to begin knitting his family back together again.

'I apologise,' he said.

'Eat your cake while I make one for me, drink your tea, and then talk,' she said. 'I know you don't know me very well, either, but I assure you I'm not a gossip. I won't repeat anything you say to me. When things are going wrong, sometimes talking about it can take the pressure out of your head.'

He didn't have an answer to that.

The tea was vile, and the cake a bit sweet for his taste, but he appreciated the kindness behind it. And the fact that she'd left the room for a couple of minutes to give him a breathing space.

'Thank you,' he said when she returned with a second mug cake and cup of milky tea.

'De rien.' She gave a half-shrug.

He couldn't help smiling. 'It looks as if we're making a Parisienne out of you already.'

She wrinkled her nose, and he thought how cute she looked.

'A Parisienne would no doubt serve this tea with lemon, not a ton of milk.'

'True.'

'And a mug cake isn't quite glamorous enough for Paris.'

'Agreed,' he said. 'Though, with a bit less sugar, it'd be nice.'

'Noted,' she said. 'Right. Tea and cake dispensed. Time for—maybe sympathy, but I think you're more the no-nonsense type. What happened?'

Maybe she was right and saying the words out loud would get them out of his head. None of the alternatives had worked yet, today. 'My brother,' he said, 'just had a baby.'

'And?' she asked, not quite understanding why Antoine would be upset about a new niece or nephew.

He looked away. 'With my ex.'

A baby.

His brother and his ex?

This was a complete minefield, and she wasn't quite sure what to say.

But Antoine clearly took the silence as waiting for him to speak, because he said, 'Of course I'm pleased for them.'

That wasn't what his face was saying. '*Are* you?' she asked.

'Yes. And no,' he admitted. 'I always thought Céline and I would get married and have children.'

Geri and Mark hadn't planned to have children. But then life had changed; and when she'd lost the baby they'd had a really honest conversation. One that had hurt both of them; Mark had been adamant that he still didn't want children, whereas the miscarriage had made her realise that her own feelings had changed.

That was one issue where there simply wasn't a middle way: one of them would've had to compromise and do something they really didn't want to. And finally, although it had made them both sad, they'd agreed that they needed to go their separate ways and find the life they wanted.

Had Antoine gone through something similar?

'I'll ask you the tough question,' she said. 'Why is she your ex?'

'Because she fell in love with my brother.' He blew out a breath. 'Neither of them wanted to hurt me. Jean-Luc even moved to Chartres, two hours away, to try and stay away from her—thinking he'd be able to forget her. And she thought she could make herself fall out of love with him.'

'But it didn't work?' she asked quietly.

'No. The morning of our wedding, she realised she couldn't go through with it.' The words tumbled out of him like pebbles churned up by the sea. 'My brother was my *témoin*—my best man, I guess he'd be in England. We were waiting outside the town hall, fifteen minutes before our slot. She called him, in tears. And he broke the news to me.'

Breaking Antoine's heart in the process.

'That's a really hard way to find out. And the timing was rough on you.'

'It could've been worse.' He shrugged. 'She could've actually stood next to me in the town hall, with all our close family and friends witnessing it, and then said no.'

But he would still have had to explain to everyone why the wedding was cancelled. 'Why didn't she say something to you before the day?'

'As I said, they thought they could fight their feelings. Neither of them wanted to hurt me. She thought she could go through with the wedding and save me being hurt.'

'And instead they hurt you very publicly.'

He inclined his head. 'We haven't spoken since. And

I hate that my family feels they ought to take sides. It's my fault the family's split.'

'But you've done nothing wrong.'

'Jean-Luc and Céline didn't do it to be malicious. They're not the bad guys. I know that.'

'But there's a difference between knowing something with your head, and knowing it with your heart,' she said.

He gave her a bleak look. 'The first step to any reconciliation will probably have to come from me. But making myself do it…' He shook his head. 'I don't expect my parents to refuse to see their first grandchild. I know they see Jean-Luc and I'm fine with that. He's their son, too. But, if I make it up with him…everyone's going to pity me. Especially now, with the baby. And I can't bear that.'

'Maybe,' she said carefully, 'they won't pity you.'

'Oh, but they will. Poor Antoine, whose fiancée fell in love with his brother.' He grimaced. 'That's not who I am. I'm a zoo vet. A good one.'

Was that the only way he saw himself—defining himself by his job? 'You're also *you*,' she said. 'Losing your brother and your fiancée, on what should've been a day to celebrate, must've been hard.' She reached out to squeeze his hand.

'It is what it is. But that's why I don't socialise much. I don't have the heart for it, any more.' He pulled away from her hand. 'And I don't enjoy being pitied.'

'I'm not pitying you,' she said. 'But I do think you're missing out, hiding yourself away in your shell.'

'You're saying I'm a tortoise now, rather than a panda?' He gave her a speaking look.

'No. Just…' She blew out a breath. 'I kind of know how you feel, because I've been there.'

'Your fiancé jilted you on your wedding day, too?'

There was a slight edge to his tone, and she realised she'd gone too far. Maybe she needed to share some of her past, too.

'No. Mark and I got married.' She wasn't quite up to telling Antoine about the baby she'd lost, and the subsequent slow and painful unravelling of her marriage. 'It didn't work out. We found out the hard way that we wanted different things.' The shock of learning she was pregnant had quickly been replaced by unexpected joy; until then, she hadn't realised that she did actually want children. Though, thanks to the disease she'd caught, she might never be able to have children. 'So we got divorced. And let's say I've learned that life's better when I'm being what you called a little ray of sunshine—if I've translated that right?'

He winced. 'I apologise for being rude.'

She shook her head. 'I wasn't fishing for an apology. I simply meant that there's another way of dealing with a broken heart that might help you more than avoidance. It worked for me, anyway.' She spread her hands. 'Fake it until you make it.'

Ant rather thought his own solution worked better. Keeping himself separate from other people was the best way to keep his heart safe. No involvement meant no chance of getting hurt again. And staying away from his family— much as he missed them—meant he didn't have to face the guilt of knowing the split in his family was his fault. Because he couldn't get past it.

But she'd said that she'd been there. She knew the same dark places he did, and he'd seen a world of pain in her eyes when she'd said that she and her ex had wanted different things. Had her ex cheated on her? Or had something else caused the split?

'Your divorce—is that why you came to Paris?'

'Partly. It's why I switched to zoo medicine.'

'Was your ex a vet?'

'No. He was a dentist. We met in our last year at uni,' she said. 'At the time, we thought we were what each other wanted. But we both ended up focused on our careers and we let the spontaneity drain out of our relationship. So I wanted to do something different. I wanted to experience another culture and live in another country for a few months.'

'Hence your Paris list.'

'Yes. I'm happy to tick things off on my own, but sometimes it's more fun to do it with someone else.' She gave him a level look. 'This isn't me propositioning you, by the way. I'm not looking for a relationship. But a friend—I'd like that. And I could be your friend, too. If you'd like that.'

A friend.

Something felt as if it was cracking, somewhere in the region of where his heart used to be.

'I was thinking, maybe you could come with me. Show me the things in Paris I might've missed on my list, and I can maybe teach you to see the city with new eyes.' She smiled. 'You never really explore the place where you live unless you're showing it off to someone else.'

'I guess that's true,' he said.

Explore Paris with her.

Could he do that?

She'd accused him of being a tortoise, stuck in his shell. Maybe she was right. He knew his sister and his parents worried about him. Showing Geri round Paris might be a bigger step towards getting some sense of normality back in his life.

'We could,' she said, 'make a start tonight. Having a drink at the Moulin Rouge, and maybe go somewhere for a pizza.'

'The traditional *French* pizza, would that be?' he asked wryly.

'Obviously I know it's Italian. But pizza's my carb of choice when I've had a tough day,' she said. 'Which it sounds like you have.'

'Be prepared for the Moulin Rouge to be extremely touristy,' he warned.

'Bring on the can-can and the accordions,' she said with a grin. 'I can even pretend to swish my skirt.'

He looked at her jeans. 'Pretend.'

'I own skirts,' she protested.

'If you want to see the show, you need to book,' he said.

'Maybe we'll do that another time, then.' She took her phone from her pocket. 'Or we could visit one of the bars where the artists used to drink.'

'I'd need to look them up, if you want to tour them,' he said.

'OK. I'll settle for the pizza,' she said.

'All right. I'll buy you dinner instead of cooking it,' he said. 'As your friend.'

'And, as *your* friend, I'll buy the wine.'

He'd let her argue that later. 'OK. We can go whenever you want.'

'I'm hungry now,' she said. 'Despite scoffing a mug cake. I've walked *miles* today. Do I need to dress up?'

'You're fine as you are,' he said. More than fine. Not that he was going to let himself think about how attractive Geri Milligan was. It wasn't appropriate, and his head wasn't in the right place; it wouldn't be fair to take this further, even if she felt the same attraction towards him.

Though the flickerings wouldn't go away. His awareness of her. The way she smiled, the way her eyes seemed to change colour—almost like a spring afternoon sky, when she was happy. The way she challenged him, making him see things in a new light instead of leaving him to brood on his problems alone.

He took her to a small pizzeria not far from the apartment, and made sure that she had the seat with a view because he was pretty sure she'd enjoy it.

'The Sacré Coeur looks amazing from here,' she said, looking thrilled.

'I'll take you round it, another day,' he said. 'And maybe you can have your portrait drawn in charcoal by one of the artists. It's touristy, yes, but it's also kind of a rite of passage.'

'I'd love that,' she said.

Once they'd ordered their pizza and a couple of glasses of wine, he looked at her. 'Tell me about your Paris list. Not that having a list says spontaneity to me.'

'I'm going to be spontaneous about when I see them,' she corrected. 'The list is because I don't want to miss out on all the big things. I want to go to the Eiffel Tower—right to the very top—and I want to see it at night when it sparkles. And walk down the Champs-Élysées.'

'To go shopping?'

'Isn't it meant to be *the* shopping street in Paris?' she asked.

'It's a tourist trap,' he said, wrinkling his nose. 'If you want luxury shopping, go to la Rue de Faubourg Saint-

Honoré. Most Parisians shop at la Rue du Commerce, near the Eiffel Tower, or in the Marais.'

She grabbed her phone and made notes. 'Got it. And I want to dance next to the Seine.'

He couldn't remember the last time he'd danced. 'We can do that,' he said. 'Though I'm a bit out of practice.'

'Everything I saw online said that it didn't matter if you were a beginner. And you *have* to do a tango in Paris, don't you? Or maybe salsa. Either will do.'

Perhaps it hadn't been such a good idea to agree to this; both dances were incredibly sensual. And he didn't dare let himself think about sensuality and Geri Milligan. 'Museums?' he said, trying to find a safer subject.

'I want to visit all of them,' she said gleefully. 'And all the art galleries. But I especially want to see the enormous Monet water lily paintings at the Musée de l'Orangerie. I missed them when three of them were exhibited in London.'

'We're both off duty on Sunday. I could drive you out to Giverny to see Monet's garden for yourself,' he suggested, and was rewarded with a smile that made the lingering shadows vanish.

'That's also on my list—but are you sure it's not too much trouble?'

'I'm sure,' he said. 'It's an easy drive. You're a big fan of Monet?'

She nodded. '*The Water Lily Pond* is my favourite painting in the whole world, and I'd love to see the actual pond he painted. I was planning to work out how to get to Giverny from Paris.'

'You can go by train, but I'll drive you and we can maybe see some of the area around Giverny, too,' he said.

'We'll book tickets tonight. Even if it's wet on Sunday, I have no doubt you'll see the sunshine.'

She narrowed those perceptive blue eyes at him. 'Are you laughing at me?'

'No, at myself,' he said. 'Because you're right. I'm used to being in my shell, in the darkness. Maybe I should try things your way. Look for the sunshine.' And fake it, if he had to. That had never occurred to him before. He'd simply blocked everything out, focused on his work and avoided social situations.

'Good,' she said.

After her first bite of pizza, she closed her eyes in apparent bliss. 'This is perfect. Proper thin-crust Italian pizza,' she said. 'And goat's cheese with rocket and chili jam is the *perfect* combination.'

She liked the wine, too.

And the limoncello ice cream he'd eschewed in favour of an espresso. 'This is amazing. You really have to try this, Antoine.'

'Call me Ant,' he said, shocking himself. He'd known Geri for three short days. He would never normally invite such informality on such a brief acquaintance. Maybe her spontaneity was catching.

'Ant,' she said with a smile, and proffered her spoon.

He shocked himself further by leaning over and actually letting her feed him the ice cream. 'It's a little sw—' He stopped himself mid-sentence. No negativity. 'It's nice,' he said.

But she'd clearly picked up on what he'd been about to say. 'Except you don't do sweet. You like things sharp—like your breakfast marmalade,' she said.

He spread his hands. 'Sorry.'

'And to think I brought you chocolates and biscuits,' she said, looking rueful.

'It was a kind thought,' he said. 'Besides, I like dark chocolate.'

She grinned. 'Of course you do. *La nuage.*'

'It's *le*, not *la*,' he said, grinning back. 'And probably that should be *le nuage d'orage*—a storm cloud. Because of course we surly Parisians will always correct your grammar and your vocabulary.'

'Actually, joking apart, I *want* you to correct my grammar,' she said. 'It helps me learn. Anyway, you're not being surly, right now. You're smiling.'

'It's you,' he said, shocked to realise that it was true. Her company had made him feel composed again. 'Thank you. For taking the shadows away. I don't know how you did it.'

She gave him a look that made his blood heat. 'I believe it's what little rays of sunshine are supposed to do.'

Right at that moment, he wanted to pull her into his arms and prove to her that he did like sweet—at least, if it was going to involve kissing her. But that wasn't their deal. She'd offered him friendship, and that was probably more than he deserved. 'Hmm,' he said, and sipped his coffee.

CHAPTER FOUR

GERI CONTINUED TO enjoy her first week at the zoo. Thankfully the okapi didn't need surgery—the X-ray showed that the problem was an infection which would be easily cleared up with antibiotics—but they did need to operate on a lemur who'd had a fight with another lemur in the enclosure, and needed sutures in the cut across his palm.

'Your stitching's very neat,' Antoine said as she finished the last dissolvable stitch.

'It needs to be. I don't want to leave him a place where he can open up that wound and we have to restitch it,' she said. 'I've had to do that before with a dog after I'd removed a strawberry lump from her leg; the owners didn't keep quite a close enough eye on her, and she took the stitches out that evening.'

'Did you work mainly with small animals before you switched to zoo medicine?' Antoine asked.

'No. Farm animals.' And she needed to head him off that subject. She didn't want to think about sheep—or the baby that would've been a toddler now. 'Once our lemur's round from the anaesthetic and recovered, what's next today?' she asked brightly.

'Bloods from Bianca,' he said. 'I'm keeping an eye on her kidneys.'

Geri knew that kidney disease, particularly in older animals, was one of the leading causes of death in tigers. 'How long has she had a kidney problem?'

'About a year,' he said. 'We noticed she was becoming a bit lethargic and spending less time outdoors, and her appetite decreased. The blood tests showed that she had kidney disease, but she's responded well to medication.'

Geri could see that Antoine was concerned, and she remembered him admitting that Bianca was his favourite animal at the zoo. 'How old is she?'

'She's fifteen now,' he said, 'which is nearly twice as old as she'd live to be in the wild. We're keeping a close eye on her and making sure she's comfortable—and that means regular blood tests to see how she's doing.'

Once the lemur was in recovery under the watchful eye of his keeper, they headed for the tiger enclosure, where Antoine introduced her to Belle, the senior carnivore keeper. 'Belle's been training all the tigers so we can handle them for routine vaccinations, health checks and blood draws—we like to avoid anaesthetics where we can, to keep the risks lower,' he told Geri. 'And it's good that we can see their gaits close up if we're concerned there might be an issue with a paw or a muscle—they'll walk steadily up and down next to the glass, meaning we can study them, and they'll offer a paw or a belly if we need a closer look.'

'And you trained them to do all that?' Geri asked Belle.

'As part of the team, yes. It takes anything from a couple of months to a couple of years to get to that level, depending on the tiger,' Belle said. 'Obviously we can't go in with the big cats like you would with a pet dog. We train them by capturing their behaviour and using positive reinforcement. When they're sitting, we'll say "sit", use the bridge word of "good" so they have a sound to associate with what we want them to do, and give them a treat immediately. They pick it up pretty quickly. We work up to "down", "up" and "roll over"—it's mimicking natural behaviour rather than doing tricks to entertain visitors, because they'll roll in scent markers anyway. Training is good mental stimulation for our cats, too.'

'Enrichment's always a good thing,' Geri agreed.

Belle stood at the wire link fence and called, 'Bianca!'

'She comes to her name?' Geri asked, surprised.

'Wait and see,' Belle said with a smile.

A few moments later, the white tigress came over to them at the wire mesh and made a soft 'brr' sound.

'Hello, gorgeous girl.' Belle gave the tigress a chunk of meat on the end of a stick.

'Hello, Bianca,' Antoine said, and mimicked the 'brr' sound.

To Geri's amazement, the tiger made the noise again, as if she were talking back to Antoine. 'I thought they only chuffed like that to greet other tigers?' she asked.

'And to the keepers and people they know, here,' Antoine said. 'I guess that makes us honorary tigers.'

The slight glint of mischief in his eye told her that he remembered she'd said he was like a panda and a tortoise, the evening before. Now he was adding a third animal to the descriptions. He was definitely as wary as a tiger, she thought. But the fact that a wild animal clearly trusted him so much…did that mean maybe she could trust him with her innermost secrets and open up to him, the way he had with her?

'Bianca, down,' Belle said.

Bianca lay down at the command, exactly like a dog

would, with her head facing Belle, and Belle gave her another treat. 'Good girl.'

The position meant that the tigress's tail was next to a small inspection hatch in the fence that Antoine could unlock; he used a snake hook to bring her tail safely through the gap, and again Geri admired the way he handled the animal, calm and confident. Antoine Bouvier was definitely the reliable type.

'Good girl, Bianca,' Belle said again, giving the tigress another piece of meat.

'She's really good about having the blood taken,' Antoine said.

'How do you train a tiger not to mind having bloods done?' Geri asked.

'We start by feeling the end of the tail gently, and then work all the way up from the end of the tail to the base,' he explained. 'When they're comfortable with that, we use a little bit of pressure with our fingertips; then we progress to using a small needle, and finally work our way up to a larger gauge—the sort for taking bloods.'

'We pay attention to how the tiger reacts to each change; if they twitch or flinch or walk away, we take it back a notch and keep trying until they're comfortable with the new procedure,' Belle added.

'And there's a command Belle didn't mention—"open". It means we can do a visual check of their teeth,' Antoine said.

He used alcohol on a wipe to disinfect the tigress's tail and felt for the vein; gently, he said, '*Poussée*, Bianca,' and Belle gave the tigress a treat as Antoine drew the blood sample.

'Good girl,' he said when he'd finished, and this time Antoine was the one to give her the treat at the end.

'That's really incredible,' Geri said. He clearly had a close bond with the tiger, and she couldn't quite get over the way the tiger had responded to him.

The tigress drew her tail back in through the inspection hatch, which Antoine closed behind her and then Belle locked it.

'All done,' Antoine said, and gave the tiger a final treat.

Bianca gave another soft chuff, then got to her feet and padded away.

'I really hope those bloods turn out to be the same as last time,' Belle said, looking worried. 'That she hasn't deteriorated even a little bit.'

'I know,' Antoine said. He gave Belle a sympathetic smile, then took a deep breath. 'I'm not ready to say goodbye to our old girl just yet, either.'

Belle's eyes glittered with tears. 'I wish…' She shook herself. 'I know we're not supposed to get attached to the animals. But how can we not? They're part of our family.' She gave a wry smile. 'Though I guess you wouldn't want a tiger weighing one hundred and fifty kilograms sitting on your lap like a tabby.'

'That's assuming you had a sofa big enough for a tiger to sprawl across in the first place,' Antoine said.

And, just for a moment, Geri could imagine the two of them sprawled on Antoine's sofa. How it would feel to lie in his arms, talking sweet nothings and stealing kisses… She shook herself. This was crazy. She couldn't let herself act on the attraction. And right now she should be focused on the tiger, not on Antoine.

'I'll let you know as soon as I get the results, Belle,' Antoine added.

He was quiet all the way to the lab, and Geri judged this wasn't the right time for small talk; he, too, was clearly worried about the tiger. He handed in the sample to the lab team and asked them to let him know when the results were ready, then turned to Geri. 'Time to check on the pandas.'

Both bears were back to their normal selves after the anaesthetic, and Pierre reported no change in Zhen's behaviour. There were no changes of hormones in her urine samples, either.

'Now we have to wait and see. The cub could arrive at any time in the next three to six months, if she did conceive on Tuesday,' Antoine said.

'I do hope it's not six months,' Geri said feelingly.

'If Zhen's definitely pregnant but hasn't given birth by the time your secondment ends, we'll sort something out to make sure you're here and you don't miss the birth,' Antoine said. 'Even if you have to take leave from your zoo.'

'Thank you.' She smiled at him. 'Having been there at the start of the procedure, I really want to be there at the end.'

'That's totally understandable,' he said.

'There was one thing I've meant to ask you all week, but I forgot in the excitement of the pandas. Do I need to start looking for a flat myself, or is that something Marie's team will handle?' she asked.

'Marie's team should be sorting it out for you. But there's no rush for you to move out,' he said. 'I don't mind you staying. Actually, if you're settled here, I'm happy for you to stay for the whole six months.'

'Really? That's so kind. I'd like that. Thank you,' she said. 'Though I think I should pay you rent.'

'There's really no need. I don't have a mortgage,' he said. 'And I was thinking, too. It's said that one of the best ways to see Paris in the evening is on a river cruise. I could book us a slot for tonight, if you like; then you'll get to see all the major landmarks lit up. Sunset's at half-past eight; you'll see the City of Light at her best.'

'That'd be wonderful,' she said. 'I'd really like that.'

'Good. I'll book the tickets. Now, it's lunchtime for you,' he said, glancing at his watch, 'and I have some paperwork that needs sorting.'

'You're not going to join us?'

'No. Paperwork is a hazard of my job. It's fine. I'll eat a sandwich at my desk. But you need a break.' He ushered her towards the staff canteen.

Geri had to damp down the flicker of disappointment that he wasn't going to join her and the rest of the team for lunch, but she enjoyed chatting to Valerie, Émilie and Jacques. The rest of the afternoon was taken up doing rounds and treating minor issues, and then she met Antoine back at his office.

'Perfect timing,' Antoine said. 'We've got enough time to grab something to eat on the way to the boats.'

'How much do I owe you for the tickets?' she asked.

'It's fine. My treat.'

'Then I'll buy dinner,' she said. And, once they'd boarded the boat, she bought them both a glass of champagne. 'I'm seeing Paris by night for the first time. This deserves proper fizz,' she said.

This wasn't a real date; Antoine was simply joining her in the sightseeing. But, as Antoine clinked his glass against hers and said, *'Santé,'* her fingers brushed briefly against his and a frisson ran through her.

Oh, help.

She'd dated a few times, since the break-up of her marriage, but nobody had made her want to take the relationship any further than friendship. Antoine, both as her host and as her senior colleague, was off limits. Why did she feel this strange pull towards him? Why did she notice that, close up, there were little gold flecks in his dark eyes? Why did his smile make her feel as fizzy as the champagne they were drinking?

'Tell me what I'm seeing,' she encouraged him, wanting to be distracted from her thoughts.

'Right now we're going past the Île Saint-Louis,' he said. 'You can see Notre Dame on the next island; it isn't open for visitors yet, following the fire, but there's something on the Île Saint-Louis I'd like to show you later.'

'Any clues?'

'Something,' he said, 'I know you'll love.'

She groaned. 'Which tells me almost nothing.'

There was a glint of mischief in his eyes. Geri tried to tell herself that it was the sparkling wine making her feel slightly giddy, but she knew it wasn't: it was Antoine's nearness. For pity's sake. Neither of them needed any complications. She was here only for a few months, and he was clearly still nursing a broken heart after his fiancée dumped him on their wedding day.

He talked her through the history of the opulent buildings of the Hotel de Ville, the city hall, as they went past. 'And you were here the other day,' he said as they reached the next building complex.

'The Louvre,' she said, enjoying the way the elegant façades were lit up.

'And there's Place de la Concorde. It's the biggest square in Paris,' he said. 'It's pretty now, with the fountains and the obelisk.'

She remembered what she'd read about the square. 'Isn't that where Marie-Antoinette…?' she began, then winced.

'And more than a thousand others.' He nodded. 'The obelisk was placed on the site of the guillotine.'

'It must have been terrifying in Paris during the Revolution,' she said.

'Not a time I would've liked to live through,' he agreed. 'There's the Petit Palais—you might want to add that to your list of art galleries, though it's worth a visit for the buildings themselves, if you like architecture.' He smiled. 'And now, on our left—something you've been waiting for.'

She looked up at the Eiffel Tower, all lit up in gold. 'It's amazing. With those lights, you can see how intricate the ironwork is.' She glanced at the top of the tower, where a beam of light stretched out across the city and swept round. 'I know it's touristy, but it's—oh!' she exclaimed in delight as the tower started sparkling. 'That's spectacular!'

'It sparkles like this for five minutes on the hour, every hour, until the tower closes to visitors a few minutes before midnight,' he said. 'The sparkling light show was originally set up for the Year 2000, and it was meant to be temporary, but it was so popular that the authorities decided to keep it.'

'I need to film this to show my family. Can I be rude?' She took her phone out and took a few seconds' video of the sparkling tower. 'This is even better than I expected.' And part of that was due to the company, though she didn't quite dare say as much.

As the boat went under another bridge, he said, 'This is the Île aux Cygnes.'

'Island of swans?' she checked.

'It's not named after actual swans, as far as I know,'

he said. 'But there's something else famous here—the Statue de la Liberté.'

She blinked as she saw the statue. 'Like the Statue of Liberty in New York.'

'It's a quarter-size replica of the one that France gave to the United States,' he said. 'The United States gave this one to France to commemorate the centenary of the French Revolution.'

'I had no idea there was a Statue of Liberty in Paris.'

'Actually, there are seven of them,' he said, 'though this one's the biggest.'

She looked at him with narrowed eyes. 'Did you know that before this week, or did you look it up in a tourist guide?'

He laughed. 'Well spotted. As you said, you never get to know your own city until you show someone else round it. I checked out the points of interest on the river trip while I was eating my lunch, and a page came up talking about all the Statues of Liberty.'

Was researching touristy things the paperwork he'd referred to, earlier, rather than something for the zoo? Geri was touched that he'd made the effort, though part of her felt guilty that he hadn't had a proper break because of her.

'I made a list,' he said, 'in case you wanted to know about the others.'

'Yes, please,' she said.

He took out his phone, opened the notes app and handed the phone to her. Again, when his fingers touched hers, every nerve-ending in her skin tingled, and she nearly dropped the phone.

'Some of the places where you can find them will already be on your list,' he said. 'The Musée d'Orsay, and the Eiffel Tower.'

'You're telling me there's a Statue of Liberty on the Eiffel Tower?' She smiled. 'I think you might be teasing me.'

'Not on the tower itself,' he said, but on a *péniche* nearby.'

'What's a *péniche*?' she asked.

'A houseboat or barge,' he said. 'And there's one Statue of Liberty on that list I'd like to see for myself because I had no idea it even existed—it's a tiny, tiny version peeping out of a centaur's breastplate on another statue.'

'Only in Paris,' she said.

'Only in Paris,' he echoed, and grinned.

When he wasn't being serious and looking slightly forbidding, Antoine was utterly gorgeous; that grin made her feel as if the whole evening had lit up.

'You can't quite see them from here, but I would definitely suggest adding the Jardins du Luxembourg to your list,' he said. 'Actually, all the parks in Paris are very pretty at this time of year, but that one's a bit special.'

'How would you recommend visiting everywhere I want to see?' she asked.

'We could break it down by arrondissement,' he said. 'Start at the first, and spiral out. Or buy a tourist map, ring everything you want to see and then make a list of places that are near to each other.'

'You work things out logically, then,' she said.

'It means you'll be able to make the most of your free time; but being organised doesn't mean that you can't still be spontaneous. I was thinking, we could visit something that's on your list, and then go off the beaten track and see what we find around it.'

'That sounds good to me,' she said. 'How long have you lived in Paris, Antoi— Ant?' she corrected herself, remembering that he'd given her permission to use the shorter version of his name.

'Since I was eighteen and came to study veterinary medicine.' He spread his hands. 'That's about fifteen years.'

Making him three years older than her, she calculated.

'I know some parts of the city much better than others—the fifth arrondissement because I lived there as a student, Montmartre because of my grandparents and obviously I live there now, and the tenth because I lived there after graduation.'

With his ex? Though it felt too crass to ask.

'What I found today intrigued me. I'm looking forward to learning more about the city I don't know,' he said.

'You really don't have to do the super-touristy bits with me if you don't want to,' she said.

He spread his hands. 'This would count as super-touristy. I've never been on one of these cruises before, and I'm not sure I know anyone who has.'

She grimaced. 'Sorry.'

'No need to apologise. It's surprising, seeing bits of the city I thought I knew well but from a different angle,' he said. 'We can climb the Eiffel Tower—though it's your choice whether we walk up the steps to first stage or take the lift all the way. It's a bit of a trek.'

'Given that I plan to try crème brûlée in as many places as possible,' she said, 'I think I probably ought to walk up.'

'D'accord,' he said. 'And here's the Musée d'Orsay.'

'You can really see it used to be a railway station,'

she said, looking at the beautiful building. 'And I love that clock.'

'If we go to the top floor, we can look out at Paris through the clock—it's an iconic view,' he said.

'I'd love that. And I can see why Paris is called the City of Light—all the buildings are brightly lit, and I love the way the lights are all reflected in the Seine,' she said.

'As a surly Parisian,' he said, 'I need to correct you a little. It's actually because Paris was a centre of scientific ideas and enlightenment in the late eighteenth century.'

'Light and enlightenment,' she said.

'Though Paris was also the first city to introduce street lighting,' he said. 'And there are twenty thousand bulbs on the Eiffel Tower alone. I guess the popular view has a point.'

'Twenty thousand bulbs? No wonder it sparkles,' she said. 'But Paris is a beautiful city. Thank you very much for organising this.'

'My pleasure. I'm enjoying it, too.'

Later that evening, Ant sat in his study and thought about it. When Geri had suggested that he join her in sightseeing, saying that she could maybe teach him to see the city with new eyes, he'd been sceptical. But even the little bit they'd seen together tonight had felt different. He'd grown so used to the Eiffel Tower that he didn't really see it any more; but, thinking how much Geri might enjoy it, he'd chosen the cruise that would go past the tower on the hour and they'd see the sparkling up close. The delight on her face had been his reward; but he'd also seen the illuminations of the stunning Parisian icon through her eyes, as if for the first time, and it had felt magical.

Sipping champagne on a Seine river cruise was something he'd never thought of doing. If he was honest, he would probably have sneered at the suggestion as being something for tourists. But, with Geri, it had been different. Fun. Carefree. And it had felt as if the lights of the city had penetrated the dark cloud that was normally wrapped round him.

He was going to have to be careful. Geri was only here on secondment. She was his colleague, and his house-guest—even if it was only temporary. He couldn't risk acting on the attraction he felt towards her and getting involved with her as more than just her friend; there were too many barriers. He'd need to be really careful. *Sensible.*

On Friday and Saturday, they were both busy at the zoo, but they'd planned to visit Monet's house at Giverny on Sunday. Antoine had suggested going early, to miss most of the crowds, and drove them out to the little village where Monet had once lived.

'Do you like simply looking at art,' he asked, 'or do you sketch or paint?'

'I can barely draw a straight line with a ruler,' she said cheerfully. 'My worst times in class as a student were when I was asked to draw things. I'm glad I don't have to do that any more.' She smiled. 'What about you?'

'Drawing didn't worry me. Though my tutors all complained about my handwriting,' he admitted ruefully.

'Medics—human or otherwise—are *supposed* to have terrible handwriting,' she said. 'Do you like art?'

'Some,' he said. 'I'm not keen on the really abstract stuff. But I like Monet. There's something about the way he paints light and water that's really soothing.' He'd never really thought about that before; Geri was definitely teaching him to look at things in a different way.

'That's what I like about his paintings, too,' she said. 'I'm really looking forward to seeing the gardens. Apparently he planted like a painter rather than a gardener—he was way ahead of his time.'

'You like gardens?'

'My mum's a keen gardener,' she said. 'And she loves visiting stately homes, but she goes to see the gardens rather than the houses. Not to mention the Chelsea Flower Show. She watches every gardening programme going, and Alex—my little sister—and I buy her an annual membership to Kew Gardens and to the Royal Horticultural Society so she gets her garden fix whenever she wants to.' She smiled. 'She's hugely envious that we're going to Giverny. I need to take a million pictures of the tulips for her.'

Ant liked the fact that Geri seemed close to her family, though at the same time it made him feel guilty that he didn't let his own family as close as he knew they wanted to be. He didn't know the circumstances around Geri's divorce, but she didn't seem to let the sadness of a breakup affect her the same way that he had.

His own mother loved flowers, too. Maybe he should send her some, 'just because'. It might help to bridge the gap he'd put between them.

When he parked the car and they headed for the entrance to Giverny, Geri's eyes were sparkling and her face was all lit up. 'I'm looking forward to this,' she said.

'Me, too,' he said, surprised to realise that he was. He'd always thought of visiting gardens as a pastime for the middle-aged, but maybe he was wrong about that.

'The spring flowers here are meant to be amazing,'

she said, 'and then in the summer there are roses and the water lilies will be out.'

It sounded as if she'd been torn between visiting now and visiting later in the summer. 'Maybe we can come back again when the roses and water lilies are out,' he suggested. 'On a weekday, when it'll be a bit less busy.'

'I'd really like that,' she said, and her smile made him feel warm all over.

Once inside the grounds, they headed for the water gardens first. They took the underpass to the other side of the road, and emerged to be greeted with purple azaleas in full flower.

'This is lovely,' Geri said.

Not only lovely, he amended mentally; it was an incredibly romantic setting, and the light in this part of the Seine valley seemed to have a special soft quality to it. The path went alongside a meandering stream, and the birds were singing their heads off. His hand brushed against hers, and a zing of anticipation went all the way through him. It would be all too easy to accidentally on purpose let his hand touch hers again, then for his fingers to curve gently against hers and slide up until he was holding her hand.

He managed to resist the temptation as they walked past the bamboos, hearing the stream bubbling and the wind swishing through the leaves. Then they turned a corner and the famous green Japanese bridge was right in front of them; the arches above the bridge were covered in gnarled ropes of wisteria, the leaves bright green and the flowers in bud, and the willow trees drooped next to the bridge.

Geri gave a sharp intake of breath; when he looked at her, he could see a tear running down her cheek. He took her hand and squeezed it. 'Are you OK, *mon petit rayon*?' The nickname—and the possessive—slipped out before he could stop them.

She sniffed. 'Sorry. They're happy tears. I can't believe I'm really here and actually seeing this.'

'Stand in the middle,' he said, 'and I'll go a little further along the bank and take your picture.'

She did as he directed, leaning on the bridge and smiling; for one crazy moment, it felt as if he was taking a touristy photo of his girlfriend, and he couldn't help wondering why her ex had let someone as lovely as Geraldine Milligan go.

Not that it was any of his business, he reminded himself, and went back to join her.

'I'll send the picture over to you later,' he said.

'Thank you. Do you want me to take one of you?'

'It's fine,' he said, smiling at her. 'Let's walk round the lily pond. The lily pads look like little islands—and I can't believe how clear the water is.'

She stopped every few metres to take pictures of the flowers surrounding the pond, the irises and tulips and little white pom-pom daisies.

At the far end of the pond, she took photographs of the bridge under the willows. 'That's going to be top of my social media pictures today,' she said happily.

Ant had teased Geri about being a little ray of sunshine, but that was exactly who she was, he thought. Her joy in her surroundings was infectious, and when they went back over into the main garden he could see the same magical things that she did.

'The whole garden's like a vast Impressionist painting. All those hundreds and hundreds of tulips—each one looks like a dot of paint on a canvas,' she said.

That would never have occurred to Ant before, but now she'd said it he could see it for himself. The tulips of all colours, the pansies and the daisies, together made up a whole that was more than their constituent parts. 'And those jonquils under the apple trees—they look like clouds drifting across the grass,' he said.

The air was sweet with the blossom of the cherry trees and apple trees, and everywhere was a riot of floral joy: a froth of forget-me-nots with bright red pops of tulips, and beds laid out like a painting box of whites and purples. The scent and the vision, combined with the birdsong, made him feel dizzy; he wanted to sweep Geri into his arms and kiss her until she was as dizzy as he was.

He managed to keep a grip on himself—just—and walked round the garden with her, letting her chatter about the flowers. But he still couldn't help wondering: *What if?*

Geri knew she was talking too much. But Giverny really was overwhelming to all the senses; the sound of the birds, the gorgeous colours of the flowers, the irresistible lure of touching some of the soft petals as she stooped to take a photograph for her mum, the scent of the blossom—so strong, in places, that she could practically taste it.

More than that, though, was Antoine's nearness.

When she'd been moved to tears by the sheer beauty of the bridge over the lily pond, he'd taken her hand and squeezed it to comfort her. His touch had made every nerve in her body shimmer, and she'd been oh, so close to turning towards him, wrapping her arms round him and resting her head against his shoulder.

This was exactly the kind of place where you'd walk hand in hand with the one you loved. Mark would've hated the way the plants spilled over the edges of their borders—if he'd visited a garden for a Sunday afternoon picnic with her family, he'd only really liked the super-formal type with box hedging and everything in its precise place. Despite his roof garden, she didn't think Antoine was the garden type, but he seemed to understand what she liked about this place: the light and the way the colours blended.

Her hand brushed against his several times as they walked through the gardens, and she had to make a conscious effort not to link her fingers with his. He'd been kind enough to drive her here, and he'd agreed to help her with her Paris list; but she knew that friendship was all he was offering. He clearly still wasn't quite over being dumped on his wedding day—an experience that would break anyone's heart but must have been so much harder for Antoine, given that his ex had fallen for his brother.

They walked under the wide archways where the roses would spill down in late summer, and headed for the house with its pink walls and bright green paintwork. Inside, the rooms were light and bright. 'I love this room,' she said when they walked into the bright yellow dining room. 'I could imagine living here.' She loved the kitchen next door, too, with the blue and white tiles on the wall in sharp contrast to the red floor and the copper pans hanging down from the shelf on their hooks. 'I could imagine cooking here—though I'm not sure I'd enjoy having to black-lead the range.'

'Actually, it's not that much of a chore,' he said. 'You simply squeeze out a bit of paste onto a rag, rub it over the cast iron, leave it to dry and then buff it with a shoe brush or a soft cloth.'

She blinked. 'Are you telling me *you've* black-leaded a range?'

He smiled. 'A fireplace, but it's the same technique. When we were small, the three of us used to help my grandmother's housekeeper. Obviously we ended up covered in the stuff, and she probably had to go round after us and do the bits we missed, but I remember it being fun. And then she'd bake us madeleines and we'd eat them warm from the oven.'

She smiled back. 'Very Proustian. I'm also a bit surprised you like them, given that cakes are sweet.'

'The ones we ate as a child were sweet. Nowadays, if I ate them, I'd choose very lemony ones, preferably on the sharp side,' he said.

She was glad that his childhood memories hadn't been ruined. Though she couldn't shift the fact that he'd talked about the three of them with such affection. 'Were you very close to your sister and brother when you were small?'

His expression clouded. 'It was a long time ago.'

'I can't imagine life without my sister in it,' she said. 'We fell out a few times, in our teenage years, but we always made up.'

'What happened between Jean-Luc and me was a bit more than a teenage squabble,' he said coolly.

'I know,' she said. 'If I were in your shoes—if Alex had fallen in love with Mark—I would've been really hurt and angry at first, but then I would've missed her dreadfully.'

'Even if she'd told you on your wedding day?' he asked.

She nodded. 'Alex is my best friend as well as my sister. We message or talk every single day we don't see each other.'

'Jean-Luc was my best friend, too,' he admitted. 'He trained as a vet. We were going to set up a practice together back in the Loire valley—he's three years older than I am—only I fell in love with zoo medicine. I told him how I felt, torn between wanting to support him and wanting to work in a different area, and he was the one who told me to follow my heart, apply to the zoo and stay in Paris.'

'Do you miss him?' she asked softly.

If anyone else had asked him that question, Ant would've given an abrasive reply. But with Geri it felt natural to talk about Jean-Luc. Because she was a stranger? Or because there was a connection developing between them? 'Yes, I do,' he admitted finally. 'I used to follow him about when I was small—as did Mélie. We called ourselves the Three Musketeers, and one of the vineyard dogs would be co-opted as D'Artagnan. Or one of the cats, if the dogs got bored.'

She took his hand and squeezed it; this time, Ant realised it was a touch of support, not of pity, and he didn't pull away.

'And you haven't seen him or talked to him since the day he left?' she asked.

'No.' He blew out a breath. 'I don't even know where to start.'

'New baby, new start?' she asked. 'I know she's the baby you should've had—but, the way I see it, babies are there to be treasured by everyone.'

There was an odd note in her voice, as if she was trying to be brave about something. But, before Ant could ask her, she added, 'And I bet he misses you just as much. Plus he must feel guilty about hurting you in the first place, and worrying that he'll hurt you even more if he makes the first move—or that you'll reject him.'

That hadn't occurred to Ant before—that Jean-Luc might be scared of rejection. 'Maybe,' he said. But he needed time to think about it a bit more. 'Shall we look at the next room?'

The expression on her face told him that she knew he was avoiding the subject—but also that she understood.

Once they'd seen everything in the house and Geri had bought some seeds for her mum and postcards in the gift shop, they took a last wander round the lily pond, and then made a detour to the nearby town of Vernon.

They ate a quick lunch of a galette with a green salad in a bistro overlooking the Old Mill—a half-timbered building straddling two piers of the ancient bridge—and when Geri looked it up on her phone she was delighted to discover that Monet had painted it.

'Now for some spontaneity,' Antoine said. 'Shall we see where the road takes us?'

It turned out to be a ruined castle, with amazing views of the Seine valley, and Geri enjoyed every second exploring with Antoine.

Back in Montmartre, he said, 'I can cook for us. Or we can go in search of crème brûlée.'

'Did you have somewhere in mind?'

'I do,' he said.

It was a small traditional bistro in one of the cobbled squares; inside, there were small tables covered with checked red and white tablecloths, bentwood chairs, and framed paintings of Montmartre on the walls. Better still, there was a grand piano in the centre of the room, and they were treated to live music. Best of all, crème brûlée flavoured with orange blossom was on the menu.

'This is perfect—it's so Parisian,' she said.

He looked pleased. 'I'm glad you like it. By the way, do you know where the word "bistro" comes from?'

'No. Enlighten me,' she said.

The glint in his eyes told her he realised she was riffing on their conversation about the City of Light, and appreciated it. 'It's probably an urban legend but, during the war with Russia in 1814, the Cossack soldiers used to shout "bistro"—or at least something that sounded like it—to make the waiters hurry up with their drinks.'

'Good story,' she said. 'I thought it'd be called after a particular dish or something like that.'

'Or a *bistraud*, an assistant wine-seller,' he said.

This was yet another side of Antoine: the urbane Parisian who took delight in wordplay. The more Geri got to know him, the more she liked him.

The steak frites were good, but the dessert was perfect. 'Is this the best crème brûlée in Paris?' she asked.

'I wouldn't know,' he said. 'But my grandmother always ordered it here. I'd guess it's one of the best.'

'I'm definitely bringing my sister here,' she said. 'Although it would be rude not to try other places.'

He laughed, and she couldn't take her eyes off him. When he was relaxed like this, Antoine was mesmerising.

'I've really enjoyed today,' she said when they got back to his apartment.

'So have I,' he said.

She was pleased that he didn't use the excuse of paperwork to back away; instead, they ended up chatting about films they'd both enjoyed. And although she'd only known him for a week, it felt like much longer.

Paris, she thought, had been one of her better decisions.

CHAPTER FIVE

IF ANYONE HAD told Ant a few days ago that not only would he be happy to join his houseguest in visiting tourist attractions in Paris, he'd actually suggest some himself, he would've scoffed.

But here he was, leaving work at a normal time on a Monday afternoon instead of finding an excuse to stay at his office or double-check on a sick animal he'd already seen earlier that day, simply because it stopped him going back to an empty apartment and brooding. And it was all because of Geri and her 'fake it until you make it' idea: because he was quickly discovering that she was right. She'd helped him remember that he lived in one of the most beautiful cities in the world, one full of light and pretty parks and stunning architecture. More than that, she'd made him realise he could still feel that frisson of attraction—something he'd thought he'd lost when Céline had left him.

That evening, they went to the Parc Monceau and its pond with the beautiful colonnade, before visiting the Arc de Triomphe to watch the daily ceremony of the flame of remembrance being rekindled on the Tomb of the Unknown Soldier, after wreaths were laid by veterans.

'It's good to pay respects,' she said softly, when the ceremony had ended. 'And something like this makes me count my blessings. How lucky I am not to have lost someone I loved to war.'

He'd never really thought about that before. 'Yes,' he said.

They climbed the spiral staircase to the top of the arch. 'Twelve roads leading off one roundabout?' she asked, looking at the traffic. 'I'd imagine driving round this roundabout is an experience.'

'That's one word for it,' he said wryly. They lingered at the top and he pointed out some of the buildings she'd already visited, and others that he knew were on her list. Then they strolled down the Champs-Élysées, window-shopping and people-watching, before grabbing a bite to eat and giving Geri a chance to try more crème brûlée.

'It's nice—but not quite as good as the one I had at the weekend in Montmartre,' was her verdict. 'I think that one's going to be my benchmark.'

'It's a tough job, finding the best dessert,' he said. 'I probably ought to point out all the different Parisian specialities you're missing with this insistence on crème brûlée.'

'You could,' she said, 'but it's my sister's favourite, and it's my sworn duty to find her the best one in Paris. I'm being a Knight of the Round Table.' She gestured to the table they were sitting at—which was indeed round.

It was utterly ridiculous, but she made him smile. 'I give in,' he said. 'The quest for the crème brûlée continues...'

On Tuesday, at the usual morning meeting going through the daybook, Belle brought up the subject of one of the tigers. 'I was doing some routine training with Sabu yesterday afternoon, and I noticed a crack in one of his canines.' She handed her phone to Ant. 'I got Rico to take the snap while I asked Sabu to do an "open".'

'Is he eating normally? Is he showing any signs of pain?' Geri asked.

'He's eating normally,' Belle confirmed, 'and he doesn't seem in pain.'

Ant made a note. 'But this isn't something we want to leave,' he said, 'because I don't want to risk that tooth breaking nearer to the gumline and him ending up with an infection. Can you send me the picture? I'll send it over to Léa—the dentist,' he explained quickly to Geri, 'and talk to her about it this morning. Then we'll decide the action plan.'

'OK. Sending it now,' Belle said.

'Got it,' Antoine said, a couple of moments later. 'I'll send it to Léa before I do the rounds.'

Once they'd finished going through the daybook, Antoine shared out the tasks and sent the information over to the dentist. He'd almost finished checking on a frog with a lacerated leg when Léa called back to discuss the case.

At lunchtime, he went in search of Belle; luckily, as she was with Geri, he didn't have to find her afterwards and repeat himself.

'Léa's had a look at the photo,' he said, 'and she recommends doing a root canal filling and repairing Sabu's tooth. She can fit us in tomorrow. It's the usual drill for anaesthetics.'

'No food or drink after six o'clock this evening,' Belle said, 'and keep him separated from the others overnight.'

'Perfect,' Ant said. 'Geri, I'll need you to help with the operation tomorrow morning. Can I put you on airway management?'

'Of course,' she said. 'Does Léa work only on animal dentistry?'

'Human as well,' Ant said. He remembered what she'd said about her ex being a dentist, but it wouldn't be kind to bring that up in front of someone else. Though he brought it up later that evening. 'You said your ex was a dentist. Did he work on animals as well as humans?'

Geri shook her head. 'We never worked together. Mark wasn't a big fan of animals.'

'Forgive me for being rude, but I don't understand why someone not keen on animals would even date a vet, let alone marry one.'

She nodded. 'With hindsight, I agree. But I suppose I always assumed that eventually we'd have children and get a dog and a cat.'

'You didn't talk about it?'

'We did. Neither of us wanted pets when we met—we were in our last year at uni—and it wouldn't have been fair to have a dog or cat when we were both working long hours.' There was a tiny pause. 'We thought we didn't want children, either.'

She'd said before that she and her ex had wanted different things. He saw the little flicker of pain in her expression, and it made him wonder what had happened. Had she realised later that, actually, she did want children, but her ex hadn't changed his mind? But before he could ask anything else, she switched the subject to the tiger's operation.

He understood where she was coming from. Talking about the past made you wonder where it had all started going wrong—and how could you be sure it wouldn't go wrong if you tried being close to someone in the future?

* * *

On Wednesday morning, they made an operating table with hay bales and a tarpaulin in the enclosure next to Sabu's. 'I don't know how you do things in Cambridge, but it's easier to work on him here—plus there isn't a table big enough in the operating theatre complex, and also it means less time under anaesthetic,' Ant said.

'We do the same with the larger animals,' Geri said.

Léa, the dentist, arrived, and Ant introduced her to the team.

With the help of Belle, Sabu lay down to let Antoine anaesthetise him through the mesh wall.

'We're going to put bubble wrap mittens on him,' Ant said, 'because he can't regulate his own temperature during anaesthesia. We'll put a duvet on him as well.' Ten minutes after Sabu had gone under, he checked the tiger's level of anaesthesia. 'OK. Ready to intubate, Geri.'

Geri sprayed the tiger's throat, made sure his jaws were kept safely open so they wouldn't snap shut on the oxygen tube—or the dentist's hand—then skilfully intubated Sabu and listened to his chest. 'OK, I'm happy,' she said. 'Ready to move him.'

Ant appreciated her professional approach and lack of fuss. 'Let's go,' he said.

It took four of them to move the two-hundred-kilogram tiger safely to the table. Belle and one of the other keepers put the bubble wrap mittens on the tiger and covered him with the duvet, and then Léa began the operation.

'This is the closest I've ever been to a tiger, and I've never seen dental work done,' Geri said. 'I can't believe how long those canines are.'

'About ten centimetres,' Léa said. 'And the root's up

to six times longer than it is in a human tooth. Do you want me to talk through what I'm doing?'

'Yes, please,' Geri said.

'OK. I'm going to take off the tip of the tooth, then re-move the pulp and bacteria in the chamber of the middle of the tooth before packing it with inert material, then repairing the tip.'

Ant had seen similar procedures done, but it was still fascinating.

Geri kept a careful eye on the tiger's airway and stats, while Valerie recorded everything; and Ant kept an eye on the anaesthetic. The dentistry took three-quarters of an hour, and overall Sabu was under anaesthetic for two hours; there was a fine line between giving him enough anaesthetic that he didn't wake up during the operation, but not enough to stop him waking up again afterwards.

Once Léa had finished repairing the tooth, the team carried Sabu back to the enclosure and laid him on a bed of fresh straw; Geri removed the intubation and Ant reversed the anaesthesia. Within minutes, the tiger was back on his feet—a little bit wobbly, but able to walk over to the water trough.

'We'll do the usual post-anaesthesia protocol,' Belle said. 'We'll keep him on his own in the enclosure for the next twenty-four hours and monitor him one-to-one.'

'Any concerns, even if it's the middle of the night, call me,' Ant said.

By the middle of Thursday, Sabu had completely recov-ered from the operation and was eating and behaving normally again; Antoine and Belle were happy to let him re-join the other tigers in the main enclosure.

On Friday, Geri and Antoine had a day off, and they

headed to see the Monets at the Musée de l'Orangerie and the Musée D'Orsay.

It was as wonderful as she expected; but Ant surprised her when they stopped to admire van Gogh's *Starry Night Over the Rhône*. 'I love this painting,' she said to Antoine. 'It's much more peaceful than the other *Starry Night*. Here, it feels like a beautiful evening and he's caught the joy of the sparkling stars and the lights from the building reflected in the water.'

'That's very you,' he said. 'Seeing the sparkle.'

His smile made her catch her breath; he was definitely paying her a compliment rather than being snippy. Did that mean he was starting to see her as something other than his colleague or his friend? she wondered. Because she was definitely starting to feel that way about him— even though it was risky and the idea of trusting her heart to someone again terrified her. She knew Antoine wanted children; so did she. But what if she couldn't have them? The Q fever that had caused her miscarriage made everything that much more complicated. It was the thing that had stopped her moving on, and she still didn't know how to get past it.

She smiled back and kept the conversation light until they got to the top floor, where they found the clock and admired the views of Paris. Antoine was taking a snap of her by the huge glass clock when a tourist asked, 'Would you like me to take a picture of you and your partner together?'

Partner. Did they look like a couple? Could they be a couple? The possibility made all her senses hum. She liked Antoine—she more than liked the man she was getting to know—but did he feel the same? She glanced at him, only to see that he looked as flustered as she felt. Better to be sensible, then.

'We're just good friends,' she said with a smile, 'but yes, please.'

Just good friends.

Ant was shocked to realise that they *were* actually becoming good friends. He felt relaxed in Geri's company, and he enjoyed their differences as well as their similarities. He liked her calmness and common sense as a colleague, and the way she found the lightness in things.

He stood next to her with his arm round her shoulders and smiled for the camera. Holding her close like that felt unexpectedly natural, particularly when Geri relaxed against him. He could feel the warmth of her skin against his, smell the light sweet scent of her perfume, and for a moment it made him feel dizzy.

When was the last time he'd posed for a simple photograph?

It was unsettling, like it had been when he'd taken that snap of Geri on the bridge at Giverny and it had felt like taking a picture of his girlfriend. He hadn't dated since Céline had called off their wedding, and he didn't think he was ready to date anyone. But, if he did, he rather thought it would be someone like Geri Milligan.

Who was he trying to kid? He knew perfectly well it would be Geri herself. He liked her. He was attracted to her. But, although she was friendly and sweet and kind, he knew she believed in faking it until you made it. Her smiliness definitely hid something that she wasn't prepared to share with him. And he didn't have a clue how she really felt about him. How to get her to open up.

She nudged him. 'Hey, Monsieur le Nuage.'

He blinked. 'What?' Her phone was back in her hand, and he'd clearly been wool-gathering while she'd thanked the tourist for taking the snap.

'You're scowling.'

'Uh—I… Sorry.'

'Is it that bad, having your photograph taken?'

'No.' He stared at her, suddenly realising what she'd said. 'Did you just call me…?'

She grinned. 'Well, hey. You call me *le petit rayon.*'

'That's fair.' He couldn't stop himself smiling back. But at the same time, it made him think. If she was sunshine and he was clouds…did it mean they were too different for anything to happen between them?

And why was he thinking about dating, anyway? That wasn't what she'd agreed to. She'd agreed to be his friend. And he needed a friend more than he needed a romance—didn't he? Except Geri was the first person he'd really connected with in two years. Someone he felt able to open up to. And he wanted more.

'You're thinking again, Ant,' she said softly. 'Stop. Just *be.* Or do you need coffee?'

'I'm a Parisian. Of course I need coffee,' he said, glad of the excuse to change the soundtrack in his head. 'Actually, if we can get a table, how about having lunch somewhere famous—where Picasso, Hemingway and Sartre used to hang out?'

'That sounds great,' she said.

After a *croque monsieur* and coffee at Les Deux Magots—though, to Geri's regret, no crème brûlée—Antoine led her through to the Latin Quarter. 'It's the second-oldest district in Paris,' he said.

'Where does the name come from?' she asked.

'The university—because the lessons were all in Latin,' he said.

'And this is where you were a student?'

'Yes.' He took her through one narrow cobbled street and pointed to a tall building. 'I used to live on the top floor. My room was the third window from the left.' He smiled. 'The roof leaked whenever it rained, and it was way too hot in summer, but I have happy memories—and I'm still friends with my old flatmates.' Though he'd made excuses not to see them, too, since the mess of his wedding day, and lately they'd given up inviting him out.

'You didn't live with your grandparents?'

He wrinkled his nose. 'Grandmère and Grandpère did offer to let me live with them, because it would save me money, but I wanted to be like all the other students.'

'I get that,' she said. 'I would've been the same. Though it's pretty round here—all those tall windows and their wrought-iron balconies stuffed with plants, the blossom on the trees, and the little bistro tables under the awnings outside the cafés. It's nothing like my student accommodation. We had soulless modern blocks.'

'We have student accommodation like that in Paris, too,' he said. 'But the people you meet make the worst flats bearable.' He'd forgotten that. She'd helped him remember: and maybe he could help her, too. 'Were you in the same hall of residence as your ex?'

She shook her head. 'One of my friends was in a band with one of his friends. We met while we watched them play in a tiny room above a pub, and when we all went for chips afterwards Mark and I ended up talking for hours in the park. It was kind of like being instant soul mates.' She looked sad. 'But things change. Were you at university with Céline?'

'No. We met at a party—a friend of a friend kind of thing.' He lifted one shoulder. 'I'd split up with someone a couple of months before, but I just clicked with Céline.' He blew out a breath. 'Maybe if she'd met Jean-Luc before I asked her to marry me... But he was spending a year in America at the time. He was polite to her when he met her, but I never really noticed that he kept his distance from her, or that he tended to see me on my own and made excuses not to see us as a couple.' He rolled his eyes. 'Which makes me as clueless as that guy in *Love Actually*. Not that Jean-Luc would have done that horrible thing with the cue cards.'

'It sounds as if they tried to keep apart,' Geri said. 'Have you thought any more about going to see them?'

'I'm still thinking about it,' Ant said. 'I don't even know where to start.'

'Maybe send them a card,' she suggested. 'It will break the ice.'

'I still need to get my head round it,' Ant said.

'In your shoes, I would, too, Geri admitted.

'You can't change the past,' he said. 'And I'm not still in love with Céline.' He glanced at her. 'What about you? Are you still in love with Mark?'

'No. He's met someone else. They're happy—and they want the same things out of life, so I think it will stay that way.

So she wasn't still in love with her ex; and Ant was slightly shocked to feel the rush of relief that her heart wasn't engaged elsewhere. 'What about you?' he asked. 'What do you want from life?'

'That's a bit deep for a sunny Friday afternoon in Paris,' she said lightly. 'Actually, what I want from life right now is an ice cream.'

The determined look in her eye made it clear that she wasn't going to tell him any more right now; but at least she was starting to open up to him. 'Good call,' he said, 'because we're near somewhere I think you'll enjoy.'

They headed back to the river, and crossed over to the Île Saint-Louis.

'This is one of the oldest ice cream shops in Paris,' he told her when they reached their destination, 'and I happen to like their sorbet *cacao amer*.'

'Chocolate?'

'Bitter chocolate,' he said.

She grinned. 'Of course. Intense and dark.' Like him. 'As you bought lunch, the ice cream's on me. What do you recommend?'

'Ask the assistant for tastes of the ones you like the look of,' he said.

She ended up choosing salted caramel.

'Try this one, first,' he said, and offered her a taste of his sorbet. Time seemed to slow down, even stop, as he leaned forward with the teaspoon and watched her close her eyes in anticipation, and then her lips parted.

There was still a tiny speck of ice cream on her lips, and it would be oh, so easy to lean forward and kiss it from her mouth…

He went hot all over when she made a tiny hum of appreciation and opened her eyes again to look at him.

'How was it?' he asked, hoping that she couldn't guess what had just been going through his head.

'Intense,' she said.

'Too bitter for you?'

'Perhaps,' she said, and then took another taste of her own. 'But this is definitely one of the best ice creams I've ever had.'

* * *

It was the perfect day discovering the city, finishing up in a tiny bistro in the Latin Quarter that Antoine claimed served the best cassoulet in Paris. When they finally got back to Antoine's apartment, she was shattered.

'I've had such a brilliant day,' she said. 'Thank you.'

'My pleasure.'

She yawned. 'Sorry. It's all the walking. And the amazing food.'

'And you have crème brûlée from the bistro for dinner tomorrow.'

Because Antoine had persuaded the waiter to let them take dessert home, on condition they brought the dishes back.

'Breakfast,' she said. 'I can assure you it's not going to last until dinner.'

'You English heathen,' he teased.

She was delighted that he'd relaxed enough with her to be comfortable teasing her; she knew he didn't mean the insult in the slightest. At the same time, she had to make a real effort to stop herself leaning over and kissing that grin from his face.

Friends and colleagues. That was the deal, she reminded herself.

But what if…?

CHAPTER SIX

OVER THE NEXT few weeks, Geri really felt that she'd settled in to life in Paris. Thanks to Antoine, Valerie, Émilie and Belle, her French had come on in leaps and bounds and she was more confident in conversation. She'd explored lots of Paris with Antoine. And she was loving her days at the zoo, because Zhen was starting to show nesting behaviour—and her urine samples showed that she might be pregnant.

'Remember, the hormone changes are the same in a pseudopregnancy, so we can't rely on them,' Antoine warned. 'Until we persuade Zhen into letting us do an ultrasound—and the foetus, being tiny, is easy to miss—we can't be sure she's having a cub.'

'And in the meantime we monitor the progesterone levels in her urine every day,' Geri said. 'When they return to baseline, either she'll have the cub or we'll know she wasn't pregnant in the first place.'

But Zhen continued to be less active than usual, and they noticed that she was licking her body and cradling things: all behaviour that was linked to pregnancy.

'We'll build her a den in her off-show area,' Pierre said. 'In the wild, she'd nest in a cave with a bed of twigs, or in the hollow of a conifer tree—something small and very cosy. Though she'll always have access to the larger enclosure.'

'Are we telling the public that we're hopeful she's having a cub?' Geri asked.

'We're negotiating that one with the PR team,' Antoine said. 'Of course we want visitors to know things that will bring them to the zoo—but the welfare of the animals comes first, and I don't want her to be crowded.'

'Which is why,' Pierre said, 'we're putting her den in the off-show area so we can keep her relaxed. We'll add a bit of insulation to reduce noise, and we'll rig up a camera so we can monitor her and share some of the feed with visitors.'

'D'accord,' Antoine said.

Geri sat on the terrace of Antoine's roof garden on her afternoon off and video-called her sister.

'You,' Alex said, 'are absolutely glowing. Paris suits you.'

'I love Paris,' Geri said. 'And I can't wait until you come over. There are so many places I want to show you.'

'Places that you've been to with Antoine?' Alex asked.

'Yes. He's been helping me with my Paris list.'

'Is that what you're calling it?' Alex teased.

'I have no idea what you mean,' Geri fibbed.

'Yes, you do. You've gone pink,' Alex said with a grin. 'And do you have any idea how often you mention his name in conversation?'

'Because he's my colleague and my friend,' Geri protested.

'I think,' Alex said, 'you'd like him to be more than a friend.'

Geri felt her face heat even more. 'Not going to happen. He's my colleague—my *senior* colleague—and I'm staying with him.'

'He's single and you're single, right?' At Geri's nod, Alex continued, 'And he likes you, or he wouldn't be spending time with you. If you like each other, what's the issue?'

'It's complicated.' Geri didn't want to break Antoine's confidence, even to her sister.

'Geri, give yourself a break. Losing the baby and then splitting up with Mark broke you into little pieces. You deserve to have some fun,' Alex said. 'Mark's found happiness. It's *your* turn.'

'I know.' But Antoine was vulnerable, too. She didn't want to risk hurting him.

'Think about it,' Alex advised. 'If you like him and he likes you… Have a mad fling.'

'I'll think about it,' Geri said. 'Now, I want to hear all about *your* date, last night.' She smiled. 'And you look glowing, too.'

'You seem a bit out of sorts today,' Geri said the following day, when she and Antoine had left the zoo and were heading back to Montmartre.

'I am. Bianca's latest bloods aren't great, and I'm worried about her kidneys,' he said with a sigh.

'I'm sorry,' she said.

'I hoped that tweaking her meds would help, this week, but it hasn't.' He looked bleak. 'I haven't got it in me to tell Belle today, but I think we're going to have to make a hard decision in the next few weeks. For now, all we can do is to keep her comfortable.'

She squeezed his hand briefly in a gesture of sympathy.

'When I started training as a vet, I realised I didn't

want to work in small animal practice, because I didn't want to have to break the news to an owner that their beloved dog, cat or rabbit couldn't be helped.' He looked away. 'Although zoo animals don't have an owner in the same way, the keepers grow attached to them as much as they'd be attached to a pet.'

'So do the vets,' she said. 'And the animals are just as attached to you. I still can't get over the way Bianca chuffs at you as if you're another tiger.'

'Yeah.' He bit his lip. 'I can't imagine the zoo without her. We came here on the same day. I mean, I don't ever want her to suffer—that's why I've been keeping a close eye on her bloods—but she's going to leave such a big hole in my life.'

'Of course she is,' Geri said. This time, she took his hand and kept hold of it, hoping to comfort him. Antoine had shut himself away from everyone after his breakup with Céline; he'd definitely started to open up and make those connections again since Geri had known him, but would Bianca's death set him back? 'But you're always going to have your memories,' she said. 'They're never going to fade.' A line of poetry drifted into her head. '"But thy eternal summer shall not fade."'

'Eternal summer. I like that,' he said. 'And you're right. I've got memories.'

'And you gave her a happy life, you and the keepers,' she reminded him. 'All the enrichment stuff you've read up on and shared with the keepers—and you kept Bianca healthy and safe.'

'Is that what you said to your farmers, when they lost a cow or what have you?' he asked.

'I've seen hard-bitten farmers in tears when a lamb or a calf hasn't made it, or when they've had to say goodbye to a sheep they've hand reared,' she said. 'So, yes. Even though it's a business and the animals aren't pets, there's still affection there. Which is how it should be—I'd hate to be in a world that doesn't have room for love.' She paused. 'I know it doesn't come easy to you, but promise me you'll talk to me rather than close yourself off?'

He was quiet for so long that she thought she'd gone too far.

And then he smiled. '*Mon petit rayon*. You have a generous heart. All right. I promise.'

'Good.'

'When does your sister plan to visit?' he asked.

'In July,' she said.

'She's very welcome to stay at the apartment,' he said.

She hadn't expected him to offer, but was delighted that he had. 'That's very kind of you, Ant.'

'*De rien.*' He looked slightly embarrassed. 'So you're close to your sister?'

'Yes. I'm really glad I can video-call her, because I miss her,' Geri said. 'Even though we see each other mainly at weekends, or when we both have a day off—Alex lives in London,' she explained, 'we talk most days. And she kept me going when I split up with Mark. Without her pushing me to do her classes, I think I would have just stayed indoors and shut—' She grimaced, suddenly realising what she was saying. 'Sorry. That wasn't a comment about you.'

'But it was pretty much what I did,' he said. 'Shutting myself away from everyone. Including my family, because it wasn't fair to make them choose between Jean-Luc and me.'

'Maybe they don't have to choose,' she said. 'Maybe they can still love both of you.'

'I think,' he said slowly, 'if my grandparents were still here, they'd urge me to reconcile. My grandmother always said how glad she was that the three of us were close. And there was no jealousy between us. I have the apartment, Mélie has a share of the vineyard, and Jean-Luc inherited investments. It was always fair.' He paused. 'Maybe you're right and I should send them a card. A gift for the baby.'

'It might be a good start,' she said. 'The baby's, what, six weeks old now?'

'You think it's a little too late to send something?'

'Your circumstances are different,' she said. 'I'd be at my sister's side for a cuddle at the first possible moment.' A cuddle with a baby who might end up being the only child in her life.

'As you say, my circumstances are different.' He sighed. 'It's weird. Of course I want to get to know my niece. If my brother had fallen for anyone else but Céline, I would feel the same way you do. But there's all this *stuff* in the way.'

'Maybe,' she said, 'you need to push it aside, because it's not helping you. If anything, I think it's hurting you more. I know it must feel like a horrible betrayal—no, it *was* a horrible betrayal—but do you want it to get in the way and suck out all the potential joy of the future?'

'No,' he said. 'But how do I push it away?'

'Fake it until you make it,' she said. Even though she knew she was a fraud, because she hadn't really made it, had she? 'In your shoes, once I'd stopped being hurt and angry, I think I'd miss them.'

'I do.' The words sounded as if they had been dragged through sand.

'Sending something's a good first step,' she said. 'As

I said before, it'll help break the ice. Take it slow—like when you and Belle and the team train a tiger to sit and not mind you taking a blood sample.'

'Maybe I could buy the baby a toy tiger,' he said.

'That'd be nice, given what you do. A plush tiger sounds great,' she said. 'Or maybe a mobile with wooden animals on it to hang above the crib.'

'Perhaps you could come shopping with me at the weekend and help me choose something?' he suggested.

Choose something for a baby.

Panic flooded through her. Then again, she'd just told him to push aside the hurt and stop it sucking out the joy of the future. Wasn't she making the same mistakes that he was?

That smile was definitely overbright.

'What's wrong?' Ant asked.

'Nothing,' she said.

He realised they were still holding hands—strange how natural that felt—so he tightened his fingers gently around hers. 'I think there is,' he said quietly. 'Talking to you helped me. Why don't you try talking to me? I'm not going to gossip, and I'm certainly not going to judge you,' he added. 'It might help.'

'I…' She was silent for a long, long time. And her voice cracked when she said, 'I had a miscarriage.'

And he'd just asked her to go shopping with him to choose things for a baby. Talk about trampling on a sore spot—though he'd had no idea. 'I'm sorry,' he said. 'That must've been tough. For your husband, too.'

'Mark was…relieved, I guess,' she said.

The words were so shocking, he wasn't sure he'd heard her right. 'Relieved?'

'He didn't want children.'

And he hadn't wanted pets, Ant remembered.

'He wouldn't ever have wished me to lose the baby—he isn't one of the bad guys, Ant. But he had a rough childhood, and it made him dead set against the idea of having children of his own. I thought I was OK with that, until I found out I was pregnant. It turned out I wasn't, because once I'd got over the shock of being pregnant I was thrilled about being a mum.' She swallowed hard. 'Sorry. I can't talk about it any more. Not right now.'

Ant had the feeling that she'd kept all the hurt inside, the same way he had. 'It's OK,' he said. 'If you decide you want to talk later, I'll be here.'

'Thank you,' she said. 'I didn't deal with it very well.'

She'd given him a pretty good clue as to why her marriage had ended. It hadn't been her fault, or her ex's. Just circumstances that had overwhelmed them both.

But maybe she'd find the strength to let out all the hurt to him, and then she could start to heal—just as she'd helped him to finally see a way forward.

On their day off, Ant made breakfast. 'Are you sure you're up to this?' he asked.

'No,' she admitted. 'None of my friends has had a baby yet, so I haven't needed to buy baby things as a present. And I never got to the shopping stage for...' She took a deep breath. 'For my baby. There wasn't time to plan a nursery, make a list of names. But it's time I made myself move on. Face what normal people do. So I'll go with you and help you choose something nice for your niece.'

'My niece,' he said. And the words didn't sting as much as he'd expected. 'I appreciate this,' he said.

'We're helping each other,' she said.

When they walked into the baby section of a big department store, she went very, very quiet for about three minutes—and then she went into sparkle mode, picking out beautiful outfits and first books and nursery accessories, full of enthusiasm and smiles.

'We don't really have these in England,' she said, picking up a flat cloth with a tiger's head peeping over the centre of one side, and knotted corners to act as paws.

'It's a *doudou plat*,' he said. 'A comfort cloth, I guess you'd call it. And that one's very cute. I'll buy it.'

'And these cot mobiles are absolutely lovely.' She stopped by one with a sun, rainbow and white fluffy clouds hanging down, and set the clockwork mechanism going; the mobile turned round to a musical box version of 'Somewhere Over the Rainbow'.

'Perfect for you, Monsieur le Nuage,' she teased.

'Actually, that's Docteur le Nuage to you,' he retorted. And then, because he couldn't help himself, he said, 'And it suits you, too, Docteur le Petit Rayon.'

'You are so bad,' she said, smiling.

But the smile didn't quite reach her eyes. Not because he'd upset her, he knew; this was fast becoming a running joke between them and she'd been the one to bring it up. She was clearly having a really hard time with this. 'Is this the sort of thing you would've bought?' he asked.

'I don't know,' she said. 'I don't usually let myself think about it.'

He took her hand. 'That was tactless of me. I apologise.'

'No need to apologise. I know I need to move on,' she said. 'But don't buy the mobile. They might already have one. Anyway, you need a panda as well as a tiger.'

'Soft toys it is.' He walked over to the display with her.

'Oh, yes!' She picked up a small plush panda and cuddled it. 'This is incredibly soft. You need this one.'

'But look, they have a white tiger,' he said, spotting one on the display stand.

'You've already got a tiger with the *doudou*. I vote for the panda.'

'Tiger,' he said implacably.

She narrowed her eyes at him and took a coin from her purse. 'Heads or tails?'

'Tails,' he said.

She tossed the coin and caught it between the back of her left hand and the palm of her right hand. 'Tails it's the tiger, heads it's the panda,' she said, before taking her right hand away. 'Oh. Tiger it is,' she said regretfully.

'Thank you. I'll get the store to wrap and deliver it for me.'

'Mind if I go and browse the craft section while you're sorting that out?'

In other words, she needed to escape from the nursery section. But she'd done well to keep there this long. 'Sure,' he said.

Once he'd bought a card and written it out, paid for his goods to be gift-wrapped and shipped and given the assistant the address for delivery, he went to find Geri in the craft section.

There seemed to be children everywhere, and she'd gone quiet again. Maybe a sunny Saturday afternoon wouldn't be the best time to take her to a park in Paris.

'I have a spontaneous suggestion for you,' he said.

'I'm listening.'

And definitely in fake-it-till-you-make-it mode, with that smile. 'It's a nice day,' he said. 'Let's get out of the city. I thought we could go to Epernay.'

'That'd be nice,' she said.

He'd make that smile a genuine one if it killed him.

'We'll take a picnic,' he said.

'With a wicker basket and a checked cloth?'

'If we take a quick diversion to the household section, yes,' he said.

She laughed. 'We can manage without a basket. But I'm curious to see what a French picnic's like.'

'What's the English version?' he asked.

'It depends. If Mum's in charge, it'll be coronation chicken and salads followed by freshly baked scones with jam and cream. If it's me or Alex, my sister, then it's sandwiches plus whatever nice things we can find in the supermarket deli.'

'In a wicker basket with a checked cloth?'

'Actually, my picnic blanket has rainbow stripes,' she said. 'But yes. And Pimm's for those who aren't driving.'

'I don't have a picnic blanket.' He'd left the house he shared with Céline with absolutely nothing, because he hadn't wanted any reminders of the life they'd made together. 'We'd better go to the household section, I think.'

Armed with a wicker basket and a checked cloth, they headed back to Montmartre. In the street next to Antoine's apartment, they bought bread, cheese, a quiche, madeleines, and a pot of aioli to go with the tomatoes, cucumber and radishes. They bought a punnet of strawberries and a bunch of green seedless grapes as well.

'A feast fit for a queen,' he declared.

'No Pimm's?'

'I have something else in mind,' he said. 'We'll have water and coffee with the picnic.'

While she packed the picnic hamper, he made a flask of coffee and checked his phone to book a tour slot, then drove her out towards Epernay, through gently rolling countryside, with the road before them like a pale ribbon through fields of vines. There were forested hills in the distance, and little villages where the houses were built of pale stone with terracotta roofs while the churches had pyramidal lead steeples.

'This is very pretty,' she said.

'At the end of next month, when the sunflowers come out, it's even prettier,' he said. 'Provence doesn't have the monopoly on sunflowers in France, you know. Van Gogh painted some of his sunflowers at Auvers-sur-Oise, a little north of where we're heading.' He risked a glance; this time, her smile was genuine rather than overbright. 'We can explore there another day, if you like.'

'I would,' she said.

They stopped in a little village and found a picnic spot overlooking the River Marne where the water looked turquoise in the sunlight.

'Good, simple food, fresh air and good company—the perfect lunch,' she said.

Knowing that she enjoyed being with him as much as he enjoyed being with her warmed him all the way through and made him feel as if the summer was blooming with possibilities. 'I'll drink to that,' he said, and raised his mug of coffee.

'No Pimm's. Not even elderflower,' she grumbled, but she was laughing. Her hair glinted in the sunlight— she really *was* the ray of sunshine he teased her about being—and that smile was definitely genuine. He knew he'd made the right call.

'Patience,' he said. 'Good things come to those who wait.'

Once they'd finished their picnic, he drove her to

Epernay. 'This,' he said as they passed the grand buildings with their wrought-iron gates, 'is the Avenue de Champagne, where all the major champagne houses have a base. Between them, they have more than a hundred kilometres of cellars under the road, and the contents are apparently worth more than the Champs-Élysées.'

She grinned. 'You looked that up.'

'Yes, because this isn't Paris or the Loire Valley.' He looked at her. 'Maybe you'd like to visit my family's vineyard at some point.'

'I'd really like that,' she said.

'Even though I know you'll end up in cahoots with my mother and my sister,' he said, 'and nag me about working too hard.'

'I might be on your side, there,' she said. 'Because we have the same job. Though I take a lunchbreak.'

'So do I,' he protested.

'A sandwich at your desk isn't the same. Learn to delegate,' she said. 'Plus having a break means you'll be fresher and more productive.'

He rolled his eyes. 'If that's what you call being on my side...'

'I am,' she said, and punched his arm lightly. 'I want you to be happy, Ant.'

'I want you to be happy, too.' All of a sudden, it felt as if the air had been sucked out round them and he felt dizzy with the possibilities. If he hadn't been driving, he would've drawn her into his arms and kissed her until she was as breathless as he felt.

'What would make you happy?' he asked.

'What would make *you* happy?' she countered.

'I asked first,' he reminded her.

* * *

What would make her happy?

What she hadn't been able to have with Mark. A relationship with someone who wanted the same things that she did. A baby. Though that was all too much to dump on Antoine. Particularly as she still didn't know if a baby was even an option. Until she tried to get pregnant, they wouldn't know how bad the damage from the Q fever had been.

'I'm happy now,' she said. 'I love my family, I love my job, and I love Paris.'

'And?' he asked.

Busted. She'd expected him to be polite and let her get away with it. Wrong. He'd give her that Parisian stare until she caved in and told him. 'A relationship,' she said. 'I think I'm ready to move on.' Just as long as she could get through this next week. The anniversary that always dragged her under the surface. 'Your turn,' she said.

He blew out a breath. 'I love my job. I'd like my family back together again, and you've helped me take the first steps in doing that.' He was silent for a while. 'And, yes, I'd like a relationship.' He paused. 'A family of my own.'

She remembered what her sister had said. Was Alex right? Should she have a mad fling? But that wasn't enough for her. She wanted something that would last. A family.

He wanted that, too. But there was the bit they hadn't talked about. The bit she couldn't handle talking about, right now: the reason for her miscarriage and the spectre of future complications. Was it fair to start something when she might not be able to deliver? It was what had held her back from dating again in England; and it stuck in her throat now, stilling her words.

She'd gone quiet on him. Maybe she, like he, was worried they were getting in too deep. Time to give her a let-out, he thought, and parked the car. 'But right now,' he said, 'I want to go on the wine tour I booked for us.'

'A wine tour? That's lovely,' she said. 'Though it might be a bit dull for you, given that your family makes wine.'

'We don't make sparkling wine,' he said. 'But I'll let Mélie tell you all the technical stuff at the vineyard. I'll quiz you afterwards. Any wrong answers mean you have to pay a forfeit.'

Oh, dear God. What on earth had possessed him to say that? He was about to apologise and backtrack when she laughed and poked him in the chest. 'If we're talking about forfeits, Monsieur le Nuage, remember that my sister is a personal trainer. And she's taught me how to do some very evil burpees.'

He'd been thinking of kisses. 'We'll discuss that later,' he said, catching her hand and feeling almost breathless at the thought of her mouth exploring his. 'I didn't have burpees in mind.'

It had been so long since he'd flirted with someone that the little exchange left him completely flustered, and Ant found it hard to pay attention to the first bit of the talk at the champagne house. But wandering round the cellars, discovering how huge the tunnels were and seeing bottles of champagne that were a couple of centuries old, was fascinating. And it felt natural to slide his arm round her shoulder, draw her close. A moment later, her arm slid round his waist. Despite the coolness of the cellars, his temperature rocketed.

After the tour, there was a chance to taste three different types of champagne.

'I'm driving,' Ant said. 'I'll take a sip of the first pour—but please have my share of the rest.'

'Thank you,' she said. 'I see what you meant now about waiting for good things. I've never done wine-tasting before, let alone tasting champagne—and this is wonderful. Pink champagne definitely beats Pimm's.'

'Good. Let me take a snap of you for your *maman*. Raise your glass in a toast.' He made sure to use his own phone for the photograph, because right then she looked really cute and he wanted to preserve the moment for himself, too.

He wasn't surprised that the rosé champagne was her favourite; and he liked the way she had the confidence to ask the sommelier questions in French, even though she needed him to translate a couple of words for her. The sommelier was charmed by her, and brought out a non-vintage bottle of rosé champagne and a sabre. 'This is the best way to open a bottle of champagne—and I shall enjoy teaching you,' he said, and proceeded to talk her through the art of sabrage.

'Am I really going to do this?' She gave Ant a worried look. 'What if I mess it up?'

'If you can anaesthetise a tiger,' he said, 'you can sabrage a bottle of champagne. You don't need brute force, you need precision—like the way you put a blade in the right place when you intubate.'

'You can anaesthetise a tiger?' the sommelier asked, looking impressed.

'We're both vets at the Zoo de Bélvèdere in Paris,' Geri explained.

'This is much, much easier—and much safer—than handling a tiger,' the sommelier said with a smile. 'Tap the blade where I show you.'

She handed her phone to Ant. 'Would you mind taking a film of this?'

'For your family? Of course,' he said.

As Ant expected, Geri executed the manoeuvre perfectly, and the sommelier gave her the cork, still embedded in the ring of the neck of the bottle.

'Bravo,' the sommelier said.

Everyone clapped, and the sommelier poured another round of champagne.

At the end of the tasting, Geri bought a couple of bottles of the rosé champagne, and Ant insisted on carrying them back to the car. Outside the gates, she tripped, and he caught her before she fell flat on her face.

He couldn't help cradling her protectively; and in turn she wrapped her arms round him. Just as she'd held him close in the cellars.

It would be oh, so easy just to dip his head and brush his mouth against hers...

'Whoops. I'm not used to drinking in the afternoon,' she said. 'I think the champagne and the sunshine have gone to my head.'

And that made him straighten up again. He wasn't going to take advantage of her while she was tipsy. If— *when*, he thought as his heart skipped a beat—he kissed her, he wanted her to be fully in the moment, too. 'It's fine,' he said instead with a smile.

Though he kept his arm round her all the way to the car—and it wasn't only to make sure she didn't fall. He liked the way she felt in his arms. And maybe, just maybe, this could be good for both of them. He just needed to find the courage to ask her.

CHAPTER SEVEN

ON MONDAY MORNING, Rico, the main keeper who looked after the cheetahs, brought up a case at the usual daybook meeting. 'I think Étoile is about to give birth,' he said.

Geri knew that in the wild cheetahs tended to hide their pregnancy until a couple of days before they gave birth, to keep the cubs safe. 'What signs have you noticed?' she asked.

'She's a bit restless,' he said. 'And her daughter from her litter last year was sniffing her belly this morning.'

'Do you think she might be lactating?' Antoine asked.

'It's possible,' Rico said. 'I'm going to rig up a birthing pen for her in the enclosure, just in case. A small pen with only one entrance, so she feels safe when she's at her most vulnerable. I'm going to put some cameras up to keep an eye on her, but I'll make sure they're high enough to avoid causing her any stress.'

'Good plan,' Antoine said. 'And will you bring her in at night this week, until we know what's going on?'

'Definitely,' Rico said. 'I'll make sure the night keeper team keeps a special eye out.'

'You mean,' Belle said drily, 'you'll find an excuse to come back and watch over her.'

Rico gave her a bashful grin. 'Maybe. But, hey, if my girl is having cubs, I want to be there. Just as you were there last year when Leylani had cubs.' Leylani was the zoo's other female Bengal tiger, who'd given birth to twin cubs the previous summer.

'And if anything happens,' Antoine said, 'you might need a vet on standby.'

'Of course, I'll call you,' Rico promised.

Geri and Antoine had almost finished dinner that evening when Antoine's mobile phone rang. He glanced at the screen.

'Everything OK? Is that Rico calling about Étoile?' Geri asked.

'No. It's Jean-Luc.'

His expression was completely unreadable. Geri decided to aim for tact. 'I'll give you some space. I'll be reading on the terrace if you need anything,' she said, heading to her room to pick up the copy of *Bonjour Tristesse* that she'd borrowed from Émilie and avoiding the dining room to give Antoine some privacy.

This would be his first contact with his brother since the day Jean-Luc had left with Céline. She really hoped that it would mend some fences between them, because she knew it had been hard for Antoine to make that first step and send a gift and card for the baby. She forced herself to concentrate on her book and made notes of unfamiliar words she needed to look up later.

Finally, Antoine came out onto the terrace, bearing two cups of chamomile tea, hers sweetened with honey. Geri suppressed the urge to ask him how his call had gone and waited for him to initiate the conversation. He was silent for a long, long time; then, finally, he looked at her. 'Thank you, Geri. Without you nudging me, I wouldn't have sent a card or a present—and the distance between us would've grown even greater.'

'It helped?' she asked.

He blew out a breath. 'It was…strange. For both of us. We were really close, and then…' He shook his head. 'It is as it is. The baby's doing well. They're all happy. Jean-Luc asked me to visit.'

'Is that what you want?'

He was silent, clearly thinking about it. And then he nodded. 'The anger's gone. And the hurt. Now, I simply miss them.'

'Then go to see them,' she said gently. 'You've done the really hard bit, taking that first step. And it sounds as if Jean-Luc's trying to meet you halfway.'

'He said he missed me. They both did,' Antoine said. 'I admit, I can be surly and I tend to keep my distance from people. But I never used to be like that.'

He hadn't kept his distance from her at the weekend, Geri thought. He'd told her what he really wanted. That moment when she'd tripped and nearly fallen over—he'd caught her, but then he'd held her close. And she'd been near to tipping her head back, inviting him to kiss her… Particularly when he'd kept his arm around her all the way back to the car.

Then she'd fallen asleep. He was back to being professional with her when she woke, and she'd lost her nerve. 'I'm glad you're starting to patch things up,' she said. 'And if you—'

But, before she could suggest supporting him when he went to visit Céline and Jean-Luc, Antoine's phone rang again.

'It's Rico,' he said, and switched the phone to speaker. 'Rico? You have news about Étoile?'

'I'm on my way to the zoo. Rémi—' one of the night keepers '—says she's gone into the pen, and he took a look at the video feed. There were ripples across her belly.'

'That sounds like possible contractions,' Geri said.

'I agree. I'm on my way,' Antoine said. He looked at Geri as he ended the call. 'Want to come?'

'And potentially see newborn cheetah cubs? Don't even *think* about trying to stop me,' she said with a smile.

Antoine drove them over to the zoo; the security guard let them in, and they headed over to the cheetah house.

Rico and the night keeper were both watching the video screen. The cheetah was pacing; then she lay down on her side, lifted her leg, and the first cub slithered out.

'Oh, my God,' Geri whispered. 'This is such a privilege.'

Étoile cleaned the birth sac off the cub, then lay down and let the cub wriggle its way across to start feeding.

'It's magical.' Rico was close to tears. 'My clever girl.'

An hour later, the cheetah covered the first cub with straw, as if to hide its scent, then gave birth to her second cub; and an hour after that, she gave birth to the third.

It didn't matter that it was half-past one in the morning. Geri wouldn't have missed it for the world.

'Look at them,' she whispered. 'They're gorgeous.' All three cubs had dark markings on their face; some spots were visible on their lower bodies, but they all had a thick greyish mane. She knew it was to help camouflage them, and they wouldn't lose that part of their coat until they were about three months old.

'We'll let her bond with them without any interference,' Rico said. 'We'll do the first health checks at about ten days.'

'Vaccines at six weeks, and then we'll be able to tell the sex of the cubs,' Antoine added. 'But for now they look gorgeous.'

Geri could see his expression softening as he looked at the cubs, and it made her feel all warm and gooey. Just then, he caught her eye, and the brief smile that made the corners of his eyes crinkle was all for her. And it felt like a deeper connection, too: they were here, together, doing what they both loved.

'I know the PR team will be dying to announce the news,' Rico said, 'but I don't want Étoile spooked or crowded by visitors.'

'We don't want her to feel she has to move the cubs. Let's limit access to the cheetah house to keepers and vets only, for the next ten days—until the cubs open their eyes and Étoile's settled,' Antoine suggested. 'And maybe we can hook the cameras up to the website for a few minutes, several times a day, to let our visitors feel they still get to share the cubs.'

'At Cambridge, we'd call it cubcam,' Geri said. 'Which is short and to the point.'

'Webcam des petits guépards,' Rico said. 'Yeah. You're right. It's too long. Cubcam is better.'

'And you three need to get some sleep before you start in the morning,' the night keeper pointed out.

'I'm not going anywhere,' Rico said. 'I need to sort some food and water for Étoile, because she's not going to want to leave the cubs. But you two—see you tomorrow,' he said.

With a last lingering look at the cubs, who were snuggled up to their mum and fast asleep, Geri and Antoine left the zoo.

* * *

The next morning, they were in early as usual for the daybook meeting, but Rico came in looking grim. 'One of the cubs is poorly—it's possible that Étoile rejected him while I took a couple of hours' nap in the rest room. Belle thought at first his mum had accidentally lain on the cub, because he was in a corner of the pen and wasn't moving at all, but then she saw him move his leg. We're luring Étoile away from the cubs with some meat so we can go in and check on him.'

'If he hasn't been with her and the other cubs, he'll be cold and hungry,' Antoine said. 'Let's get him into the surgery, and we'll give him a feed and warm him up; then we'll see where we go from there.'

Fortunately everything on their list that morning was routine and could be worked around the cheetah cub. Geri was in the surgery, getting the heat pads prepared and some formula mixed with a colostrum supplement before putting the bottle into a jug of hot water to warm through, and Antoine brought the cub in from the pen, tucked into his shirt to let the cub get some of his body heat.

Geri checked the cub's temperature with a thermometer gun. 'He's too cold for his temperature to register on the thermometer,' she said.

'I wondered if that might be the case.' Antoine looked grim. 'And he's floppy because he's cold. Let's give him a feed and see if we can warm him up a bit. Then we'll check him over to see if there are any problems.' He wrapped the cub in a towel with heat pads while Geri double-checked the temperature of the formula.

'OK. It's ready,' she said.

'Let's get this into you, little one,' Antoine said softly, and rubbed a couple of drops of milk onto the cub's mouth.

To their relief, the cub responded, sniffing for the teat and then sucking a few mouthfuls of milk.

Geri's heart squeezed, when she saw how gentle Antoine was with the tiny cub. Just as he'd be with a baby...

She had to swallow the lump in her throat. 'What are we going to do with you, little one?'

'Put him back in the den, once he's warm and fed. We need to give Étoile a chance to bond with the cub. If we hand-rear him, we'll have to find him a home because he won't fit into the pack here—he'll be seen as a threat and they'll kill him,' Antoine said. 'But first, we need him warmed up until his pads are the same temperature as his body, and his mouth and tongue are both pink.'

They took it in turns with Rico and Belle to sit cradling the cub, and by the afternoon his temperature was back up and he'd taken some more milk.

'Let's get him back to his mum,' Antoine said, handing the cub back to Rico.

'I'll stay tonight,' Rico said.

'You stayed last night,' Antoine said. 'And you haven't been home yet. I'll stay tonight, and I promise I'll call if there's any change.'

'And I'll stay with you,' Geri said. 'I'm not going to settle until I know the little one's doing all right.'

That evening, Antoine and Geri made themselves comfortable in the staff room, with a monitor hooked up to the cubcam to let them see Étoile and the babies.

'Have you done many night vigils like this?' Antoine asked.

'I've done a few callouts that turned into all-nighters where we had a cow with a difficult first labour,' she said. 'And, at the zoo, we had a rota system for a couple of nights when we had a lioness we needed to keep an eye on.'

'The zoo's strange at night,' he said. 'The calls of the howler monkeys at sunset—it always makes me think of an animatronic dinosaur my grandparents took me to see when I was young.'

'I'd never thought of that before,' she said, 'but you're right.'

They kept the conversation light and uncomplicated; but eventually she could feel her eyelids drooping.

'Have a nap,' Antoine said.

'Only if we set an alarm for an hour's time; then I take over watching while you have a nap,' she said.

'Two hours is probably better,' he said, and set an alarm on his phone.

Geri drifted off to sleep; when the alarm woke her, she realised that her head was pillowed on Antoine's shoulder and his arm was round her. It felt absolutely right; she allowed herself a moment to savour it. But was she too close for Antoine's comfort? Since the afternoon when he'd admitted he wanted a relationship, he'd kept her firmly in the friend zone. She sat up straight. 'Sorry for draping myself over you.'

'De rien,' he said. Though she couldn't tell a thing from his expression.

'How's our cub doing?' she asked.

'Étoile's let him cuddle up with the other two, which is a good sign. He hasn't fed, yet, but maybe soon,' he said.

'Let's hope,' she said. 'Now, it's your turn to sleep. I'm going to set my phone and grab a drink of water.'

When she sat down again, Antoine had drifted off to sleep. A couple of minutes later, she felt him shift next to her, and his head ended up on her shoulder. Again, it felt *right*, and she enjoyed the closeness.

In the few short weeks since she'd known him, she'd grown to like him. More than like him. She was pretty sure that he felt the same way that she did—attracted to her, but scared to trust his heart to anyone. Although she could name a dozen reasons why getting involved would be a bad idea for both of them, she still couldn't help wondering: what if they gave in to the temptation? Would it help to heal them both?

When the alarm went off, two hours later, he was awake immediately. 'Sorry for using you as a pillow.'

'De rien,' she said with a smile. 'Still no feed, but he's still sleeping as part of the litter.'

'That's good.' He stretched, then slid his arm round her shoulders. 'My turn for pillow duty.'

Every nerve-end zinged and her pulse rocketed. All she would have to do was turn her head slightly and reach up, slide her palm along his cheek and tip his head down so his mouth met hers...

But they were at work. This wasn't appropriate, she reminded herself. Instead, she rested her head against his shoulder, telling herself that this was what any colleague would do in the circumstances.

He woke her forty minutes later.

Bleary-eyed, she looked at him. 'What's happening?'

'You really won't want to miss this.' He gestured to the video monitor.

All three cubs were lined up, feeding from their mum.

'She's accepted him,' Geri whispered in awe.

'I think it's going to be all right, now,' he said.

It was natural to hug him in the sheer joy of the moment. And even more natural for their cheeks to press together. For their heads to turn very, very slightly towards each other. For their lips to graze each other's. Once. Twice.

And then they were really kissing. He had one hand tangled in her hair and the other arm wrapped round her waist, and she was holding him tightly. Little sparkles of pleasure ran through her as his mouth moved over hers, nipping gently and urging her to open her mouth and let him deepen the kiss.

Desire surged through her, making her feel dizzy. She was glad they were sitting down, because she was pretty sure her knees had both turned to jelly.

When he broke the kiss, they were both shaking.

'I'm sorry—I shouldn't have done that,' he said, taking his hand out of her hair and dropping his arm from her waist.

But there was yearning in his eyes, not distaste.

'I think it was both of us,' she said. If Antoine was backing off, she had nothing to lose. She took her courage in both hands. 'We could say it was the heat of the moment, and blame it on the joy of seeing the cub accepted by his mum. But I think it's been coming for a while.'

He was silent for such a long time that she started to think she'd got it very badly wrong, and horror seeped through her. Oh, God. Work was going to be awkward in the extreme, now—and she'd have to move out. No way could she stay with him after what she'd said.

'You're right,' he said. 'It's been there for a while for me, too. But I...' He dragged in a breath. 'You know my situation. I think yours might be a little complicated, too.'

It was. And she hadn't told him everything about the baby. She'd been too focused on trying to block out the fact that the anniversary was ticking round: a day that always felt like lead and where it was as much as she could do to put one foot in front of another. 'Yes,' she whispered.

He stroked her cheek, his dark eyes full of emotion. 'Then we should be sensible.'

She knew he was right, but at the same time her shoulders sagged with disappointment. 'I'll make us some coffee,' she said, wanting to put a little physical distance between them while she got her head in the right place.

'Thanks. I'll take some film of this for Rico and Belle.'

If she thought about it logically, she definitely shouldn't get involved with him. They lived in different countries. What would happen at the end of her secondment? Would he be prepared to give up everything for her and live in England? Or would he expect her to give up everything and settle in France?

She'd been here before, in a situation where there wasn't a workable compromise. Her marriage had broken up as a result. It would be crazy to get involved with a man who was still coming to terms with being dumped on his wedding day. Maybe instead of helping to heal each other, they'd only make things worse.

They needed to be strictly colleagues and friends. Even though part of her wanted more, she was going to be sensible. And she was glad she'd made that decision, half an hour later, when Rico walked in to check on the cub's progress. Supposing he'd walked in when she and Antoine had been kissing?

'I know it's barely dawn,' Rico said, 'but I couldn't sleep.'

'Worrying about the cub?' Geri asked.

'Yeah.' He looked up at the monitor. 'They're all asleep. Together. That's a good sign.'

'Better than that,' Antoine said. He flicked into the photos app and handed his phone to Rico. 'I took this earlier because I thought you'd want to see it.'

Rico was silent as he watched the film of all three cubs lined up and feeding, and although he was smiling broadly by the end his eyes were full of tears. 'Our cub's got a fighting chance, now.'

'It looks like it,' Geri said.

For a moment, her eyes met Antoine's. She could see he was glad about the cub; but was that a hint of regret she could see in his face, or was that wishful thinking?

By the end of the week, Étoile had accepted the cub completely, and the cubcam had become the most popular page on the zoo's website.

Ant had arranged to visit Jean-Luc, Céline and baby Maya at their home in Chartres on Saturday.

'I know this might be a big ask,' he said to Geri, 'but you're welcome to come with me. You don't have to meet Jean-Luc or Céline or see the baby. Just have a wander round Chartres, because it's pretty there and I think you'd like it.'

She stared at him, saying nothing.

Of course it had been stupid to ask her.

But then he realised there was a tear running down her face. And another. And another. She was crying silently, and to him it looked as if her heart was breaking.

'What's wrong?' he asked.

She scrubbed at her face. 'Nothing.'

It didn't look like nothing to him.

'This happens once in a while,' she said.

And that was even more worrying.

How did he get her to open up to him? She'd been a

bit super-smiley with him since the night they'd ended up kissing and he'd called a halt; and she'd kept him at a slight distance, too.

He busied himself making her a milky cup of tea, exactly the way she liked it.

'The English solution to everything?' she asked wryly.

'It's obvious something's wrong, Geri. Talk to me.'

'It's not important. And you're supposed to be leaving for Chartres, or you'll be late.'

She had a point. Seeing her in tears had made him forget everything else. 'One moment,' he said.

He quickly texted Jean-Luc.

Something's come up and I need to reschedule. Apologies for late notice. Will call later today. NOT cutting you off.

The reply came back moments later.

D'accord.

'All sorted,' he said.

'But you—' she began.

'But nothing,' he said. 'Take a sip of tea, then take a deep breath—and tell me what's wrong. I'm not going to judge, just listen.'

She shivered, and took a sip of tea. And then she paused for such a long time that he thought he wasn't going to tell him a thing. But, finally, she started speaking. 'Today's the anniversary.' She swallowed hard. 'Of the day my life turned upside down.'

'The day you lost the baby?' he guessed.

She squeezed her eyes shut. 'My life started turning upside down a few weeks before then, I guess, though I didn't know it at the time. I worked in a practice dealing with farm animals. One of our clients had problems with a ewe, and I was on call, so I went to help.'

A ewe.

A few weeks ago from now would have meant late April.

Lambing season.

Ant had a nasty feeling he knew exactly what Geri was about to tell him. If he'd been the senior vet at her practice, he would never have allowed her to go on that call.

'I didn't have a clue I might've been pregnant, and Mark and I weren't even trying for a baby, or I would've asked someone else to take the call for me,' she said, almost as if she'd read his mind.

What had she contracted? Campylobacteriosis? Chlamydia? There were a number of zoonotic diseases in sheep that could cause women to lose a baby, Ant knew, which was why pregnant women were advised to avoid sheep at lambing time.

'If I'd had any idea there was *coxiella burnetii* on the farm...' She shook her head. 'But the flock had no symptoms of Q fever whatsoever. As far as I was concerned, I was simply helping a ewe with a difficult birth—a lamb that was stuck. We had a good outcome, and the mum and the lamb were both doing well. I had a mug of tea with the farmer; we discussed how the new lambs were doing, and whether he was expecting difficulties with any of the other ewes. There was no reason to think that anything else might go wrong.'

Ant remembered from his training that Q fever spread by contact of abrasions with bodily fluids, or by inhalation of spores. He was pretty sure that Geri would've used gloves if she'd had a cut on her hands; she must've caught the infection through simply breathing normally while she was treating the ewe. A symptomless flock meant that nobody could have known there was a potential problem and taken precautions to avoid it.

Her face was filled with anguish, and he couldn't stay on the other side of the table from her any longer. She needed to get the words out, but he was also sure that she needed comfort—and that was something he could do for her. He pushed his chair back, walked round to her, scooped her up and sat in her chair, settling her on his lap and holding her close. 'I'm here,' he said quietly. 'I'm listening. None of this was your fault, Geri.'

'It feels like it,' she whispered.

'It absolutely was *not* your fault,' he repeated. 'Keep talking. Remember, you told me how sometimes talking about things can take the pressure out of your head. You were right. Talk to me and let it out, instead of letting it squash you.'

She slid her arms round him, and he was glad that she was clearly taking comfort from his nearness.

'Two weeks after I delivered the lamb, I went down with what I thought was some kind of spring flu. I was bone-deep tired, I had a banging headache and my muscles ached all over. I couldn't shift it. The covid test was negative; my GP—my family doctor—took bloods to see what was going on.' She closed her eyes for a moment, clearly haunted by the memory. 'The results came back positive for *coxiella burnetii*. She said I had Q fever, and asked me if I was pregnant because the usual treatments are dangerous for unborn babies. I was about to say no— but then I realised I hadn't had a period for a while.' She grimaced. 'Which isn't me being scatty. My periods have always been all over the place.'

'You're the least scatty person I know,' Antoine said, stroking her hair.

'Thank you.' Her breath shuddered. 'The doctor asked me to do a pregnancy test before she could prescribe anything. I was utterly shocked to see that second blue line come up. And I was utterly horrified to realise I'd put a baby at risk.'

'You couldn't have known about the *coxiella burnetii* or the baby,' he said, holding her close. 'It's not your fault. It's not anybody's fault. It was simply bad luck.'

'The doctor started treating me with cotrimoxazole,' she said. 'But it was too late. I lost the baby two weeks later, at what we think must've been about ten weeks.' She closed her eyes. 'Three years ago today.'

'I'm so very sorry,' he said, holding her more tightly.

'It's like being wrapped in lead,' she said. 'Most of the time I'm OK. But this day of the year—it just flattens me. It feels full of shadows. Whatever I do.'

'Of course it does. It doesn't matter that it was early on, or that you hadn't planned the baby; it's still a loss and of course it's going to hurt.'

She leaned her forehead against his. 'Thank you. For understanding.'

'I'm here.' He stroked her hair.

'And then afterwards, it made me realise that actually, I *did* want children. But Mark still didn't. He'd had a fairly miserable childhood, and his parents had an acrimonious divorce. Even though he'd met my family and they were proof that family life didn't always have to be difficult, he still didn't want children.' She grimaced. 'He liked things ordered and pristine. We even had white furniture and white carpets—which absolutely aren't sensible to have with small children or pets. We talked about it, but he was shocked by the idea that we might've been parents. And then it got worse. He said he didn't have a role model, growing up, and he couldn't see himself as a dad. Ever.' She sighed. 'We kept going round and round in circles. I think losing the baby changed us both; it made him more adamant that he didn't want children. But I did, and there wasn't a real compromise. You can't have half a baby. One of us had to give up our dream, and it wouldn't be fair on the other. Eventually we agreed it would be better to end our marriage, and we split the house and everything down the middle. Mark was fair about it—he wasn't selfish.'

Not selfish? Ant wasn't quite as sure about that. Financially, her ex had been fair; emotionally, could he have done more? 'Though he wasn't prepared to raise children with you?'

'Mark was—*is*—a good man,' Geri said. 'We loved each other, but in the end that turned out to be not quite enough. He didn't want to hurt me, but how could he force himself to do something to please me that would've made him hugely unhappy? And in the long run it would've hurt us more—if we'd had a child and *then* split up, it would've hurt our child, too. He'd been collateral damage himself, and he didn't want to be the one inflicting that on a child of his own.' She spread her hands. 'We talked and talked and talked about it, and in the end this seemed the fairest solution for both of us.'

'I'm sorry,' he said, holding her close.

'He's found someone else now and they see things the same way. Neither of them want children, and they're happy together.' She gave him a watery smile. 'And

I'm truly glad for him. I didn't want to see him lonely and miserable.'

Of course she didn't. Geri was lovely—and she *cared*. It was one of the things he liked so much about her.

'I didn't want to go back to working with farm animals—not when working with the sheep had made everything go wrong for me. That was when I decided to switch specialties,' she said. 'I did my Masters in London, living with my parents while I studied, and then I got the job at Cambridge.'

'And you're happy in your new role?'

'I am,' she said. 'I really do love my job.'

'But what about you?' he asked. 'You said you wanted a relationship.'

She nodded. 'But, before I get properly involved with someone else, I want to make sure that my future partner and I really do want the same things.'

She'd met *him*. Could he be her future partner? Did she want the same things that he did?

'And you still want children?' he asked carefully.

'I do—but it's going to be a bit more complicated now,' she said. 'Because of the Q fever, it's possible that I'm at a higher risk of losing my next baby. And it's also possible that the Q fever might be reactivated during pregnancy. I know the doctors will give me more blood tests to check, and they'll keep a really close eye on me, but...' She grimaced. 'If I ever get pregnant again, I'm going to be worrying all the way through the pregnancy.'

'Which is only natural, considering what happened to you,' he said.

'The doctors gave me medication for a year after I lost the baby. I know at least I'm not at risk of developing endocarditis,' she said. 'But they told me it might be tricky getting pregnant and staying pregnant.'

'That's understandable, given what's happened,' he said.

'I hope my future partner will think that way,' she said.

He did; but now wasn't the right time to push her to consider him as a future partner, Ant thought. Particularly as he knew he was as damaged as she was. But maybe, just maybe, he could help her through today. And then they could see where this took them.

'I'm sorry that happened to you,' he said. 'Losing a baby and then losing your marriage. That's hard.'

She nodded.

'You told me you always looked for the sunshine— how, when this happened to you?'

'I was really low for a couple of months after I lost the baby. My sister was brilliant; she bossed me about and made me do her classes. And eventually I realised I could either stay miserable, and people around me would worry about me all the time and it'd be a vicious circle; or I could try and look for the bright stuff in life. That's how I learned to fake it—to stop everyone worrying about me.' She shrugged.

Except suppressing her feelings hadn't helped her move on. It had kept her stuck. He kept his arms wrapped round her, and gradually her tears dried.

'Thank you for listening,' she said.

'Any time. And I'm sorry this happened to you, Geri. You lost more than I did.'

'No. I think we both lost what we wanted,' she said, 'and it wasn't either of our faults.'

'Maybe,' he said, 'we need to spend a while in a green

space. Somewhere quiet where you won't have to face families with children. Go and splash your face with water, give me ten minutes, and I'll take you somewhere.'

Geri was grateful that Antoine had given her some space. Splashing her face with water made her feel better; by the time she heard the front door close, she felt a bit more in control.

She headed back up to the kitchen to join him, and blinked in surprise when she saw he was holding a bunch of white roses and a pair of scissors.

'The florist didn't sell dried petals,' he said, 'but I thought maybe we could drop fresh ones into a stream in remembrance of your baby.'

'That's...' The tears welled up, clogging her throat; she had to swallow hard before she could speak again. 'That's really thoughtful.'

'It's what I do on my grandmother's anniversary,' he said. 'But the place where I normally go in Paris will be full of children, and it'll be hard for you. We'll go out of the city.'

'Thank you,' she said. 'Though I feel guilty, because you were supposed to be seeing Céline and Jean-Luc and mending some bridges.'

'It's fine. And this is just as important,' he said.

She helped him cut the petals from the roses and fold them into a paper bag; then they drove north of Paris, out towards the Forest of Compiègne, and he parked the car in a pretty village. They walked past a row of cottages with pale stone walls, terracotta roofs and painted wooden shutters at the windows; climbing roses covered the trellises around the doors, and a few buds were starting to peep out. It felt almost as if they were walking back through centuries, and at any minute a carriage and horses would come down the cobbled street.

At the end of the street there was a fortified gate; a stone arch stretched between two towers with conical tiled roofs. Geri half expected it to lead to a castle, but it turned out to be a church.

'It's what's left of an old Benedictine abbey,' Ant said.

They stopped in the middle of a small stone bridge that crossed the stream, where he gave her the bag of rose petals. She scattered a handful, then offered the bag to him.

'Sleep peacefully, little one,' he said softly as he scattered the petals.

It was as if he knew the words in her heart, and she felt lighter—as if the weight of misery that normally shrouded her on this day was finally starting to dissolve.

When they finished scattering the petals and left the bridge, he took her hand; she knew this was his way of letting her know without words that he was there if she needed to lean on him, and she really appreciated it.

They walked in a comfortable silence back to the car, not needing to speak.

At the car, she squeezed his hand. 'Thank you, Antoine. For understanding. For caring. It means a lot.'

'Any time,' he said, and the warmth in his eyes made her feel as if there was brightness left in the world.

CHAPTER EIGHT

THE NEXT DAY, Geri felt as if the huge weight of grief had slid from her shoulders and she could breathe again.

'I'm sorry for sobbing all over you yesterday,' she said to Antoine over breakfast.

'It's fine,' he said. 'I understand.'

'Thank you. It's that one day in the year when it just overwhelms me,' she said. 'The day afterwards, I can cope again. But you did a lot to help. I appreciate it.'

'You're welcome,' he said. 'I've got a half-day today. Maybe we can do a bit of exploring, this afternoon—and go dancing by the Seine, this evening. Tick another thing off your list.'

'I'd really like that,' she said.

After dinner, they headed down to the Jardin de Tino Rosso, a pretty park on the left bank of the Seine. It was filled with flowers and modern sculpture, but best of all for Geri was the series of little amphitheatres by the edge of the river. There were people sitting on the curved stone steps to watch the dancers in the centre—and it seemed to be open to everyone. Some wore proper dancing shoes, some wore trainers, and others still danced in bare feet.

'You wanted to dance the tango in Paris,' Antoine said with a smile. *'Voici.'*

Geri eyed the dancers, who all seemed to know exactly what they were doing. 'I've never actually danced the tango,' she said.

'I learned here as a student,' he said. 'It was fun.'

'Maybe I should sit and watch,' she said.

'It's an open dance thing. If you sit down, someone will ask you to dance,' he said. 'You might as well dance with me.' He smiled. 'Hey. If you can anaesthetise a tiger…'

'Then I can take the cork off a champagne bottle with a sabre, and I can dance the tango,' she said.

'That's *mon petit rayon*.' The warmth in his eyes sent heat sizzling through her veins. 'Now, your sister teaches aerobics. I'm guessing you know how to follow a routine?'

'I do,' she confirmed.

He drew her over to a quieter spot. 'Let's run through the basics. Remember you'll be alternating your feet. Stand facing me, feet together,' he said. 'Take one step back with your left foot, then one to the side with your right.' He nodded in approval as she followed his instructions. 'Two steps back—left and right—then cross your left foot in front of your right.' He smiled. 'Last bit: right foot back, left foot left, close with your right, and you're ready to start again.'

'Got it,' she said.

'Good. Now do it again, and this time you'll be more or less mirroring me,' he said. Once they'd run through the sequence three or four times, he said, 'Now let's try it in hold. Put your right hand up, and hold my left.' He smiled. 'That's fine. Your left arm goes round my shoulders, and your hand goes just below my neck.'

When she'd followed his instructions, he slid his right arm round her shoulders, pulling her close to him.

'Follow my lead. We'll do the basic step,' he said.

It felt very different, when he was up close and personal. She'd never realised how broad his shoulders were, how defined his muscles were. Not only his back: his legs, too. She could feel her breath growing shallower and her pulse speeding up as they danced.

'Ready to add a bit?' he asked.

'Uh-huh,' she said, not trusting herself to use proper words. Dancing with him was definitely scrambling her brain.

He taught her how to swivel her hips, and it made her catch her breath.

She'd had no idea that the tango was *this* sensual.

'Let's try it down with everyone else,' he said. 'Follow my lead. I've got you; you won't fall.'

She had no idea how they got down to the main dance floor; all she was aware of was the sound of the music, the heat of the late spring evening, the scent of the blossom and the feel of his body close to hers.

Even though she knew there was a crowd of people in the little amphitheatre, it felt as if it was only the two of them, the music and the reflection of the streetlights shimmering on the river.

He'd dipped his head far enough to rest his cheek next to hers. Every time they turned a corner, his leg slid between hers and he held her more tightly before releasing her again. Every swivel of their hips stoked her desire higher and higher. If he didn't kiss her, and soon, she was convinced that she was going to spontaneously combust.

She tilted her face slightly, so her lips brushed the corner of his mouth; and she felt the immediate tension in his body.

'Geri, if you do that again,' he whispered, 'I can't be responsible for what happens next.'

It sounded like a challenge.

How could she resist?

She kissed him again; and this time he kissed her back, his mouth hot and sensual beneath the stars.

It wasn't enough.

Not anywhere near enough.

'Let's go home,' she whispered. 'Dance with me in your roof garden.'

'D'accord,' he said, his voice sounding as shaken as she felt.

He held her hand all the way on the Métro. Kissed her under every streetlight between the station and the row of houses where he lived. Kissed her in the lift up to his apartment.

'Hold that thought,' he said as they reached his front door. Once he'd unlocked it, he scooped her into his arms and carried her up the stairs and through to the kitchen. Then he let her slide down until her feet were touching the floor, before kissing her again.

'You wanted to dance,' he said, and opened the door to the roof garden. 'I don't think we have room to tango.' He found some sweet, slow music on his phone, then drew her into his arms and danced with her cheek to cheek.

The tango had felt like dancing through fire. This felt like dancing through an orchard full of blossom, with the petals gently dropping over them. And this time, when he kissed her, it was sweet and slow and made her ache.

'Antoine,' she whispered. 'I want you.'

'I want you, too, *mon petit rayon*,' he whispered back.

'Take me to bed.'

His dark gaze held hers. 'You're sure?'

She nodded. 'I've wanted you since the day we met.'

'It's the same for me,' he said. 'But—'

'No buts. We'll think about things tomorrow,' she said. 'Tonight—let's just *be*.'

He brushed his mouth against hers, sensitising every nerve-end, and she shivered. 'Ant. *Now*.'

He scooped her up, carried her back into the apartment, and then down the stairs to his bedroom.

The next morning, the alarm shrilled on Antoine's phone.

Geri woke, warm and comfortable in Antoine's arms— and then the previous night flooded back into her head.

Oh, help.

What did they do now?

They'd been carried away by the music and the dancing, and they'd both wanted each other. It had been a moment out of time. One she was glad they'd shared; but now it was Monday morning. Time to go back out of their bubble and into their normal lives.

And all of a sudden she felt ridiculously shy.

He switched off the alarm. 'Good morning.'

His voice sounded carefully neutral. Did he regret last night?

And where did they go from here?

She still felt ridiculously shy, but she wasn't a coward. She'd face this. She took a deep breath and looked him in the eye. 'Good morning.'

It wasn't only his voice that was carefully neutral; his expression was, too.

Sink or swim, she thought. 'What happens now?'

'That depends.'

Two could play at equanimity. 'On what?' she asked coolly.

'Touché,' he said. 'Last night—I have no regrets.'

Relief flooded through her. Maybe they could find a way through this that wasn't awkward. 'Me, neither.'

'Good.' He kissed the tip of her nose. 'But I'm not ready to share that with anyone else, yet. Not until we both know what we want. Perhaps at work we can let everyone think we're just friends?'

'Is that what we are?'

'I don't know,' he said. 'There are all kinds of reasons why we should be just friends. You're here for six months. We live in different countries. We both have scars across our hearts. The sensible thing would be for us to be just friends.'

'There's a "but" in your voice,' she said.

He nodded. 'I like you, *mon petit rayon*.' He paused. 'More than like.'

Her pulse kicked up a notch. 'I wasn't expecting this. I wasn't looking for another relationship.'

'But?'

She smiled. 'I like you, too. A lot. More than like. And I want to be with you, see where things go.'

'Then let's keep this between us, for now.' He stole a kiss. 'Though, this very minute, we need to get a move on or we'll be late for work.'

'And that,' she said, 'might let the cat out of the bag.' She kissed him back. 'First one to the kitchen puts the kettle on.'

'D'accord.' His eyes glittered. 'And, much as I'd like to scoop you up and carry you to my shower, I think you'd better use your own bathroom.'

'About the shower? Maybe we can do that tonight,' she said, and was gratified to see colour bloom across his cheeks. It was enough to remove the last vestiges of her shyness; she climbed out of his bed, scooped up her clothes and sashayed to the door, enjoying his sharp intake of breath.

In the kitchen, they had a perfectly civil breakfast of coffee and *tartine*.

But then Antoine kissed her by the front door, enough to make her knees weak.

'Hold that thought,' he said. 'Now we go into colleague mode.'

'Colleague, flatmate and friend,' she corrected.

Even so, he held her hand all the way to the Métro station, and halfway to the zoo. But then they strolled into work as if it was a perfectly normal Monday morning. Geri liked that Antoine put professionalism first and concentrated on the animals, and she was even more thrilled at the daybook meeting when he and Pierre agreed to tempt Zhen with some treats in the hope that they could do an ultrasound.

'We'll definitely know if she's pregnant?' Geri asked.

'Hopefully,' Antoine said.

Once they'd done the rounds and sorted out the morning's problems, it was time to give Zhen an ultrasound. There was an inspection hatch on the bars of her enclosure, similar to the one Antoine had used when taking bloods from Bianca's tail, and Pierre was carrying a bucket of sweet potato cubes.

'Do you want to feed our girl?' Pierre asked.

'I do—but I also want to see the ultrasound,' she said.

'Feed our girl while Ant feels her tummy,' Pierre said, 'and then when he does the ultrasound you can take a film of the screen for the zoo.'

'All right,' she said.

Zhen came into the enclosure and lay down in front

of the bars of the training chute on her right side, facing them.

'I assume you do the same sort of training as they do with the tigers?' Geri asked.

'We do,' Pierre confirmed. 'Zhen and Bohai are both happy to put their paw out and grasp a bar to let us do a blood draw. We use a tennis ball on a pole as our target, and reward them with sweet potato or honey water in a squeezy tube.'

He fed Zhen a cube of sweet potato. 'Good girl,' he said. 'Paw up.'

Zhen put her left paw on the bar, and received another treat and more praise.

'Leg out,' he said, and the panda stretched out to bare her tummy.

Geri took over, soothing the panda and feeding her more potato as Antoine undid the inspection hatch. 'I can't believe how gentle she is,' she said. 'This is like giving treats to a dog or cat.'

'We all enjoy training,' Pierre said.

Antoine felt the panda's abdomen, as Pierre gave Zhen another cube and praised her.

'Time to film?' Geri asked.

'Yes,' Antoine said, and squeezed gel onto the transceiver head. 'We've warmed the gel so it isn't a shock to her,' he said.

Pierre kept soothing the panda and feeding her cubes of sweet potato while Antoine pressed the transceiver against her stomach.

'Someone's full of bamboo,' he remarked. 'Don't hold your breath, because we're looking for something the size of a marble. It's only the last two weeks of pregnancy where we get a decent view of a foetus.'

Geri held her breath as she filmed him doing the ultrasound, then switched view to the portable screen.

Would it show the amniotic sac—or was it a pseudopregnancy?

Ant moved the head of the transceiver. 'Well, now. I think we might have a sight of foetal tissue.'

The triangular image showed the denser muscles and tissues, and then the wavy dark space of Zhen's uterus, and finally the tiny white shape Antoine had mentioned earlier.

'And that's our panda foetus?' she asked.

'Probably,' Antoine said. 'We can cautiously say, as long as she doesn't resorb the foetus, with luck she'll have a cub next month.'

'I feel almost as proud as when I saw my son's ultrasound,' Pierre said feelingly. 'You clever girl, Zhen. You clever, clever girl.'

Geri stopped filming and took over feeding the sweet potato to Zhen while Pierre looked at the screen.

The keeper wiped his eyes. 'Look at me, crying like a baby.'

'I can hardly believe this,' Geri said. 'Today's a perfect day.'

Antoine stroked the panda's abdomen and took the transceiver away. 'Good girl,' he said. 'You were very patient with us.'

Pierre gave Zhen a couple more treats. 'Well done, sweetheart,' he said. 'Now go and have your bamboo.'

The panda grunted as Antoine closed the inspection hatch, and then stood up and ambled away.

* * *

That evening, Ant and Geri caught the Métro back to Montmartre. He took her hand as they left the station, and it felt so right.

'Want to go exploring, or have a quiet night in?' he asked.

'I think we'd have to toss a coin for that one,' she said with a smile. 'Either way, I'm going to talk your ears off about pandas. I've been reading up.'

He couldn't resist her enthusiasm and the way her eyes sparkled. 'Early dinner,' he said, 'then the terrace and a glass of wine.'

'Perfect,' she said. 'Did you know that a panda cub can't regulate its body temperature? That's why the mum will keep the cub tucked under her chin or her arm for the first few weeks, and breathe on it to keep its environment warm and humid.'

He did know, actually, because he'd worked in zoo medicine for a few more years than she had, but he wasn't going to stifle that enthusiasm. 'Baby pandas are hairless and blind,' he said. 'They need that warmth and humidity.'

'I really hope Zhen has that cub,' she said. 'It's incredibly exciting.' She paused. 'Today couldn't get any more perfect.'

'That sounds like a challenge,' Ant said. 'And one I fully intend to meet.'

Her eyes widened. 'I like the sound of that...'

After dinner, they strolled through the streets holding hands; he kissed her at every street corner on the way back to his apartment.

On the roof garden, he scooped Geri onto his lap and held her close. 'I've wanted to do this all day.'

'Me, too.' She stroked his face. 'I like being with you.'

'I like being with you, too. You make the world feel full of sunshine.'

'Careful. You're starting to sound like a poet,' she warned teasingly. 'Oh, wait—isn't French poetry melancholy?'

'A lot of it is,' he said. 'But some aren't. There's the Rostand poem about a kiss being the pink dot you put on the I of the verb "to love".'

'That sounds fabulous,' she said. 'Do you know the full thing?'

'I'm a scientist,' he said. 'I didn't really learn much poetry. Hold on, and I'll find it.' He took his phone from the table and checked the internet. 'Here.'

She scanned it swiftly, then tried translating it.

'That's a good attempt,' he said, rewarding her with a kiss.

'Read it to me in the original,' she said. 'You have a beautiful voice.'

Nobody had ever said that to him before. Nobody had ever asked him to read poetry to them before. And he'd pretty much forgotten most of his literature lessons from school. But he smiled and read it to her.

'That's lovely,' she said.

'It's actually from *Cyrano de Bergerac*,' he said. 'The scene where Cyrano wins a kiss for Christian from Roxane. The film won Depardieu an award nomination.' He found the clip on the internet.

She watched it, her pupils growing darker. 'He should've won the award for that,' she said. 'But I like your version better. The words won a kiss, did they?'

'*Un bisou,*' he confirmed.

'Then that,' she said, 'should be your reward, too.'

The kiss was slow, long, and sent his pulse hammering. By the time she broke the kiss, he couldn't think straight. All he could think of was how much he wanted to kiss her again, make love to her, make her see stars.

And he only realised he'd said the words out loud when she whispered, 'Do it.'

What could he do but carry her to bed?

CHAPTER NINE

IT WAS ALMOST a perfect week, Ant thought. He loved his work at the zoo; and he loved spending time outside work with Geri, exploring the hidden corners of his city and making love with her. He couldn't remember the last time he'd been this happy.

When they both had a day off on Thursday, he took her to Versailles. It had been a while since he'd visited, and he'd forgotten how big the building was.

'This is breathtaking,' Geri said as they walked into the Hall of Mirrors. 'Those huge arched windows reflected in those enormous mirrors, and the chandeliers—all that light! It must've seemed even more stunning when it was built.'

'Nearly three hundred and fifty years ago,' he said. 'Louis XIV was determined to prove that the French could make mirrors as well as Venice.'

She loved the lightness of the Queen's bedchamber, too, with the exact replicas of the original fabric.

But her favourite bit was the Grand Trianon, with its pink marble columns, chequered floors and stunning gardens. Ant liked it, too, because he got to hold her hand all the way through their visit, and to kiss her in a quiet arbour of roses.

It was another day out of time, where he felt they got closer still; but Friday was more worrying.

Matthieu, head of the primate section, looked grim. 'It's Shabani.' Shabani was the silverback—the leader of their small troop of gorillas. 'He's not been eating much, this week.'

Given that gorillas spent half their day eating, that was a bad sign. 'Is there any physical reason why he's not eating?'

'He's not been touching his favourite browse—' fresh tree trimmings '—and I wonder if he has a tooth causing pain,' Matthieu said.

Ant nodded. 'We're going to need to sedate him, to take a proper look at him.'

'Are the gorillas trained in the same way as the tigers?' Geri asked.

'No. We'll need to use a dart,' Ant said. 'One of the vet team will do it, Matthieu; we don't want to risk damaging any of the keepers' relationships with him.'

'I was hoping you'd say that. I've kept him apart from the others,' Matthieu said, 'and no food or water since last night.'

'We'll put him top of the list,' Ant said. 'Geri—airway or sedation?'

'Airway,' she said. 'And I'll do the darting. He doesn't know me, and I don't want him associating it with you in case you need to do treatment while he's conscious.'

'Thank you,' Ant said.

Shabani was in one of the indoor enclosures. Geri darted him, but Shabani pulled the dart out immediately.

'It needs to be in for a couple of seconds to get enough anaesthetic into his system,' Ant said. 'But we don't want too much, either.'

'Not on top of what he already might have had,' Geri said. 'Let's use a half dose with the second dart.'

This time, it worked. As soon as he was unconscious, a team of four keepers moved him onto his back, and Geri intubated him to keep him breathing.

Ant assessed Shabani's mouth. 'I can't see anything,' he said. 'We need an X-ray.'

He X-rayed the gorilla's jaw, but all thirty-two teeth were fine.

Gently, he explored the gorilla's face. 'There's a lump here, under his jaw,' he said.

Matthieu dragged in a breath. 'Are you thinking cancer?'

'We'd need the lab to tell us that,' Ant said. 'At the moment, it feels like soft tissue. I'm going to remove it, and we'll get it tested.'

He sterilised the area, and made only a small hole, meaning that Shabani would be less likely to pick at the stitches afterwards. He excised the lump and put it into a sample container for the lab team, then concentrated on suturing the wound.

The whole procedure took almost an hour.

'OK. We're going to reverse the anaesthetic now,' he said.

Geri removed the tube, Ant gave the injection, and they stayed outside the enclosure to monitor the gorilla.

'I think his airway might be blocked,' Ant said. 'I'll go in.'

He cleared Shabani's mouth; the gorilla growled, and Ant backed out of the enclosure.

Shabani growled again, and Matthieu gave a smothered sob.

Geri clearly noticed, because she put her arm round his shoulders. 'It's going to be all right,' she said.

'It's just seeing him lying there, helpless... I've known him since he was a baby,' Matthieu said. 'I cuddled him when he was tiny.'

'We needed to check him out to find out what was going on, and Ant couldn't have removed that lump without anaesthetic,' Geri said. 'He's coming round, the same way as a human when they mumble a bit and it doesn't mean anything. We're here to keep an eye on him.'

She really was lovely, Ant thought. Empathetic, instinctively knowing when someone needed kindness and saying the right words to make them feel better.

After half an hour, Shabani was conscious but still a little drowsy.

'I'll keep an eye on him,' Matthieu said.

'It's nearly lunchtime,' Geri said. 'I'll get you a coffee and something to eat.'

'I'm not sure I could eat anything,' Matthieu admitted. 'I'm too worried. I'd rather stay with Shabani.'

'I'll keep you company,' Ant said.

'We both will,' Geri said. 'I'll get the equipment back to the surgery, take the lump to the lab, and bring you both some lunch.'

Matthieu gave them a watery smile. 'Sorry. But my gorillas...they're like part of the family.'

'Of course they are,' Geri said. 'I used to work with farm animals—and every single cow, sheep and pig had a name. The farmers could tell them all apart, even those who looked identical to me. They all had characters. Just because the animals here aren't domestic, it doesn't mean you don't get close to them.'

By the next morning, Shabani had his appetite back

and had been reunited with his brothers; and by the middle of the week the lab came back with the good news that it wasn't anything sinister, merely an infected salivary gland.

The following Saturday, Antoine asked Geri to go to Chartres with him.

'If it's too soon for you to be around a baby, I understand,' he said. 'I don't want to reopen your scars.'

'It's not my dark day of the year. I can cope,' she said. 'But are you sure Jean-Luc and Céline won't mind me being there?'

'Jean-Luc asked me to invite you.'

Antoine had mentioned her to his brother? That felt like a huge step. 'All right,' she said. 'Provided I can take flowers and something for the baby.'

'And I'll take champagne,' he said.

Antoine was quiet on the drive, and Geri put her hand briefly over his on the steering wheel and pressed lightly. 'Are you sure you're up to this?'

'Once we're over the first awkward moments,' he said, 'I think it'll be fine. The anticipation's the worst thing.' He paused. 'Jean-Luc and I—we've been texting quite a bit, since I got back in touch. Little things, nothing deep. But it feels as if I'm getting my brother back.'

'I'm glad,' she said.

Finally, they reached Chartres and he parked on the drive; carrying the flowers, champagne and the fabric book of zoo animals Geri hadn't been able to resist, they waited on the doorstep.

Jean-Luc answered the door. For a second, everyone was frozen; and then Jean-Luc gave Antoine the biggest hug. 'My little brother,' he said, his voice thick with emotion. 'I'm so glad to see you.'

Geri was surprised by how similar they looked. The only real difference between them was in the shadows under Jean-Luc's eyes, which could all be down to the new baby. Still with his arm round Antoine's shoulders, Jean-Luc turned to her. 'You must be Geri. *Enchanté.*' He shook her hand.

'Pleased to meet you,' Geri said. *'Merci de m'avoir invitée.'*

'Come in,' Jean-Luc said, standing aside to usher them in.

Céline was walking up the hallway, carrying the baby. She looked nervous, but glanced at Jean-Luc, who gave the tiniest nod.

'Welcome,' she said.

Antoine went very still, and then he smiled. 'She's beautiful, Céline. I can see both of you in her.'

'Ant. I'm…' She blew out a breath, clearly searching for the right words. 'I'm sorry. For everything. For not telling you earlier, for hurting you.'

'It doesn't matter any more,' Antoine said. 'It's in the past. We've all changed. And I'm glad you're both happy—and that you have the little one.'

Her eyes filled with tears. 'Thank you.'

'This is my colleague, Geri,' Antoine said. 'She's on secondment in Paris from our twinned zoo in Cambridge.'

Colleague. The word felt like a papercut, even though she knew it was sensible. They'd agreed to keep their relationship to themselves, after all. And introducing her to his ex as his girlfriend would be awkward. But at the same time she wished it could be more than this.

'*Bienvenue*, Geri,' Céline said. 'Are you enjoying Paris?'

'Very much,' Geri said. 'We brought a little something for you both, and for Maya.'

'Oh, this book is so lovely. Thank you so much. See, Maya? *Les animaux.*' She turned one of the pages and smiled. '*Le tigre.* Of course. Bianca.'

'Thank you, Geri. Come and sit down,' Jean-Luc said.

Céline handed the baby and the fabric book to him. 'I'll make coffee,' she said, 'and put these beautiful flowers in water.'

'Can I help?' Geri asked; apart from being polite, she had a feeling that Antoine and Jean-Luc might need a moment to themselves.

'Thank you. That would be kind.' Céline led her through to the kitchen, and put the flowers in water before putting the kettle on; she'd already shaken grounds into the cafetière and put cups and saucers on a tray, clearly prepared for the visit.

'Are you Ant's girlfriend?' Céline asked.

It was blunt, and Geri knew she and Ant should've expected this and discussed her response. Caught off guard, she resorted to the facts. 'I'm his colleague, here on secondment. There was a problem with my flat, and I ended up staying with him.'

'I see.'

Geri could feel the heat rising in her face and knew it was giving her away. 'He was a bit prickly to start with, but we work well together and I think we've become good friends. He's helping me tick off my list of things I want to see in Paris, and also find the best place for crème brûlée for when my sister visits.'

'He said you helped him find the *doudou plat* and the tiger for the baby.'

Geri smiled. 'Yes. We had a squabble in the shop and had to toss a coin. If I'd had my way he would've sent you a panda—the pandas are why I came to Paris, to work on the breeding programme. I've loved pandas ever since I was tiny.'

Céline nodded and gave her an assessing look. 'I assume he's told you everything?'

'About the situation? Yes.'

'I never wanted to hurt him,' Céline said softly. 'Neither did Jean-Luc. I loved Ant. But when Jean-Luc came to Paris and I met him for the first time, it was like fireworks going off in my head. Like nothing I'd ever felt before. I tried to fight it—and I was never unfaithful to Ant. I thought as long as Jean-Luc wasn't in Paris, I could ignore my feelings and be the partner Ant deserved.'

'I'm not judging you,' Geri said. 'You can't help who you fall in love with.'

Céline gave a sad smile. 'But we handled it badly and we hurt Ant. I don't think either of us will ever be able to forgive ourselves for it.'

'I think he's come to terms with things,' Geri said. 'I know he misses Jean-Luc—and you. The baby was the catalyst for him to make contact with you both again.'

'I think,' Céline said, 'he would still have kept his distance, if not for you.'

'Maybe,' Geri said.

Céline gave her a hug. 'Thank you for whatever you said to him. The times Jean-Luc has wanted to call him, but it felt as if we'd be rubbing our happiness in his face and that wasn't fair. We knew we had to wait until he was ready to contact us—on his terms.'

'Ant said Jean-Luc has been texting him.'

Céline nodded. 'He says he feels as if the family can

come together again. We both know it's our fault that the split happened.'

'Ant thinks it's his fault.'

Céline shook her head. 'If I hadn't called off the wedding...'

'Then you would both have been unhappy,' Geri said. 'You spared him that.'

'I wish there'd been a way to do it so nobody got hurt,' Céline said. 'And I hope we will become friends.'

'I'd like that,' Geri said.

When they took the coffee through, Ant was sitting on the sofa, holding the baby. Geri's heart squeezed. Right at that moment, she could imagine him holding his own child. It made her wonder if it would be better to go back to being purely colleagues and friends; Ant was clearly a born father, and having children might be complicated for her. He'd already been hurt. How could she potentially put him through the anguish of losing a baby, or not being able to have children?

Or maybe he saw her as his transition person, and thought he was doing the same for her.

So she smiled. A lot. Even though her heart squeezed even more when it was her turn to cuddle the baby; the warmth, the weight and the little sleepy snuffles Maya gave when she fell asleep all made her think of what she'd lost. Of what might never be.

Jean-Luc insisted that they stay for lunch, and gradually Geri found herself relaxing.

'Thank you for coming to see us,' he said, kissing her cheeks, when they finally left. 'It's been good to get to know you.'

Céline followed it up with a hug. 'Thank you for bringing Ant back to us. And maybe we can come to see you in Paris.'

'I think we'd both like that,' Geri said, hugging her back.

Antoine was quiet as they walked round Chartres; but once they were in the cathedral grounds, he took her in his arms and held her close. 'Thank you,' he said. 'For giving me perspective. For persuading me to bridge that gap when I was being stubborn.'

'My pleasure. They're lovely. As is the baby.'

'I saw your face when you held her. It hurt,' he said softly.

'It did,' she admitted. 'But at the same time I think it was good for me to have close contact with a baby.'

'We're healing,' he said. 'It's going to get better.'

It was, particularly when Antoine did another ultrasound on Zhen later the following week and this time they got to see the foetus.

'Look—there's a spine,' he said, 'and the foetus is kicking. It's about four centimetres long; I'd say we'll have a panda cub at some time in the next couple of weeks. We'll need a rota to be on panda watch in about ten days' time.'

Between work and exploring Paris with Antoine—and waking up in his arms every morning—Geri couldn't have been happier. Maybe she was storing up trouble for herself in the future, but for now she was enjoying the moment and not having to go into issues that she'd find hard to face. It would be easy to let herself love this man, but she didn't want to saddle him with the burden of her infertility. And maybe their affair would come to a natural end when her placement was over. So she was just going to enjoy her time with him and ignore the shadows.

She managed that until the day the lab gave them the bad news about Bianca's bloods.

'Her kidneys have deteriorated a lot more since the last tests,' Antoine said. 'I can't give her any meds to make things better. I know they've had success with kidney transfers in cats, but I don't know of any in tigers—and even if a kidney was available from another tiger and we could do some pioneering surgery, there's no guarantee the transplant would work or give her a better quality of life.' He took a deep breath. 'I can't let her suffer. I need to speak to the directors; they need to ratify my clinical decision.'

She knew the decision he meant. The one that all vets hated having to make. 'Do you want me to go with you? For moral support, I mean?' she asked.

'No. But I think Belle could do with a hug,' he said. 'I'll come and find you when I've spoken to the directors.'

When he came to find them, he was grim-faced. 'It's agreed. We need to say goodbye.'

'She came to the zoo the same day you did,' Belle said. 'A year before I joined.'

He nodded. 'This will be hard. But we need to do it, for her sake.'

Belle's eyes filled with tears. 'I know.' She called Bianca, who came padding over to the bars where they stood and made a soft chuffing noise.

'My lovely girl,' she said. 'It's going to be hard, not having you saying hello to me every day.'

The tiger chuffed at her.

'We've been here together since that first day,' Antoine said. 'I can't imagine the zoo without you. But we need to let you run free and be out of pain.'

'Down, girl,' Belle whispered; as Bianca lay down, she gave the tiger a treat.

Antoine had already prepared the syringe. 'Good girl,' he said, and Belle gave her another treat.

'I know you're tired, my lovely. So tired. And we'll miss you very, very much. But now it's time for you to sleep,' Antoine said.

The tiger made a soft chuff as if to say goodbye.

Belle was shaking with the effort of not sobbing out loud and distressing the tiger, and Geri slid an arm round her shoulders.

Antoine knelt next to the tiger. '*Poussée*, Bianca,' he said and slowly eased the tip of the syringe into her vein. This time, Geri wasn't on intubation duties, because this time the tiger wasn't going to wake up, and she had a lump in her throat.

'Run free, *ma petite*,' Antoine said, and stroked the tiger's flank before withdrawing his hand and the syringe.

His eyes were wet, and now Belle was sobbing openly.

Geri put her arms round both of them, trying to comfort them as best she could.

She wasn't sure how any of them got through the day. Antoine did his rounds while avoiding everyone as much as possible; Belle had the other tigers to look after, but was clearly hurting; and Geri was worried about Antoine.

The only thing she could think of to do was the same thing that he'd done for her. She popped out to the nearest shops and bought flowers; then found him in his office at the end of the day.

'Come on,' she said gently. 'You need to get out of here.'

'I just...the world feels flat,' he said. 'And I know it's ridiculous, being this upset about a tiger.'

'A tiger who joined the zoo the same day that you did. A tiger who knew your voice and came and chuffed at you, as if you were one of her pack. That's not any old tiger,' she said. 'Come with me.'

'Forgive me, Geri, but I'm not in the mood for exploring Paris tonight.'

'We're not exploring,' she said. 'I have petals.'

His eyes glittered in recognition of what she meant. 'That's…'

'You don't have to speak,' she said. 'I know.'

With the help of the map on her phone, she took him to the Parc Monceau and found the Venetian bridge. 'I thought here might be a nice spot to remember her,' she said.

'Very nice.' He took a handful of flower petals and scattered them on the water. 'Vets aren't supposed to have favourites.'

'In theory, but we all do. My best friend at my old practice has a jar of dog treats in her consulting room, and any springer spaniels coming in for a check-up or inoculations or investigations get an extra bit of fuss.'

The anecdote made him smile, as she'd hoped it would.

'I connected with Bianca,' he said. 'My apartment isn't suitable for keeping a dog, but maybe I should get a cat.'

'A black and white one,' she suggested.

'Called Bianca,' he said. 'Though I think you'd name a black and white cat "Panda".'

'It's a great name for a cat. Short for Pandemonium,' she said. 'Which is what all the best kittens will cause.'

'Yeah.' His voice thickened, and he sprinkled more petals onto the water below. 'Or maybe I could adopt a rescue cat.'

'Maybe,' she said with a smile.

He sprinkled the rest of the petals in silence, and she knew in his head he was saying goodbye to the white tigress who'd been there for his whole time at the zoo. And it would hurt as much as saying goodbye to a beloved pet.

He didn't say much on the way back to his apartment, though when she reached for his hand his fingers tightened round hers. When she offered to cook them both dinner, he shook his head. 'I'm not hungry.'

She stroked his face. 'I would offer to make you a mug cake, but you hated the last one.'

'I appreciated the kindness,' he said.

'I'm going to make an omelette,' she said. 'Which won't be anything like a proper Parisian one, but you're welcome to share it. Even if you only take one mouthful.'

He slid his arms round her and held her close. 'You're one of a kind, Geri Milligan. A very special kind. And you make the world a better place just by being in it.'

She caught her breath. 'I think that's the nicest thing anyone's ever said to me.'

'It's true,' he said, drawing back to look her in the eye. 'You've changed my world. You've brought me out of the dark little shell I was hiding in. You've helped me to start rebuilding my relationship with my brother. You've helped me to open up to my colleagues at the zoo again—even Sylvie with her relentless barrage of terrible jokes.'

'You would've got there yourself in the end,' she said.

He shook his head. 'It's more than that. You've reminded me that the world is full of sunshine. In Monet's garden, you taught me to see spring flowers like his paintings. You've made me remember how much I love Paris, from the little hidden corners right through to the Eiffel Tower sparkling at night. And even today, when my heart's sore and I'm out of sorts, you're like this warm light welcoming me home.' He drew his hand up to her mouth. 'Over the last few weeks, I've come to realise that I love you. And I know what we said about there being all sorts of reasons why we shouldn't do this—but there's a bigger reason why we should. Why we can work things out between us. Will you stay with me in Paris and maybe make a family with me, Geri?'

Stay with him.

Make a family with him.

But what if she couldn't? What if the Q fever had caused irreversible damage and they couldn't have children? What if all the strains of miscarriages and IVF treatment ripped them apart?

Panic flooded through her.

She liked Ant. More than liked him. If she was honest with herself, she'd fallen in love with the quiet, formal Parisian with his hidden depths. Kissing him beneath the spring blossom made her pulse beat faster and filled her head with starlight.

But.

He'd been badly hurt by Céline not being honest with him. Geri knew Ant wanted children; so did she, but that was something she couldn't guarantee.

It would be fairer to walk away. Give him the chance to meet someone else, someone who could share his dreams without complications.

'I can't,' she whispered. 'I'm so sorry. I *can't*.'

He stared at her, looking shocked. 'But—I thought you felt the same way I did.'

She did.

Which was what made this so very hard.

If she talked it through with him, he'd make everything sound reasonable. But how could she be sure they'd be able to overcome the obstacles? She'd loved Mark and their marriage had worked—until they'd lost the baby and discovered there was such a huge gulf between their hopes and dreams. Their marriage had failed because they both wanted different things; but her relationship with Antoine could fail because they both wanted the same things—and it might not happen.

And she couldn't risk going through that.

'I can't,' she said. 'I'm not perfect and I can't do this to you. I just can't.'

'But, Geri—'

'I can't,' she said. Overwhelmed by misery and needing space, she rushed out of the room in tears.

CHAPTER TEN

IT WAS JUST as well she'd only brought one suitcase to Paris, Geri thought, because it meant it was a lot easier for her to pack. To move into a hotel that night—because it really wasn't fair to keep staying with Antoine when she'd turned down his proposal. To find a flat in the next couple of days: a tiny apartment in an Art Deco building in the sixteenth arrondissement, a beautiful building full of curves, with pale cream bricks and its tall windows, shutters and balconies painted pale green.

Her flat wasn't far from the Eiffel Tower, and she got to see the sparkles every single night. If she'd found the place during her first week in Paris, she would've loved living here; but, although the apartment was much smaller than Antoine's spacious duplex, it felt echoey and empty. She'd grown used to sharing breakfast with him, asking if he wanted a drink before she put the kettle on—or having him surprise her with a cup of tea, precisely the way she liked it. Cooking dinner with him, if they weren't going out exploring Paris. Curled up on the sofa together, reading. All the little things of a shared life added up to much more than the whole.

Travelling to the zoo was strange, too: on her own rather than having Antoine to chat to and to point out things, and having to remember to catch a different train and change lines halfway through the journey. And work was excruciating. Antoine was cool and professional with her, and he'd gone back to eating lunch at his desk rather than joining the team; she was guiltily aware that he was slipping back into his old isolation, and she knew it was her fault. Everyone seemed aware that something had happened between them: but nobody asked. An invisible barrier had gone up, and Geri no longer felt part of the team; she was a stranger in a strange land. All she could do was simply do her job to the best of her ability.

And it was all her own fault that she felt utterly miserable. She'd panicked and pushed Antoine away—and, in the process, she'd hurt him and broken her own heart. Worse, she'd hurt him on a day when he'd already been vulnerable. She'd never be able to forgive herself for that.

'You look terrible,' Sally Milligan said. 'I'm getting on the next train to Paris.'

'Mum, no. You've got work tomorrow,' Geri protested.

'My daughter's more important,' Sally said, 'and anyway I can work extra hours next week, to catch up.'

'Mum, I love you, but you really don't have to rush over here,' Geri said.

'I know something's up, because your texts stopped being sparkly,' Sally said. 'What's happened?'

Geri gave in and told her mother the whole sorry story.

'It sounds to me,' Sally said, 'as if you haven't given him a choice.'

'He's been hurt before. I don't want to put him through having a proper relationship with me, only to find I can't give him the family he wants.'

'Apart from the fact that you have other options, such as fostering or adoption,' Sally said, 'he wants the same things that you do. It's not like it was with Mark. If he loves you, and you love him, you'll find a way to sort things out—*together.*'

'But that's the point, Mum. How do I know he really loves me? How do I know he didn't just ask me to stay because he was trying to make himself feel better after his favourite tiger died?'

'You don't. So talk to him,' Sally said. 'Be honest.'

But Geri couldn't find the words. Even Zhen giving birth to a tiny nine-hundred-gram cub didn't raise her spirits. Geri had been looking forward to seeing a newborn panda and watching it grow, seeing the white fur start to cover its pink skin over the first couple of days, followed swiftly by the black markings around its eyes and on its body. She should've been thrilled by its loud squeals when it wanted to nurse or for Zhen to reposition it, knowing that regular loud squeaks were signs of a healthy cub. And even taking part in the first assessment of the cub—checking its heartbeat and lung sounds, checking the umbilicus, palpating the abdomen—didn't delight her as much as it should've done. Antoine didn't seem as excited and thrilled about the cub as she'd expected, either; though, given how much she'd hurt him, she wasn't surprised that he'd gone all detached.

Guilt at how much pain she'd caused him, and misery at how much she'd wrecked everything between them, spoiled everything.

Geri definitely wasn't herself, Ant thought. She'd always been professional at work, but she'd been bubbly too, full of enthusiasm. He'd been prepared for her to watch the cubcam every minute of the day on her phone when she wasn't at work, in case she saw a glimpse of the cub, and to tell him snippets of facts she'd learned—how quickly panda cubs grew, how their eyes didn't open until eight weeks and that for the first two weeks they couldn't urinate or defecate unless their mum licked them to stimulate them. How panda dads were incredibly hands off and never actually had anything to do with their cubs.

Instead, she was quiet at work. The sparkle had gone from her eyes.

The sparkle had gone from his life, too. The apartment felt hideously empty without her. And everywhere he looked, there were lovers holding hands, kissing, sharing a smile, enjoying the city.

He missed doing that with Geri.

He missed *her*.

Did she miss him as much as he missed her? Was that why she was quiet and cool and professional instead of *le petit rayon* he'd teased her about being?

Maybe he should ask her. Get her to really talk to him. Persuade her to tell him why she'd backed off, when he'd been sure they felt the same way—and then work out how to overcome every single barrier she'd put up. She'd taught him something important after he'd let the gulf between him and Jean-Luc grow instead of trying to bridge it; he knew if he repeated that mistake with Geri, she'd go back to England and he'd lose her for good.

He knew he'd pushed her too far, too fast. Now, he needed to let her know that he'd wait until she was ready. That he was prepared to work at this. But, to do that, he had to get her to talk to him. How?

He knew she loved romcoms, because he'd overheard her talking about movies to Belle and Valerie. Maybe there was something he could do connected to a film.

Something she wouldn't expect him to do, and it would make her lower her guard.

An hour's browsing on the internet decided him.

That evening, he headed towards the building where she lived. Throwing stones at a window was a bad idea; but he could throw roses. Particularly as she was only on the first floor; and, even better, it looked as if she'd opened her window to let the heat out of the room.

Everything was cued up on his phone, and he had one earphone in to help him keep vaguely in tune.

Ignoring the curious glances of passers-by, he threw the first rose in through her window.

Geri heard a soft thud, and looked up from the French text she was reading. Rostand's *Cyrano de Bergerac*, even though the balcony scene made her throat feel scratchy with unshed tears because she remembered Antoine telling her about it, and she *missed* him.

A second thud.

She saw the rose coming in through the window just before she heard the third soft thud as it hit the wooden flooring.

Who on earth was throwing roses through her window? Was this some kind of Parisian publicity stunt?

Frowning, she put the book down and crossed over to the window.

Red rose number four came hurtling her way, and she caught it before looking out to see who'd thrown it.

Antoine was waiting beneath the window, and he gave her a slow, slow smile. One that made her heart miss several beats.

Then, to her shock, he held the remaining roses up to her, almost as a toast, and began to sing.

She'd never heard him sing before, but his voice was beautiful. And the song he was singing gave her goose-bumps. Classic Charles Aznavour—'She'—but it sounded more like the Elvis Costello version from one of her favourite films. And Antoine was singing in English rather than in French.

People were gathering in a semicircle around him, but he ignored them; he was entirely focused on her, singing his heart out to her.

She blinked back the tears as she listened to him sing. Antoine Bouvier was the last person she would've expected to make a public declaration like this—particularly as she'd already turned him down—and it made her knees weak. That smile, those intense looks, the way he sang the words as if every single one burst from his heart...

He finished singing, and all the onlookers clapped and cheered.

'Je t'aime, mon petit rayon,' he called. *'Je t'aime.'*

I love you.

The crowd fell silent, clearly as eager for her answer as he was.

And her throat felt clogged with tears, to the point that she couldn't speak. Instead, she gestured to him to come up.

A few moments later, her intercom buzzed. She pressed the button to release the door, and then he was there at her doorway.

'Ant... I...'

'I know.' He enfolded her in his arms.

For a long time they stood there, simply holding each other, not talking.

Then she pulled back to look him in the eye. 'I'm so sorry I hurt you.'

'It's my fault. I know I rushed you,' he said. 'And I'm probably rushing you now—but I can't help myself. I don't want you to leave, Geri. I want to be with you. I want to make a family with you.'

'But that's the point,' she said. 'You know about the Q fever. I might not be able to have children. What if I can't give you the family you want?'

'Then we adopt,' he said. 'Or foster. Or be extra "parents" to the zoo babies. There are all kinds of families. We'll make ours the best we can.'

She didn't doubt his sincerity, but it wasn't enough to allay her fears. 'I've been married before, Ant. It went wrong, when Mark and I realised that we didn't want the same things. And the end of my marriage ripped me apart. I can't face going through that again.'

'Let's talk about this. Find out what we both want, where we can compromise, and how we can make it work,' he said. 'Sit. I'll make you a cup of tea, and we'll talk.' He groaned when he walked into her kitchen and opened the cupboard door above the kettle. 'Instant coffee?' He gave a theatrical sigh. 'What a shame. Well, as it's you, I'll manage.'

'You're such a coffee snob,' she said, relieved that he'd lightened the atmosphere.

'This is Paris,' he reminded her with a smile. 'We're all coffee snobs here. Apart from weird English zoo vets, it seems.'

He walked back into her living room, carrying two mugs, and handed one to her. 'Where do we start?'

'I don't know.'

'Telling me how you feel about me would be a good place,' he said. 'Given that I just sang my heart out to you, in front of a crowd of strangers, you already know how I feel about you.'

'If anyone had told me you'd sing up to my balcony, I would never have believed them,' she said. 'And I love that film.'

'The actress and the bookshop guy had to overcome a lot of differences to be together,' he said.

'You've seen the film?'

He wrinkled his nose. 'I read the synopsis. Their lives were very different: she was a famous film star, while he was an ordinary guy who worked in a bookshop. There was an ocean between their countries—a bigger one than the English Channel. But they believed in love enough to give each other a chance.'

And there was the iconic bit where Julia Roberts asked Hugh Grant to love her. Which was kind of what Antoine had done to her, except he'd sung it. Such a private man, baring his heart to her in front of everyone—it was a huge, huge deal. And if he could do something that was so far from his natural way of doing things, just for her, then it gave her hope that maybe they could make this work.

'I love you, Ant,' she said.

'Good,' he said drily, 'because I've been a little concerned about that.'

With good reason. She'd hurt him. 'I'm sorry I pushed you away.' She bit her lip. 'I guess I panicked.'

'My timing was way off,' he acknowledged. 'I should have taken it more slowly. Prepared you. Talked more about how I felt, so you knew what was in my heart before I offered it to you.'

Instead, she'd stamped on it.

'But I was...' He searched for words. 'In a dark place, I suppose, and I wanted the sunlight.'

'So you did ask me to stay with you, just to make yourself feel better.'

'Is that what you thought? Is that why you turned me down?' He shook his head. 'It was more than that. Specifically, I wanted the sunlight you've brought into my life. I wanted *you*.'

'Is that past tense?' she asked warily.

'*Mon petit rayon*, I sang the most romantic song I know to you, in English,' he pointed out. 'You can't possibly have misunderstood the message.'

She smiled wryly. 'Even little rays of sunshine get paranoid.'

'I love you, Geri,' he said. 'And I want to be with you. I want to make a family with you. I know it's not going to be easy, and I'm prepared for that. If you can't have children, there are other options we can explore.'

Her heart skipped a beat. Could it be true?

'What about all our other differences?' she asked. 'For a start, you live in Paris and I live in England.'

'It's a little too far to commute,' he acknowledged. 'But one of us could move. We can toss a coin for it. Or we could spend half the year in Paris and half the year in Cambridge. Our zoos are part of the same organisation; we'll simply ask them to accommodate us.'

'And if they can't?'

'Then we consider doing consultancy work,' he said.

'Freelance.' Financially, that'd be precarious.

As if her worries showed on her face, he said, 'If you're worrying about a salary and how we'll manage, it's not an issue. I don't have a mortgage.' He looked away. 'I, um, own the rest of my building, too. I rent the other three apartments to tenants.'

He owned a whole building in an upmarket part of

Paris? That meant he was a lot wealthier than she'd thought. And that threw up another barrier. 'I, um… What if your family thinks I'm a gold-digger?'

'My family,' he said, 'will think nothing of the kind. You've already met Jean-Luc, and he likes you very much. I've told my sister and my parents about you, and they're dying to meet you.' He looked at her. 'How will your family react to me?'

'I've talked to them a lot about you,' she said. 'They already like the sound of you. When they meet you, they'll love you. And that's a definite.'

'Good. Next obstacle?' he asked, clearly intent on finding every single one and dealing with it.

'I…' She blew out a breath. 'This whole thing about us being colleagues—it's not really an issue, is it?'

'No,' he said.

'What about your obstacles?' she asked.

'I don't have any,' he said. 'Because I want the same things that you do. To love you for the rest of my days, to make a family with you, and to work with you in a job I love. Where we live and work don't actually matter. We can live anywhere you like—as long as we're together.'

He'd do that for her? Move from Paris? Hope began to flare in the deep hollow space she'd thought would stay empty for ever. She put her hand to his cheek. 'But you love Paris, Ant.'

'I admit I've fallen back in love with my home city, thanks to you,' he said. 'But Paris won't be enough for me if you're not here. For me, home is where you are. If that's England, then it's England.'

She could see in his eyes that he meant it.

'I know we have differences,' he said. 'The way you

drink tea is appalling. And your mug cakes make an utter mess of the microwave.'

'You're way too fussy about the way cheese should be cut—and served,' she retorted. 'Crackers are one of life's joys.'

'Good bread,' he said, 'is better.' He grinned. 'Our differences will make life more interesting. I *like* bickering with you. And we can always toss a coin if we can't agree—like we did in the shop.'

'Our nursery will be themed with pandas,' she said.

'Our nursery will have tigers,' he corrected. 'And we'll have that mobile you liked. The one with the clouds and the sun and the rainbow.'

'That's us. You all brooding clouds, me all sunshine.' The flicker of hope was becoming a steady flame now, growing brighter. 'And together we'll make rainbows.'

'The mobile had fluffy clouds, not brooding,' he said. 'Perhaps you can teach me to be fluffy.'

She grinned. 'Docteur le Nuage... What's French for fluffy?'

He grinned back. *'Duveteux.'*

'No way! You're making that up,' she accused.

'No, really it is. Look it up. Or *pelucheux* might be better,' he mused.

'Docteur le Nuage Pelucheux,' she said.

He groaned. 'Please don't call me that at work.'

She laughed. 'I wouldn't be that mean.'

'You'd better not be. Any more obstacles?'

There was the big one. 'Ant, I... I love you, and I love the way you understand me, and the way you made my dark day of the year bearable for the first time since it happened. You make me feel brave—and with you I don't have to fake it any more.'

'Good,' he said. 'Though I can see there's another "but".'

She held him more tightly. 'What if I can't have children? What if the Q fever comes back?'

'Then we'll deal with it,' he said. 'And we'll deal with it *together*.' He stroked her face. 'As I said before, we have options. Maybe we could think about adoption or fostering. And you have my backing, always.'

She could see the sincerity in his eyes.

'So is there anything else worrying you?' he asked.

Geri scrubbed the threatening tears away with the back of her hand. 'With you by my side, I can face anything.' She took a deep breath. 'I know it's a lot to ask, that I've made you jump through hoops.'

His eyes narrowed. 'But?'

She stroked his face. 'Antoine Bouvier, I want to learn French poetry and how to cut cheese the way you like it. Will you live with me and be my love?'

'Yes,' he said. And then he dropped to one knee. 'Though I want more than that. I don't have a ring, but I'd rather choose it with you in any case. Geri Milligan, will you marry me and make a family with me?'

'Yes,' she said. 'Though we need to seal the deal.'

'I think we might agree on how we do that,' he said, rising to his feet, and kissed her.

There was only one answer to that. She smiled. *'D'accord.'*

EPILOGUE

Two years later

GERI WALKED HAND in hand through the Zoo de Bélvèdere with her husband, their six-week-old daughter strapped into the sling on his chest.

'Louise, here are the pandas. This is why your *maman* came to France,' she said.

The baby gurgled.

'Though she stayed for your *papa*,' Antoine said.

'Because I fell in love with pandas, with Paris, and with your *papa*. Not in that order,' Geri said with a smile.

'I should hope not, Dr Bouvier,' Antoine said reprovingly, though his eyes were full of laughter. 'It's been an amazing two years.'

'The anniversary of the day you threw roses in my window and proposed to me,' she said.

'We'll have champagne tonight,' he said.

'I thought the French were fussy and insisted on rosé for their barbecues?' she asked.

He laughed. 'The barbecue's tomorrow night. Our parents are babysitting tonight.'

Since they'd moved to a house in the fifteenth arrondissement—in a leafy street, with a sunny living area—Antoine's parents had moved into his old apartment, and his sister had taken over the vineyard completely. Her parents and sister visited often, and their living room and kitchen were usually filled with family and friends. Including Jean-Luc and Céline, whose second baby was due in a month; Geri and Céline had become firm friends. Along with a black and white cat called Bianca and a dog of undetermined parentage called Blue, they'd made the family Geri had dreamed of.

'Babysitting, hmm?' She gave him a sidelong look. 'What did you have in mind?'

'I was planning,' he said, 'to take my beautiful wife for dinner, on a rooftop terrace with a good view of the Eiffel Tower.'

'And dancing?' she asked.

'Oh, I guarantee there will be dancing,' he murmured in her ear, his voice low and husky.

Desire shimmered through her. 'Perfect. *Je t'aime*, Dr Bouvier.'

'And I love you too, Dr Bouvier,' he said.

* * * * *

COMING SOON!

We really hope you enjoyed reading this book. If you're looking for more romance be sure to head to the shops when new books are available on

Thursday 6th July

To see which titles are coming soon, please visit
millsandboon.co.uk/nextmonth

MILLS & BOON

MILLS & BOON®

Coming next month

BROUGHT TOGETHER BY HIS BABY
Kristine Lynn

"Why don't you stay here?"

He hoped the look he shot her—confusion mixed with something less inhibited—implied that it wasn't a good idea. And if he was an artist, he'd commission a whole piece in the shade of red her cheeks turned as she realized how her question had come across.

"I mean in the cabin I have on the property. It's not being used, and you can make it your home as long as you need."

"Why would you offer that to a stranger?"

"You aren't a stranger; you're Emma's dad. And you're trusting me to help raise her. For now," she added when he opened his mouth to reply. "And if I'm being honest, it serves my designs, too. I don't know how to be away from her for very long, and if you're here I won't have to. And if you ever need help with her, I'll be next door."

He considered that. It checked a lot of boxes. It would probably be cheaper than any of the dumps he'd find in town. He knew the landlady already—and trusted her. But the stone tipping the scales was that he'd never be far from Emma either.

"I'll insist on paying rent."

"Fine. If that's what you need. It's furnished, but you can make it your own."

"And, to be honest, I'm not sure I'll be comfortable taking her overnight—not until we find our rhythm, anyway."

"That's fine. Just let me know when you're ready."

Liam sipped at his water, looking out over the expansive deck to the ocean below. It was more than he deserved.

"Thank you. I've put the end of my marriage behind me, but I know I've still got work to do to build your trust—and Emma's, too. I don't take that lightly."

"Good. Me neither. Now, let's talk about getting you a job. Are you set on downtown?"

Liam smiled so hard he felt it in his cheeks. He hadn't been sure at all about coming out here, about meeting Emma and what would come of that first meeting, but now, deep in his soul—the one he'd built from scratch after the first one had been obliterated in combat—he rejoiced.

Things were shaping up for the better for the first time in his life, and he had a feeling he owed a lot of it to the beautiful woman holding his child.

But imagining her as more than that was as off-the-table as imagining how he was going tell his dad to find someone else to fill the Everson Health board seat. Because Liam wasn't going home anytime soon.

Continue reading
BROUGHT TOGETHER BY HIS BABY
Kristine Lynn

Available next month
www.millsandboon.co.uk

LET'S TALK
Romance

For exclusive extracts, competitions and special offers, find us online:

f MillsandBoon

🐦 @MillsandBoon

📷 @MillsandBoonUK

♪ @MillsandBoonUK

Get in touch on 01413 063 232

MILLS & BOON

THE HEART OF ROMANCE

A ROMANCE FOR EVERY READER

MODERN

Prepare to be swept off your feet by sophisticated, sexy and seductive heroes, in some of the world's most glamourous and romantic locations, where power and passion collide.

HISTORICAL

Escape with historical heroes from time gone by. Whether your passion is for wicked Regency Rakes, muscled Vikings or rugged Highlanders, awaken the romance of the past.

MEDICAL

Set your pulse racing with dedicated, delectable doctors in the high-pressure world of medicine, where emotions run high and passion, comfort and love are the best medicine.

True Love

Celebrate true love with tender stories of heartfelt romance, from the rush of falling in love to the joy a new baby can bring, and a focus on the emotional heart of a relationship.

Desire

Indulge in secrets and scandal, intense drama and sizzling hot action with heroes who have it all: wealth, status, good looks…everything but the right woman.

HEROES

The excitement of a gripping thriller, with intense romance at its heart. Resourceful, true-to-life women and strong, fearless men face danger and desire - a killer combination!

To see which titles are coming soon, please visit

millsandboon.co.uk/nextmonth

JOIN US ON SOCIAL MEDIA!

Stay up to date with our latest releases, author news and gossip, special offers and discounts, and all the behind-the-scenes action from Mills & Boon...

 @millsandboon

 @millsandboonuk

 facebook.com/millsandboon

 @millsandboonuk

It might just be true love...

MILLS & BOON

Desire

Indulge in secrets and scandal, intense drama and plenty of sizzling hot action with powerful and passionate heroes who have it all: wealth, status, good looks…everything but the right woman.